"You know what you are."

"I know what I am not."

"No," Morgiana said. She spoke slowly, as if to measure each word. "I understand now. This is not the old battle over your Frankish woman, or the new one over your brother. They are but pretexts. This is the oldest of all our battles. You are a Frank. I am a Saracen. If I will not yield to your world and your ways, if I will not fight with you in your war, then you will drive me away. It must be I who goes. Less division in your soul, that you must go to war against my people."

She was calm, quiet, utterly reasonable. It seemed perfect sense, as she said it. And yet—dear God—

Aidan wanted to weep; he wanted to howl aloud. He reached for her, to draw her to him, to break down the wall that his madness had raised between them. She was not there. She stood on the floor in her Muslim garb with the turban wound about her head: all alien, and all apart. "I shall not again trouble your peace. Not while this kingdom stands."

"Morgiana—"

He clutched at air. She was gone. Truly, utterly gone. Where she had been in the heart of him was only emptiness, and four stark words.

I keep my promises.

Books by Judith Tarr

Alamut

The Hound and the Falcon Trilogy
The Isle of Glass
The Golden Horn
The Hounds of God

Avaryan Rising
The Hall of the Mountain King
The Lady of Han-Gilen
A Fall of Princes

Ars Magica

A Wind in Cairo

THE
DAGGER
AND THE
CROSS

A Novel of the Crusades

Judith Tarr

BANTAM BOOKS
NEW YORK • TORONTO • LONDON • SYDNEY • AUCKLAND

THE DAGGER AND THE CROSS
A Bantam Spectra Book / published by arrangement with Doubleday

PRINTING HISTORY
Doubleday edition published February 1991

Bantam edition / November 1991

SPECTRA *and the portrayal of a boxed "s" are trademarks of Bantam Books, a division of Bantam Doubleday Dell Publishing Group, Inc.*

All rights reserved.
Copyright © 1991 by Judith Tarr.
Cover art copyright © 1991 by Tom Canty.
Library of Congress Catalog Card Number: 90-44106.
No part of this book may be reproduced or transmitted in any form or by any means, electronic or mechanical, including photocopying, recording, or by any information storage and retrieval system, without permission in writing from the publisher. For information address: Doubleday, 666 Fifth Avenue, New York, NY 10103.

ISBN 0-553-29416-4

Published simultaneously in the United States and Canada

Bantam Books are published by Bantam Books, a division of Bantam Doubleday Dell Publishing Group, Inc. Its trademark, consisting of the words "Bantam Books" and the portrayal of a rooster, is Registered in U.S. Patent and Trademark Office and in other countries. Marca Registrada. Bantam Books, 666 Fifth Avenue, New York, New York 10103.

PRINTED IN THE UNITED STATES OF AMERICA

RAD   0 9 8 7 6 5 4 3 2 1

Part One

ACRE

April 1187

1

If there was an inch of breathing space anywhere within the walls of Acre, there was a pilgrim in it: gaping at the sights, battling the crowds, or giving thanks to God that he had come at last to this land across the sea, this gateway to Jerusalem. Byzantium might be greater, Damascus might be older, Jerusalem infinitely more holy, but Acre was the port to which every pilgrim in Europe was best advised to come, if he would salve his soul with the greatest of all pilgrimages.

Acre was the gate, and this was the season. Fine sailing weather, the furnace heat of summer some weeks off, and Easter just past: most holy of feasts in the most holy of places. The outer harbor seemed all ships and scarce a glimmer of water. The inner harbor, safe in its walls and its chain, warded the thronging fleets of the city's own. Even the landing of the Ordemer, the unsheltered shore that faced the westward sea, had all the traffic it could bear.

In that press, even a king might find himself compelled to wait his turn. And a prince, to pace a vanishingly narrow strip of quay, even that much won for him by determined guards and the exercise of his justly notorious temper. The fleet was there, crawling past the Tower of Flies—such a city: its harbor warded by a tower named for Beelzebub, and its land wall anchored by a tower called Accursed. Five slender graceful ships sailing under the devil's tower, each with a seabird carved on the prow, and on the foremost a crown; and he was here, landbound, walled in noise and stench and thrusting, thronging humanity. He could not even prowl properly. There was no room.

Something blocked what space he had, halting him. He glared down. The obstacle glared up, magnificently fearless. All at once he laughed. He caught her in his arms, swung her high, held her level with his eyes. Her glare more than matched the one he had forsaken. "Put me down," she said, each word icily distinct.

"Not without a ransom," he said.

Her jaw jutted. It was a most determined jaw, although she had not even ten summers to put behind it. "I am too old for children's games."

He raised a brow. "Are you, now? And when did you come to that decision?"

"This morning," she said. "When you told everyone else to wait at home. I decided to be grown up, and decide for myself."

His brow rose a fraction higher. "Is that logic, milady? The others are quite sufficiently grown up, and they obey me."

"They choose to." She wriggled, to little effect. "My lord uncle, will you put me down? If it pleases you?"

He obliged her then, for courtesy. She settled her skirts and pushed her tousled hair out of her face. She was not a pretty child: too pale, too thin, all eyes and angles. What she would be when she was grown, not many had the eyes to see.

Which was, he reflected, a mercy. She had her mother's coloring: storm-blue eyes, brown curling hair with lights of red and gold. She seemed to have her mother's face, if not that lady's robust Norman bones. The rest of it would come clear later. Much later, God willing.

Once she had won back her dignity, she made her way to the end of the pier, and poised there. The guard nearest maintained an impressive calm, but his eye was keen, even as he spared his lord a smile.

Prince Aidan smiled back a little wryly, and went to stand beside her. After a sufficient while, her hand crept into his. A little longer and she leaned against him. The ease of it, the perfection of trust, caught at his heart.

He shook his head. She had distracted him admirably; and he had not even threatened to tan her hide for disobedience. The fleet was a whole shiplength closer. That would be the pilot on the flagship's deck, the lean whipcord man in the turban of a Muslim. The mariners about him seemed strange after so long in this alien country: two breeds of them, they seemed to be, tall and narrow or short and solid, pale under the weathering of sea and sun or nut-brown from head to foot, hawk-keen or stone-blunt, but all black-haired, sea-eyed, blue or grey or misty green. Home faces, faces bred under another sky, on grey stone and grey sea and mist-grey moors and headlands. Rhiyana, Rhiyanon, Rhiannon. Armorica once, Less Britain after, but the magic that was in it, and the line of kings that ruled it, had changed its name and given it another patron; and even the Christians could not deny or destroy her. For a moment he seemed to breathe that air, cold and clean, and taste the edge of strangeness that made it wonderful.

He gasped, coughed. Ysabel regarded him in concern. He smiled at her. She was dubious, but she let him be. He took a shallow breath of the fetor that was Acre, and raised his eyes again to the ship. There was one face of them all, one that his heart cried for a sight of; one that was not there. Some he might have known, a dozen years agone, and some of those sadly aged in human fashion, and one, a woman's, made him gasp. But it could not—she could not—

Gwenllian was an old woman. He knew it; as he knew that she had not come. Elen, this had to be, just past twenty, and the image of her grandmother when she was young, slender and tall, hair as black and eyes as grey and skin almost as white as his own. She had grown up willful and proud enough for a queen, standing under the canopy in what seemed to be full mail.

Cloth of silver, cunningly cut and sewn. The sun caught her briefly, dazzling him.

Then he saw the one who had come up beside her. No matter what they were, no matter how close minds and hearts might be, they whose bodies had slept twined in the womb could never be wholly content save in each other's living presence. He met his brother's eyes across the narrowing expanse of harbor. A long sigh left them both.

"Allah!" came a mutter behind him in the accent of a Kipchak Tartar. "As like as two hairs on the same dog."

"That is not," said a voice almost exactly like it, "how I would put it. One being a prince, after all. And the other a king."

Aidan kept his back to the two of them. They would know better than to think that he had not heard; though they might cherish a glimmer of hope. Their captain's hiss was considerably more distinct, and the muted clatter of two armed men snapping to attention. Aidan swallowed a smile. Timur and Ilkhan had never quite believed that any pair of brothers could be more alike than they themselves were. Now they were learning the error of their ways.

As long as it had taken the fleet to make its way through the harbor, the last moments seemed to pass in a blur of speed. Shouts from the ships; shouts from the shore; space cleared, lines flung, sailors clambering up masts and over sides. The passengers waited in tight-leashed patience.

Aidan had no such virtue. He damned prudence, damned dignity, damned his own princely finery, and leaped the long stretch over and upward, onto the deck. His brother was there. Who reached first, who caught whom, neither ever knew or cared.

Gwydion was the quiet one, the water-twin, the merest shade taller, the merest whisper more slender. A smile from him was like a shout of laughter. He was smiling now, holding Aidan at arm's length, drinking him in. His hand brushed Aidan's face, half cuff, half caress, ruffling the close-cut beard. "Gone Saracen, have you, brother?"

Aidan eyed Gwydion's own beard—new since they

parted, and most becoming. "What is this, then? A new fashion?"

"A bow to kingly dignity," said Gwydion.

"And besides, how else can we drive people mad trying to guess which of us is which?"

"That's easy," someone said behind Aidan.

Aidan spun. Ysabel perched coolly on the rail, looking from one to the other with a narrow eye.

"We are," said Aidan with taut-strung patience, "indistinguishable."

"You are wearing your black coat, the one the sultan gave you, and he is wearing a blue cotte," she said, "with silver birds all over it. You do have the same face. That's amazing. But you're two different people."

"We are that," Gwydion granted her. "Is it so obvious, then?"

She nodded. Then, as if she had remembered at last who he was, she slid down to the deck and curtsied. "My lord king."

The King of Rhiyana bowed, all gracious, and hardly laughing at all. "My lady. You would be Ysabel?"

"Ysabel de Mortmain," she said.

Gwydion inclined his head. "You honor us."

There were grins here and there at the spectacle of a crowned king offering full courtesy to a small tousled girlchild. Not an excessively clean one, either. Aidan judged that she had come up one of the hawsers. Her cotte would never be the same for it.

She, having paid tribute to courtly manners, returned to herself with a snap, and cast a curious eye over the ship. "Is this yours? Do you sail it yourself? Are you the captain, or do you have someone who does it for you?"

Gwydion came as close to laughter as he ever came. "Yes, it is mine, and I have ample help to sail it, but yes, I am the captain, and the admiral, too, since this is a fleet and I command it. When time is not so pressing, would it please my lady to examine it?"

"That means," Aidan said, "that his majesty has duties, and you are keeping him from them. Here, milady. Since you are so determined to go where you are expressly forbidden to go, you may atone for it by practicing patience."

Her glare was eloquent regarding his own failings in that quarter, but she knew better than to say it aloud. He bowed to her wisdom and took her by the hand, turning toward the high ones who waited still, in just such patience as he preached, under the awning. The lady who led them seemed much amused, even as she came to his embrace.

"Elen," he said. "Elen, I'd never have known you."

"I would always know you, uncle," she said. Her voice was silver-sweet, and the lilt of their people was strong in it. So too, now, a ripple of mirth. "Even without your lord brother to remind me. You don't change."

"No," Aidan said, very still. "No. We never do."

Her eyes, so like her grandmother's, looked levelly into his. She was not bitter. No more than Gwenllian had ever been; or Gereint her mother's brother, who died in a castle near Jerusalem, the night before Aidan came to share his Crusade. Now Gwenllian grew old, as Elen knew that she herself would. But Aidan who was Gwenllian's brother, Aidan would not, no more than Gwydion who was called the Elvenking. A mortal king had loved an immortal woman under the boughs of Broceliande, and his sons had inherited her magic, but his daughter had inherited his humanity.

Human eyes met eyes that were not human at all, and smiled. "Did you think that I would grow up ugly?"

"I knew that you would grow up beautiful." Aidan kissed her lightly on the brow. "You are most welcome in Outremer."

"I am most happy to be there."

She was: it sang in her. He caught her, to her startlement and sudden delight, and spun her about, and set her down as lightly as if she had still been a child. "Come, catling! See what a kingdom we have for you to shine in."

Ysabel did not know if she liked these strangers who had come to claim her prince. The king—he was bearable; he was like the other half of Aidan, the half that was quiet, and knew all the uses of patience. He needed them, in the customs house of Acre. Where Aidan would have lost his temper and done something regrettable, Gwydion spoke softly, leveled his calm grey eyes, and got what he wanted. Ysabel decided that she could approve of him.

The others, the knights and nobles from Rhiyana, were nobodies. Some had handsome faces; some had pleasant voices. They were not as rough as the usual lot of newcomers. They were a little shocked by Aidan's guards, but never as shocked as the raw recruits who came in with every ship from Normandy or Anjou or Anglia. Those were always appalled, and always trying to a pick a fight over the presence of turbaned infidels in good Christian company. They were even more outraged when they were told that those infidels had been mamluks of the Syrian sultan: soldier-slaves of Saladin himself, and now of a Christian prince, who never made the least effort to convert them to the one true faith. Aidan was always defending his honor in passages of arms, and always winning. He was the best knight in Outremer; Ysabel knew that he was the best knight in the world.

The Rhiyanans were not exactly comfortable in front of so many turbans. But they had practice in accepting the unacceptable. Their king was something even worse, in some minds, than a Saracen, and he kept odd company. The man who was closest to his right hand, backing him in everything he said to the king's officers, was no more a Christian than Arslan or Raihan, though he was no Muslim, either. Simeon bar-Daniel could not be his majesty's chancellor—that was not allowed a Jew—but he could be his majesty's advisor, and his privy secretary. Ysabel could see that the king was his friend; they were easy with one another, even preserving appearances in front of strangers.

No; they were all pleasant enough. It was Elen whom Ysabel could not warm to. Aidan called her *catling*; and that was Ysabel's name, never mind that she flew into a rage whenever he called her by it. And he talked to her the way he talked to Ysabel, as if he had known her from a baby, and loved her, and thought of her as his favorite niece.

"She is his favorite niece," said the boy who had been standing next to Ysabel for rather longer than she had deigned to notice.

He was hard to ignore, once he had spoken. He was some inches taller than herself, and some few years older, and the cap on his head and the riot of curly hair under it, with the striped gown, marked him another Jew. And—

"You weren't supposed to hear that!"

He did not even have the sense to blush. "You were shouting it for the deaf to hear."

"*You* aren't—" She stopped. Stared. Peered close. He stared back. His eyes were as big and liquid-dark as a fawn's, but never as gentle. There was a spark in them; it kindled green. "Who are you?"

He swept a bow. "Akiva bar-Simeon, at my lady's service."

She was bursting with questions; she could tell that he would be all too pleased to answer. Therefore, she asked none of them. "Do you mean that?"

"I always mean what I say."

She snorted, not delicately. "So, then. Promise you won't do it again."

"What if you want me to?"

"Then I'll tell you."

"That's fair," said Akiva. He must have been studying the king, to be so flawlessly calm. "Elen *is* his favorite niece. Also his only one."

"Not here, she isn't," Ysabel said darkly.

Akiva started to say something, thought better of it. Which was very wise of him.

"He is my uncle," said Ysabel. "He loves me best. He belongs to me."

"Have you asked him what he thinks of that?"

"He knows," she said, as loftily as she could.

Akiva had sense. He did not argue with her.

*   *   *

The house was, as always, in an uproar. Joanna had, as always, made a valiant effort to settle it, then given in to it. It always managed to find its own peace, whatever she did. Even today, at the height of the pilgrim season, with the King of Rhiyana expected at any moment.

Ranulf had fled, pleading business that could not wait. Lucky man. He would come back in his own good time, and expect to find everything in perfect order.

As, she vowed grimly, it would be. The kitchen was well employed in preparing the banquet. The hall would be ready as soon as the steward finished howling dirges over the cloth for the high table, which had been abducted to serve as a pavilion when the children played at Franks and Saracens. It was hardly their fault that Ranulf's wolfhound had chosen to pursue the kitchen cat straight through the makeshift tent, right after the dog had had a long and thorough roll in the midden. But now they were one cloth short, and Aimery had been sent to the market for another, and knowing that lad, he would be most of the morning about it.

The younger children, at least, were safe in the nursery, with ample occupation. She could hear them now and then, when one of them struck a high note in the chorus. Once she heard a crash and a bellow. That would be Conrad, in his office of concertmaster. Sour notes appalled him; an excess thereof induced him to throw things, preferably at the offender's head. Since he was a mamluk when he was not a music master, he seldom missed.

She caught a page flying doorward, and deflected him hallward. "My lord's best cups," she said. "Fetch. Polish. Now!"

The imp vanished. He would do as he was told, or his backside would remember it.

She continued her march on the solar. Her back was aching already. She set her fist against the pain and willed it away. Six children living, two more dead in infancy, a ninth big enough now to kick: one should expect to pay a price for such singular good fortune. One did not have to be happy with it.

There was someone waiting in the wide cool chamber

with its tiles from Isfahan. Joanna forgot the aches in back and head, and remembered only joy. "Mother!"

Lady Margaret de Hautecourt rose for her daughter's embrace. Joanna laughed as always to find her so small and herself so large, a little round dumpling of a woman beside her great Norman tower of a daughter. Margaret was half a Saracen. Joanna was all of her father's kin, as tall as a man and broad to match, broader now with the baby in her belly. She kissed her mother soundly on both cheeks, and embraced her again for good measure. "Oh, Mother! I'm so glad you've come."

"As am I, to be here," Margaret said, once Joanna let her go. Her smooth braids were unruffled under the veil, her dark plain gown uncreased. Joanna, who could never keep tidy when she had things to do, brushed half-heartedly at hair and gown, and gave it up.

"It's all in order," she said, "though it doesn't look it."

"To me it does." Margaret sat, as serene as if she had not just ridden up from Jerusalem, and favored her daughter with a smile. "You have an art all your own. Order in chaos. One word, and all of it falls into place."

"It's not that easy," muttered Joanna; but it warmed her, that praise. Margaret never dispensed it lightly.

"Now," said Margaret. "What would you have me do?"

"Sit here," Joanna answered her promptly. "Rest. Keep me company while I untangle these accounts. They'd have been done days ago, but the bailiff had a fever, and he didn't bring them till this morning, and of course they can't wait." While she talked, she readied book and ink and pens. "Will you have wine? Water? Sherbet?"

"I've been seen to," Margaret said.

As Joanna beat her way through the thicket of figures, she glanced now and then at her mother. Margaret was a haven of quiet, sitting where the sun slanted through one of the high narrow windows, perhaps drowsing, perhaps telling the beads which glowed honey-gold between her fingers. She could have been of either world, of Christendom or the House of Islam; a peaceful, aging woman in somber black, nodding in the sun.

She was not so terribly old, nor so very unlovely under the widow's weeds. She was still sought after for her lands and her wealth, and not a little for her person. But that part of her duty, she had decided long since, was done. One husband to please her father: he gave her Joanna, and the son who had fallen to an Assassin's dagger nigh eleven years ago. One husband to please herself: the young knight from Rhiyana, whom also the Assassin took. There would be no other. She ruled her demesne in her own right, and answered for it to no man, except the king in Jerusalem.

Joanna stifled a sigh. Not for envy, not exactly. She had married to please her mother, and learned to please herself. Ranulf was a good husband. He respected his wife, and when he had other women he did not flaunt them where she could see. He was proud of his sons; he doted on his daughters. Even the odd one. Even—

She did not let herself think of that. It was done. There was no mending it. Nor would she, could she, regret it. Ranulf loved the one he called his princess, never knowing how close he came to the truth. He did not need to know. The others since were proof enough, and surety. Joanna was all that a wife should be. She had given him sons to be his heirs, and daughters to trade in fine marriages. And one who was his in the ways that mattered, and called him father, and never knew the truth.

The line of figures blurred. Joanna blinked fiercely. Eleven years. Seven children since. And it could still twist her vitals.

He had never said a word. Once the bargain was made, the lines drawn, he never stepped outside of them. She was a baron's lady of Acre. He was her proper, royal kinsman. The children called him *uncle,* though he was only that by courtesy: Margaret had wedded his sister's son. Canon lawyers would reckon that close enough. For Joanna it was appallingly close, and deadly far away. The width of a child's body, or a woman's marriage vows.

She bit her lip until it bled. The pain helped a little. She was a lady and a wife, and many times a mother. He was preparing for his wedding.

More fool she, to offer her house and her hospitality, since his brother must come through Acre. It was both generous and proper. It was also a penance. She would see him happy, and not with her. She would, within the fortnight, see him wedded to another woman.

It shocked her, how much it hurt. She had had ten years and more to learn to bear it; to see them together; to know that there was no parting them. But they had never properly been husband and wife. They had taken oaths, and being perfectly matched in stubbornness as in all else, had held to them. Prince Aidan was a Christian. The Lady Morgiana was a Muslim. She would not forsake her faith. He would not compel her. Neither would he take her to wife, except with the blessing of holy Church.

Which it, in the person of the Patriarch of Jerusalem, would not grant while she remained an infidel. Lovers they might be, and a long joyous life of sin they had led in their castle of Millefleurs on the marches of Syria, but married, they were not. That needed the pope's decree.

And now it was won. Aidan's brother brought it on the ship which Aidan had gone to meet. They would present it in Jerusalem on the wedding day; the Patriarch would perforce accept it; and the Church would bless the union. And Joanna would smile bravely, and pray that no one noticed her clenched teeth.

At least she need not dance at the wedding. Her condition was good for something besides an aching back.

She straightened it and yawned. Her mother glanced at her. She bent over the ledger, glaring at it. *From Hakim Ali the rais of al-Rabat, four ells of fine muslin cloth, two being white, two dyed with indigo . . .*

Morgiana had no patience with the nigglings of a lady's duties. In Millefleurs the bailiff did it, or more properly the bailiff's wife, whose head for figures was nothing short of miraculous. What Morgiana did was keep those figures in a proper balance: high enough coming in and low enough going out to suit Rashida. Morgiana, as her Frank was fond of saying, was a true Muslim: a merchant to the marrow.

Her Frank, as she was fond of telling him, had not the faintest notion of what a merchant was. Lady Margaret and her kin were merchants. Morgiana was a traveler and a haggler and a magpie for treasure. Booty was best, but he objected, and called it stealing. Buying at bone-pared prices was well enough, and sometimes better sport.

The prices in Acre were ridiculous, on both sides of it. Franks had no conception of commerce; they were shockingly easy to cheat. The merchants from the Italies, who had studied in the markets of the east, took shameless advantage of such innocence. Time was when she would gleefully have abetted them, but she was of Outremer now, and in a fortnight she would be a baroness of the High Court of the Kingdom of Jerusalem.

She hugged herself and danced a step or two, not caring who stared. The Christians' pope had commanded it. Allah knew, it had taken five of them, and two not even proper popes, and then the King of Rhiyana himself with all the power that he could bring to bear; but now at last it was done. She would be in name what she had been in fact since a night in the desert of Persia which could still warm her with the memory; and he would be happy, which mattered more than anything.

She stopped. The crowds parted to pass her; she barely noticed. Maybe when the words were said, Allah would allow and the Christian God would listen, and she would have the child she wanted. That great Frankish cow in her house near the winter palace—she had a whole herd of them, and always another coming, and even, most unforgivable of all, one of his. And Morgiana had none. Not even a lost one, to show that she was not barren.

The Frank never balked at sharing the cuckoo in her nest. Easy generosity. She had more than enough to spare.

"She should have been mine," Morgiana said aloud,

unheard amid the clamor of Acre. "*I* should have borne and suckled her. She should have been my daughter!"

Soon, Allah willing, there would be one who was. Morgiana began to walk again, her temper calming, her joy coming back. Joanna had Ysabel, but Morgiana had her prince; and he had no eyes, now, for any other woman.

She looked about. She hardly knew what she was looking for. Aidan would have been glad to have her with him at the quay, but she was learning arts and courtesies. This was her gift to him: a reunion with his brother, without the distraction of her presence. She did not want to be where Joanna was, if there was anywhere else to be. Therefore she was here, wandering the markets of Acre.

She had a trinket or two, bought on a whim, and her eye on a particularly fine ruby that might, if the price went low enough, make a signet for a groom-gift. She already had the cottes made of Ch'in silk, three of them, and the cloak lined with sable, and the belt of gold, and . . .

A ring would please him, and the ruby was his stone. She knew a jeweler who could carve it, and a goldsmith who could set it.

She turned with sudden decision and went back the way she had come. No one jostled her or got in her way. That was part of what she was. Humans knew in their bones, even when they saw only another of themselves: a woman in dusty black with a veil over her face. Sometimes a pilgrim, raw with newness, would think of cursing her for an infidel. He never did it, nor need he ever know why.

The merchant with the ruby was shrewder than most, but he was no match for her. The price she won was almost half the fair worth of the stone; and even at that, he made a kingly profit. She could hardly keep him from cheating poor feckless knights on their way back from Crusade, but she could take her own small revenge, and teach him a lesson besides. They grew soft, these robbers of pilgrims. It did them good to match wits with their betters.

She left the shop, well pleased with herself. A little distance down the street, where a cloth merchant displayed his wares, she saw a face she knew. In part for good humor, in part for curiosity, she drew closer.

Joanna's eldest son was the image of both his parents: man-high even at twelve years old, with his father's bright gold hair and his mother's grey-blue eyes, and a face that, young though he was, was already waking sighs among the women. He made Morgiana think of a half-grown lion.

Pure Norman though he seemed, he had sufficient in him of his Saracen kin. He bargained well and cannily, and he knew how to use both his youth and his size. The object of his labors, a fine damask cloth, made Morgiana smile behind her veil. She had wondered what would happen when the steward discovered the wreck of the children's pavilion.

When he came out with the cloth wrapped in muslin and then in a bit of sacking, Morgiana fell in beside him. His glance was nervous, with an edge of white; it eased hardly at all when she said, "Good morning, Messire Aimery."

He started slightly, and peered. "My lady? Morgiana?"

"To the life," she said.

Born to this sunstruck country as he was, he was as deeply bronzed as any Saracen; but a blush was still perceptible. "M—my lady."

"What, did you think I was something less respectable?"

His cheeks were crimson. His eyes were furious. He would not look at her. "Did my mother send you, my lady?"

Morgiana stopped short. "Since when have I run errands for any dog of a Frank?"

He spun, startled, turning angry. She watched him remember what she was. He did not crumble at once into terror. He never even thought of it. In that, he was his mother's son. But he was a little more careful than he might have been, in saying what came into his head.

"My lady, you are noble and a kinswoman, but my mother is my mother. I would thank you to speak of her with greater respect."

She inclined her head. "Well and wisely said, messire. They will make a courtier of you yet."

He shrugged uneasily and became a great gangling lad again, reduced to incoherence by the presence of a lady.

She took pity on him. "Come, you must be hungry: young things always are. I know a place where the honeycakes are famed in Paradise."

It was beyond him to resist her, though he trembled like a colt in a new saddle. She led him to a street which even he, born in this city, hardly knew, and down an alley which she would have wagered gold he did not know, to an utterly unprepossessing doorway. He was in a fine state at the end of it: thinking that, after all, he had been waylaid by a bandit.

It was a perfectly ordinary shop in which they found themselves, but the scents which filled it were not ordinary at all. Aimery drew a breath. His eyes went wide. He sat without a word on the bench to which Morgiana led him, and took a long moment simply to breathe.

The shopkeeper was as vast as her wares were excellent. She greeted Morgiana with deep respect and Morgiana's companion with restraint, and brought them the best of what she had. There were others in the shop, but most did not stay; they bought and left, often pausing to exchange gossip with their neighbors.

"But," said Aimery when he had a breath to spare from devouring Fatimah's cakes. "This is an infidel place. How can it be here?"

"Maybe it isn't," said Morgiana.

His eyes went wild.

She patted his hand. "Hush, child. It's the best place I know. Does it matter where it is?"

It did. Profoundly.

"Think of it," she said, "as an adventure."

He swallowed hard, trying not to choke. "You—this —you brought me here by witchcraft!"

She lowered her eyes. Aidan would not be pleased. He would tell her, again, that she would never learn; that she must learn. And never mind that this mortal child knew what she was. Most of them did, sooner or later. She was not a good liar.

She rose. "I'll take you back," she said.

He caught her hand. He seemed surprised that he had done it; but he did not let go. "No. No, my lady. It was just . . . you never . . . I didn't know you could do that."

He did. But he had never believed it. He was getting over his shock; he was beginning to enjoy himself. An adventure, he was thinking. A tale to widen eyes among his siblings, and among the pages and the squires when he went back to Tripoli. "Where are we, my lady?"

"That," she said, "is my secret."

He let her keep it, though he was burning with curiosity. A mystery, too. He was in bliss.

She sat down again and watched him eat. He paused. "Lady. Won't you have some, too?"

She shook her head.

"Is it because I'm a Christian?"

"Hardly that," she said, "when I break bread with unbelievers every day."

"I'm not—it's you who—" He stopped, tangled in it. "Father Robert says you're in—irre—unregenerate."

She laughed. "That's not all he says I am! He tried to baptize me once, did you know? He reasoned that since a baby needn't know or consent, a grown witch might not need to submit, either. I think he rather hoped that I'd sprout horns and a tail at the touch of the holy water, and fly screeching out the window."

"Did you?" Aimery went crimson again. "I mean, did he really do it?"

"My lord talked him out of it. Not gently."

Aimery looked as if he would have laughed, if he had dared. "I can imagine. Uncle—his highness can be very persuasive. I saw him in the tournament last winter. Count Raymond says there's never been a better man of his hands in Outremer."

"There hasn't," Morgiana said. "Bohemond was a great fighter in his day. King Amalric was notable; and his son, the leper king, would have been, if he had lived."

"You *knew* Bohemond?"

Morgiana shook her head. "I heard of him. He was seven feet tall. Even for a Frank, that's big."

Fatimah brought a cup of a sherbet cooled with snow. Aimery drank it blindly, fascinated. "They called him that, you know. Bohemond. Because he was like the giant in the story. The infidels must have thought he was a devil."

"A jinni. A spirit of earth, as my prince and I are spirits of air. That's not a devil, exactly. We can accept Islam; we can win salvation, though it's harder for us, and longer. Iblis—the Adversary—is our forefather, you see."

"You are children of Satan?" Aimery's eyes were round.

"No," she said, willing herself to be patient. "We are our own creatures, less than angels, but sharing somewhat of their substance. So we never grow old, and we never sicken; but we have free will, like men. Except that men have pure souls apart from their flesh, and we are both spirit and flesh, and so it's harder to divide the two. It's in holy Koran."

"It's false scripture. Though Mother tells us to be polite to it, and to people who believe in it. So does Count Raymond."

"Your count is a wise man, for an infidel." She did not say what she thought of Aimery's mother. "I'm neither devil nor damned, and my prince is as good a Christian as any I've seen."

"But you're witches," said Aimery.

"What, like old women muttering over their cauldrons? We are white enchanters. We work magic in Allah's name. Or in God's. You might say we *are* magic. We can no more help working it than you can help being almost as big as Bohemond."

"I'm hardly—" He looked down at himself. "I'll never be as big as that."

"Close enough," she said.

His eyes measured her as she sat there in her veils and her smallness. Odd: she never felt small when she was among Muslims. She often wore men's clothes, and passed for a man, or a eunuch at least; and not a little one, either. But a tall Muslim was merely a middling Frank, and she was a woman besides. This hulking boy made her remember that. He was beginning to understand what women were for, though he was young enough still to blush when he understood it.

She let fall her veil, which was revenge for the names he had called her, and smiled, which was to soothe him. A woman should always know how she looked to a man. Morgiana knew that she was beautiful; she knew that it was not a common beauty, nor a comfortable one. Gentleness was no part of it. Perhaps that was why her smile did not have the effect she wanted. Aimery blanched and stammered. "Lady. Lady, I—"

"Messire, I don't bite."

"But," he said, "you're so beautiful."

Now it was her turn, at last, to blush. It made her furious, but it comforted him. He gulped what was left in his cup and set it down.

"I'm glad you're going to marry my uncle," he said in a rush, as if he had to get it all done at once or never do it at all. "I'm sorry it took so long. I'd like—I'd like to be your squire. When I'm raised to it. If your grace will accept me."

"But aren't you already given to Count Raymond?" she asked.

He shook his head, sharp and short. "That's not what it is. My lady. That's the allegiance of the world. This is a higher thing. Like—riding in tournaments, and wearing your token on my helm, and making you Queen of Beauty if I win."

Ah, she thought. He had been listening to troubadours. "My prince might object."

He wilted visibly. "Yes. He would, wouldn't he? And he always wins."

"There will be a lady for you," she said. "I'm sure of it."

"But never one as fair as you."

"Beauty is greatest in a lover's eye." She did not expect him to understand; she hoped that he would remember. She rose again, held out her hand. "Come, messire. It's time we went back to Acre."

2

The merchants of Genoa had their own quarter in Acre, like a city within the city, warded by its own wall and closed off by its own gate. Where the citizens of St. Mark and the trader princes of Pisa had little more in their quarters than a hostelry and a church or two, the Genoese, who had aided the armies of the first Crusade in the capture of the city, had taken the best of it and made it their own.

In the heart of the quarter, in a house that had sheltered merchant princes since the city was young, five men gathered, ostensibly to examine a new shipment of spices. Jars and vials and packets waited on the table under the awning, should anyone happen upon their meeting.

"Wine?" asked the master of the house.

There were no takers. The youngest of them, who was his son, looked longingly toward the pitcher, but knew better than to ask. The wizened man in the monk's habit sniffed disapprovingly. His companion seemed asleep. The man in mail had a cup half-full, which he set down to pace along the portico. The others watched him warily. He had an odd, unfinished look, as if there should have been more to him: not quite handsome, not quite ugly; neither tall nor short, neither dark nor fair, neither remarkable nor rightly nondescript. One would lose him in a crowd, unless it suited him to be noticed. Then he could draw every eye.

He paused by the table, crumbled a bit of saffron in his fingers, chose a clove and set it on his tongue. He came back still engrossed in the sharp, pungent taste, and sat where he had been before, lapsing into immobility.

Guillermo Seco, merchant of Genoa, shook himself as if from a doze. "So, then, sirs. Are we agreed?"

The plumper of the monks opened an eye. There was no sleep in it, and a fair degree of mockery. "When have human men ever agreed on anything? Be polite, Guillermo. Tell Brother Thomas what we do here."

"You were to tell him—" Seco broke off. "Very well. As kind as you are to come here so soon, reverend Brother, with your ship barely moored at the quay, you are kinder still to lend us your aid in what we propose."

"Not exactly," said the wizened monk. "I said that I would consider your proposal. I never promised to accept it."

Seco stiffened, but he kept his smile. "Indeed, Brother. Indeed. You know why we are here?"

"Suppose that you enlighten me," said Brother Thomas.

Seco's eyes narrowed. He drew a breath, and let it out, focusing his irritation in the words which he intended to say. "We stand against a common enemy: a rival in war and in commerce, and no friend to the King of Jerusalem. If you choose to call us a conspiracy, you may. I prefer to call it a defense of the kingdom against a subtle and deadly threat."

"Subtle?" the plump monk said. "There are many things which I would call the Prince Aidan, but that is not one of them."

"Subtle," said Seco, "in his very unsubtlety. All the world knows what he is and where his sympathies lie, yet no one has ever dared to touch him. While the leper was king, he was the leper's sworn brother, and no man was permitted to speak against him. When the leper died, when our lord Guy was the rightful regent—husband as he was and is to the Princess Sybilla, and stepfather to the child king—the leper's favorite cast in his lot against us, and favored the regency of the Count of Tripoli. When the child died, would he acknowledge Sybilla queen, or Guy king by right of law and marriage? He would not. He has made no secret of his contempt. He will not swear fealty to a king who has, he professes for any to hear, no more substance than a poppet on a pole."

Seco's son stared. "He actually said that?"

"Word for word," said the man in mail, "to my brother's face."

"He's mad," the boy said, awed.

His father quelled him with a look. " 'Mad' hardly begins to describe him. He lairs in his castle on the border of Syria, among his heathens and Saracens, with infidels in his hall and an Assassin in his bed. The Sultan of Syria is his boon companion; the Old Man of the Mountain has struck bargains with him, and sealed them with the witch's body."

"He is also," drawled the portly monk, "unconscionably rich."

"The devil's riches," Seco said. "He has his hand in the river of Saracen gold."

"And when you would have dipped your own finger in it, he laughed in your face." The portly monk yawned. "Leave the sermons to us, Messer Seco. You hate him because he has what you would give your soul to have; what you strive for endlessly but never win, he gains simply by being what he is."

"A king's son," said the boy. "Kin to the House of Ibrahim, who are merchant kings."

His father did not strike him, but he shrank, paling. "If that were all he was," Seco said through clenched teeth, "he would be easy prey. Even if he were only a damned traitor, we would know how to deal with him. The Master of the Assassins has never been one to let a prior commitment interfere with present expedience."

"I gather you tried it," the portly monk observed.

Seco's face was crimson; yet he smiled. "I did, Brother Richard. Would you have dared?"

Brother Richard shuddered. "I leave daring to you men of the world. What did the Old Man say?"

"Sinan," said Seco, "was not minded to interfere. There were reasons, he said. Such as that no wise infidel will cross wits willingly with the jinn."

"Now we come to it," Brother Richard said. "You

believe that this prince and his tamed Assassin are—
what? Minor devils?"

"I know what they are." They all stared at Brother
Thomas, even the motionless and hitherto impervious
knight. He swelled under their regard, lifting his narrow
chin. "They are," he repeated. "Devils, witches, unnatu-
ral creatures. I know them. I have seen what they can
do."

Seco leaned forward. "Have you, Brother? Have you,
indeed?"

"I have studied them," Brother Thomas said, "since
I was sent into Rhiyana as a young man, when Abbot
Boniface was the pope's legate to the Rhiyanan king. I
have returned there often since, and observed them as
closely as any man may. They are witches, sirs. Have no
doubt of that. In their own country they make no secret
of it. Any child can see what their king is. I came to
Rhiyana as a youth of two-and-twenty, and so did the
king seem when first I saw him. Now I count twice that
and more, and how does the king seem? As his brother
does, sirs. A pretty lad of two- or three-and-twenty."

"We notice that," the boy said. "They never change.
You'd think they'd have the sense to pretend."

"Why should they?" said Brother Richard. "They
must be, by my reckoning, a good threescore and ten. Or
a bad, if you prefer; and the Assassin is older than that.
Who has ever touched them?"

"A few have tried," Brother Thomas said. "None has
succeeded. Their people surround them; even their
Church defends them. And they have their magic."

"You talk of it." The knight sounded eminently
bored. "I see no use in it—and no terror, either. The dog
and his bitch are devilish young for the years they're
given: granted. Maybe he has help to be as good on the
field as he is; maybe she is as deadly with a dagger as
rumor makes her. What does that make them but comfortably dangerous? I want that thorn out of the kingdom's side, before it tears a hole wide enough to let the
Saracen in. Unfortunately the two of them are powerful
enough to make removal difficult unless we catch them

in outright treason; and even then we'll still need them,
and the men they can bring to the field."

"If they bring them at all," said Seco. "My lord. That
is what we do here. If we can separate them from their
power, show them to be witches and worse, remove the
threat of treachery . . ."

"A perfectly ordinary impossibility," said the knight.
He stretched out his legs, hands folded over his belt. He
did not, for all of that, look like a man at ease. "You
want to draw his fangs: well and good. I fail to see what
witchcraft has to do with it."

"Everything," said Brother Thomas.

The knight's brows went up.

"Everything," the monk said again. "What you want,
yes, that I can see. The prince and his Assassin may
endanger your kingdom; they certainly endanger your
king, whose right to the throne they are not eager to
accept. Now the brother comes, and he is a crowned
king: an all too plausible rival, should he choose to become one. I hear that King Guy is a fair knight but no
general, and a wretched statesman. Gwydion of Rhiyana
is knight and general and statesman, and enchanter besides.

"No," Thomas said before the knight could interrupt,
"you do not see it. You see only what they wish to reveal.
Their beauty and their agelessness—that is the very least
of what they are. Even that may be enough in such a
kingdom as this is, balanced on the sword's edge. If the
devil raised an army against the Saracen, would you accept it?"

The knight shrugged. "That would depend on the
price. If it cost my brother his throne, then no, I
wouldn't. Guy may not be much better than the idiot
your witch-prince calls him, but he's my idiot. I prefer to
keep him."

"Then, my lord, you must take thought for witchery.
I know—I know for a certainty—that if one of them
wishes to know what we do and say here, then he will
know. They can walk in your mind, my lord. They can
read your every thought."

The boy gasped. His father was green-pallid and had

begun to sweat. Even Brother Richard seemed uncomfortable.

The knight shivered, but his expression was skeptical. "Why conspire at all, then, if the enemy is omniscient?"

"They are not God," Thomas said frigidly. "There are ways to elude their scrutiny. Prayer is one. Knowledge is another—if it comes without fear. Their powers are great, but hardly infinite; they are not easily deceived, but they can be distracted. As they must be, if this plot of yours is to succeed."

"How do you know," demanded the knight, "that they aren't spying on us at this very moment?"

"I do not." Thomas was calm. "I trust in God that they are well occupied with the king's arrival in the city; too well to care what mere mortals do."

"Yes," the knight mused. "They would be that arrogant." He fixed the monk with a hard stare. "If you're telling the truth."

"He is," Brother Richard said.

"Even so," said Seco. His voice shook; he struggled to steady it. Bad enough that the one he wanted to break was a witch. It had never occurred to him that that witchery could come to him from far away, and strip his mind bare, and leave him shivering in the dark. Now he understood all his failures, and his enemy's scorn. The memory burned. "Even so, we have to try. That is why the good Brother is here; apart from his other skills. To teach us how to stand against the sorcerers."

"If I agree," said Thomas. "You may escape them if you fail. I must live within their reach."

"You've done it for years already," the knight said.

"Never so close. Never with so much at stake."

"True," said Brother Richard. "You have to consider what this will win you. Death if you fail. If you succeed . . . maybe only the Elvenking's discomfiture and his brother's enmity. Prince Aidan is a bad enemy. His Assassin is worse."

Seco's temper flared. "Are you with us or against us?"

"With you, of course," the monk said placidly.

"Someone should be the voice of reason, no? Even with my lord Amalric to help."

"I admit," said Amalric, "that I fail to see what you can gain from this. Messer Seco wants profit. I want a threat removed from the kingdom. Your brother monk has his long campaign and, I judge, an old score to settle. What have you?"

"The pleasure of the hunt," Richard answered him. "And a certain degree of greed. I have a way to make in the world and in the Church. This may make it for me. I found Brother Thomas for you, did I not? Is he or is he not more than you ever dared to hope for?"

"Only if he throws in his lot with us, and sticks to it."

Brother Thomas sat still under their eyes, refusing to be hurried. "What you ask me to do, I can do, if you will supply me with the wherewithal. Whether I will do it . . . I have lived my life to bring these demons to the justice of holy Church. Should I chance defeat by striking too soon?"

"It will be a worse defeat if you strike too late." Amalric measured him. "Whatever the King of Rhiyana may be, you're no boy. Would you wait so long for just the right moment, that it never comes at all?"

Brother Thomas stiffened. That blow had struck home. Amalric's mouth stretched with the beginnings of a smile. "They never grow old; they may never die. Can you outwait them?"

"I can judge my moment," Thomas snapped. "Very well. You can do nothing without me, innocents that you are in the ways of witchkind. For Christian charity, I will help you."

"For Christian charity," said Amalric, nodding sagely. "Yes. Indeed. How else?"

Thomas's look was not kind, but he was a man of God, and a man of his word. He held his peace.

3

The cloth was on the table at last, the hall hung with silk and scented with rosewater, the servants in fresh livery and the children in their best clothes. The dogs were banished to the kennels, Ranulf's falcon to the mews. Ranulf himself was caught, scrubbed, and bullied into a cotte befitting a baron of Acre. He looked well in it, if not precisely comfortable. Age-softened wool and well-worn leather would always suit him better than silk.

Joanna, whose own rich gown was rather tighter in the middle than she would have liked, gave it a last, exasperated tug, and turned to her husband. "How terrible is it?" she asked.

Ranulf looked her over. "You look," he said, "magnificent."

"Angry, you mean. Like a sausage in a casing."

"Sausages look angry?"

He was laughing at her. She aimed a cuff at his head, stopped short of ruffling his newly combed hair. It was thinner than it had been, and the gold was fading to dun and grey, but he was still a handsome man. She bared her teeth at him. "And it's all your fault, sir."

"I'm doing penance for it," he said, flexing his shoulders in the cotte. "Don't you think—"

"No! I won't, and you won't. Quick, out, or they'll be here before we're ready for them."

As it happened, they were not. The lord and lady of Mortmain were in the courtyard when their guests rode in, as calm to look at as if a king dined at their table every day. Aimery, stiffer with pride than with his new cotte, was there to take the king's bridle. Joanna took note that he did not stare, though there was plenty to stare at.

It was true. They were exactly alike. It was dizzying to see one on the tall grey gelding and the other on the tall grey mare; one in the Saracen coat and one in blue embroidered with silver; one bareheaded, the other with his hood on his shoulders. They had the same long-limbed grace, the same light touch on the rein, the same effortless ease in the saddle.

Joanna's knees wanted to melt. Twins were nothing uncanny. Aidan's Kipchaks were imps out of Hades, but they were human enough for all that.

These looked it, well enough: tall, white-skinned, black-haired young men with eagles' faces. There was a glamour on them, blurring their fierce alien beauty, dimming the light that shone out of them. But she knew. She saw what they were, with doubled intensity.

One of them smiled at her. That was Aidan. It caught her breath in her throat, and then it steadied her.

How had she imagined that they were indistinguishable? The other was quiet, almost muted, with a fierce edge beneath; fiercer maybe than Aidan's own. He dismounted without the flourish that his brother put into it, and greeted her in a voice, with an accent, so like the other's that she glanced aside, half expecting trickery.

The king's eyes glinted. She smiled before she knew it, and sank down in the best curtsy she was capable of. His hands as he raised her were narrow and uncannily strong. Familiar, and utterly different.

Then he was past, greeting Ranulf, Margaret, the children in order. There was a gap in the ranks; she looked harder, and it was filled. Ysabel seemed flushed and a little breathless. Later, Joanna promised herself, she would find out what the child had been up to.

"Don't trouble," Aidan said in her ear. She started, caught herself. He was at his ease, damn him, and so happy that he shone. "She was with us."

"All this time? But—"

"But." He leaned a fraction closer. Not quite touching. He never, quite, touched. "No harm done, though one fine day I'll take a strap to her. She's getting too clever for her own good."

Ysabel, demure between her smaller, plumper sisters, was engrossed in the king's greeting. Joanna's brows lowered. "I never even knew that she was gone."

"You were busy." Aidan sighed a little, shrugged.

"She did want to see my brother. I expect she'll behave herself now that she's done it. For a while."

"For just as long as it takes her to find some new bit of mischief." Joanna drew herself up. Her back was aching. Again. "Enough of that. Where's Aimery? Ah. Here, sir, run to the hall and tell the steward to be ready. We'll be in directly."

She was running away, and he had to know it as well as she. He did not try to stop her. He never did.

This time, she supposed, he had cause. Of course the Assassin would have waited to make her entrance until she could draw every eye. Shameless though she could be when it pleased her fancy, running about dressed like a boy, on high occasions she was always the perfect Muslim lady: wrapped, swathed, and muffled in veils. Only her hands were visible, white and slender, and her cat-green eyes. No one in the High Court had ever knowingly seen her face, though once, and only once, they had come close to it: the first time she went before them and claimed Aidan for her own. But then she had had her back to them, and only King Baldwin had seen what there was to see, and he was years dead. They told tales of her, exactly as she intended. That she was hideous, or hideously scarred. That she was unbearably beautiful. That she had a demon's fangs, or a cloven hoof. They never matched the green-eyed Saracen eunuch who was often in the prince's company, with the mysterious lady of the Assassins.

Her lover's brother greeted her as a king should, with royal courtesy. Joanna did not hear what she said, but Gwydion's response was clear enough. He was as smitten with her as all the rest of them, snared by eyes and hands and a low pure voice.

Joanna did not hate her. Oh, no. Joanna was merely jealous of everything that she was. Beautiful—because she was that; a beauty to break the heart. Clear and witty and wise. Aidan's, beyond hope of changing it.

He was with her. Joanna had not even seen him move. He had her hand in his. She never leaned or clung: she was a wild thing, and even for him she would not be either soft or pliant. But her eyes on him, even at that

distance, were burning-tender. He bent over her, tall beside her Saracen smallness, and said something that
made her laugh. The sound was fierce and sweet. Still
hand in hand, with the king beside them, they went into
the hall.

The children were not supposed to take part in the
feast. It was the nursery for them, and Nurse's hard eye
lest they dirty their clothes, and later they would sing for
the king. Ysabel knew she could not stretch the morning's ruse to cover an afternoon's absence: Prince Aidan
obviously had not given her leave to sit with him, and
Nurse knew what Mother wanted. Ysabel thought of giving Nurse's mind a nudge, but she stopped short of it.
That was the Sin, Aidan had taught her. Tricks and
sleights were one thing; at worst, one got one's behind
paddled, and that was that. Mind-twisting was ugly, a
devil's trick. It smirched the magic, and took all the
beauty out of it.

Still, it was sorely tempting. Mariam and Lisabet
were little better than babies; all they wanted to do was
play with their dolls. Baudouin, the youngest, was asleep
with his thumb in his mouth. William was a page; like
Aimery, he was judged worthy to serve in the hall.

It was not fair. William, at seven, could wait on the
king. Ysabel would be ten on the Feast of the Conquest,
and she was shut up with the babies. *Help Nurse look
after them,* Mother said.

As if Nurse ever needed help. Ysabel glowered at the
piece she was supposed to be embroidering, and thought
of setting it on fire. The needle seared her fingers. She
yelped and dropped it. Nurse thought she had pricked
herself. Nurse was adept at thinking round the humanly
impossible. Not at all like Dura. Dura was mute, and
Mother's. She saw everything, and understood it, the
way cats did, under her skin.

Ysabel thought of going to find her. Nurse might not
object to that, with all the others to occupy her.

Mariam and Lisabet began to quarrel. This was a

hotter fight than most: it came rapidly to blows. Nurse sprang into the fray.

Ysabel took a bare instant to take it in, and to thank Blessed Mother Mary for it. Then she was gone.

The hall was full to bursting, between her father's people and her uncle's and now the Rhiyanan king's, and such of the pope's men as had not gone to keep the bishop company. All of Aidan's mamluks were there, though some only pretended to eat. Ysabel, in her favorite spying place behind the phoenix tapestry, watched them watch their prince. He had Morgiana on his right and Elen on his left, and he had never looked as happy as he did now. He dazzled her, he was so splendid.

Ysabel was happy for him. She would have been happier if she had been William or Aimery: stiff and proud in livery, waiting on him and hearing what they all said. She could do that, but she had to listen underneath, and be careful about it. Aidan might not care if he noticed, but Morgiana could be merciless. Though she seemed happy enough, these days. Laughing at nothing, dancing for no reason at all. It was all a great deal of fuss for a few words on a parchment; even if they were the lord pope's.

She did not notice Simeon the Jew anywhere, or his son. She was a little disappointed, though of course they would not eat at a Christian table. The mamluks only did it to be near their lord. She was glad she was a Christian. She could eat anywhere, and never worry about being unclean.

Watching them eat made her hungry. She stood it as long as she could, but her stomach began to growl menacingly. They were not doing anything, after all, but eating and talking of nothing in particular. She left them to it.

Cook roared at her, but let her filch a trencherful of dainties and carry them to the garden. She settled there, well content, with the kitchen cat to keep her company.

She was not surprised when Akiva sat on the other

end of the bench. "Have you had anything to eat?" she asked him.

"The king saw to it," he said. "We have our own cook."

She nodded. "My uncle's people have one, too. One of them married her to keep her with them. Or so Dildirim says. He's getting fat on what she feeds him."

Akiva grinned. His teeth were white and sharp. Animal teeth. She eyed him sidelong. He stretched, turning his face to the sun. He was not much prettier than she was, with his great hooked nose and his too-big eyes and his pointed chin, but something was starting to change. The way Aidan said she would, when she was older. Like a cygnet turning into a swan.

"It's warm here," he said. "My bones like it."

"Your skin won't, if you're not careful."

"I am." But he sat up straight again and looked at his hands. They were very white. Hers were whiter, but not by much.

He looked up. She stared back. "Are you the king's son?" she asked him.

He flushed angrily, but he laughed. "No! Nor his nephew, either."

It was her turn to flush. "He's only my uncle by marriage. Grandmother married his sister's son—Lady Elen's uncle. After my real grandfather died. Because Mother and her brother needed a father, and she liked him. Very much."

"Ah," said Akiva.

Her brows lowered. "I don't like what you're thinking."

"You don't know what I'm thinking," he said calmly. "You're not looking."

Nor was she about to let her. He was strong. Not as strong as Aidan, but strong enough, and trained. She drew back.

"I'm why my father went to Rhiyana," Akiva said. "Besides the fact that we're welcome there, and treated like human people. He's a wise man, my father. He saw what I was, and he knew that I was his, and my mother's, too, and yet I wasn't; I was something else. He'd heard about the king; he thought he might know what to do with me. And so the king did. They're fast friends now, and not just because of me."

"I can see that," said Ysabel. She chewed her lip. He was telling secrets. That was a gift, and it expected a gift in return. But she was not sure she wanted to tell him. He knew the part that was less important. How not? He was like her. She said slowly, "I've always known I was different. It never mattered, much. He was always there to help me: my uncle. My—" She tried, but she could not say it. "People don't know. They count to nine and look at my father—the one who thinks he's my father. They don't know to count to eleven, to get one of us. My mother thinks I don't, either. She thinks I don't know." Her hands were fists. "I'm not a bastard. I'm *not*!"

"I'm not calling you one," said Akiva.

Ysabel barely heard him. "I am, though, aren't I? Father is Aimery's father, and William's and Mariam's and Lisabet's and Baudouin's and the new baby's. I'm the one Mother lied about. Because she loved someone she shouldn't have; and still does. And he's going to marry Morgiana. *She* says I'm silly, and if I were a Muslim it wouldn't matter who my father is, because where Allah is, every child is the same."

"I think I like Morgiana," Akiva said.

"You don't *like* Morgiana. You love her or you hate her. Usually both at once."

"Morgiana is more absolutely *us* than any of us. Isn't she?"

Ysabel blinked. "Well. Yes. Yes, that's exactly it. There's no human in her, to take the edges off."

"She frightens people," Akiva said.

"Even you?"

He grimaced. "Even me. I tried to slip around a corner and see what she was thinking, and she almost took my thought-finger off. Not even thinking about it, mind. Just swatting me like a fly. I've still got the headache."

"No wonder, if you were that stupid."

He twitched, offended.

She bit her tongue. If he had been one of her brothers, it would not have mattered. Brothers were for driv-

ing wild. But he was certainly not her brother. "I mean,"
she said, "nobody tries that with Morgiana twice. Even
my uncle had to learn the hard way."

He accepted the peace offering, after a little thought.
He held out his hand. "Friends?" he asked.

She wiped her own hand hastily on her skirt and gave
it to him. "Friends," she said.

Aidan was well aware of the spy behind the arras.
Something would have to be done about her, he reflected,
not for the first time. Perhaps if she were granted a woman's privileges, made a part of everything, given what she
persisted in taking: that would put paid to her rebellion.

He would speak to her mother. Which was never as
easy as Joanna might think it was. Blessed humanity; it
made her blind to what it cost him, to keep the distance
he must keep.

She was pregnant again and happy in it, her rich
body grown richer with years and childbearing. After the
first, which had been bitterly hard, she had settled to it.
She bore well, and as easily as a human woman could.

Maybe he had a little to do with that. Some of his
magic was in her still, woven with her substance, from a
time when she had almost died, and he had given her all
the power he had, to make her live.

The one who had almost killed her sat beside him, a
faceless figure in swathes of green veils, but under them
she was thrumming with joy. Morgiana ran a teasing
hand up his thigh. He caught it, twining his fingers with
hers. "What, madam! Can't you wait until the Church
hallows it?"

"No," she said, clear and definite, as Morgiana always was. Even when she doubted, she made no bones
about it.

He raised her fingers to his lips. He heard the slight
catch of her breath. When they were the most notorious
sinners in Outremer, they had been less circumspect by
far than they were now, with their wedding before them.
It changed things. It made them matter more.

Sometimes they forgot that there was a world outside

of them. Aidan woke to it with a guilty start, as he often did of late. People were indulgent. It was a new thing, to be predictable. He did not know that he liked it.

There was a stir at the entrance to the hall. A latecomer, and one of rank, from the magnitude of the flurry. The steward hastened toward the high table and bent to Ranulf's ear. Aidan eavesdropped shamelessly. "A guest, my lord," the steward said. "Messire Amalric de Lusignan."

Ranulf's expression altered not at all. "Let him in," he said, "and clear a place for him."

"At the high table, my lord?"

Ranulf hesitated the merest instant. "Yes," he said.

Aidan had to admire his aplomb. Ranulf de Mortmain would greet the devil himself with quiet courtesy and offer him a place at his table.

Messire Amalric was hardly as illustrious a personage as that. Merely the brother of Jerusalem's upstart king, and Constable of the kingdom in his own right, and no friend to the house of Mortmain. Ranulf, like any other baron with a brain in his head, had resisted Guy's regency when the child king was alive, and stood with the Count of Tripoli: firmly enough that his eldest son was Raymond's page, and soon to be made his squire.

Amalric had gall, Aidan granted him that. He advanced as calmly as if this were a friend's hall and he an invited guest. His eyes scanned their faces, flickering from Aidan to Gwydion and back again. For a moment he was hard put to choose; but he, unlike his brother, was no fool. He bowed to the Rhiyanan king and said clearly, "I bring you greetings, my lord of Rhiyana, in the name of my lord of Jerusalem. He regrets that he cannot greet you in his own person; he begs your indulgence."

It was all perfectly correct, and deeply, subtly insolent. Gwydion, who had known all the nuances of insult when this pup's father was in swaddling bands, inclined his head a precise degree.

Aidan spoke for him with rich pleasure. "My lord of Rhiyana accepts the apologies of the lord from Lusignan. Is he, perhaps, indisposed?"

"A slight fever," said Amalric easily, keeping his eyes
on Gwydion, betraying no anger at the title which Aidan
gave his brother. "No cause for alarm."

Or, his mind said clearly, for joy. He was a jarring
presence to such senses as Aidan's: plain forgettable face,
clever eyes, mind darting from thought to thought with
dizzying quickness. He relished this game of kings, and
the spice of fear that was in it.

Aidan preferred a good clean battle. He raised his
cup and drank rather more deeply than might have been
wise; not that it could befuddle him as it would a human
man.

"We hope," Gwydion said to Amalric, "that your
brother recovers swiftly from his indisposition. A kingdom is never well served when its king is ill."

Amalric crossed himself piously. "Your majesty is
kind. My brother would be pleased to speak with you
when you come to Jerusalem; and the lovely lady"—he
bowed to Elen—"perhaps would consent to bear the
queen company."

"It would be my pleasure," said Elen, coolly and
flawlessly courteous.

Aidan smiled to himself. The hoyden had grown into
a great lady. Maybe, after all, there was hope for Ysabel.

He was pleased enough, almost, not to mind that
Amalric accepted the place which had been made for
him; even though it was beside Elen. Joanna was on his
other side, and she was well able to keep him in hand.

He seemed content to be the skeleton at the feast; he
essayed no further insolence, nor played any game that
Aidan could discern, unless this was all of it: to be here,
and welcomed, and accorded courtesy. Aidan put him
out of mind. Let him bear the tale to his fool of a
brother. They did nothing here that was not perfectly
proper. Even Guy might be capable of comprehending
that.

Elen was glad when the feast was over. Bred as she
was to courts, she had no fear of great gatherings and the
dance of thrust and parry which was conversation in

their midst, but even royal blood could grow weary of it. And she was more than weary. She was wrung dry.

Riquier had been no great marvel of a husband. She was given to him at fourteen, to seal an alliance which her father reckoned indispensable. She gave him three children, none of which lived past infancy. Now he was dead, and she shocked herself. She grieved for him. She wanted him back.

Sometimes she wondered if Gwydion truly understood, or if he had brought her with him simply because she asked. That too had been a shock: how keenly she wanted to be away from any place which reminded her of Riquier. Rome was almost good enough. Outremer might even heal her. They said it could, if a pilgrim's heart was pure.

She grimaced as her maid undressed her in the room which the two of them must share. It was an eastern room, not large but airy and cool, with a door that opened on the garden. This part of the house, Lady Joanna had said when she showed Elen to it, had been the harem when Acre was a Saracen city. It was not a gilded and scented prison, as she might have imagined. It was merely separate, and quiet.

Quite unlike her heart, or her unruly body. Whatever Riquier's shortcomings, he had been a skilled and frequent lover; and she had learned to be his match. The fall that killed him was quick, and therefore merciful, and of that she was glad. But she could not forgive him for abandoning her.

Someone rapped lightly at the door. Joanna, casting a shrewd eye over the room and its occupants. Elen flushed, as if that patently human lady could know what she was thinking.

"You're well?" Joanna asked her. Simple courtesy; there could be no more to it than that. Elen murmured something. The lady nodded, but she did not withdraw. Such a tall woman, and so strong, with a firm-jawed, level-browed face. No beauty, but not ugly, either; handsome in an inescapably Norman fashion. It was hard to believe that her mother was half a Saracen.

Elen spoke before she thought. "Won't you sit down? Or do you have duties?"

"You were the last of them," Joanna said, blunt enough, but with a smile in it. She sat down gratefully on a cushion that Elen had seen no visible use for, and leaned against the wall. "Ah. That's better. I'm run off my feet."

Elen smiled. "We'd never have guessed it, as cool as you were, and everywhere at once. Were those all your children, who sang to us?"

"Every imp of them," she said. "And no sour notes, thank Our Lady. It would never have done to have Conrad throwing things in front of the king."

"Conrad is their tutor?"

"He's been teaching them to sing. You'd have noticed him: the Viking in the turban."

Elen most certainly had. "He's . . . rather noticeable. Why does he dress like a Saracen?"

"He is one."

Elen's disbelief was palpable.

"He's a mamluk," Joanna said. "A soldier-slave. They come as children from all over the world; they're bought by the sultan's men, and trained as knights are— knights of Islam. Though mamluks from the Rus are rarer than most; usually they're Turks, or Tartars like the twins. They're all Aidan's, that lot, though he set them free."

"Aidan's Saracens." Elen liked the sound of that. "And one a Viking. Take off his turban, put him in a cotte, and you'd have a perfect Norman."

"So he does, now and then, mostly for mischief. He won one of his wives that way. It was a terrible scandal. She was a good Christian, a sergeant's daughter; he wooed her and won her, and she never seemed to mind that there were two others before her."

"Two . . ." Elen eyed Joanna narrowly for signs of mockery, but there were none. "How can a man have three wives?"

"If he's a Muslim, he can have four. All that's required of him is that he be able to support them, and treat them all alike."

"The women don't mind?"

"Who asks them?" Joanna's tone was surprisingly bitter. "It's better than lying and sneaking and keeping mistresses on the sly."

"I couldn't do it," Elen said.

"Nor I," Joanna admitted. "Nor, I think, if they had a choice, most of them. Morgiana would kill before she'd share her prince."

She spoke as if she knew it for a certainty. Elen was not quite bold enough to ask how. Morgiana, Elen was learning rapidly, was strange even for one of the Folk. Elen had yet to see anything of her but her hands and her green cat-eyes.

She shivered a little. "I can imagine that she kills as easily as she breathes."

"No," said Joanna with startling vehemence. "No, she doesn't kill easily. But quickly, yes, and sometimes without stopping to think. She's purely like a cat, is Morgiana."

"You don't like her, do you?"

"Liking has nothing to do with it." Joanna stood, straightening with care, bracing her hands in the small of her back. "I was her prey once. No fault of hers that I survived. Forgiveness is easy enough; it's forgetting that I can't do."

Elen bit her lip. "I'm sorry."

"For what?" Joanna was sharp, but not angry. She even managed a smile. "She's a hunting cat and I'm a dog of a Frank. We'll never love one another, but neither need we be enemies. We go our own ways; we cross as seldom as we can. It works well, all in all."

Well, but not entirely comfortably. Elen bit her tongue to keep it from working any more mischief.

Joanna left her then, with an embrace that was somewhat more than dutiful, and a smile that warmed her for a good while after. It even, a little, eased her longing for Riquier.

4

Aidan had no use for sleep, with Gwydion to share the night with him. Even Morgiana trailed off at last, leaving them to themselves in the lamplit dimness of the chamber. Gwydion's squire snored softly just outside the door; but for that, there was no sound. For a long while neither moved to break the silence, with mind or tongue.

Gwydion laid his head on his brother's shoulder and sighed. "Never," he said. "Never so long again."

Aidan settled an arm about him. "No," he said. "Never. How did we stand it?"

"Did we?"

"I thought I did."

"I, too. Until I realized that there seemed to be too little of me. I kept groping for my other half. I even missed your temper."

Aidan grinned and ruffled his hair. "Does you good to have to fly into your own rages now and then."

His brother shivered. "You know why I don't dare."

Aidan's grin faded. He held Gwydion close, shaking him a little. "I'm here now. I won't let you shatter."

"No; you'll do it for me." Gwydion laughed: a quick hiss of breath. "Ah, brother, God knows I've needed you. Maybe it's true what they say, and there's only one of us, but in two bodies."

"Does that make me half a man?"

"Surely that's for your lady to say."

Aidan ran his hand down his brother's back. "Saints, you're as stiff as a stone. Here, lie down. Don't you know by now to let it out before it sets solid? You don't need a rage. A good, loud howl would do."

"What, on shipboard?" Gwydion lay as he was bidden and let himself be coaxed out of his shirt. He gasped as Aidan attacked a knot. "I was well enough until I went to Rome. Maura was with me then. You know how she dislikes to leave the land which she has made her own: how she pined when I brought her to Caer Gwent, until her beasts came, and she made her garden, and put down roots in the new earth. In Rome it was worse. She hid it from me; she gathered all her strength, and used it all, and worked miracles in the papal curia. One day she fainted at a cardinal's feet. She was alive and blooming, but she was dying: like a flower cut from its root."

Aidan's hands stilled. "You didn't tell me."

"What was there to tell? I prevailed on her to return to Rhiyana. She was most unwilling. She wept that she should be so weak; that she had failed in a thing that any mortal child could do. But she was fading, and in the end even she could not deny it. I sent her back to Caer Gwent, to rule in my place, and grow strong again. So she did, and so she has."

"And you've been alone."

"And I've been alone." Gwydion's voice was inexpressibly weary. "Now I understand why Maura wept."

"Prices," Aidan said, easing the tension out of him, stroke by long slow stroke. "We have blessings beyond the reach of human men: beauty, agelessness, great magic. But there is a price. She is bound to the land, and I to you, and all of us to one another. And there are so few of us; so pitifully few."

"It keeps us from growing too proud."

"Or too vain, or too spoiled."

"Power can be a sore temptation," Gwydion said. "Everything can be so easy: to make, to heal, to speak not in empty rattling words but in the truth behind them. Yet it's never enough. The world is so great, and I —even I—so small. . . ."

Sleep was claiming him, though he struggled against it. The weariness in him was bone-deep. It dragged at Aidan. He thrust it away, pouring out his own bright, glad strength. "Rest," he said. "Sleep."

When Gwydion gave up the fight at last, Aidan stretched out beside him. His warmth was beast-warmth, his presence a joy so profound that for a moment Aidan could not breathe. He laid his arm across his brother's back, body to gently breathing body, and matched the rhythm of his magic to the slow pulse that was Gwydion's. Sleep came with it, sweet and deep.

Ysabel, looking for mischief in the hour before sunup, found Aimery instead. He was full of himself as usual, ordering the bath-servants about because, as he put it, "His majesty wants to bathe. Again. All over."

"Prince Aidan bathes every day," Ysabel said, unimpressed. "Don't you do that in Tripoli?"

"We live like Christians in Tripoli," said Aimery haughtily.

"In filth?"

He snarled and tried to push past her. She was solider than she looked; he could not move her.

He stopped, furious. "Will you get over? His majesty is waiting."

"His majesty is so happy to be with his brother, he's not noticing how long anything takes."

"How do you know?"

Ysabel was not about to tell him. "I'll get over if you promise to take me riding after."

"I can't take you riding. I have to wait on his majesty."

"What if his majesty wants to go?"

"Then I'll go with him. And you," said Aimery with enormous satisfaction, "will stay home with the rest of the babies."

Her eyes narrowed. She kept her voice quiet. She was proud to hear how quiet it was. "I'm not a baby."

"You're a girl," he said.

"Is that what they teach you in Tripoli?"

"In Tripoli," he said, "women know their place."

Either he was an idiot, or he had been away too long. She thought that maybe it was both. She smiled at him with poisonous sweetness. "Prince Aidan always lets me ride with him. He says I ride better than any boy."

Aimery went stiff. He was even more horrified than she had hoped.

She laughed and danced out of his way. He almost ran away from her.

* * *

He fetched up against a wall, no matter which wall it was, and drove his fist at it. The pain was sharp, and welcome.

She always knew exactly what to say. Exactly where to drive the knife. Exactly where to twist it.

He was the oldest. The heir. The one who mattered most. And it was always Ysabel they talked about, Ysabel they thought of, Ysabel they fretted over. She was the one they noticed. She was their favorite.

He would give his heart's blood for a moment of the prince's attention. And did he ever get it? For a vanishing instant, maybe. Then Ysabel would come, and Aimery would be forgotten. He was only another of the tribe. She was the one Aidan loved.

He cooled his burning cheek against the wall. His hand throbbed. "I hate her," he said.

It sounded silly, said aloud. *Of course you don't hate your sister,* his mother would say, impatient as she always was with foolishness. *You're jealous, that's all. Someone's always jealous in a family. That's the way the devil tempts us.*

Maybe he hated his mother, too. Maybe he hated everybody.

His mood was beautifully black. He was almost sad that it had to lighten. He had duties, after all, and a king to wait on. That much, even Ysabel could not take away from him.

It was cool in the garden, almost cold, with the sun barely risen to warm it. Elen paused under a flowering tree. She would have to ask someone what it was. Its scent was sweet and potent, more purely alien than anything she had yet known: truly, at last, Outremer. She broke off a spray and tucked it in her hair. Her veil had slipped to her shoulders; she left it there. The sun lay on her like a warm hand.

The garden was larger than it looked, with paths and hedges and bowers, and a fountain playing where roses bloomed. Sometimes she could not even see the house, so clever were the contrivances of paths and hedges.

She saw the man long before he saw her. A gardener, she supposed, clearing weeds from a fishpond. He wore a turban, which made him a Saracen; he was not as small as most of them were, though he was dark enough. His sleeves were rolled high, baring long strong arms the color of bronze. He swept up a handful of weed and tossed it toward a goat which waited as if expectant. The beast caught it neatly; he laughed and said something in what must have been Arabic. She liked the sound of his voice. Warm and deep, with a ripple of mirth.

She watched him feed the goat. It was a young one, and seemed to be someone's pet: its fawn coat was brushed to silk, its amber eyes mild, for a goat's. When he stopped feeding it, it blatted. He answered it in tones both regretful and firm. The goat butted him peremptorily.

There was a moment of stunned astonishment; then, a resounding splash.

She leaped. Too late by far for his dignity, but she got a grip on his hand and pulled him, gasping and spluttering, out of the pond.

He had lost his turban. His hair was in braids, three of them. His face was as bronze-dark as his arms. Water ran in streams from his beard. A strand of weed was wound in it. She reached to pluck it loose.

His eyes opened, blinking through the wet, and froze her in midmotion. They were blue. Blue as the Middle Sea; blue as a fire's heart.

And utterly, devastatingly appalled, as he saw her clearly.

She finished what she had begun. It was her own kind of defiance. He stiffened at her touch, as if he could not believe that she would dare it; all at once he recoiled. She caught him before he fell in again.

His face went an astonishing shade of grey: bloodless under the bronze. She wondered if he had hit his head. She was sure of it when he staggered and, abruptly, went down.

Not in a faint. He was groveling. Or whatever Saracens called it.

It made her angry. She dragged him up. He was taller than she had thought, almost as tall as Gwydion. "Never," she said, not stopping to think if he would understand her, "never do that to me."

He flushed. There was nothing subservient in his expression. From the look of it, his temper bade fair to match hers. "My lady," he said in quite passable Frankish. "What would you have me do?"

"Face me like a man," she said. "Did you hit your head?"

He turned it gingerly on his neck and explored it with long supple fingers. "No," he said, "my lady." His black brows met. "May I ask what my lady is doing here?"

"Saving your life, I rather thought." She tossed her head. "I still think so. Even if you do not."

"I thank you for my life," he said as if he recited a lesson. "My lady."

"Your life, but not your pride. As for your dignity . . ." She offered him her veil, and when he would not take it, proceeded to dry him herself.

He wriggled like a small child, though the words he muttered—even in Arabic—did not sound like anything a child would know. "Would you rather drip?" she snapped at him.

"Yes!"

She laughed. That stopped him. Even without those improbable eyes, he was a handsome man. And young; but not a boy. He was more than five-and-twenty, less than thirty: a good age for a man.

She dried him as much as she could, and enjoyed it rather more than she should. He suffered it grimly. No doubt it was agony to be handled so by a woman, and a Christian at that. That he was not a gardener nor a menial, she was beginning to be sure of. That kind of touchy pride never lived out of childhood, unless its owner ranked high enough to foster it.

"Are you one of Aidan's Saracens?" she asked.

He drew himself up. "I am his mamluk," he said.

And proud of it, too. This time he met her grin with one of his own, though it was brief, a white flash in his dark face. "And I am his sister's granddaughter," she said. "Elen."

He inclined his head, gracious, if not quite ready to forgive her. "Raihan," he said.

She accepted the gift as courteously as he had, and as coolly. "You speak the *langue d'oeil* very well."

"My lord taught me." His tongue stumbled just perceptibly, as if praise made it awkward. "Strangers are not to know. That we understand them."

"That's wise. You hear more, that way."

His eyes glittered. "Oh, we do, indeed."

"Too much?"

"Never while it serves my lord. He is never sullied, whatever men may call him."

There was faith as pure as any saint's. They gave it a moment's silence. Then, with a squawk, Raihan dived toward the goat. It surrendered its great sodden mouthful and resumed its exploration of the pond.

Raihan looked in dismay at the tattered remnants of his turban. Suddenly, unexpectedly, he laughed. It was amazing laughter, rich and full and direly infectious. He was still laughing as he bowed to her—in western fashion this time, with a prince's grace—and walked away, with the goat scampering at his heels.

Ysabel got her ride after all, with everyone in the house who was minded to go, and that was most of them, except for Mother, who was too big with the new baby, and Grandmother, who never rode if she could help it. Gwydion was no better in cities than Aidan was, though he was quieter about it. Once he had his bath and heard mass in St. Perpetua's and ate as much as his kind would ever eat, they all fetched their horses and went in search of clean air.

Aimery was conspicuously not speaking to her. She refused to pay attention. Her mare was new, a gift from her uncle and his lady, and fine: Arab-bred, and fiery enough to make Joanna intensely nervous whenever

Ysabel rode her. Ysabel was inordinately proud of her. She could keep up easily with Aidan's gelding; she loved to arch her neck and flag her tail and dance. People stared as she went by.

That was not all there was to stare at. They were all in riding clothes, nothing splendid except for the odd idiot who thought one went hunting in silk, but there was a small army of them, and Aidan's mamluks with them, and Morgiana playing the eunuch again. Ranulf had a brace of hounds; some of the others had falcons. The Turks had their bows. There would be meat for the pot tonight, and some pleasure in the getting of it.

It was almost impossible to tell Gwydion and Aidan apart without looking inside. They were both in hunting green, and both riding tall greys, and both sparking with delight in the ride and the company. Aidan smiled more, that was all, and Gwydion almost never laughed, except with his eyes. Most people gave up trying to decide which was which, and addressed them both at once.

Morgiana knew, deeply and surely, which was her lover and which his brother. It was strange, dizzying, to see Aidan whole. What she had thought was all of him was only that part of him which was not Gwydion. And yet he was not diminished, nor subsumed into that other self. He was brighter, stronger, more truly himself than she had ever seen him.

She was not jealous, she decided, riding behind them, watching them together. Whether she liked Gwydion, or disliked him, or was indifferent to him . . . that needed time and reflection. That beloved face, that body which she knew in every line and angle, though doubled, was only one to her, the one with Aidan's soul beneath it. The other was a stranger.

A courteous one, to be sure, and quite unperturbed by either her faith or her history. Aidan had that gift, too, of accepting a creature for itself, without heed for what the world might say of it.

"But of course," Gwydion said, falling back beside her as Aidan sprang in pursuit of a roebuck. "We aren't human, to succumb to human divisions. We have to make our own."

The hunt passed them and left them behind. They slowed to a walk, to the disgust of Morgiana's stallion; but he eyed Gwydion's mare and decided that, all in all, he preferred to linger. She kept a light firm rein, letting him dance as he pleased, but holding him well in hand.

"A fine horse," Gwydion said.

"He comes from Egypt," she said. "They breed good horses there; though they prize mares over stallions. This one sires fine foals. Ysabel's mare is one of his."

"I could see," he said. "Both bays, with the star on the forehead. And the head, it is distinctive."

"That is the Arabian head. The large eye, see, set well down from the poll, and the profile curved inward, and the nostril half a handspan wide when it flares. They drink the wind, these horses."

"They are beautiful. So light as they move; so fiery. Alas that I'm too tall for their smallness."

"They could carry you easily," she said.

"If I didn't mind trailing my feet behind me." Gwydion was laughing, though his face was quiet. He ran his hand down his mare's neck, smoothing her mane. "This lady will do for me. Such a gift she is, and half an Arab, too, like her cousin who carries my brother. She would be greatly prized in our country."

"So she would," said Morgiana. "Aidan talks of taking a small herd back with him when he goes: a stallion or two and a few mares of Arab breeding, to cross with your own horses. Your mare is one of his testings, as his gelding was Gereint's."

Gwydion's bright mood darkened at the name of his sister's son. Whom she had killed; for whose death she had paid, and would pay down all the long years.

He did not say it. For that, he won her approbation, if not yet her heart. He gazed ahead across the wide plain of Acre, with the hunt in exuberant cry upon it and the ridge of Carmel blue beyond. The land was losing the green of spring, going dun and brown where there were no people to till it. The orchards, the fields of cane, the cattle in their pastures, were fenced and bordered with

desert. Rich land, but dry and forbidding, if one was
born in the west.

She, whose first memory was of the desert of Persia,
would never perfectly understand a country where rain
fell, sometimes, every day. Sometimes even for days on
end.

"It's very green," said Gwydion, following her
thoughts as she allowed, "and often grey above it with
clouds and mist. But the bones of the land show through
on the moors and the headlands. There's strength
enough there, for all the water that runs over it."

"Water can be as strong as any force that is."

Gwydion's mare slipped the rein and began to graze.
The stallion was not hungry, except for her. Morgiana
persuaded him to halt. He tossed his head and stamped,
but surrendered abruptly and snatched mouthfuls of
grass between eye-rollings and yearnings toward the tall
grey beauty.

"I am glad," said Gwydion out of nowhere that she
could discern, "that you suit my brother so well."

"Do I, then?"

"Perfectly." He leaned on the pommel of his saddle,
at ease, so much like Aidan that she blinked. "I admit, I
had my fears. You were the hunter, after all; and he has a
penchant for trapping himself in oaths which he will not,
or cannot, break."

"Yes," she said, amused. "I did trap him, didn't I? In
front of the whole High Court, with King Baldwin himself called upon to make the judgment. Whether a bargain we struck, that I should settle his account with the
Old Man of the Mountain, and he should give himself to
me until he satisfied me, was in fact fulfilled by a night of
his . . . service; or whether satisfaction should encom-
pass more than a few hours' pleasure. Whether he had
sworn to be my night's lover, or my husband." She
smiled and shook her head. "It was hardly wise of him to
strike a bargain with a Muslim, and he a Frank and a
prince, and no merchant at all."

"All Muslims are merchants, he tells me." Gwydion
ran his fingers through his mare's mane, idly, eyes low-

ered. "He should have known better. He knows enough of kings and princes."

"No king in the world can outmaneuver a good trader." She looked to see if he was offended. He was not; not at all. The corner of his mouth curved just visibly upward. "He did well enough by the bargain. He's a wealthy man, as wealthy as any in Outremer; and much of that is Assassin gold."

"And he has you."

She shrugged, one-sided. "I'm no advantage in this kingdom. I breed rumors, but no children."

His compassion rocked her almost out of the saddle. "That will come as God wills. My brother thought that he could sire no children, no more than I; and there is Ysabel."

"Her mother is human."

"Even so," said Gwydion. "Perhaps you are too young."

She laughed, harsh and brief. "I am, at the very least, sixscore years old. I think I may be much more than that. How old must I be before I'm old enough?"

"When did your courses begin?"

"My—" She closed her mouth, mastered her shock. She was used to indelicacy from Franks, and Allah knew, Muslim women could be blunt enough among themselves. But this went beyond indelicate. It was indecent.

Except that there was nothing immodest in the way he asked it. He was like a physician, cool, honestly desirous of an answer.

Simply to be outrageous, she gave it to him. "Is that what that is? Once in a great while, when the moon is waxing? Then I've had it a score of years or so, one a year, maybe, or twice."

He nodded. "Young, then, no matter the count of your years: like a maid just come to womanhood. I think we come into ourselves late, and then we don't either bear or beget easily. It comes with what we are. If we were as fecund as humankind, we would overrun the earth."

"Better we than they."

"No," he said. "I think not. How much magic can one world hold?"

"More by far than is in us."

"I wonder," he said. "In a world the humans share . . . my brother says that in Islam he is much more welcome than he is among Christians. Your world allows us, as ours does not. But if it were known, truly, all that we are, what mortal man would not learn to hate us?"

"There are many who love us. Too well, I sometimes think."

"Ah, but even they have moments of bitter envy."

"I envy their fertility. And yes, even their mortality. They know that there is an end to their living. They will see Paradise long before us, and be far more welcome there, because they are mortal men, and we are but spirits of fire."

"Your Allah does not welcome every soul alike?"

"We are told that He does. But mortals are greater than I: that also is in His Book."

"Ours gives us no place at all," Gwydion said. "Therefore our priests set us among the devils. They would destroy us if they could, and count it a holy act."

She regarded him steadily. "You have your own Crusade."

"To make my kingdom safe for our kind. Yes. And for any other who suffers persecution at mortal hands."

There was a fire in him, all the fiercer for that it was so quiet. "We call it *jihad,*" she said. "Holy war. War that is just; war in God's name."

"Even if it is bloodless, as I would keep it?"

"Even then." She paused. "You are a strange man."

"Stranger than my brother?"

"My lord is explicable enough. He is fire, that is all: bright, burning, terrible when he is let run wild. He runs away from reflection, because it might seduce him into damping his fire. He is most predictably unpredictable."

"Most would tell you that I am dull beside him. Plain water, quiet and rather cold."

"Water quenches fire; and water, raging, can break stone. How many have reckoned that they knew you, and striven to deceive you, and discovered too late that they themselves were deceived?"

"I always tell the truth," he said.

"All of it?"

His eyes glinted. "All that is necessary for the purpose."

"I think," she said, pondering it, "that I may come to like you, O my brother."

"Indeed, O my sister?"

"Indeed." He smiled at her. She grinned, wide and white, like the boy she seemed to be, and gathered the reins. The stallion began a dancing canter. As the mare stretched to match him, he leaped into a gallop. Morgiana flattened herself on his neck, still grinning. The mare was a pale blur in the corner of her eye. Gaining, by the Prophet's beard, and her rider laughing. Aloud. Gwydion. Who would ever believe it?

She laughed with him, light and wild, and gave her mount his head.

Part Two

JERUSALEM

May 1187

5

Jerusalem was a city of domes and towers, set upon the
heights, blazing white in the pitiless sun of Outremer. No
green betrayed itself, no garden within those walls, unless it were a garden of stone, and its own sun blazing
out of it: the Dome of the Rock in the west of the city,
roofed with pure gold.

From the Mount of Olives, above the grey-green ter-
races, across the bleak dun ravine of Kidron, the pilgrims from Rhiyana looked down upon the Holy City.
Some of them wept. Some prayed on their knees.

Gwydion stood silent. His eyes drank it in: the city
that was there for human eyes to see, and the city that
was beyond the mortal city. Holy, high Jerusalem. The
city of peace, for which men had warred for years out of
count.

A tremor rocked him. It came upon him so, not
often, sometimes not for years together; but when it
came, there was no stopping it. He could only brace for
the storm, and endure until it passed.

Blood and fire. Armies innumerable, inexorable as
the sea, shrilling their war-cry. *Allah-il-Allah! Allahu akbar!* The walls fell before them. No army stood against
them. A pitiful few of knights rode out, made what stand
they might, were swept away. The muezzin's voice
wailed over the dome of the Holy Sepulcher.

He gasped, shuddering. The sun blinded him. Christian voices babbled about him; somewhere, someone was

chanting a psalm. *Deliver me, O Lord, from evil men, preserve me from violent men.* . . .

His brother's shoulder braced him; his brother's voice sounded in his ear, soft and blessedly calm. "Peace; it's past."

The humans had not seen, or else had taken it for simple excess of emotion. His own folk stood round him like guards, his brother closest, Morgiana at his back, Akiva in front of him with Ysabel. None of them had thought; they had simply chosen their places. They moved apart as the moment passed, with no word spoken, no thought exchanged.

There was something in that, something potent. There had never been so many of them together, in such a place. Almost without willing it, he could reach, draw them together, make of them—

They scattered. The world burst upon him. People waited, human and otherwise, because he was king, and where he went, they must follow. For a moment he could not. Would not.

But that passed. Years and training rose up in him and mastered him. He led them down from the Mount.

The entry of the King of Rhiyana into Jerusalem was not the quiet passage he might have wished for. His knights, his squires, his men-at-arms, his servants, the pilgrims afoot and on muleback, the priests and the monks and the pope's legate, Aidan's small army of Saracens and his Christian soldiers and servants, the whole tribe of Mortmain: they were a royal procession, and they received a royal welcome.

Aidan had a house near the Dome of the Rock; so near that the great golden dome cast light upon it after the sun had left the rest of the city. From its roof and from some of the upper chambers, one could look down into the jeweled beauty of the courtyard and see the Knights of the Temple in their white robes and red crosses, going about their duties.

"We've given his majesty something to think of," Aidan said with considerable pleasure as he sat with his brother on the roof, watching the sun go down. The house hummed below them, full to bursting with all the people they had brought to it; and that not even all of them. The Mortmains had their own house near the Holy Sepulcher, and the priests had lodgings in the Patriarch's quarter.

Gwydion turned an orange in his hands. He was quieter even than usual, had been since he left the Mount of Olives. His mood did not lighten to match Aidan's. He said somberly, "Yes, his majesty will think. So will his less contented barons. There is another king in the kingdom; another stallion in the herd. And I wait to greet him. I choose the company of my kin, and make no haste to seek a palace that is not my own."

"He can't touch you," said Aidan. "Or fault you for wanting a day to settle yourself. He'd do worse than that if he were the stranger in the city." He leaped up from his seat and began a circuit of the roof, skirting the orange trees in their basins, the rose-briars that twined into a bower for summer evenings, the jasmine waking with the sunset to send forth its sweet strong scent. He plucked a handful of blossoms and scattered them on his brother's head. Gwydion made no move to shake them off; made no move at all. "Gwydion *bach,* our noble king is just capable of doing up his own hose, if someone shows him how. He's no match at all for you."

"What is he for Jerusalem?"

The pain in Gwydion's voice gave even Aidan pause. He dropped down at his brother's feet, took the white cold hands in his. "I saw, too," he said. "I saw Jerusalem fall. But I won't believe that it must be. Not while we live to forestall it."

Gwydion shuddered once, deeply. His hands tightened on Aidan's with sudden, bruising force. "Would to God I had your faith."

"It's not faith. It's blind obstinacy." Aidan grinned up at the face that was his own. The stars of jasmine were caught in the blue-black hair. They were not, somehow, incongruous, even as grim as he was, even as fiercely inhuman as those bones were, with no glamour to soften them.

"This kingdom was founded on the sword's edge," Aidan said. "It has endured a hundred years against odds no sane man would contemplate. One thin line of fortresses from Kerak to Banias: that is all that stands between us and the infidel. More than any kingdom in the world, this is a camp of war, held by folk to whom war is their life's breath. They will not yield while there is strength in them to fight."

"God grant," said Gwydion.

"Would it be so terrible if he saw true?"

Aidan raised his head from Morgiana's breast. "How can you say that?"

"You can ask?"

Their eyes met, clashed, disengaged. He sat up. She lay unmoving, slender ivory body, cloak of wonderful, improbable hair. In lamplight it was almost black, with ruddy lights; in sunlight, the color of wine. She was heartbreakingly beautiful.

And utterly maddening. "We are," he said, "defenders of this kingdom."

"You are. Are you going to swear fealty to Guy, after all?"

"Not if I can help it."

She stretched, sinuous, and coiled on her side, head propped on hand. The lamplight struck fire in her eyes. "Well then. Suppose that the sultan takes Jerusalem. He's a better king by far than Sybilla's fancy man."

"He's an infidel," Aidan said.

"So am I."

"I'm not marrying him."

"I should hope not." She traced an idle, tingling pattern on his thigh. "Why should it matter which God a man prays to, if he rules well?"

"It does matter," he said. "Here of all places in the world. This is our holy land; our Christ who lay in the Sepulcher. We defend it for his sake."

"What of us? That is our Dome out yonder, which your Templars have outraged by setting a cross atop it; our Rock from which the Prophet, on his name be blessing and peace, went up to heaven. It's our land, too, our holy place."

"And Simeon would tell you that your Dome is built on the Temple of Solomon. Maybe we should give all this country back to the Jews, and have done."

"God forbid!"

"God probably will. Allah, too. If He's all the same, who's to say that even He knows which of us has the most right to this city?"

"You are appalling," she said.

He bent to kiss her. She caught him as he drew back, wound her fingers in his hair. "Uncounted multitudes of Muslims," she said, "and any one of them more than willing to taste my sweet white body; and with what should I fall in love? A howling infidel."

"Whereby we know that God can laugh."

Her fingers unwound from his hair, traced the shape of his face, ruffled and then smoothed his beard. He shivered lightly under her touch. He was the first lover she had ever had, and the only one. She had never lost that edge of wondering joy, to find him so different from herself, and yet so perfectly matched. Made for her. Man to her woman; heart to her heart.

"So beautiful," she said, marveling, as if she had never seen him before.

"You are insatiable."

She laughed and tumbled him onto his back. "What, sir! Am I too much for you?"

"Ten men would barely be enough."

"Ah," she said. Her eyes gleamed. "Now there's a thought."

"Good. Then I could sleep."

She stopped short; she hissed. "You wouldn't."

"I might wake up later," he mused, "and dismember them one by one."

"I hope so," she said. "I'd hate to think that you'd let anyone else touch me."

"Touch you, maybe, if you didn't take his hand off for trying. Keep you, no. I'm not that magnanimous."

She shook her head. Her hair was a curtain about them both, cool and silken-soft. "Frankish honor," she said. "Any decent Muslim would kill a man for looking at me."

"He can look all he likes, and envy me as much as he pleases. If you ever deign to show your face."

"I shall do that," she said calmly, "when I am your properly wedded wife, and it is your right to command me."

It was growing difficult to think, with her astride him so, and her face above him, and her lovely round breasts, and her strong smooth thighs. "What if I won't command you?"

"Then I shall do it because I choose."

She bent. Her face filled his world. All Persia was in it: the elegant oval, the cheekbones curved high, the long nose with its suggestion of arch, the lips fine-molded and astonishingly tender. Yet it, and she, was nothing human. The tilt of the wine-dark brows; the great eyes beneath them with their pupils wide now, green-gleaming within, that would slit narrow when the sun was high; the moon-lit ivory of her skin. The scent that was on her, imperceptible to human senses, dizzyingly sweet to his own. The light in her, the sheen of her power, woven with his beyond any unweaving.

She shifted above him, poising. He knew better than to snatch. She took him joyfully, fierce as a cat and fully as wanton.

Just before she fell asleep, she said, "It would not be so ill at all, if Allah had Jerusalem."

6

Courtesy commanded that a king, in another king's city, should pay his respects to that monarch. Gwydion was nothing if not courteous.

Aidan loved to look splendid, but he had little patience with the madder extravagances of court dress. Gwydion had both patience and, when he chose, the flair to carry it off. Blue and silver were his colors, eastern

silk and western silver, and a great cloak like a field of
stars, lined with ermine, and belt and chain of silver set
with sapphires, and a sword in a damascened scabbard—
almost plain, that, wrought for use, its blade forged by
the prince of smiths who had made Aidan's own—with a
sapphire in the pommel, carved with the seabird
crowned. His crown was on his head, the great state
crown of his father, silver and sapphire, with a glimmer
of moonstone and diamond.

Aidan, in the black coat which Saladin had given
him, and all the rest scarlet, and a golden coronet, for
once was almost pleased to efface himself. "You look,"
he told his brother, "like the night in full flower."

Gwydion was amused, though he tried not to be. The
monks who had failed signally with Aidan had tri-
umphed with him. He was modest. It was not vanity of
his beauty but pride of his kingship that kept his head so
high under the cruel weight of the crown. If he wearied
of it on the slow ride from the Dome of the Rock to the
Tower of David, even Aidan was not to know. He dismounted with a panther's grace despite all his encumber-
ing splendor, and waited serenely for the pages to
straighten his cloak, smooth his robes, ready him for the
stares and whispers of the court. Both were Joanna's
pups, the younger hardly less composed than the elder.
Aidan would praise them later, when it would not throw
them off their stride.

His eyes flicked over the escort. It was all Rhiyanan
today: another of Gwydion's courtesies. It would not do
to flaunt Aidan's infidels, or Aidan's refusal to swear
fealty to the upstart king. One or two of the mamluks
were there, it was true, but Raihan and Conrad looked
perfectly at ease in Frankish dress, like the knights of
Outremer which after all they were.

The rest were as they should be. Ysabel was nowhere
in sight, though Aidan did not quite trust her to stay at
home where she belonged. Her mother and her mother's
husband were within at court, as a baron and his lady
ought to be if they were in Jerusalem.

The King of Jerusalem did not come out, which was
somewhat less than proper, but his servants admitted

Gwydion with every show of courtesy. The court, such of it as was not scattered in the castles and strongholds of the kingdom, awaited him in the great hall and bowed low as he entered it. There were knights enough, and more barons than Aidan might have expected outside of a formal court, with their ladies and their kin and their hangers-on. They made a brave show for the honor of Jerusalem.

The king sat with his queen under the gilded canopy, he in white and gold, she in imperial purple, which suited her wheat-gold beauty. She at least had the look of a woman well content with herself and her world: queen as she was born to be, bereaved of a son but consoled in the daughter who had not, please God, ruined her figure, and certainly she would be vouchsafed another son. And meanwhile she had her beloved husband.

Guy de Lusignan, King of Jerusalem, Defender of the Holy Sepulcher, was the very image of a king: tall, broad-shouldered, ruddily handsome, with corn-gold hair falling in curls over those splendid shoulders, and a beautiful golden beard, and eyes as blue as flax-flowers. He was not, for all of that, a pretty lad. There was a manly light in those clear blue eyes and a virile grace in that tall body, and his voice when he spoke was deep and firm, the voice of a man among men.

It was unfortunate that all that virile beauty had no more wits than Queen Sybilla's lapdog.

Peace, brother. Gwydion's voice in Aidan's mind, gently reproving. *Where is your charity?*

Where it belonged: and not on the throne of this embattled kingdom. Aidan set his teeth and kept his thoughts more scrupulously to himself.

The reality of a king and the image of a king came face to face before the throne. Winter's king in stars and darkness, summer's king in light and splendor; the pale king and the bronze king, grey eyes meeting blue with a shock like two blades clashing.

Guy blinked and looked away. "Your majesty is welcome in our kingdom," he said as if he meant it. At the moment he did. He rose and came down, smiling widely, opening his arms for an embrace. Gwydion returned it, and the kiss of peace that followed it.

Guy stood back, still smiling. "I see that my brother brings new swords for the defense of the Holy Sepulcher."

Gwydion inclined his head, turning it into a greeting of the queen as well. She bloomed under his regard.

He was not half cool enough, to Aidan's way of thinking. When Guy linked arms with him, drawing him into the gathering of courtiers, he went with all apparent willingness. He did not look meek; he looked as a king does when he is being gracious.

That, when it came to it, was why Gwydion was king and Aidan was not. Gwydion had a knack for suffering fools.

Hardly as much a fool as that, Gwydion thought. Aidan had a propensity for swift and damning judgments; and he had loved the one whom Guy thought of, when he could stand to think of him at all, as *that stinking leper*. As indeed King Baldwin had been when Guy knew him: a handless, faceless, shrouded monstrosity, blind and ravaged with his sickness. Beauty meant much to Guy, perhaps too much; ugliness revolted him, and sickness horrified him. That most hideous of sicknesses, in one who was a king, shocked him out of all charity. He could not see what was in the rotting body. The brilliance; the bravery; the strength in the face of afflictions that would have broken another man. Baldwin was hardly more than a boy when he died; king at thirteen, warrior and general from his crowning, victor at seventeen over the wily Saladin, leader of his people even when he must lead them, dying, from a litter, dead at four-and-twenty with as much of life and suffering and kingship behind him as if he had attained his full and natural span. Guy only knew that he was a leper, and that he deplored the love match which his sister had made. Had Baldwin lived, Guy would never have come close to kingship. He knew it, and he did not forgive it.

No more than Aidan forgave him for winning the crown
at last and in despite of them all.

Gwydion forbore to judge. Guy was no marvel of
intellect, but he had charm enough, and a full repertoire
of the courtier's arts. He presented Gwydion to each of
his great lords who were present, and to their ladies as
well. The latter were quite enchanted with him, even
when their husbands were not. He knew the virtue of a
white smile and a limpid stare and a word uttered
sweetly, with fetching sincerity. Every woman was beautiful if Guy decreed that she was, and every man his
loyal servant.

And Gwydion was his dear and loyal brother. "Your
strength will turn the tide," he said. "Because there will
be war, and soon. The Saracen is readying to march.
We'll give him a surprise, you and I. Two kings where he
looked for one; two armies on the field against him."

"Hardly that," Gwydion said. "I came for a wedding,
not a war."

"Ah," said Guy, not pleased to be reminded. "Yes.
But still, you have how many knights? Thirty? And men-
at-arms enough, and the power of your name. That's
worth an army in itself." He paused, struck with a
ghastly thought. "You are going to fight with us, aren't
you?"

"If needs must, yes."

That was enough for Guy. He clapped Gwydion on
the shoulder. "Of course you are! What was I thinking?
Here, you have to meet Lord Balian, he has a cousin in
Rhiyana—yes, Balian?"

No; but the tough old soldier was too polite to say so.
His eyes met Gwydion's levelly, matching him to the
tales and to his brother's face, reckoning the years in
which he had kept Rhiyana at peace. Looking for softness. He seemed to find none. He smiled slightly, and
bowed. "Sire," he said. From him, that was tribute.

"Remarkable," said the young lord who stood beside
Aidan. He was not *pullani*, not a halfblood Syrian, but
he was dark and slender and silken enough to be one.

"What a picture they make! Someone should write a song about it."

"What, 'The Hawk and the Peacock'?"

The young lord winced. "I was thinking of something a little less . . . satirical."

Milord Humphrey of Toron was a poet and a scholar, a fluent speaker of Arabic, and already, young though he was, a skilled master of diplomacy. He was not, in this nation of warriors, even a passable fighter; which was the more galling for that he was the grandson and namesake of a Constable of the kingdom, who had been a warrior of note in his day. Newcomers from the west, and veterans who had won their titles on the field, despised him. Older men, high in the counsels of the kingdom, envied him his youth and his intelligence. Younger ones, with a way to make in the world, objected to his presence in it. Women admired his smooth dark face but scorned his ineptitude in a fight.

Aidan liked him. He knew and understood Islam, and he was always exquisitely courteous to Morgiana.

"They're a handsome pair, our two kings," Aidan said to him. "May I be pardoned if I'm partial to my brother?"

"Surely," said the man who had married the queen's sister. Who could have been king himself instead of Guy, but who, unlike the knight from Lusignan, knew his own shortcomings. When the crown was offered him, he had given his oath of fealty to his sister's husband. "Guy may be no general," he had said, "and not much of a king after Baldwin, but he can hold his own in a battle. Which is more than I can do."

He smiled now and looked about. "Where are your mamluks, my lord? Did you actually leave them at home?"

"I actually did."

"That couldn't have been easy."

Aidan bared his teeth. "Easy enough, once I'd knocked a few heads together. And," he confessed, "picked out a pair to play at being Franks."

"So that *is* Conrad," Humphrey said. "And is that

Raihan? He looks hardly *pullani* at all, outside of a turban. You'd almost think he was Rhiyanan."

"Wouldn't you? Until he opens his mouth. His accent is still ripe Damascene, even in the *langue d'oeil*. I told him to play mute if he can."

Humphrey laughed. "Someday, my lord, the world is going to wake and find you devious."

"What, I? I'm as honest as the day."

"Simple, too, and as harmless as a leopard in a deer run."

"We're all predators here," Aidan said.

"Predators at bay. There's peace in the House of Islam. You know what that means."

"Even his majesty can guess. Saladin has risen to rule two sultanates, in Egypt and in Syria, for no other cause than this: to drive the Franks into the sea. Now that his realm is secure, he'll raise the jihad."

Humphrey was calm, but he was white about the lips. "This year, do you think?"

"God grant!" That was a knight from Poitou, a new one, raw and blistered by the sun and bursting with zeal. "I came for a war. Poor recompense for my passage if I don't get one."

"You will," Aidan said.

The Poitevin stared at him. "Aren't you the one with the paynim wife?"

Aidan smiled sweetly. "Within the week, I shall be."

"Don't say it, Gauthier," said a man who had been a year or two in Outremer.

Aidan kept his smile till it cloyed.

Gauthier said it. "Which side will you be fighting on?"

"Don't be a fool, Gauthier," said the veteran. "He's one of us. Ten years' worth, and then some. He got his castle after Montgisard, for his bravery in the battle."

"Ten years?" The Poitevin was hard put to believe it. But there was Gwydion, whose name and tale were known in Francia, and there was no mistaking the likeness, even at the hall's length. Gauthier's eyes went wild.

It was sorely disappointing how quickly he mumbled an apology and fled. Gwydion's presence was going to lose the veterans a few wagers. Tyros could always be relied on for a challenge or six before one of them caught on to the jest. They never expected the champion of many battles to look all of three-and-twenty, with never a mark or a scar, and skin as white as a maid's.

"Your reputation goes before you," said Humphrey, not without regret. He liked a good wager as much as the next man. He shrugged, sighed. "Ah well. We'll all have fighting enough, if the year goes as I forebode it will."

"Deus lo volt," someone said, softly enough, but clear as a war-cry: "God wills it."

While the king played host to Gwydion, it was left to Queen Sybilla to make the king's kinswoman welcome. She was gracious about it, conducting Elen in the kings' wake but departing from it soon enough to settle in an alcove. There was a cushioned divan for their comfort, and a servant with wine, and a remarkable degree of quiet. The ladies who arrayed themselves about were as decorative as they were discreet. Sybilla, like her husband, had a predilection for beauty in her companions.

Intelligence, Elen reflected somewhat uncharitably, seemed to be no part of it. "Such a lovely gown," Sybilla said. "Surely that's Ch'in silk?"

Elen smoothed the gleaming skirt. It was silver grey, embroidered with blossoms, white and fragile pink. "It is a gift," she said, "from my uncle and his bride."

Sybilla's eyes chilled slightly. "Ah. Yes." Just like her husband. They were much of a mind, it seemed, when it came to Aidan and his Assassin.

The queen recovered herself quickly and smiled. "I understand that you are yourself recently widowed. How unfortunate. Have you given thought to a new marriage?"

"My husband died scarcely a year ago," said Elen, carefully and rigidly controlled. "It would hardly have been proper."

"Ah," said Sybilla, not a whit dismayed, "but grief is seldom a luxury permitted us who are royal. My first

dear lord was hardly cold in his grave before the hunt
began for his successor."

"How unfortunate," Elen murmured.

Sybilla sighed profoundly and tilted her head at
what, no doubt, was reckoned a fetching angle. "It was
necessary. Our kingdom needed a man who could be its
king."

"You found him yourself, I understand."

The queen smiled. Her eye sought her husband where
he stood amid a circle of barons, with Gwydion tall and
shadowed at his side. "Yes, indeed, I found him and I
chose him; but I took care to choose a man who would
look well upon the throne."

"He does look well," said Elen with no particular
emphasis.

Sybilla took Elen's hand with a great air of sharing
confidences. "We have splendid men here. Not all as
handsome as your Rhiyanan lords—they are beautiful,
do you breed them for it?—but the sun and the air and
the fighting make them strong, and the court teaches
them the gentler arts. We can hardly spare time from the
wars for a proper, courtly court, but we do our best with
what we have. Maybe one will catch your eye. Or two, or
three." Her glance was wicked. "You see how rare a
jewel a woman is here, and a woman of pure western
blood, and beauty with it—there's no doubt of it. You'll
have your pick of our fairest knights."

"I had thought," said Elen, "to be a proper pilgrim."

Sybilla laughed, high and consciously sweet. The others took up the note like a chorus of birds. "Oh, but your
grace! Our knights will be desolate. Surely it's a Christian's duty to console them."

"Did you have any in mind?"

Elen meant it for irony, but Sybilla took her at her
word. "I knew you were a woman after my own heart.
Come, I know just where to begin."

Elen would have given much to be as heedless of
royal wrath as Aidan was, and as ready to speak bluntly;
or simply to walk away. But she was too well trained, for
too long, under Gwydion's firm hand.

She was also, and somewhat guiltily, curious. Now that she had been both wife and widow, she realized that she much preferred the former.

Unless there was a way to have them both. A widow's freedom and power to rule her own possessions; a wife's pleasures of bed and body.

Shocking thoughts for a lady of breeding as she walked hand in hand with the Queen of Jerusalem, making a gracious circuit of the court. They paused often, wherever there was a man who might be the better for the company of a wife.

Elen could not recall exactly when King Guy's brother appeared. He had not been in the hall when she began; she was sure of that. He took shape on the edge of her attention, obtrusive in his very unobtrusiveness. He was at her elbow, watching as a baron of a certain age and considerable girth, and a handsome fief near Banias, labored to be captivating.

In remarkably little time the baron was gone, and his lumbering courtesies with him. The queen had withdrawn on the arm of someone young, handsome, and betrothed. Elen was alone but for Messire Amalric.

"It's a pleasure," he said, bowing over her hand, "to greet you again."

She murmured a word or two and resisted an inexplicable urge to wipe her hand on her skirt. It was not that Amalric was ill to look at, or that she had any care for the shape of a man's face: God knew, Riquier had been no beauty. Amalric was a plain man, plain-spoken, with none of his brother's conspicuous charm. She should have found him easier to like. If he reckoned her wealth and her lineage and saw in her a chance to gain a throne, as his brother had before him—why not? It was an honest ambition.

He spoke in her silence, words which, with a start, she struggled to recall. "You're brave to have come so far on such a pilgrimage, with war in the air."

"Isn't it always?"

"More now," he said, "though we're never completely at peace. This is no country for the weak."

"I hardly reckon myself strong. I wished to see my kinsman wed, that is all; since I had some small part in it."

He did not choke as the others did at the mention of Aidan's wedding. He smiled with every appearance of ease and said, "A joyous occasion, and long in the making. Was it you, then, who worked the wonder in the papal curia?"

"Indeed, no. That was my lord king, and her majesty the queen. I helped them as I could, which was little enough. I know somewhat of canon law, from an excess of curiosity in my youth; it was useful in its way. The sons of holy Church find learning disturbing in a woman, and appalling in one who has no calling to religion."

"It is unusual," Amalric said.

"And, no doubt, unnecessary." She made little effort to keep the malice out of her voice. "Are you versed in the law, sir?"

He spread his hands, smiling. "I'm but a simple knight, my lady, come to defend the Holy Sepulcher."

Simple, she thought. Indeed. "There is wealth to be won here, I'm told," she said, "and more than wealth, if one is clever."

It was impossible to shake his composure. He looked, if anything, delighted with her rudeness. "Of course, my lady. There's the soul's wealth, for the pilgrimage. And it's a great virtue to divert the riches of the east from the infidel's clutches into good Christian coffers."

"Where they can do good Christians as much good as possible," she said. "Or is it Christian to hunger after gold?"

"Why not, if it's Saracen gold?"

"Ah, then you are of the school which teaches that nothing is evil if it thwarts the infidel."

"I might balk at alliance with the devil," he said. "Or I might not."

His eyes rested, not by accident, on Gwydion. Elen smiled, cool to coldness. "Indeed; and if the kingdom falls, he might offer you a refuge."

"A warm one, no doubt," said Amalric.

"I wish you joy of it." She caught a listener's eye over Amalric's shoulder. Blue in a dark face, and for a moment—angry? Amused? Both at once?

He came as readily as if she had called him, bowed extravagantly, overwhelmed her with eloquent nonsense. As neatly as she had been trapped, she was freed. He bore her away before Amalric could say a word.

His babble stopped as soon as they were well away. He did not withdraw his arm from beneath her hand. She would have liked to throw her arms about him and kiss him; she had instead to pace coolly beside him with her head at a regal angle and all her laughter trammeled in her eyes. "I am grateful," she said, "for the reprieve."

"You seemed to be holding your own," said Raihan.

She showed a gleam of teeth in what might have passed for a smile. "Is that why you rescued me?"

Above the heavy shadow of his beard, his cheeks glowed ruddy bronze. "I happened to be nearby," he said. "My lady. And I did not like what he had to say of your kinsman."

"It's not what he said. It's what he was being careful not to say." She frowned slightly; her fingers tightened on his arm. "No. It's not even that. He is his brother's man, after all; he'd be a poor partisan if he failed to defend him. It's just . . . I don't know what it is. I simply can't abide him."

"Maybe it's the reek of jackal that surrounds him."

His tone was frankly venomous. She regarded him in surprise. "I thought," she said, "that Saracens never spoke freely if they could avoid it."

He showed his teeth as she had, with nothing of humor in it. They were excellent teeth. "Ah, but I'm corrupted: I've been raised in a Frankish castle. Or maybe it's blood that will tell. My father, insofar as my mother ever knew, was a man-at-arms from Tripoli."

"She didn't—" Elen stopped herself.

Raihan finished it for her. "She didn't know for certain. One doesn't, when one is diversion after a battle. Her husband was kind: he kept her afterwards, and let her raise me, and when I was old enough to be worth something, sold me for a decent price."

He was perfectly calm about it. No doubt he had to be. His eyes on her were level, daring her to recoil, or to say something regrettable. He could not help but know what Christians thought of birth outside of wedlock.

She was neither shocked nor repelled. She did not even pity him. "You've done well for yourself," she said.

He laughed, light and free. "So I have! My lady, you are wasted on these dogs of Franks. A Muslim, now: a Muslim would appreciate you."

"What, as a beast in his menagerie?"

"As a jewel in his crown." His cheeks had gone ruddy again, though his voice was as smooth as ever. "That one only wants you for what he thinks you can give him."

"Most men do," she said. "Why not? I know what I am. Rhiyana's succession is clear enough. Neither my lord nor his brother has an heir. Their sister has a daughter, and the daughter has Rhodri, who is man enough and heir enough, but as mortal as any; and I am his sister. May God forbid that I ever come closer to a throne than I am now, but I am close enough, for a man of some ambition."

"I should like to see him touch my lord or his brother," said Raihan through gritted teeth.

"I doubt that he would," said Elen.

"Do you, my lady? I wish that I could be so certain. That one never means to live out his life in his brother's shadow, you can be sure of it. If he saw a way to a crown, he would take it, even if the price for it was a life. Or two. Or four."

"Two at least of those lives may not be so easy to take," Elen said. "No; he's more likely to gamble, and pray for a stroke or two of fortune."

"He may pray all he likes," said Raihan, as sweetly poisonous as ever Aidan could be.

"And," said Elen, "if I'm to be given away, it's my lord the king who will do the giving."

He seemed to agree with her that that concluded the argument. He deposited her in the company of the lord and lady of Mortmain, who were quite sincerely glad to see her, and went to attend his prince. She did not know why, for an instant, she should feel abandoned. He was only being a good servant.

And, no doubt, a good Muslim.

7

"It is certain?" the Patriarch asked.

"Incontrovertible," said the pope's legate.

There was a silence. Patriarch Heraclius was a Byzantine Greek—a Roman, he would insist. Abbot Leo was Roman in truth, of a line that went back unbroken to the Republic. Of the two of them, he was the elder, the smaller, and the more visibly saintly: a sweet-faced old man in rusty black, who affected no mark of his rank. Heraclius beside him seemed a true prince of the Church. His eyes were dark and deep, his beard long and beginning augustly to silver, his body—regally slender in youth, thickening as it aged—set off to best advantage in patriarchal white and scarlet. If Abbot Leo objected to the presumption of equality with the pope in Rome, he did not express it.

Leo sat back in his chair and folded his hands over his middle. "The Holy Father left no doubt of it. The dispensation is granted. The marriage will take place."

"It could not have been an easy decision," Heraclius said.

"Easy enough in the end," said Leo, "the petitioner being an anointed king on behalf of his brother, who is not only a faithful son of the Church but a defender of the Holy Sepulcher."

Heraclius' expression was sour. "You have the document, then."

"In a locked coffer, under guard." The legate smiled. "I thought it best to take no chances."

"I should examine it," said Heraclius, "if I am, as I presume, the one who must perform the rite."

"You are," said Abbot Leo. "The bridegroom himself requested it, as he professed in his petition, 'so that there may be no doubt in any man's mind that this union is valid and binding.'"

"I could choose to be flattered."

"Indeed you should." Leo cocked his head, birdlike. "The dispensation shall be read publicly before the wedding. That is the Holy Father's instruction. I may not, until then, break the seal, to which the fortunate couple should bear witness as whole and unbroken. Will my word be sufficient that all is properly in order?"

"I can hardly offend you with a refusal."

The legate smiled his sweet, vague smile. "Oh, but I am impossible to offend, when I understand perfectly. Still, I am his holiness' man. You do understand, your eminence."

It was not a question. Heraclius took it with such grace as he might.

"Tell me," Leo said after a while, when Heraclius had poured and drunk a cup of wine. "What is there that makes you so reluctant to perform this marriage? They are hardly the first to cross the wall of faith and creed."

"They are the first of royal blood," said Heraclius. The wine slowed his tongue somewhat, but did not calm him. "The woman, of course, is unspeakable; though he seems to have tamed her slightly since she presented herself before the gathering of the High Court and proclaimed that he had sold himself to her in return for her power over the Master of the Assassins. He is to be applauded for insisting on a proper Christian marriage, if not for suffering her to persist in her unbelief. One may argue that she is, after all, only a woman."

"So was it argued in the curia," Leo said.

"Successfully, I presume." Heraclius stroked his beard, frowning. "Do you know the prince at all?"

"Somewhat," Leo answered, "long ago. I was in awe of him then. I was a novice, and young for it. He," said Leo, "was but a little older than he seemed."

"That does not trouble you?"

"Not while the Holy Father is content."

Heraclius' teeth clicked together, painfully: they were

not of the best. The pain burned away his shock. A prince of the Church was not well advised to wonder at anything a saint chose to do. "It troubles me," he said. "As does the necessity of accepting it."

"You dislike him, then."

"He can charm wine out of a stone. Men do battle for a place in his following. He keeps no more state than a baron should, prince royal though he is; this is not his kingdom, he says, and he will not demand the right of his birth, only what he can earn in service to the realm. He is scrupulous in that service. Even"—and Heraclius did not say that easily—"in his refusal to offer liege oath to the king in Jerusalem."

"That is no longer a difficulty," Leo said, "for him at least, now that his brother is present and holds a prior oath."

"And Guy does not strip him of his lands, for fear of losing the men who come with it; and more than they. He has allies in all quarters. The Knights Hospitaller themselves stand behind him, and they bow to no man."

"Not even to God?"

Heraclius shot him a glance. "You see how I am constrained. He is a power in the realm. I will not of my own accord sanction this wedding, but I accept the pope's decree, since the petitioner comes from a land under Rome's jurisdiction."

"A powerful concession," Leo said, "and a laudable obedience."

Heraclius said nothing, so that he might have nothing, later, to regret.

Just as Leo was rising to depart, a clerk brought word of one who would speak with them both. The man's eyes were wide and somewhat startled. "He says that he is the King of Rhiyana, your eminence, father abbot."

He was, although he came in no great state, with only a squire for escort. By his garb he could have been a simple knight; he carried himself quietly enough, and offered these princes of the Church all due respect.

Abbot Leo greeted him with delight. "My lord king! You look well. And the Lady Elen, is she prospering?"

"Like a flower in the sun," Gwydion said. "You had the right of it, father abbot. This pilgrimage has taught her to smile again."

"Good, good." Leo did not wait for Heraclius; he beckoned Gwydion to a chair. "Come, sit, be at ease. Will you have wine? I believe there are cakes—are there, your eminence?"

Gwydion sat, but refused food or drink. Heraclius watched him under lowered lids. He had none of his brother's restlessness; he knew how to sit still, and how to wait. His face was quiet; serene.

Deadly; because it seemed so young. The eye could not accept what the mind knew, that this was no young knight new to his spurs, no innocent in the ways of the world, but a king both ancient and subtle. What else he might be was told in whispers. No natural man could live so long unchanging. There was sorcery in that; and, surely, in more than that.

Abbot Leo was snared in it. He babbled happily, addressing the witch-king as if he were an old and cherished friend. "All these years, and would you believe it, this is my first sojourn in the Holy City? So high and so holy; so many blessed places. It seems that I am always weeping, for joy or for grief, or for both together. Have you climbed the rock of Calvary? I went up, and hard it was on these old bones; then down the steep narrow stair past all the pilgrims' crosses into the vault of Golgotha. Saint Helena found the True Cross there, but then, you must know that, my lord. And past the Place of the Skull, in such beauty that it breaks my heart—but so simple itself, after all, a plain stone, an empty tomb: the Holy Sepulcher."

"Yes," said Gwydion softly. "I have seen it."

Leo smiled, all innocent delight. "Why, of course you have! You would have done it as soon as you decently could. Are you in comfort here? Is your brother as well as you had hoped?"

"Better," Gwydion said.

"And his lady? Is she well chosen?"

"Remarkably well." Gwydion seemed close to smiling. "And yes, I am relieved to know it. My brother has found his match, in more ways than one."

"I shall have to cultivate her acquaintance. A word or two at a banquet, spoken to a pair of eyes within a veil, is hardly enough to judge a woman's character."

"That is her modesty," said Gwydion.

"Muslim modesty." Heraclius broke in with unByzantine impatience. "She concedes nothing to Christian manners. She is altogether a perfect Saracen."

" *'Car felon sont Sarazin,'* " Gwydion sang, soft and heart-stoppingly sweet. "She is that no longer, your eminence. She has chosen the west, and my brother. The east has lost her."

"All of her that matters," said Leo. "Except her soul. Has no one tried to teach her the truth of our faith?"

"Many a man," Heraclius answered, "and not a few women. She hears them all, and if she speaks, it is only to profess her own false faith: 'There is no god but God, and Muhammad is the Prophet of God.' "

"How beautiful," Leo said. "How exquisitely simple. I can see that she might prefer it to our endless intricacies. Three Gods in One, and God's son dead upon a tree, and 'Love thy neighbor' and 'Sin no more,' and surely she would take no pleasure in our vow of chastity."

Heraclius glared. "Perhaps, father abbot, rather than seek to convert her to our religion, you should convert to hers."

"Why, has anyone done it?"

"No." The Patriarch bit off the word. He did not add that one zealous abbess had been restrained, with difficulty, from pronouncing Muhammad a true, but minor, prophet. She was still under discipline.

Gwydion did not move, did not speak, but suddenly he was the center of the room. His eyes, Heraclius thought. He had raised them, that was all. They were the color of good steel. There was nothing of youth or of gentleness in them. "It would set my heart at ease," he said, "to know that no obstacle remains between my brother and this marriage."

Heraclius' fists were clenched. With an effort he un-
clenched them. "To my knowledge there is none. Have
you cause to suspect otherwise?"

"The dispensation is in good hands?"

"Under guard," Heraclius said with a glimmer of
pleasure.

"You are yourself prepared to uphold it?"

"To the letter."

Gwydion paused. For a moment it was as if Prince
Aidan sat there: tensed, fierce, glaring with a falcon's
mad eye. It blinked, veiling itself. The soft calm voice
said, "It is not that I mistrust you. But this has been no
easy road; nor shall I deem it ended until the rite is done.
As I fear even yet it may not be."

"You fear?" Leo asked. "Or you foresee?"

Gwydion regarded him with wide pale eyes. "Fear
only, father abbot, but all the worse for that. If I knew, I
would know how to prevent it."

"There is nothing," Leo said. "I promise you. You
know what is written beneath the seal; you have seen it
laid in its coffer. My own monks stand vigil over it. None
shall touch it, nor speak against it."

Gwydion crossed himself. "God grant," he said.
"There is no reason to fear, father abbot. I fear—I know
not what. I have come so far, after so long a battle, and I
cannot believe—I cannot trust—that all will be well. The
air is full of war. Where better to begin than with this
union of Christendom and Islam?"

"Therefore we guard against it." Leo smiled and patted his arm. "No, no, my son. You have your victory. It
is yours; no one will take it from you."

Gwydion seemed unoffended by either touch or
words. Uncomforted, but unoffended. "I pray that no
one dares. Not for my sake, father abbot, nor even for
my brother's. His lady is no gentle creature; and when
she is angered, she knows no mercy."

"She kills," said Heraclius.

"If she must. If there is cause."

"There will not be," said Abbot Leo.

*   *   *

The inner courtyard of Aidan's house had a fountain in it, and a lemon tree, and a family of cats asleep in the sun. One of them woke long enough to pour itself into Gwydion's lap. He stroked it as it asked, not too gentle, not too slow. His free hand stretched to catch the spray from the fountain. He was calmer now, with the abbot and the Patriarch sworn to defend Aidan's dispensation.

As if they could do otherwise. He was fretting over shadows. His mind, seeking, found nothing to fear. Aidan had enemies; what great lord did not? None was so rash as to thwart him in this. Most would come to the wedding to see the deed done at last, and to feast at his expense.

Gwydion filled his hand with water and laved his face. The coolness was blissful. He glanced about a trifle guiltily and dropped cotte and shirt. The cat departed in disgust. He refused to pity it. He plunged his whole head into the basin, and rose dripping, and shook like a dog, in a shower of spray.

A strangled sound brought him about. Morgiana was there, struggling valiantly not to laugh.

She had been nowhere in the courtyard a moment ago; nor anywhere in the house.

Her face glistened with spray; sparks of it glinted in her hair. He blushed. The laughter burst out of her. "Why, brother! You're no more dignified than Aidan is."

"That is a secret I would rather you kept."

His stiff reply made her grin. She danced round the fountain, as graceful and fierce as a she-leopard on the hunt, and whirled to a halt on the rim beside him. Her cheeks were nigh as brilliant as his; her eyes brimmed with mirth. "Three more days," she said.

"Only three."

"Three too many." She hugged herself and rocked. "Do you know what I ran away from? Harpies! I can prepare myself quite satisfactorily. Why in the world do I need an army of servants to help me do it?"

"Because your betrothed is a prince," Gwydion said, "and you will therefore be a princess."

"Ya Allah! Is that what a princess is? Shepherd to a flock of bleating women?"

"You might say that."

She hissed through her teeth. "Then I suppose I should endure it." Her brows knit. "It's not that I mind women's talk. It's that they think they own me. I am my own woman!"

"And theirs, if you would wed their prince."

She reached out with perfect ease and worried a tangle out of his hair. "Before it dries," she said, "and sets in knots." She set to work on the rest with a comb plucked out of the air, and a light deft hand.

His hair was thick and not quite straight; it loved to knot and tangle, and it never submitted meekly to discipline. Morgiana muttered over it, but happily enough; it was something else which put the growl in her voice. "I'm not to see my lord again until the wedding. For propriety, they tell me."

"And because he has been seized and sequestered by the hordes of his servants."

"That would never stop me," she said.

"Why not, for the game's sake?"

"What if I wake in the night and want him?"

"In three days' time you shall have him, and no force in earth or heaven shall sunder you."

"As Allah wills it." It was a sigh. She smoothed the last stubborn knot. "It might be good for my lord, at that. He can cleanse his soul with self-denial."

"That is a suitably Christian penance," said Gwydion.

She laughed. "For him, certainly. For me . . . what grace in heaven, that I have two such faces to look at, and one is not forbidden me." She paused. "Or is it?"

"Only if you want to do more than look."

"Would you let me?"

"As I love my brother," he said, "no. Or would you have the priests forbid you ever to marry him at all?"

"They wouldn't dare."

"If they could prove that we had been more than brother and sister, they would not merely dare. They would bind us with it."

"Allah!" She looked at him, bare but for his braies and hose, and at herself in chemise and drawers such as a Muslim woman wore in privacy, and went gloriously scarlet.

He brushed her cheek with a finger, cooling the fire in it. She raised a hand to it, surprised. "How did you do that?"

He showed her. There were no words for it. One sensed the hurt, *so;* one reached, *so;* and it was done.

"Ah," she said in sudden understanding. She reached, *so;* and went out like a candle's flame.

His mind snatched at the emptiness where she had been, a stroke of pure terror.

She staggered out of air and fell into his arms.

He steadied her carefully. She barely noticed. Her eyes were furious. "That," she said, "was not what I meant to do."

"What did you do?"

She showed him. One focused oneself, *so;* one reached, *so.*

If one had the gift.

"I can ease pain, a little," she said.

"I can only vanish as humans do, by being quick and quiet."

She measured him, narrow-eyed. "Aidan can do it if he tries. It makes him ill."

"He told me," said Gwydion, "when he wanted to come to Rhiyana, if only for a night, and found that he couldn't."

"Poor love, he wanted so much to have the art, and the price on it is too high."

"Yet you do it as you breathe."

"That is not always an advantage."

"No," he said. "I can see that it is not."

"One is never solid," she said. "The earth is always shifting. One dreams a place, and wakes in it, and sometimes the people there are not pleased."

"It might startle them somewhat," he said with a touch of irony.

She nodded. "They shriek, you see. Even the men. And snatch bedclothes, if they have any."

"And send thanks up to heaven for sending them so splendid a dream."

"Some of them," she said. "Your brother did, before he knew me."

"And often since."

"He curses me, too, sometimes, and wonders what he did to deserve me."

"Every man should do penance for his sins."

"So he says. So should I do: the better to sin hereafter." She swooped toward him. Her kiss was brief, but it burned. "For remembrance," she said.

She was gone. He was speechless. And, he discovered, no longer sunk in gloom. Whether he wanted to laugh or to curse her, he had lost the fine edge of his melancholy. He was almost fit for human company again.

Or at least for Aidan's. The prince did not know yet that his bride had decided, late as it was, to be properly chaste. When he learned it, he might need his brother's steadying hand.

Gwydion knew duty when it beckoned. He put on shirt and cotte, and followed where it led.

8

By the morning of his wedding, Aidan had reached a fine pitch of temper. Morgiana was taken away from him, walled up in Lady Margaret's house. He should have had diversions enough, with all the mischief the young bloods of court and city could devise for a new bridegroom, but he did not want mischief. He wanted Morgiana.

He had at least got rid of most of the army that had haled him out of bed. There were enough still to make a princely number, first in the bath, then to cut his hair and beard and to be growled at when they would have curled and scented one or both, and to stand over him while he resisted a sop of fine white bread in wine and spices.

"Eat it," said Gwydion, sitting by him and taking his own advice. "You may not want it now, but your stomach is sure to object, loudly, when you most need it to be still."

"What, do you think I've never been out in public before?" But Aidan took the bowl, regarded its contents without favor, choked down a bite or two. His stomach clenched.

Gwydion came round behind him and worked deft, merciless fingers into the knots of neck and shoulders and back. His stomach settled, only a little, but enough to accept what he fed it. There was cheese with the bread, and an orange from his own trees. He found that he had an appetite after all.

Gwydion's approval flowed warm and tingling through Aidan's skin. "You were always more sensible than I," he said.

Aidan slanted a glance over his shoulder.

"Truly," said Gwydion. "Do you remember the morning of my wedding?"

Aidan snorted. "Remember it? How could I forget? You drank enough wine at dinner the night before to sink the fleet, and never mind that it was no more to you than a moment's dizziness; then you refused to sleep, because, you said, if you did you might wake and find it all a dream; and when we came to dress you, you had decided that Christian marriage was not what you wanted at all, and you tried to convince me that I should take the crown and you should elope with the lady. I proposed an exchange—you keep the crown, I take the lady—and you did your best to throttle me. You wouldn't eat, either. Or sit still. Or let anyone near enough to you to dress you. You were almost late to the wedding."

"You see? Now, you have sense. You drank no more than you should, you roistered only halfway till cockcrow, then you actually slept. And here you sit as calmly as you ever can, with breakfast in you."

"It would serve you right," Aidan muttered, "if I lost it all over you." He swallowed. "Gwydion, do you think we need all this? Muslim marriage is so much simpler. One calls the *qadi,* he approves the contract, one says the words, it's over."

"That's no more than Christian marriage is," Gwydion said. "As this is, under the pageantry. Come, brother, would you disappoint all the people who have come to see you wedded?"

"You above all," Aidan said. "No, I can't turn coward now, can I? The Patriarch would be too purely delighted." His smile was ripe with malice. "That's one pleasure I shouldn't forgo: to make Heraclius say the words he least likes to say, with the Holy Father's bidding on him, binding him to it. And knowing all the while that I know what he is; how he intrigued to dispose of my lord Baldwin and set Guy in his place. He failed then; it took Baldwin's death to give him his victory. But I don't forget."

"You are not the most charitable of men," Gwydion said.

"Why should I be? I'm not a man." Aidan stood, stretched. His back had tensed again, but the knots were out of it. It was a pleasurable tension, an edge of excitement. "It's time," he said in dawning delight. "It's really time. I'm going to have her as I wanted her, for all the world to see."

Morgiana knew no barrier to her own gladness. She could even endure the flutter of women about her, because soon it would be over, and she would be as beautiful as she could be. The maids shared her mood. They loved to be in the secret; not one had betrayed it, though it was a sore temptation. The Rhiyanan, the princess, who never needed to remind herself not to be afraid of the infamous lady of the Assassins, caught Morgiana's eye in the mirror and grinned, as wide and white and irrepressible as Aidan himself.

"He is going to fall in love with you all over again," Elen said.

One of the others giggled. "As if he needed to! My husband tells me he was pawing the ground last night like a stag in rut, and threatening to storm the house and snatch you away. I wish he had," she said wistfully. "It would have been a sight to see."

"So would he, when I was finished with him." Morgiana turned her head from side to side, frowning. "Are you sure I should have my hair in all these braids?"

Elen smoothed the last one into its coil and beckoned. Two of the deftest maids came with the veil, a drift of the finest cobweb silk, and settled it over the woven intricacy of Morgiana's hair. "You look like a queen," Elen said. Her grey eyes glinted, wicked. "Only think. How delighted he will be, to take it all down."

Morgiana blushed. The others laughed. They all knew what a wedding was in aid of; and they all, even those who had husbands with whom they were well content, were a little in love with her prince. *The young moon in Ramadan,* the Muslims said of him. The fairest knight in the world, the Franks decreed. Even beautiful, hollow King Guy was no threat to his sovereignty.

By the noon prayer it would be done. He would belong to her and she to him, before God and man. God knew it already. Man, being slower to understand, needed proof: this rite and this panoply.

The veil was settled to the maids' satisfaction. Morgiana met her own eyes in the silver mirror as if they had been a stranger's. They had decided not to paint her face, after some discussion: it was too pure an ivory, paint would only sully it. There was paint about her eyes, a shimmer only, a whisper of kohl.

She looked like a queen. She, the nameless spirit out of Persia, the Assassin's servant, the Slave of Alamut. She shivered, cold in her splendor. What was she doing? How had she let it come to this? He was Frank, prince, infidel. He had hated her before she taught him to love her; before he learned to forgive her the murder of his kin. Did he love her now? Or did he only bow to the inevitable?

"There," said Elen. "There now, it's perfectly proper to be afraid; and better now than in front of the priest. Cry, even, if you need to. There's time yet."

"I can't cry. I'll smear the paint."

"Then we'll simply put it back on again."

"No," said Morgiana, stiffening her back. "I'm no quaking virgin. He will still be he, when we speak the words; and I will still be I. This was decided the first time I saw him. There's no changing it."

"Nor do you want to," said Elen as if she had power and could know. She set a kiss on Morgiana's cheek, light and warm. "For luck, and for kinship. I'm pleased to have you in our family."

Morgiana almost broke then. But her temper was stronger than tears. She quelled them with a formidable scowl, and then with the shaky beginning of a smile. "I'm pleased to be in it," she said.

No one, seeing the Prince of Caer Gwent ride in procession to his wedding, would have suspected the depth of his morning terrors. They were still there, but buried deep, with his foot set firmly on them. He was all royal, and he knew what beauty he had, he in scarlet silk and cloth of gold, crowned not with gold but with flowers. His mount was a wedding gift from the Sultan of Egypt and Syria, from Saladin himself, a blood-bay mare of the Arab blood, rare for both her height and her quality; she danced beneath him, tossing her head, so that the bells on her caparisons sang silver-sweet. The canopy over him was gold, the bearers his mamluks in scarlet and gold, the rest before him to open his way, and behind him the riding of his friends and his allies and his kinsfolk. He had been astonished to see how many they were. Conrad was up to his tricks again: he had found the best voices among them, men and boys both, and prevailed upon those to ride together, singing. A moment ago it had been a song to set his ears to burning. Now they were chanting as slow and sweet and solemn as monks, and it was good Scripture, but it was hardly meant to cool his blood.

> *Let him kiss me with the kisses of his mouth: for*
> *thy love is better than wine.*
> *Because of the savour of thy good ointments thy*
> *name is as ointment poured forth, therefore do*
> *the virgins love thee. . . .*

And that was only the beginning of it. Someone had got at Conrad; he knew nothing of Scripture, only holy Koran. Someone was going to pay, and dearly.

Even, he said in his mind, *if that someone is my brother.*

Gwydion's laughter, as silent as the words, was all the answer Aidan won.

And after all it was a wedding procession, with all of Jerusalem come to see it pass, and beggars and pilgrims scrambling for the largesse which the pages cast. Copper only, for the ride to the Holy Sepulcher. When he came back with his lady beside him, it would be silver, and at the wedding feast, gold.

Even copper was something to be glad of, if one were a penniless pilgrim. That gladness warmed him; and the blessings that came with it. Simple folk were not as given to cursing him, or to calling him witch and infidel, as were their alleged betters.

He was marveled at, exclaimed over, even loved. It startled him, how many of them had more than liking for him. He did no more for them than a prince should, if certainly no less.

They came down the Street of the Temple and through the market that paused to see them pass, and into David's Street, and turned right on the Street of the Patriarch, with the dome of Holy Sepulcher high on its hill before them. Another company advanced toward them, singing as they sang, but in the high sweet voices of women.

> Whither is thy beloved gone, O thou fairest
>   among women? whither is thy beloved turned
>   aside? that we may seek him with thee.
> My beloved is gone down into his garden, to the
>   beds of spices, to feed in the gardens, and to
>   gather lilies.
> I am my beloved's, and my beloved is mine: he
>   feedeth among the lilies.

Aidan's heart leaped. She was there under a canopy which was the mate of his, on her blood-bay stallion that

for looks could have been the brother of his mare: a
shimmer of green in the bright field of her women,
wrapped in veils as she always was, and closed away
from his mind. She wanted to come to him all new, as a
maiden would; as she had come that first night, and
come through fear to lasting joy.

It was all Aidan could do not to spur toward her,
scatter all their attendants, sweep her away. His mare
would have been glad to do it. She had no more love
than he did for this crawling pace.

There was only a little more of it. The hill of Calvary
waited, and a path opened for them, cleared of pilgrims;
though there were throngs enough of them about, glut-
tonous for spectacle. He reached it first, as was proper,
and left his horse there, and mounted up to the most
holy precinct in Christendom.

He hardly saw it, or the great ones crowded into it.
His mind, and then his eyes, were all for the figure which
guarded the inner gate: the Patriarch of Jerusalem in
splendor to rival his own, in a phalanx of acolytes. He
was not, despite appearances, forbidding entry to the
church. Those who would wed must wed before the
door, since what they would do was reckoned both sin
and sacrament. Once they had spoken their vows and
received the blessing, then they were permitted within.
Aidan had insisted on that. There could be no nuptial
mass for a bride who was an infidel, but she could hear
the day's mass, and share as much of it with him as her
faith would allow.

Heraclius was making the best of it. He was not smiling, but neither was he scowling as blackly as he usually
did on sight of Aidan. Aidan loathed him cordially, but
today he almost—almost—could love him, because he
was going to say the words which Aidan had done ten
years' battle to hear.

Aidan paused in front of him and bowed, and kissed
his ring. Heraclius endured it with rigid composure. He
did not give Aidan the blessing. Aidan, for the moment,
forgave him.

Morgiana had mounted the steep hill and passed
through the outer gate between the pillars from Byzan-

tium. Her women fell in about her, but she walked as if she were alone, very small and very erect in that most Christian of holy places, wrapped in her veils. Even her hands and her eyes were hidden. The women's voices wove through the heavy air, chanting softly now, but clearly.

A garden inclosed is my sister, my spouse; a
spring shut up, a fountain sealed . . .
A fountain of gardens, a well of living waters,
and streams from Lebanon. . . .

It was not Aidan who came to take her hand, but Aidan's brother, acting for the family which she had never had. Aidan, seeing them, was briefly dizzy. This was what folk would see when he stood beside her: that tall young man with his eagle's face, towering over her, bending his head to murmur a word. Within the shrouding veils, she nodded. Two of her women came behind her—one of them was Elen; Aidan had not even seen her —and lifted the veils.

A gasp ran through the court and up to heaven. One veil was left, fragile as a spider's weaving, floating atop her hair. The sun turned the woven coils the color of wine in crystal, with a shimmer of copper and gold. Her face shone beneath it, an image carved in ivory. Her gown was a Frankish gown, as her bared face was a Frankish custom, but it was made of golden silk and of cloth of gold, and all her jewels were gold and emerald.

She glanced once at him, and then away. Shy, now that it was almost done; or as afraid as he that she could not bear these last few moments' parting. They could not join hands, nor do aught but stand just out of reach, until the Patriarch should give them leave. He was in no haste to do it, damn him. He seemed as staggered as all the rest, to see her face at last, and to know that she was beautiful.

Aidan almost laughed. A finger's length of dainty slippered foot peeped from beneath her gown. It was patently no hoof, nor ever cloven.

Heraclius cleared his throat. The women's singing

died away. It was silent in the precinct but for the inevitable sounds of folk living and breathing and doing battle with the flies. Aidan gave them a gift: the flies departed in search of other prey. Then, for a moment, there was no sound at all.

"We gather here, O children of Jerusalem, to witness the binding together of two who are high in your counsels." Heraclius' voice did not quite match the rest of him, being thin and rather high, but it carried well enough. "Yet, since they are of differing faiths, and she is a worshipper of the false prophet Mahound, it has been judged advisable to seek the dispensation of Rome, to remove the impediment which otherwise would sunder them."

Morgiana was not pleased to hear herself so described or her Prophet so named. Gwydion's hand closed ineluctably upon her arm; she contented herself with a fierce and carrying whisper. "Muhammad is the Prophet of God!"

Heraclius pretended not to hear. "Therefore," he said, "before we begin the rite, his holiness' reverend legate has instructed that we present the document as it was given him from the hand of the Holy Father, and that it be examined and read, so that none hereafter may question the validity of this marriage."

Aidan drew taut. Morgiana, he noticed, was whitely intent. Abbot Leo, for once clad in his proper and princely splendor, came forward on the arm of a sturdy young monk. The youth carried a coffer of no particular richness, carved of cedarwood and bound with iron. They halted on the step, from which Heraclius had perforce retreated. The monk held the coffer; but it was not Leo who opened it, but the man who had walked behind them, another monk, older but no less sturdy. Both of them looked as if they would have known what to do in a fight.

They could also, it was evident, read and write, and do them well. The elder monk opened the coffer with respect but with dispatch, took out what was in it, turned it over. "The seal is intact," he said, "and untampered with."

So it was. Aidan was shown it, and Morgiana, and Gwydion who would speak for her when the dispensation was read and disposed of. So too Heraclius, and the abbot himself. When they had all seen it, Leo cut the threads that bound the fine vellum. The monk unfolded it, drew a breath, and read.

"Urban, bishop, servant of the servants of God, to Aidan, Prince of Caer Gwent in the kingdom of Rhiyana, Baron of the High Court of the Kingdom of Jerusalem, Defender of the Holy Sepulcher. In that he would ally and wed with that one called Morgiana, of rank and lineage unknown, servant once to the Master of Masyaf in the land of Syria, Slave of Alamut, infidel and unrepentant, we have determined that impediment exists, to wit, disparitas cultus, disparity of faith. To the petition that such impediment be set aside, and that the petitioners be joined in holy wedlock with the blessing of Mother Church, we respond: No."

The monk read on as if his tongue had outstripped his mind. Aidan heard him, but did not hear him. He had not said what Aidan had heard him say. That one word. That one, impossible, unbearable word.

"We deny dispensation. We refuse the sanction of holy Church. We condemn that one who calls himself our faithful son, who defiles his bed with the flesh of an infidel, in contravention of all the laws of man and God. Let him set her aside; let him harken to our pleading; let him turn again to the faith of his fathers, lest he be cast out into the nether darkness, and flung into the Pit."

Aidan shook his head, back and forth, over and over. Morgiana's face was very white and very far away. Her eyes were blank, flawed emeralds, dulled with shock.

The monk read more slowly now, stumbling over the words, but unable to stop. *". . . Witchcraft, sorcery, heresy and black enchantment: with these charges we indict her, and him who would unite with her. For the murder of Christian souls, the denial of our faith, the bewitchment of our servants, let her suffer due and proper punishment. Only by recantation, by conversion and by penitence, may she—"*

The monk could not go on. His face was ghastly.

Perhaps it was Gwydion who struck such horror in him, for simple presence before his face; for likeness to Aidan. The king was quiet, cold, and still. "May I see?" he asked gently, but it was as much as any man was worth to refuse him. The monk did not begin to try.

Gwydion took the vellum with its pendant seal, and read it swiftly, in silence. No sound broke in upon him. He looked up. "This is a forgery." He turned the terrible calm of his stare upon the pope's legate. "Father abbot, it were best that you ascertain the whereabouts of the proper document, and swiftly."

Abbot Leo looked wan and old, but his voice was steady enough. "My lord king, there is no other. That is the coffer which we brought from Rome, and which has been guarded night and day since it was set in my hands." He held them out. They shook, but it might have been only the palsy of age. Gwydion set the lying thing in them.

Leo looked long at it, and hard. He examined each seal; he scrutinized every phrase. He passed it to the monk who had read it, who though nigh prostrate with shock was scholar and theologian and secretary in the papal chancery. Their eyes met. Wretched; sorely baffled; but agreed.

"I saw it written," Leo said. "I saw it signed and sealed. This is not what his holiness commanded to be set down. And yet . . ."

"And yet," said the monk, "it is all in order. All is as it should be. There is no forgery that we can see."

"You know that it is," Gwydion said. He took back the lying thing, turned it. His finger traced the face of Saint Peter upon the leaden seal.

Paused.

"My lords," he said. "My lords, what is this?"

Leo stared at him. The monk frowned, wondering transparently if he had forsaken his wits. "That is the Holy Father's seal," the man said, "majesty."

Gwydion shook his head sharply. "No," he said. "This." He tugged at the cord from which hung the seal. A slender cord, a twisting of silken thread.

"That is the cord," said the monk with careful pa-

tience, "with which the Holy Father seals his dispensations." He stopped. "With—which—" He snatched the
vellum out of Gwydion's hands, suddenly and utterly
forsaking propriety.

Gwydion came very close to smiling. "The silken
cord with which he seals his dispensations. Anathemas,"
he said, "are sealed with hemp."

Monk and abbot looked again at one another. "A
forgery," said Abbot Leo in rising joy. "Indeed and certainly, a forgery."

Gwydion turned upon the Patriarch. "Do you hear,
my lord? Do you see?"

"I see a bit of thread on a seal," said Heraclius. He
might be struggling to keep the malice out of his voice. If
so, he was losing the battle. The Patriarch took the false
anathema from the monk's slack hands, and made a
show of reading it. Rather a good one, for a man who
was not remarkably fluent in curial Latin. "Here is the
seal itself as prescribed, and the signature, which I know.
This surely is what his holiness wishes, though only God
may know why he has done it so."

"He does not wish it," said Gwydion, still softly, still
quietly, but his calm was cracking. "I myself saw the
words written: the dispensation granted, the blessing
given, the order set down that the rite should be per-
formed by the Patriarch of Jerusalem, or in his incapac-
ity, by a priest of his choosing, with the legate's
approval. His holiness was not greatly pleased, but he
was willing, and mindful of my brother's devotion. He
would not have perpetrated so foul a sleight as this. Nor
ever sealed it with a seal that is a lie."

"That may be so," Heraclius said. "I know only what
is written here, and that is clear enough. The dispensation is denied. The marriage is void. I cannot bless what
Rome will not sanction."

He loved to hear himself say that; he rolled the words
on his tongue, savoring them.

He was not party to the deception. Aidan stabbed
deep in his mind, deep enough to sway him where he
stood, and dim his eyes; but there was no knowledge
there, no complicity. For him this was a godsend, and he

would use it with pure pleasure, but he had had no hand
in it.

Someone had Aidan by the arms, was shaking him,
calling his name. He shook his reeling head. His hands
were clawed. Heraclius cowered against the doorpost,
clutching his throat. Aidan snarled and struggled. "Let
me go. Damn you, let me go!"

Gwydion would not. There were others with him,
holding grimly. Mamluks. Ranulf. Somewhere on the
edge of awareness, Aidan laughed. A dozen men, it took.
He was as strong as that.

They had forgotten one who was almost as strong:
small as she was, and female, and seemingly struck down
in the wreck of her joy. Morgiana was Assassin trained,
and Assassin still, though she had forsaken it. She sprang
not on the foolish quivering Patriarch but on the monk
who had read the false letter. She did not claw him, or
throttle him. She met him eye to eye and held him till he
stiffened and convulsed and fell. Her eyes darted, glittering. Seized Leo. Drew him stumbling, staring, helpless. She was gentler with him, or he was stronger. He
did not topple. He went down slowly, as if his knees had
failed him.

"Nothing," she said, sharp and distinct through the
rising clamor. "They know nothing. Who knows? *Who
has done this?*"

It was a cat's scream. She poised to leap again, to
strip another mind bare, to find what she must find before she went truly mad. Aidan's captors would not let
him go. Would not understand.

Except Gwydion. He left Aidan to the rest, and
caught her before she sprang, and held her. She did not
fight him. Her mind was not her body's slave; it could
move when she could not. He gasped as he felt the power
that was in her, but he stood against her. He swayed her;
he turned her aside. "No, sister. No. This is no time, no
place."

Her every line denied it, but she drew in upon herself.
She ruled her rage; she gave him that gift, because he
was her kinsman and her king.

It should have been joy, that acceptance. Not pain on

top of pain. Aidan shook free of his captors, but he did not go to her. She would have turned on him.

He faced the Patriarch. The Patriarch blanched, but he was adamant. "I will not say the words without firm and proven dispensation. Which this not only denies; it casts out any who dares defy it."

Lies. All lies. And no mind here that sparked with guilt; no flicker of betrayal. Some were glad enough, as Heraclius was; some were even exultant. But none had done it, or would admit to it.

This time he mastered himself. He could hardly rend them all limb from limb, though he would happily have begun with the king and descended through the ranks. Guy had all he could do to maintain an expression of shocked disapproval, and not to laugh aloud. His queen was less delighted. It was a pity, she was thinking, that that beautiful creature must be denied what he clearly wanted most in the world; but perhaps it was for the best. She would find someone for him, she would put her mind to it: someone suitable, malleable, and irreproachably Christian.

He choked on bile. He wanted no one, nothing, but Morgiana.

Calm, he willed himself. Calm. Whoever had done this had hoped no doubt to drive him mad. He would not give the satisfaction. He would find the one who had plotted this, and make him pay, slowly. Then he would find the true dispensation, and make Heraclius accept it, and wed Morgiana as God and the Holy Father had ordained.

"I swear it," he said. "By God and His son and His holy Mother, by the stone of Holy Sepulcher, I swear: This shall be traced to its root and expunged. I will have my blessing and my bride. And if I fail in this, may the earth gape and swallow me; may the sea rise and cover me; may the sky fall to crush my bones."

9

The great oath thundered into silence. The silence held for a stretching moment; then burst in tumult.

Aidan did not have to be dragged away. He went under his own power at speed which nothing human could match, and which nothing inhuman was minded to stop. He should, no doubt, have stayed and faced the uproar. He dared not. He had almost killed Heraclius once. He would happily have drunk the man's blood and gone after the one who had forged the pope's decree, but he was too sensible—little as anyone but his brother would have believed it. Heraclius was better alive than dead. Alive, he could have his nose rubbed in his own shame when the dispensation was found.

"We will find it." Aidan flung the words over his shoulder, pacing the hall with the fierce restlessness of a leopard in a cage. It was not his own hall, with the wedding feast spread and now abandoned, all its dainties given to the poor and the pilgrims. This was a smaller space, and quieter: Lady Margaret's house near the Sepulcher, with its peaceful inner courts and its iron-barred gate.

The others watched him in silence. Margaret herself; her daughter; Elen; Gwydion; Simeon the Jew with his son and, firmly ensconced upon a cushion, Ysabel; and Morgiana. Everyone who knew the full truth of what he was, and what he could do, and how he could do it. His mamluks stood with Margaret's guards without, holding off the importunate and the curious. The city was buzzing with the scandal.

"We will find it," he repeated. "However we must; whatever we must do."

"What if it's been destroyed?" Joanna asked.

He spun. She did not flinch. "It cannot be. It must not be."

"We could," said Elen slowly, "send to Rome, and

have a copy made. Unless the dispensation is here. Then we simply have to look for it."

"Simple," said Morgiana, almost spitting it. "Yes, it should be simple, shouldn't it? Except that I've been looking constantly, and there is nothing. No hint, no clue, no faintest suggestion of the truth. Not even a flicker of guilt, to lead me to the source."

"Then the source must be in Rome," Elen said.

Gwydion shook his head. "No. I saw the dispensation written and sealed. I had it on my ship; I assured myself more than once that it was intact and untampered with. Whoever, whatever did this, he has done it since we came to Acre."

"Still," Elen said. "If you can't find it, we may have to go to Rome after all. Or . . . send to Rome." Her eyes were on Morgiana as she said it.

"No." Gwydion was gentle but immovable. "Don't think it. It would be simple, yes, but for how long? People can count. They can reckon distances and days of travel, and human probability. They will know surely then what we can little afford to let them know; and if the pope is told, we gain no more than our enemies have made for us: denial and anathema."

"You Christians," said Morgiana, "are impossible. In Islam I could go, set my dagger to the appropriate throat, and put an end to all this mummery."

Aidan stopped short and whirled upon her. "Yes. Yes, it's my fault. If I hadn't sworn—if I hadn't insisted—"

"Hush," Gwydion said. "This is no place and no time for casting blame. We have enemies capable of skillful and all but undetectable forgery; we have a wedding destroyed, a city in turmoil, a war in the making. Who knows but that this is a stroke in that war? It would suit neither side to permit such a show of amity between Christendom and Islam as this should have been."

"This is no work of Alamut," said Morgiana. "Nor of any in Islam. The stink on it is a Frankish stink."

Aidan bit his tongue. The others did not look angry. Joanna was flushed, but that might be no more than pregnancy.

As if she could sense his thoughts on her, she heaved herself up. "I don't see that any of this is getting us anywhere. We have to find the dispensation; that's obvious. I gather that you've been searching out secrets among the pope's men—"

"And the king's," Morgiana said, "and the Patriarch's."

Joanna's brows drew together. "You've been searching, and you've found nothing. You'll keep on with it, I'm sure. But what use is that to us? We can't help you in any way that matters."

"You can," said Gwydion, though Morgiana's glance denied it. "You can search by human means, with human senses. Ours are different; that difference may be the cause of our failure. We trust too much to the ways of power. We forget how much can be gained within the mortal world."

"But what can escape power?" Akiva asked.

His father would have quelled him, but Gwydion forestalled it. "Power is not omnipotence. We can be deceived; we can succumb to overconfidence. We can fail to see what is before us."

"Particularly when we don't know where to look." Aidan's hands, reaching to rake through his hair, found the crown of flowers. He flung it from him, viciously. As it spun through the air it kindled, and fell burning to the tiles. He flung words in their goggling faces. "Powers of heaven and hell below! What mortal man can do this? What mortal man would dare?"

It was not a question that any of them could answer. Joanna broke the silence, her voice as low as ever, determinedly calm. "I think," she said, "that I can do more good elsewhere."

"Yes," said Morgiana. "You can."

Joanna's lips thinned, but she did not rise to the bait. "Ranulf may have heard something in the city while we've been sitting here being angry. Or I may be able to learn something useful myself." She held out her hand. "Come, Ysabel."

Ysabel dug in her heels, but Joanna was having none of that. She said her farewells, even, pointedly, to Morgiana, and took her leave, with Ysabel mutely furious behind her.

This silence was the longest of all. The garland smoldered into ashes; they watched it, transfixed. Aidan moved suddenly to quench the last of the flame, to swirl the ash into the air. "Damn them," he said almost gently. "Oh, damn them."

"Damn them to their own hell!" The King of Jerusalem was nearly as furious as Aidan, and much less quiet about it. What set the veins to bursting in his temples and heated his face to burning was hardly the scandal of the morning—that had been a profound and completely unexpected pleasure—but another outrage altogether, and one much closer to his kingship.

Reynaud de Châtillon, younger son of the Count of Gien in Francia, lord of Kerak in Moab, Prince of Antioch that was second only to Jerusalem, had, like Guy himself, sailed out of obscurity to win a princess. Unlike Guy, he had wits and to spare: the mind of a fox and the heart of a bandit lord, people said of him, not without admiration. Though past sixty, he had the vigor of a man half his age, and a flair for treachery which put the Byzantines to shame. They loathed him: they could never stomach a foreigner who excelled in their native arts.

Saladin more than loathed him; he despised him. Reynaud, gleefully aware of it, had let himself be bought, and been paid more than handsomely for a truce, so that the caravan from Cairo to Damascus might pass in safety by his castle of Kerak. The sight of so much wealth rocking and swaying under his gate and the sound of Muslim voices calling peacefully to one another in his very ear were more than he could bear. Like the bandit he was, he seized the caravan, stripped it of its treasures, and sent the merchants staggering, naked and afoot, back to their own lands.

Saladin could be as ruthless as any king born, but his honor was inviolable. An oath to him was sacred; the breaking of a man's given word, the most mortal of sins. When word of Reynaud's oathbreaking came to him, the brittle thread of his forbearance snapped. He called up his armies. He laid siege to Kerak. He ravaged the lands about it, clear down to the Jordan. He raised the jihad.

"If that were all," Guy lamented, flinging himself about the solar, wreaking havoc with the more fragile of its furnishings. "If that were *all* anyone had done—"

It would have been enough, Amalric finished for him, watching him rant. But of course God was not so merciful, and men were not so simple. Even as Reynaud succumbed to temptation, Count Raymond of Tripoli made a mistake. That was a rarity, Amalric granted him that. It was Raymond who should have been king, and not this poor distraught fool: Raymond the wise, Raymond the circumspect, Raymond who had been King Baldwin's own favored choice to rule after he was dead. But even Raymond was mortal, and could on occasion choose awry. Like every great lord in Outremer, he had his own, sometimes contradictory net of agreements and alliances; and those could close to trap him if he let down his guard. As, a very little while ago, he had.

Perhaps he had had no choice. It had seemed a reasonable request, in its way. Saladin requested leave to make a show of force across the Sea of Galilee; a show, no more, a promise of what was to come, a repudiation of Reynaud's treachery. And Raymond granted it, with strict conditions. For one day only, from sunrise to sunset, Saladin's men might ride in Frankish lands.

That, they had done. Seven thousand of them, with the sultan's son at their head.

"I heard of it," Guy said, biting off the words. "You know what I did. I sent my strongest lords to head them off. And what did they do? They dawdled. Someone's horse lost a shoe. Someone else wanted to tup the serving wench, for all I know. They came too late, and there was the enemy, the whole heathen horde of them, taking their ease at the springs of Cresson, as cool as if they owned them."

"It would have been better," Amalric said, bluntly enough since there were only the two of them, "if you had kept the Master of the Templars on his leash, and not sent him with the others."

"But it was you who said—" Guy broke off. He had learned through long and sometimes painful lessoning, when not to remind Amalric of a palpable truth. "Well then. What could I do? He insisted that I let him go. He promised to do what he judged was best. How was I supposed to know he'd think it was best to take twoscore Templars and ten Hospitallers and a hundred of my own knights, and fall on the Saracens?"

"Gerard de Ridefort has no sense at all when it comes to infidels," Amalric said. "One glimpse of a turban and he foams at the mouth. Seven thousand of them were more than his sanity could bear."

"Yes, he is mad. A hundred and fifty knights against seven thousand, three only escaped alive or untaken, the Grand Master of the Hospital dead on the field—O sweet Jesu, we can't even spare one, let alone sevenscore!"

"It will," said Amalric, "teach Raymond not to swear pacts with the infidel behind our backs."

"There is that," said Guy, but he was little comforted. His brows met over his fine straight nose. "Ridefort ran away, Amalric. As soon as he saw the tide turn against him, he turned tail and bolted."

"He can't afford to be a hero," Amalric said. "Not as high as he stands. He is Grand Master of the Templars, after all."

Guy nodded. His frown had faded slightly. "Still, that was a cowardly thing to do."

He would have gone on, but there was a page at the door, flushed with haste and full of news. "Sire! Sire, look who's come!"

Guy strode past him, oblivious to the impudence. Amalric made note of the child's face for punishment later. These *pullani*; worthless, the lot of them. But pretty to look at. They were certainly that.

There was indeed a guest. Even white with the dust of the road, even unsteady on his feet from riding straight, barely pausing even for remounts, he kept his regal bearing, his air of sublime superiority. But what he had come to do was all that Amalric could have wished and more.

Count Raymond of Tripoli had made a mistake. And,

being a wise man, he was able to see that it far out-weighed his earlier error of refusing to accept Guy as king. The words came hard, as if round bile, but they were sweet to hear. "Sire," he said, clear and proud in front of the court, "I have sinned. I cannot say in all truth that I repent. But I have opened my gate to the Saracen under a bond of truce, and he has ridden beneath it with the heads of Christian knights upon his spears." His voice rose, ringing to the roof. "My lord, my king, I will serve you faithfully, if only you will grant this that I ask. Avenge your knights who have fallen so foully. Take up the banner of Crusade. Raise the chivalry of Outremer against the Saracen. God wills it, my lord, my king. Will you lead us to war?"

Guy's head came up. His eyes shone. His voice rang out, deeper than Raymond's, clearer and stronger and immeasurably more potent. "Yes, my lord of Tripoli. I will lead you. Who else will follow me? Who will take arms against the infidel?"

"*I!*" his knights and his barons roared back; and if not to the last man of them, then close enough. "God wills it! *Deus lo volt! Deus lo volt!*"

Deus lo volt!

The cry of it rang through the evening, reaching even into the sanctuary of Margaret's house, where Aidan still was, sunk from the first flush of rage into a bleak stillness. The others had gone about their business, even Morgiana. He sat alone in his forgotten splendor, staring at a smudge of soot on the floor.

A light hand laid itself against his cheek. He did not start, or even look up. Morgiana knelt in front of him. He had to look at her or turn away.

She was dressed as a Muslim youth again, except for the turban. Her hair was plaited in a single braid, her face scrubbed clean. She looked small and young and rather forlorn, but her eyes were agate-hard. "You should put on something more comfortable. Or eat, at least. You haven't touched a thing since morning."

"Later," he said.

She frowned, but she let it be, for the moment. "Aidan, beloved, we can't let them conquer us. It's bitter, this blow, and unconscionably cruel, but we are stronger. They can only slow us. They can't stop us."

He stretched out a finger to trace the shape of her face: narrow oval, pointed chin. "It's not that I'm weak," he said. "It's that they are so petty. What possible profit can anyone gain from striking us down at the church door?"

"Of profit, little," she said. "Of pleasure, much too much."

"Is that why they do it? For pleasure?"

"Maybe they believe that they're punishing treachery. Or witchcraft. Franks are given to that."

"I am a Frank," he said, a little tightly. Not much, not yet.

"You are yourself." She leaned against his knees. He opened them; she came into his embrace. She was much more lightly clad than he was. He ran his hand down the sweet familiar line of her back, and up to her nape. She caught his free hand and held it to her cheek. "We'll find the pope's letter. We can go back to Millefleurs, recover our senses, set about a proper hunt."

"Millefleurs?" He was puzzled. "How can we go to Millefleurs?"

"What can we do here? We only came for the wedding. We were going back home after. Or don't you remember?"

He remembered. But. "We can't go back now."

"Now more than ever. You know how you hate cities; and this one has gone mad."

"This one is about to go to war. Can't you hear them in the streets? Saladin has raised the jihad. Count Raymond is here and has sworn fealty to Guy—God help the man, he should have more sense than to pile an error on top of a mistake—and his price is Crusade. The king has called the *arrière-ban*. The muster is in Acre within the fortnight."

"You don't have to go," she said. "You owe Guy no service."

"Guy, no. But Raymond and the kingdom and the cross—yes, they bind me."

She pulled back, the better to see his face. "You only stayed after Baldwin died, because you had too many debts both owed and owing, and because you were stubborn; you wanted to marry me in Jerusalem. We were going back to Rhiyana with Gwydion after the wedding, when we'd settled all our affairs. As we will, and in as short order as we can: as soon as we find the dispensation."

Aidan shook his head. "It's not that simple now. The war has come. Gwydion has seen Jerusalem fall; and I, on the wings of his prophecy. How can I just walk away from it?"

"How can you stay? Baldwin kept you because he loved you. You made allies enough, even a friend or six. But you also made enemies; and this puppet king is one of them. They won't hesitate to turn on you, simply because there's a jihad in the way."

"Guy is an idiot, but he's not mad. He needs me and he knows it. I swore to defend the Holy Sepulcher. I can't break that oath."

"I find myself wishing," she said through gritted teeth, "that you were a little less honorable, and a little more like a Frank. Look at Reynaud. What was an oath worth to him? He broke it, and he's rich and he's happy. Raymond kept his, and he's had to crawl at Guy's feet, because Guy's dogs didn't have the sense to stay out of a battle when they were outnumbered fifty to one."

"All the more need for a knight with some vestige of sense."

"You can't," she said. "I let you go before, dreading every moment of it, and even fighting beside you when I could, because you love a fight so much. But this isn't errantry. This is holy war."

"Yes," he said.

She seized a double fistful of his hair and pulled his head down. *"Allah!* Are you mad?"

"I am a Christian and a knight of the cross."

"Mad," she said. "Stark mad."

"You knew what I was when you set your chain on my neck."

"When did I ever—" Her breath hissed between her teeth. "I trapped you. Is that what you are saying?"

"I am saying that we had a bargain. You initiated it, and you held me to it. It was never any part of it, that I should turn my back on this kingdom and let it fall."

"*I* started it? *I* held you to it? Did you have no say in it?"

"Precious little," his tongue said for him.

Her lip curled. "How like a Frank. Lose a wager, get the worse of a bargain, and blame it all on the filthy Saracen."

"As I recall," he said icily, "it was never I who insisted on calling us by those names. Or who used them to cut, when no other weapons were to hand."

"Frank!"

"Assassin."

She caught her breath. Her face was bloodless. "There. There we have it. Maybe our enemies were wise, after all. What did they say, *dispar—dispass—*"

"*Disparitas cultus.* Disparity indeed, and no hope of changing it. Do you know how I feel when you grovel at your prayers, five times a day, every blessed day? Do you know what it does to me when you fast in Ramadan, and read the Koran daylong, and snap my head off if I venture to touch you? I gave up eating pork for you, I gave up shaving my beard for you, I did everything I could to make myself as you would have me. And how did you ever repay me?"

"By loving you."

That gave him pause. But his temper was up; it boiled out of him, all of it, years of it, and with it the bitterness of this day that should have been the best of his life, and had become the worst. "Loving me? Is that what you call it? Setting your mark on me, keeping me like a prize stallion, indulging such of my whims as suit your fancy. Now I have oaths to keep, and you bid me break them. Do you even care that that would break me?" She said nothing. Stunned; or afraid to speak. "Did

you ever love me? Or was it never more than owner-
ship?"

"Is that what I have been to you?"

He faltered. That made him angry. "It's what I've
been to you! I—fool that I am, I loved you."

"And now?"

"And now." His throat was tight. He forced the
words through it. "I am still a fool. And I will ride in the
Crusade."

"Even if I beg you?"

"When have you ever begged?"

Never, and she knew it. She backed away from him,
slowly. "And I? What will I do?"

"Whatever you please."

"Even if I please to fight in the jihad?"

He snapped erect. "You can't."

"Why not?"

"Because—" Because she belonged to him, as much
as he to her. Because she was a woman, and he was a
man, and it was his part to fight, hers to wait at home
and pray for his soul. Except that he did not know if he
had a soul, and her prayers would not be Christian
prayers, and she was never one to wait anywhere, for
anything.

"Because I don't want you to," he said.

She laughed, sharp and deadly. "What I want is as
nothing, is that not so? But what you want is ever to be
obeyed."

"What does your Prophet say? Our Evangelist says,
'Wives, obey your husbands.' "

"How wise of him, and how convenient for you. It's a
pity that I'm not your wife, and not about to be, as Allah
and our enemies have willed it."

That was more pain than he could bear to speak of.
"If you fight in the jihad, we will be fighting against one
another. Is that what you want? To kill me, and call it
holy war, and go to Paradise?"

She sprang to her feet, wild, so wild that her voice
was hardly more than a whisper. "Yes. That would be
like heaven's black humor, to make me kill you. But
Paradise—no, if I took your life, I would not have that;

for I would kill myself thereafter, and forfeit all right to salvation." She held out her hands. Almost—almost beseeching. "My lord. We knew that this would come, in the way of this world. Yet there is a way to escape it. Millefleurs, first, to see that our people are taken care of; then Rhiyana. Let the humans wage their wars. We shall make our own peace, and live in it, for as long as Allah gives us."

Peace, yes, and quiet apart from men, and the love that was between them across all the walls of faith and pride and custom. She would give up her own war for him, leave this country that was hers, go away to Rhiyana where even the sky was strange.

He shook his head, though it tore at his heart. "We can't," he said. "Not yet. When this war is settled, then, yes, we can go."

"But not now."

"Not now." He tried to be gentle. "I promised to leave Outremer when we were wedded; but not before. And if I stay, then I must fight."

"And I," she said, inexpressibly bitter, "am a stone about your neck. But for me, your heart would be whole. You would suffer no whisper of treachery; nor ever any scandal among your people."

"You are worth any pain."

"Yet there is pain," she said. "You are torn. But not enough. I am but your lover. Your war is your war."

"Never mine."

"No?" She was out of his reach now, mind as well as body. Her voice sounded dim, as if it came from far away. "Go, then. I'll not stop you."

"But what will you do?"

"What does any woman do? I can hunt. I promise I'll not kill until you've seen who did this to us."

"Morgiana—" he began, stretching out his hand.

She departed, for once, as anyone else might: through the door, and not slowly. By the time he mustered his wits for pursuit, she was gone.

10

The brightness had gone out of the world.

Ysabel sat on the bed she shared with her sisters. They were out doing whatever children did when they did not understand why all the grownfolk were so grim. She, who understood, who had been part of it until her mother dragged her away, had gone so far as to shout at her mother for doing it. This was her punishment: a behind still smarting from the spanking, and confinement to bed without supper. The dull ache of hunger was nothing to the great black knot that was her middle.

It had all been so beautiful. Aidan had looked like a prince out of a story, and Morgiana had been his princess, and both of them so happy that the whole world seemed to sing. Then the monk read the horrible letter, the one full of lies instead of the pope's blessing, and the brightness broke like a lamp flung on the floor.

Her throat ached. She had been crying, but she was tired of that. There were hours yet till dark, and then Nurse would come with Mariam and Lisabet, and she would have to pretend to sleep or be plagued endlessly with questions and frettings and nonsense. Nurse would want to dose her. She hated Nurse's doses. The other children loathed the taste, but never seemed to take any harm from them. They did odd things to her; sometimes they made her sick. It was because she was different, Morgiana said.

She hugged her knees, sniffling. Morgiana was different, too. And Aidan. They were proud of it; glad of it. Even with all the lies about witchcraft and sorcery and heresy.

She made a mirror out of air, which was her art and her secret, and even Aidan did not know about it. It was easy to do. She made a circle with her hands, and told the air to gather there, and brought in a little fire and a whisper of earth. It hung where she put it, just in front of her face. She passed her palm over it, and it quivered and glimmered and flowed, and there was a circle, all silver and perfectly smooth, with her face in it. She was even less pretty than usual, with her nose red and her eyes swollen with crying. Aidan said she would be beautiful when she grew up, the way Morgiana was, and Gwydion, and himself. None of them had looked like anything when he was a child; they were all eyes and knees and elbows, and much too pale for comfort. Just as she was. Even if he was not simply telling her that to make her feel better, she had a long way to go yet.

She glowered at her reflection. Nurse said her skin was something to be proud of, so perfectly white, and never a splotch or a freckle, no matter how much time she spent in the sun. Nurse did not know how Aidan had taught her to make a second skin out of power, when she was old enough to know how to do it for herself, as he had done for her since she was born; or how he had shown her what the sun could do to her. They were moonlight-and-darkness people. The sun was their enemy. It would flay them alive if they let down their guard.

She narrowed her too-big eyes and called light, to make them do what they always did; go all blue, with only slits for pupils. Cat-eyes. That was another thing she had had to learn when she was old enough to do it for herself: not to let people see what the light did to her eyes. She dimmed it, and watched her pupils go wide and round and eat up all the blue; but that was not safe, either, because when the blue was gone, the red came out. It was green in the others. She was different even from them. But they all had night-eyes, like animals. She could see perfectly well in the dark, when other people stumbled and cursed and groped blindly at nothing.

She made a fierce cat-face. It would have been more impressive if she had not been in between her milk teeth and her grown teeth. The best ones were just growing in, or were half there or not there at all. When they did come in, they would be very white and very sharp— "Don't bite your tongue too often for a while," Aidan said, laughing but meaning it—and some of them would be longer and more pointed than human teeth. Aidan knew how to horrify troublesome people simply by smiling at them, and giving them time to notice that there was something odd about the smile.

She swept her hand through the mirror, scattering it into nothing. "It's not *fair* to make him so unhappy!"

Suddenly she could not bear to be shut up in walls, not for one more instant. She pulled a cotte on over her shift, barely noticing which one it was, and called her shoes. They ran from under the bed and onto her feet. She snatched a cloak; by good luck it was the one with the hood sewn on it, one of her mother's more useful oddities.

It was never hard to slip out when one was determined, and had power to hide behind. She could have walked boldly out the front gate, and no one would have noticed. But there was no bravado in her now. She went out the back way, through the garden and over the wall. By the time she came out of the alley onto a wider street, she had begun to cry again. She pulled the hood over her head and went where her feet took her.

In a while which she did not measure, she found herself near the Temple. Aidan's house was not far from there, but he was not in it. She thought of finding one of her hiding places there, almost decided to do it, then stopped. It was no good without Aidan. Nothing in the world was better than to climb into his lap and feel his arms close about her, warm and strong, and know that he was there and that he loved her and that he would never let her come to harm. But he was in her grandmother's house because he could not bear to be in his own, and he was even more miserable than she was. He would have no comfort to offer her.

There was a gate in the wall, not far from where she was. A Templar stood guard in it in his mail and his surcoat with the red cross on his breast. He was young: his beard was thin and wispy and hardly longer than his jaw, and he gangled in all directions. He also stank to heaven. Templars always did.

"Do they think it's holy to be filthy?"

Ysabel jumped like a cat, a good yard high, and came

down spitting. Akiva backed away to a prudent distance, but he could not keep the grin off his face. "Where did you come from?" she snapped at him.

"I wanted to see the Temple," he said. "Or what's left of it."

"And pray at the wall?"

"And pray at the wall." He paused. "Do you think they'll let me in?"

"Not here," she said, sure of it. Her temper was gone as quickly as it had come. "The young ones are always a little crazy. They go after Jews and Muslims, sometimes."

"They always go after Jews," he said.

"The older ones don't," she said. "Or most of them. They've learned to live here."

He shrugged. He did not believe her.

"The Wailing Wall is on the outside," she said, "down by the tanners. If you can stand the stink, you can do anything you like there."

He could stand the stink. She went because she was curious, and because she was tired of her own company. She had seen the Jews in their shawls and their beards, let in sometimes in spite of the ban on their living in the city, rocking and mourning in front of that single bit of wall, but never a Jew whose name she knew.

Akiva did not rock and mourn. He did stop and stand for a long moment. Then he covered his head with the shawl and walked forward slowly. He set his hand on the pale stone where one great block gave way to another. His mind was a white silence. He was emptied of everything but prayer, and in the prayer, grief, and in the grief, hope. The Temple was fallen. His people were driven into exile. They could not even dwell in their own city; the pilgrims who came, came only on sufferance. But someday—someday—

Tears were running down her face. Again. A thought pricked at her. Someone was thinking that she was a Jew, because she was wrapped in the dark cloak and standing by the wall, crying.

The tears stopped when they were ready. She felt almost as empty as Akiva, aching but clean. When he

came back into himself, she was calmer than she had
been since morning. He looked at her and knew; she did
not even mind.

They went in by the Beautiful Gate, which was as
pretty to look at as the air was rank. The guards there,
like the people outside, took Ysabel for a Jew, since
Akiva was so obviously one, but they did not say anything. One even smiled, the way big rough men could
when they looked at children.

The great, empty, sunlit space, and the mosque with
its golden dome and its golden cross and its jewel-bright
tiles, and the little mosque by the Wailing Wall with its
silver dome, where the king sometimes lived and the
Templars had a barracks, struck Akiva dumb with awe.
Ysabel could not entirely see why. He could see most of
it from Aidan's house, if he took the time to look. She
supposed that it was different to be inside; and the Dome
of the Rock could take even her breath away as she stood
outside its door and looked up.

Inside was the most beautiful place in the world. It
had eight sides around the circle of the dome, and then
three rings of walls and pillars. The pillars looked like
trees turned to stone: they were made of marble, and the
walls around them and the arches above them were covered in mosaics and paintings of Christ, made since the
Christians took Jerusalem, and the dome that floated
over them all was carried up on arabesques of blue and
gold. It was like an explosion of flame, except that no
flame ever kindled would twine itself into such intricate
perfection of curves and windings and circles: red and
gold and black and silver.

Under the dome was one of the holiest of the Muslim
holy places: the Rock itself, as rough as all the rest was
perfect, a plain pale-golden outcropping with what Morgiana said was the footprint that Muhammad made when
the angel took him up to heaven. Christians and Jews
said that it was a piece of the Temple, and that there had
been an altar there, where the priests offered sacrifices,
because that was where Abraham had gone to give Isaac
to God; which made it as holy as any place in the world,
except the Holy Sepulcher. The Templars had put an

iron wall about it and carved steps in it and paved it over with marble, and set an altar on it, which made Morgiana hiss and spit; but they had only done all of that to keep people from chipping the rock away and selling it to pilgrims.

Akiva thought it very beautiful, but he did not like it. "Too many religions on top of one another," he said, "and mine on the bottom, all crushed and trampled."

She was glad enough to go outside. She kept forgetting to breathe in the splendor of the dome; and they were being stared at a little too steadily. Someone would come soon and want to know where their parents were, and why they were out by themselves.

They went out the north way, past Bethesda Pool to Jehoshaphat's Gate. The sun was sinking and the shadows were growing long, but Ysabel did not want to go home. All those people crowding and squabbling and simply being alive, and all being human, and mind-blind, and kin but not kin. None of them understood her. Not one. Not even her mother.

She was going to cry again. Akiva reached out and took her hand. He did not say anything, and he did not think at her. She swallowed hard and made the tears go away.

They went through the gate, up from the valley to the Mount of Olives, turning toward Gethsemane. The stream of pilgrims was thinning with the evening, and most were coming instead of going. They all looked solemn and sanctified, or tried to. On another day she might have burst out laughing, just to shock them, but now she had no heart for it.

She stopped beyond the garden and sat down under an olive tree, setting her back to the gnarled trunk, staring at the sky through the silvery leaves.

"The sun's going to go down soon," Akiva said, "and then they'll close the gate. Are you planning to stay the night here?"

She had not thought about it. Now that he had said it, she thought, why not? She could hardly get a worse beating than she had coming already.

"You might be surprised," said Akiva. He sat beside

her and fished under his shawl. He came out with a
leather bag like a pilgrim's scrip, and a skin of what
turned out to be water. There was bread in the scrip, and
cheese, and a napkinful of dates. He divided it carefully
in quarters and gave her a share and kept one, and put
the rest away. "For the morning," he said.

She scowled. "Who told you you had to play nursemaid?"

"Nobody. I want to stay out here. I hate cities. Even
this one. Especially this one. It chokes the breath out of
me."

"It does that to all of us. We get used to it after a
while. It never gets easy."

"I noticed." He took a bite of cheese and chewed it
slowly. His eyes were on the city's walls, and on the
Dome of the Rock. "My father says he can feel it, too.
All the years and all the wars and all the holiness. If this
were our city again, he says, it wouldn't hurt us to be
here. It would be ours; it would embrace us like a
mother."

"My people hold it, and I don't feel that it's glad of
us."

"That's because you conquered it. You didn't build it;
you haven't made yourselves one with it. It's your captive, not your mother."

"It's ours." The cheese was good. The bread could
have been fresher, but she was hungry enough not to
care too much. "Tonight I think I hate it. It hurt my—
my father." He barely twitched, though she had never
said it aloud before. "There's war in it now. All anyone
can think about is killing Saracens."

"Or being killed by them."

"My father—" It was a little easier to say, the second
time. "My father will go to the war. I can feel him thinking about it. Thinking maybe someone will kill him and
put an end to all this nonsense." She shuddered. "He
hurts too much. Even from here."

Akiva put his arm around her, and his shawl with it,
making a tent out of them both. "Can't you stop reading
him?"

"I can't help it. He's been part of me since before I

was born. When his feelings are too strong or his walls
are down, I find him everywhere I turn. He says—he
says it will get better as I get older. I'll learn to shield
better, and I'll be stronger. He says it's because he
trained me. That's half a lie. It's the blood that does it.
He's *in* me. He made me."

"Didn't your mother help?"

Temper could be useful. It made a wall, and Aidan
was on the other side of it, away from her. "My mother
is human."

"So she is," Akiva said.

"I *don't* despise her!" Ysabel said sharply, though he
had not said it aloud or, for all she knew, in his mind.
"She's always at me to be ordinary. To behave myself. To
be human. But I'm not. I can't be."

"One has to pretend," he said. "To stay alive."

"I'm sick of pretending."

"So am I." He sighed and moved a little closer. The
sun was sitting on the horizon; the day's heat was fading
as fast as the daylight. Jerusalem looked washed in gold.
He said something to it. Something foreign. Hebrew. A
bit of a psalm. " 'How beautiful are thy dwelling places,
O Lord.' "

She gave that a moment's silence. Then she asked,
"Are you studying to be a priest?"

"We don't have priests the way you do."

"Well. Whatever, then."

"A rabbi. A scholar. Yes, I want to be that. After
Rosh Hashonah I shall be a man and be called to the
Torah; then I'll begin to study in earnest."

"A man? You? Your voice hasn't even broken yet."

He was annoyed, but not enough to move away from
her. "It will when it's ready. That's not what a man is,
after all. A man is what he knows, and what he does
with it."

"I know a little about what Jews study. Torah and
Talmud and a great deal of bickering. The Ramban, and
the Rambam, and one says this and another says that,
but someone else says no, it can't be either, but if it is, it
has to be thus and so, because—"

Akiva choked. Half of it was fury. The other half was laughter. "You are blasphemous!"

"Well, isn't it like that?"

"Yes," he admitted after a while. "But you make it sound silly. It's not. It's the most important thing in the world."

"Chopping logic into mincemeat?"

He cuffed her, not too hard, and still trying not to laugh. "Finding out exactly what God said, and what He meant by it."

"Oh," she said. "Theology. I'm not supposed to know anything about it, being too young, and a girl. But I listen to the chaplain when he reads, and sometimes when he finds someone interesting to talk to. He was talking to the king the other day. He was so happy afterwards, he was dizzy."

"The king has a very subtle mind," Akiva said. "He can set my father's head to spinning, and my father is as good a student of the Law as any I know of. They argue by the hour, sometimes, sounding as if they're about to murder one another, and loving every minute of it."

"The chaplain wasn't arguing. Not really. Not once he'd got going. They were picking apart how Anselm proved that God is. Then they got on to Aristotle. The king says the Church will go his way in the end, though it's been trying to ban him in the schools. Father Stephen ended up agreeing with him, though he was shocked at first. He didn't expect someone who looks like that, to be as wise as that, or as good at talking people round."

"He should have known better. He knows Prince Aidan, after all."

"Prince Aidan is always doing his best to seem less than he is. And he's not interested in theology."

"No," said Akiva. "He isn't, is he? He'd rather make a song than a syllogism."

She laughed, startling herself. It was growing dark. There were still people on the Mount, beggars and pilgrims who had, or wanted, no other place to sleep. If she had been alone, she would have been afraid. But there were two of them, and they both had power, and they were warm and fed and surprisingly comfortable. "Father Stephen thinks my father is a bit—well, light-minded. My father never does or says anything to change his mind for him." She shifted to peer into Akiva's face. "Do you think he's frivolous, too?"

"No," said Akiva. "Just worldly. Why shouldn't he be? He's a knight and a prince."

"That's what he says. We can't all be scholars. Someone has to do the ruling and the fighting."

"He does it better than anyone, except the king."

She nodded. She did not hurt inside anymore, or not enough to matter. The black roil in her middle was gone.

It was the quiet. And the stars coming out. And Akiva. He was warm next to her; he felt right, sitting there, with his shawl around her and his mind flowing gently beside hers, sometimes touching it, sometimes curving away. She liked the way his thoughts ran. They were very clear, like water running, but they went down and down like a deep pure spring. She was more like light on the water, darting-quick, with sudden shadows in it.

She felt the tug of sleep. Akiva was wide awake as far as she could see, but his mind was on Jerusalem again, thinking in Hebrew, half praying, half running over his lessons. He was thinking that if he died here he would be spared a great deal of trouble, since this was where all his people were supposed to come on Judgment Day. She almost laughed at the picture in his mind, everybody tunneling like busy rabbits, hurrying to come to Olivet before the Trump stopped sounding.

He spared a little thought for what would happen much nearer to home when they came up missing; but not too much. No more than she did. That would happen when it happened. *Inshallah,* as Morgiana would say. Ysabel could be that much a Muslim.

11

Brother Thomas was not pleased to discover that he had guests. Brother Richard he might have expected, since the man was one of the Patriarch's following, and always about, whether by accident or design. The Constable of the Kingdom was no surprise, under the circumstances. But the other—

Guillermo Seco looked about at the meticulous order of the scriptorium. It was empty at this hour, with the monks at recreation, and none minded to linger over his work. The desks stood in their rows with the tall stools drawn up to them and the array of inks and paints, brushes and pens, rulers and scrapers, set as each man preferred to have them. The desk nearest had the makings of a mass-book on it, half a yard high, the letters inked in, each large enough even for dim old eyes to read. The task which the limner had left was an initial woven with vines and flowers and fantastical creatures, sketched in delicately in black ink, with the first touches of color: blue, a speck or two of scarlet.

Mass-books were worth nothing to a trader in spices. Seco glanced at it with mild interest, but the brunt of his attention fell on Thomas. Thomas met his smile with a cold stare. He smiled on, oblivious. "Success!" he said, almost crowing it. "A complete success."

"Was it?" Thomas asked none of them to sit, though there were chairs in the alcove where the book-press was.

"Utterly," Seco said. "I was there, and able to hear every word. It went exactly as we planned. The legate produced the coffer, they all inspected the seals, the legate's secretary read the document. Our document. The expressions on their faces—not one of them suspected."

"One of them did," Thomas said. "The King of Rhiyana came to the legate and the Patriarch, some days ago. He had suspicions, but no certainty. He bade them be on guard. It was unfortunate for his cause that the deed was already done."

That quelled Seco, for the moment. Thomas let him ponder the thin edge on which they walked, which clearly he had not believed in; then said, "You were not wise to come here. While we are separate, we present no clear target. Together, we blaze like a beacon."

"Did you lie to us, then?" Seco demanded, falling back on bluster as such men did when caught in the wrong. "I did all that you taught me. I kept out of their sight, I did nothing to attract their attention, I thought the nonsense you bade me think until my head was like to burst."

"I taught you truly. But these are witches of great power, and you are a simple man, with a mere few days' teaching in arts that, for true mastery, require years of training and discipline."

"Such as you have?"

Thomas ignored the suggestion of a sneer. "Such as I have. You know how I learned it: the stranger in Naples with his arts that came, he said, from the land of Prester John. I began my study of them when I was a very young man. I am still no more than a journeyman; and I am not at all assured that I can elude such a hunt as these creatures have raised, now that they are pricked to anger."

"You said they would not know where to look."

"Then they will look everywhere; and if the devil is minded to aid them, they will chance upon the truth. Your coming to gloat over their discomfiture is just such folly as the Adversary loves to exploit."

Seco flushed darkly. "I have business in the city, and a rich trade in the offing. Would you have me lose it for your fears?"

"Would you prefer to lose your soul for your folly?"

"It may not be as bad as that," Amalric said. He perched on a stool with his elbow perilously close to a page and its newly applied gold leaf. He shifted away from it; Thomas breathed again. "I've not only been in the city, I've been in their company, and none of them has stripped me of my secret. They know I'm their enemy; they expect me to thwart them; but they haven't the slightest suspicion that I'm part of this."

"No doubt they believe it too subtle a plot for a plain man of war," said Brother Richard. "But for the one cord which you would not alter for fear of betraying the ruse too soon, the forgery is flawless. The pope's legate himself has said so."

"That is the truth," Thomas said. "I am, after all, one of the scribes in the chancery, when I am not sent on embassies with the Holy Father's legates."

"Or studying the arts of Prester John." Richard raised a brow as a thought struck him. "Is he one of them, do you think?"

Thomas did not like to dwell on that. "We have what we sought: the wedding is delayed, the witches are discomfited. We—"

"Delayed?" Seco scowled. "Why only delayed? If this forgery is perfect, why can it not stand?"

"There are copies in the chancery," Thomas said, not quite as if he instructed a child. "I expect that they will send there for a new dispensation while they pursue their hunt here."

"Delayed, then, but for a goodly while." Seco paused. "You did destroy the document. Didn't you?"

"No," Thomas said.

Only Seco seemed appalled. Amalric looked simply interested. "Why?" he asked.

"Several reasons. We may need it in bargaining, if they discover who we are. If they do not, it may suit us to produce it; it may even behoove us to pretend that we are allies and not enemies."

"Subtle," said Amalric. "Collect a ransom and persuade them that it's a reward. I like that. If we could find another target for their anger, produce him as the forger, let them do with him as they will . . ."

"I will not be party to the destruction of an innocent soul," Thomas said tightly.

"Not innocent," Amalric said. "Not of anything but this."

"You forget that they read souls. They will know that he is not the forger."

"Ah," said Amalric, "but if your arts are all that you proclaim, then surely you can take care of that."

Thomas's mouth set in a line. This man was much more dangerous than he seemed. He had taken to the eastern art as though born to it, mastered in hours what had taken Thomas months to learn. He did not, as yet, show signs of wishing to know more than the concealment of secrets. Thomas hoped that he never would.

"By God's grace," Thomas said, crossing himself, "there will be no need for such a sin as you speak of. For sin it is, to trap the innocent."

"No doubt," said Amalric blandly. "I don't suppose you'll want to tell us where you've hidden the dispensation. In case of accidents, of course."

Thomas understood him too well. "In case of accidents, yes. My lord."

"Well then," said Seco, deaf to the undertones or judging it wise to disregard them. "Now that we have what we planned for, we had best consider what to do hereafter."

"For the moment, nothing." Amalric rubbed his shaven jaw idly, almost caressingly, eyes narrowed in reflection. "We've thrown a cat among the rats; they'll provide us with sport enough for a while. Later . . . I do like your proposal, Brother. One of us, out of concern for truth and justice if not for friendship, finds and reveals the missing document. He is, of course, most careful what he thinks of when he does it. For reward he takes— whatever he pleases. The king has wealth and power. The prince has more wealth than he and, in this country, rather more power. Both might be pleased to share some of each with the one who gives the prince his heart's desire."

Seco's eyes gleamed with greed. Thomas, watching Amalric, saw satisfaction, quickly masked.

"There is somewhat that we can do," Richard said, "while we wait for the proper time. Rumors are easy to plant; they grow like no other crop. It is no secret that these our adversaries are witchfolk, but no one has come out and said it. Until now. If it can be spread abroad, and kept abroad, that the Holy Father himself condemns the Assassin and all who traffic with her, as sorcerers and black enchanters . . ."

Thomas's heart leaped. Yes. Yes, that was what he had hoped to hear. If Richard had not said it, he would have been obliged to do so himself. He would pay dearly to see Gwydion of Rhiyana revealed for what he was, and punished for it. To create a false anathema, to forge the pope's signature and his seal—those were sins, yes, but sins in the cause of a greater good. It burned his soul to see such creatures as those in the bosom of holy Church, kneeling before her altars, accepting the bread of the Eucharist and turning straight from it to their sorceries. Gwydion was a canny beast: he had taken a commoner for a queen, but she professed to be a Christian, and played as cleverly at devotion as her husband himself. Aidan was the wilder, and the less prudent. He betrayed himself utterly in this that he would do, allying not only with an infidel but with an Assassin. They would burn for it. And it would be Thomas who brought them to the stake.

His brow was damp, his breath coming hard. No one seemed to mark his loss of composure. Amalric was speaking, and the others were listening. "A witch-hunt might be useful, at that: it will distract them from their own hunt. But we have to be careful that it doesn't get out of hand. We need the king and the prince for the men they command. Once the army is mustered, it might be possible to dispose of them. They don't grow old and they don't catch fever, but they can be killed."

"You know that?" Seco asked.

"I saw the prince wounded in a fight once. It was bad enough to put him out of action for a while; and I heard his woman railing at him. I know little enough Arabic, but I could piece together what she said. They're devilish hard to kill, but it can be done."

"How—" Seco said faintly.

"Burn it to ash. Sever its head. Stop its heart. Anything that would kill a man instantly, will kill one of them."

"Bleeding takes a while," Richard said, "but a man bled dry is a dead man. As no doubt she told him. She has none of her race's reluctance to call a spade a spade."

"Her race is the race of witches," said Thomas, "and they are seldom circumspect."

"Except when they need to be." Amalric slid from the stool. "You underestimate their cunning, I think. There's more to them than mind-reading and looking a fraction as old as they are. They know how to use the latter. I have to keep reminding myself that I'm not talking to a raw boy."

"I never forget," Thomas said. "And I know what they are. I have had years to learn." He met the knight's steady, colorless stare, and suppressed a shiver; but he spoke to Seco. "Messer Seco, you might consider the wisdom of returning to Acre for a little while, until the king comes to it and raises the levies. Then you were best advised to take yourself elsewhere. Perhaps, if you deferred your business in Jerusalem . . . ?"

"Yes, I am your weak link," said Seco with surprising perception and even more surprising equanimity. "I can delay my negotiations for a week. Would that be adequate?"

"Ample," said Thomas.

Seco nodded briskly. A little too much so, perhaps: his only indication of temper. "Then I had best go about it. Brothers, my lord."

"That one will need watching," said Richard lazily when he was gone.

"He did give in too easily, didn't he?" Amalric sounded amused. "He won't turn on us, I don't think. Not as long as he sees a chance at the prince's gold."

"Or his highness's life?" Richard inquired.

"Maybe. If it doesn't endanger his profits. And meanwhile he is useful. He brought us together, didn't he? He's good at spreading rumors; he can afford to pay for the best."

Thomas eyed him warily. It was, in the beginning, Seco's conspiracy. Or perhaps it was not. Thomas did not need witchcraft to perceive that Amalric was playing more sides than he chose to admit. The merchant had conceived the plot to dispose of the prince whom he envied so bitterly, but Thomas did not think that the method was his. Richard would have known how to go about it; but who had brought in Richard?

Amalric stood in the Patriarch's scriptorium in his plain and rather rumpled cotte, with mail showing under it, and a razor-nick on his chin. He looked like any knight in Outremer: a rough soldier, out to win his fortune and not caring overmuch how he went about it. The cross over his heart and the vow that went with it were but the means to his end.

Which was always and inescapably his own advantage.

Thomas did this for God and for holy Church. It was unfortunate that his allies must be a merchant greedy for gold and a monk with a bent for intrigue and a knight who would stop at nothing to get what he wanted; but they were what God had given him. He would have to make the best of it.

A bell rang, faint but clear. He swallowed a sigh of relief. "That, my lord, is the summons to chapel. Will you come with us to hear the office?"

For an instant Thomas feared that Amalric would accept. But he shook his head with no pretense of regret. "I'm wanted at the palace. Good day to you, then, and good hiding."

"To you also," said Thomas. He could not quite bring himself to raise his hand in blessing. It was for Richard to do that; and he did it with devotion that bordered on parody.

Thomas suppressed a second sigh. Such allies, he had. But the game was worth the candle. Oh, yes. By God and His angels and all His saints, it was worth the price.

12

By evening there could be no doubt of it. Ysabel was missing. The children's nurse, long inured to the vagaries of her most fractious charge, did not trouble Joanna until she had searched the house and the garden and questioned anyone who might know where the child had gone. Joanna greeted the news with hard-won calm, and no fear, not quite yet. Anger, yes; and when she found Ysabel, she would indulge it.

She sent out the hunters in a pattern that was all too familiar. A party to the house by the Dome of the Rock, another to her mother's house, a third with torches to traverse the city. Then, perforce, she waited. Sleep was beyond her. Ranulf led the searchers in the city; but for the burden in her belly, she would have gone with him. Forbidden that, she sat in the solar and glared at a bit of needlework, and rehearsed the greeting she would give the truant.

Ysabel was not in Aidan's house; but then, neither was he. The men-at-arms who had gone to ask, brought news, and a companion. Simeon the Jew had little of his usual wry composure. He looked as if he had been tearing out his hair. He had, it seemed, misplaced his son.

Joanna kept calm by an effort of will. She sat him down, coaxed wine into him, extracted as much as he knew. "We came back to the prince's house," he said between gulps of wine, "somewhat after midday, with tasks to do that were not well put off. My son was restless and could not settle to his work. He asked leave to go into the city; I was distracted, I must have given it, though I meant to bid him keep to the house and its garden. He left. He has not come back."

"They may be together," she said. "They seem to have taken to one another."

Simeon set the cup down empty, but would not let her fill it again. He seemed to have mastered himself. "So they have," he said. "I wish I could say that it comforts me."

"So do I." She took the cup and filled it, and drank it herself. The wine was strong and sweet, sharpened with cinnamon. It cleared her head a little. "I've got searchers out. If they're in the city, they'll be found." If it was not simply childish rebellion that had taken them; if they had not come to harm. Two children in a city on the edge of war, crowded with pilgrims from all over the world, and some who were not pilgrims, but folk who preyed on pilgrims . . .

She closed her eyes to that. Ysabel had vanished before. She had always come back, or been brought back, intact and unrepentant.

She was with Aidan. That was all. Whenever she was in disgrace, she went to him for sympathy. She usually got it; even if he took her mother's side, he broke down soon enough and let her have her way.

"Little minx," Joanna muttered.

Simeon managed a dim smile. "Your aplomb is admirable, my lady. I, alas—I only have the one, and he drives me to distraction."

"You think she doesn't?" Joanna shook her head. "She runs away whenever it pleases her. I'd take a whip to her if I thought it would do any good at all."

"I threaten my hellion with my lord king. That holds him for a while."

"I can't threaten her with my lord prince. He aids and abets her."

"Then perhaps," Simeon said, "she has gone to him."

But she had not. Nor had Akiva.

Which left the searchers in the city and Joanna in the solar. Simeon took one or two of those who had come back, and went out with them. It was harder this time not to follow them. "Someone has to be home," she told herself sternly. "In case she comes back by herself. Someone has to be ready to tan her hide."

Aimery was not pleased to be scouring the city for his sister. The adventure was all very well, and the ex-

citement of stalking the streets with torch in hand, startling the rats and the beggars asleep in doorways, passing
the lights and clamor of the taverns, once surprising a
pack of footpads about their business and driving them
off. His father went about it as a good soldier should, not
too fast, not too slow, with a minimum of fuss. Aimery
was proud of him. That was what he wanted to be when
he was a man. Strong. Looked up to. Worth something in
the world.

But to waste it all on a chit of a girl . . .

King Gwydion's Jew met them near the Temple wall
and told them that his son had vanished, too. That gave
them two targets to aim for. Ranulf was polite to the
Jew, though Aimery would have told him to go back to
his prayers and leave the hunt to proper men. The Jew
went away toward the cattle market; Ranulf's party
paused, debating. Some were minded to go back and see
if Ysabel had come home by herself. Ranulf told them
grimly to go on hunting.

Aimery had time to think. He was angry and he was
tired and he was disgusted with all of it, but his mind
was clear enough. They were not going about this in the
right way. They were thinking like grownfolk; not like a
child.

He kept on thinking, trudging in his father's wake,
peering into doorways and alleys, sometimes calling his
sister's name. Suppose that he was a girl, and Ysabel,
and mad at her family for expecting her to act like a
properly brought up child. He would want to run away,
and do it thoroughly. Which, since she was Ysabel,
meant very thoroughly indeed.

The others were afraid that she might not be staying
away of her own will. Aimery doubted that. Another
girl, maybe. Not Ysabel. Ysabel never did anything she
did not want to do.

They stopped by Lady Margaret's house, and the
porter was waiting for them with wine and a bite to eat,
but no news. Aidan had not been told. Everyone agreed
that that was best. He had troubles enough without this;
and, said the porter, he had been persuaded to sleep a
little, with his brother watching over him. The Lady

Morgiana was gone, no one knew where. No one suggested that Ysabel might be with her. Which was as well,
thought Aimery. If Morgiana had her, she could be anywhere in the world.

He preferred to think that she was in Jerusalem.
Somewhere no one thought to look. Not in a church—
that was not like Ysabel; especially if the Jew's son was
with her.

The men were starting to stumble. His father was as
steady as ever, but Aimery could see that he was tired.
He was thinking of giving it up; of waiting for morning.

Almost as soon as Aimery thought it, Ranulf said it.
"Back." His voice was rough. "It's no use. She'll turn up
on her own, or we'll go out again in daylight. God
knows, it won't be the first time."

No one tried to argue. Aimery held his tongue. He
knew he should say something of what he was thinking,
and where he thought Ysabel might be. Maybe his father
would agree; maybe he would refuse to listen. It would
be out of Aimery's hands. Just as it always was.

He kept quiet and followed obediently, the good,
dull, unnoticed eldest son, doing what his father told
him. His mother was waiting up for them; all she could
say was, "No?"

"No," said Ranulf heavily.

She hardly saw Aimery at all. Her thoughts were all
for Ysabel. She hugged him gingerly against her bulk,
kissed him with a preoccupied air, and said, "Bed, now.
You've done enough for one day."

Just as if he had been a child, and not a favored one,
at that. He went where he was bidden, where William
was already, sound asleep with the lamp flickering low.
He had all the blankets, as usual. Aimery lay down in his
clothes. Just for a while, to rest his tired feet. Just until
the house went quiet.

He started awake. William was still asleep, still
wrapped in blankets. All Aimery could see of him was a
tuft of straw-colored hair.

It was dark beyond the lamp's light, but the air

through the opened window had a tang of morning. Aimery combed his hair with his fingers, groped under the bed for his boots.

Cook was up, baking bread. Aimery's stomach growled, but he did not stop to appease it. Hakim the porter, as Aimery had hoped, was snoring in the gate. Aimery stepped gingerly over him and eased the gate open. It creaked; he froze. Hakim's snores never faltered. Aimery slipped out and eased the gate shut. He pulled on his boots. His heart was thudding hard. He had never done anything like this before. A good boy, people said. No rebellion in him.

Dull.

He would show them what he was made of.

The city, like the Mortmains' cook, woke early. The devout went to mass at dawn. The hungry went in search of food, and the vendors and the shopkeepers obliged them. The gates opened at sunup with the changing of the guard: the night guards yawning off to bed, the day guards coming bright-eyed to their posts. They were not usually so alert, but there was war in the air. That roused them wonderfully.

They took no notice of Aimery. He was not the only one going out. The first eager pilgrims were straining at the leash, and from the look of them had been doing it for half the night. "We have to do it now," he heard one of them say in some agitation. "Before the Saracens come and kill us all."

He could have thought better of the chivalry of Outremer, Aimery thought. He did not trouble to say it. It never did any good to tax pilgrims with truth.

Aimery's step was light as he started up the Mount of Olives and took the turn that led to Gethsemane. He outdistanced the pilgrims soon enough: they kept stopping to marvel, or to burst into tears, or to pray. He was born in this country. He knew how holy it was, but he had to keep on living in it. And, now, hunting for his sister.

She was not where he had thought she would be. He sagged. He had been so sure. It was what he would have done, and where he would have gone, if he had been Ysabel.

A sound brought him about. He had his dagger out before he thought.

The Jew's son blinked at him sleepily. The head on his shoulder was sound asleep, hopelessly tangled, and indisputably Ysabel's.

Aimery let his breath out slowly. They had taken shelter under a tree, half-hidden behind it. Clever of them. He wondered which had thought of it.

He sheathed his knife and stood over them. He ignored the Jew. He dug his toe into his sister's side. "Wake up," he said.

She came up spitting. Aimery got out of the way. Akiva got hold of her skirt and pulled her down again, and sat on her.

She settled quickly enough, once she had a chance to wake up. Akiva let her go. She glared at them both, but especially at Aimery. "Where did you come from?"

"Where do you think?" He planted his fists on his hips. "We've been hunting all night. Father is worn to a rag. Mother is furious. Couldn't you have picked a better time to run away?"

She went red. Good: he had scored a hit. "They locked me up. I couldn't stand it."

"And why did you lock you up? Because you were acting like a spoiled brat."

She scrambled up. "I was *not*!"

"You were. You couldn't think of anybody but yourself."

"Was *not*!"

"Was." Aimery curled his lip. "You made a bad day worse. I hope you're proud of yourself."

He thought she might leap at him; but she stood still, shaking, with her fists at her sides. "I hate you," she said.

"Not half as much as I despise you." He turned his back on her. "You can stay here for all I care. I'll tell Mother where you are."

"That's all you want, isn't it? To get some attention from her."

His back snapped straight. "Maybe it is. At least I don't do it by keeping her up all night and making her afraid I've been kidnapped. Or worse."

He started walking then, toward the city. He refused to look back.

She caught up with him halfway down. The Jew came more slowly, moving as if he was stiff with sleeping in the open. Aimery ignored them both.

Ysabel stayed next to him, glaring at the ground in front of her feet. He hoped she felt good and guilty. He doubted she did. She looked purely angry.

"You don't hate me," she said.

"I didn't say I did."

She let that go for a step or ten. Then: "I don't like to be despised."

"Then stop doing things to earn it."

"You're horrible."

"You're a spoiled baby."

"I'm not," she said. Not as loudly as she had before; not as furiously. "You don't know what I am. You don't know—why—" She stopped. "You don't understand."

He would have liked to hit her for sounding so condescending. "Maybe I don't want to."

"You never liked me. Not from the first, when you stopped having Mother all to yourself."

He would not answer that. She was baiting him; she was pricking his scars to see if he would bleed. He would not give her the satisfaction. He would not even walk faster, to get away from her.

"She doesn't love me any more than she loves you. You're the good one. The one who never gives her trouble. The one she always throws in my face. 'Aimery listens,' she says. 'Aimery knows how to behave. Aimery is what a child ought to be.' "

Aimery set his teeth. "And of course you would never want to be like that."

"I try." She even sounded as if she meant it. "We aren't all born good. Some of us have to work at it."

"Not very hard, from the looks of it."

She kicked a pebble viciously. It skipped down the

hill, over a pilgrim's foot, into a tuft of grass. "Why don't you just shut up?"

He shut up. They went the rest of the way in silence, with Akiva trailing behind, offering no intercession. Wise of him. Between the two of them, just as between the Christians and the Saracens, there would never be more than an armed truce.

13

Aidan flung the pen across the room. It pierced the plastered wall as if it had been a dagger, with a splatter of ink raying out from it. He thrust himself up and away from the table with its ledgers, its rollbooks, its manifold minutiae of a prince's preparation for war.

His seneschal watched him, a little pale about the eyes, but carefully calm.

And that drove him as wild as any of the rest of it. They were all indulging him with heroic patience. Coaxing him back to his house; giving him ample tasks to occupy his mind; sitting quiet through his blasts of temper. Time would settle him, they told one another sagely. Time and a good fight, which he would get, once the king had called up the levies. His portion of which, he was purportedly attending to now, this morning that should have been the morning after his wedding night, with his wedding denied him and his lady hunting without him and only the war left to console him.

Aidan stalked from table to wall and back, snatching the pen as he passed, dropping it under Master Gilbert's nose. "What in the world can I do here," he demanded, "that you cannot do better?"

"Wield the authority of your position," Master Gilbert answered, "my lord."

Aidan snarled at him. "What authority? What position? What do I have at all, that matters in the slightest?"

"Your life." That was not Gilbert, and well for him that it was not, or he would have taken a stroke for it.

Aidan turned on his brother. Gwydion had a look about him that Aidan almost welcomed: of patience carefully sustained, and calm that had nothing in it of passivity.

"You need," said Gwydion judiciously, "to hit something. Will I do?"

Aidan regarded him, narrow-eyed. Something was blooming in him; something black, with fire in it. "A match, brother?"

Gwydion inclined his head. "A match."

They could have done it naked, without weapons, as they often had: wrestling to a fall, or dancing to best of three. But Aidan's mood wanted something deadlier, and Gwydion was minded to oblige him. It was not, by God's bones, indulgence. It was temper needing to match itself with temper, and body with body, more perfectly equal than any other in the world.

They put on mail and took up the heavy practice swords, blunt beside the fine steel of their Damascus blades but quite lethal enough. Neither was minded to ward his head with a helm, though they wore the padded cap under the mail-coif. Image looked at image and grinned, white and fierce. "Already I feel better," Aidan said.

Gwydion smiled. "We'll see how you feel when I'm done with you."

"I'll try not to gloat over my victory."

"Victory, would it be? *En garde,* then, braggart, and may the devil take the hindmost!"

Aidan laughed and fell to.

The sound of blade clashing on blade would have been guide enough, even without the mask-faced Saracen who had conducted them from the door. Evrard de Beaumarchais, who considered himself King Guy's friend, glanced at the brace of lordlings who accompanied him, and then ahead, to the light at the end of the passage and the bare swept courtyard and the two who fought in it. There were others about: more Saracens, a Rhiyanan or three, a scatter of servants.

Evrard neither liked nor disliked the lord of Mille-fleurs. This was a kingdom of fighting men, and Prince Aidan was as good a fighting man as any in it. That made him worthy of respect, whatever else he was; and whatever he chose to share his bed and his board.

He was in fine form this morning. Both of him.

Evrard blinked and shook his head. Of course the other would be his twin, the Rhiyanan king. It was like watching a man and his shadow, or a battle of mirrors. Without blazons to mark them, without any distinction of expression or movement or skill with the sword, there was no telling which was Aidan and which was Gwy-dion.

This was no simple practice bout. There was real force in those sweeping blows. Almost, Evrard would have said, real anger; real enmity. Neither held back, and neither gave quarter. They were faster than anything nat-ural should have been, weighted down with mail in the sun, and wielding the great coarse cudgels that were the two-handed broadswords. Even as Evrard stared, one of them melted from beneath a stroke that should have clo-ven him, and flashed round as quick as a cat, and struck at the other's neck. But there was cold steel between, and eyes the color of steel, and a smile like a sword's edge. They froze so, blade crossing blade, eye crossing eye. "Yield?" said one.

"Never," said the other.

The first laughed. The second smiled. They lowered their blades and closed in a sudden, breathless embrace.

Still with their arms about one another's shoulders, bright-eyed, streaming with sweat, they thrust back coifs and caps from wetly matted heads, and seemed for the first time to notice that they were not alone. The one who had smiled raised a brow. The one who had laughed shook his hands out of their sheaths of mail and ran them through his hair. Both his brows went up. "Sir

Evrard. Sir Thierry; Sir Wulfram. To what do I owe the honor?"

Evrard was surprised to realize how much it mattered that he know which of them was which. Now that they were still, he could see how truly still the king was, and how subtly restless the prince, like a flame in a windowless room. He bowed to the elder first, but it was to the younger that he spoke. "We give you greeting, my lord prince. Perhaps you would prefer to recover yourself before we speak? Privily," he added with a glance about, but not quite at the king.

Aidan's frown deepened, and Evrard went briefly cold. If the tales were true—if he could know without being told—

But he seemed quiet enough, and while he was not visibly delighted, he was sufficiently courteous. He saw them settled in a cool and airy room with wine and cakes and sherbet and a servant to wait on them, while he went to divest himself of his armor.

He did not keep them waiting unduly long: only long enough to wash and put on cotte and hose, plain enough both, but rich enough not to insult their dignity. He brought no one with him; once he had accepted a cup of sherbet, he sent the servant away. He raised the cup to his lips, but barely drank before he set it down. "Well?" he said.

Evrard cleared his throat. It had seemed a wise course when he was persuaded to follow it. Now he was not so certain. He found himself wondering why he was chosen, and not someone of greater rank; not one of those who had contrived the message. He was good with words, he knew that. He was not notably inclined to cowardice. And yet . . .

He had commanded troops in the field. He knew what he was being used for. His folly for being so blinded by the honor that he could not see it sooner.

Whatever else he was, he was no coward. He clung to that as he looked into the white hawk-face. He had never seen it so close or so clear. It was not so young after all. Or so pretty. There was something disturbing in the cast of it; in the set of the eyes in it, in the way they looked out from under the slanting brows.

He swallowed hard and made himself speak. "My lord prince, I come with these my fellows, not as a single man—though I believe in what I have to say—but as one who speaks for a number of those in the High Court. A very fair number, my lord. You may be assured of that."

The prince waited. It was not patience.

"We share your distress in what has befallen you, and regret that it should have come upon you. We deplore the deception, if deception it is. Yet, for all of that . . ." Evrard paused to draw a breath. Still the prince did not move or speak. "For all of that, my lord, under the circumstances, might it not be for the best? You must be aware of what is said by those of little wisdom and less perception, but more power in the kingdom than can readily be ignored. That a great lord should be so closely allied with the Saracen; that he should have tamed an Assassin. That there might be more than alliance. That there might be—" Almost, he could not say it. "That there might be treachery."

The prince laughed. It was a sound exactly like that of his blade upon his brother's. "Yes, I know what people say. More maybe than you think. What you're admitting to—that is a lie."

"No doubt," said Evrard uneasily. "On your side, no doubt at all. On another . . . my lord. This is not a pleasure, you must believe me. But that it is necessary— that I know."

"Then why don't you come out and say it, and get it over?"

Sweet, those words; one remembered that the one who spoke them was a singer. One also remembered that he was the best knight in Outremer. And maybe more than that. Very likely more than that.

Evrard did as he was told. "My lord, I speak no word of betrayal, not without proof. That is, of betrayal of the kingdom. What else there may be—my lord, it has been brought to our notice by those whose veracity can be tested, that there may be more than the impediment of religion between yourself and your betrothed. That she may be—"

Aidan's laughter now was full and free. "You're trying to tell me that she's been accused of taking another lover? Evrard, Evrard! You were always a pleasant enough booby, but this is ridiculous."

Evrard bridled. He had expected anger, even physical attack, but this mockery was uncalled for.

The prince shook his head, still smiling. "Evrard, who put you up to this? Are you trying to make me feel better by telling me she isn't worth the trouble?"

"No one 'put me up to this,' " Evrard said stiffly, and not entirely truthfully. "I am not attempting to comfort you in so backhanded a fashion. I am telling you the truth as I have been made to see it. God knows, any perfidy is possible with a Saracen, and this was an Assassin. Is still, for all any of us knows. But what she has been observed in the act of—my lord, even if the pope's letter is a forgery as you claim, and the marriage is not annulled by the disparity of your religions, have you received any dispensation for consanguinity?"

Aidan regarded him blankly. "Con— Evrard, whatever she is, she is not related to me in any of the forbidden degrees."

"I was not thinking of her. I was thinking of the one with whom she has been seen in circumstances which admit of no ambiguity. Which would forbid her to marry you, since she has shared carnal relations with one of your close kin."

"What?"

He was visibly stunned. Evrard had no pity to spare for him. Not since he laughed, and made clear exactly what he thought of Evrard. "She has been seen," Evrard said—to his credit, not with any great relish, even now— "and more than once, in more than one place, in close and intimate embrace with the lord your brother."

Aidan's head shook. "That's nonsense. We look exactly alike. Is this the worst you can do? Accuse her of consorting with me, and call me my twin?"

Evrard hesitated. It might be true. He rather hoped that it was. "Was it you, then, in the court of the fountain in this house, three days before your wedding? You were in blue," Evrard said. "And wearing a ring with a sapphire."

The prince frowned. "I never wear blue. It's my brother's color. His ring—his signet, the king's signet, with the seabird carved on it—" He stopped. "Someone has been lying to you, Evrard."

"He swore to it on holy relics."

"No," said Aidan.

It was sinking in slowly, as such shocks did.

"She wouldn't," he said. "Not with my brother. She couldn't. He couldn't. He told me—"

"I'm sorry, my lord," Evrard said, meaning it. Hating what he had been persuaded to do, and hating himself for being even so briefly glad of it. Prince Aidan had a rough tongue, everyone knew that. It was no cause to cut him to the bone.

But was there any gentle way to do it?

Evrard tried to find one. "My lord, it may be for the best. If she would betray you with your own brother, what would she not do? He is not at fault, I'm sure; she bewitched him. Our witness swore to that, as to the rest."

Aidan rose slowly. He seemed calm; undangerous. But Evrard's belly knotted. "Get out," the prince said.

"My lord—"

"Please." Aidan's voice was soft. "If you value your life. Go. Now."

The other two were already edging toward the door. Evrard stood, but he could not make himself walk. "My lord, I am sorry. I wish I had not had to bring you such news on top of the rest. But we felt that you should know; that you should consider it in the light of what has happened."

"Out," said Aidan. The softness shredded. There was edged steel beneath. "Out, damn you to hell. *Out!*"

The king's pi-dog fled. And none too soon for his skinny neck. Aidan's hand found a goblet. It shattered most satisfyingly. The shards, alas, flew wide; none came close enough to touch him. He would have welcomed the sting, and the blood that would follow it.

Morgiana and Gwydion. Preposterous. Another woman—maybe. One had, once, and none of them had seen fit to tell the priests that she who wedded Gwydion had once shared Aidan's bed. But that was before any betrothal, when a village witch loved two princes and could not choose between them, and all three knew, and loved one another, and never stained it with jealousy. Not even—not excessively—when she chose the gentler of them and consented to be his lady, and afterward his queen. Aidan had not touched her since; not in that way.

As Gwydion would not have touched Morgiana. As he had said that he would not, lest it be discovered, and the marriage be forbidden for yet another cause. Gwydion never lied; not to his brother, the half of his self.

Nor would Morgiana have seduced him. She wanted Aidan, and only Aidan. She never lied to him.

Did she?

He turned in the room, seeing none of it. He was half mad with the wreck of his wedding. This was but another sleight, a new and clumsy blow, delivered by a wide-eyed innocent. Evrard honestly believed that he had done it for Aidan's own good. Those who had sent him . . . not so honest, they, and never so benign. What they wanted was clear enough. To weaken him; to confuse him; to sunder him from his Saracen, whom they had good reason to fear, and from his brother, who might raise himself up as rival to the upstart king.

Except that Morgiana would never betray her lover, and Gwydion would never claim any kingdom but his own. They were not ambitious in any way a mortal would understand; these mortals least of all.

All the good that the bout in the courtyard had done him was gone. His mood was more foul than ever. He could not even venture another bout. He would kill the one who fought with him, even if it was Gwydion. Especially if it was Gwydion.

He could not face his brother in this state. He thought of going out. Yes. He would go afoot, alone, and let the city take him where it would. For once its numb-

ing clamor of minds and voices, its seethe and stench of
humanity, its agelong burden of holiness, seemed truly
welcome. It would hammer away his black mood; make
him anew.

In his plain clothes, with a hood to draw up if he saw
anyone he knew, and no weapon but the dagger he always carried, he was no more notable than any other
knight or squire in a city full of them. That would
change in a week's time when they were all gone to Acre,
but today they were much in evidence, going about errands for their lords or for themselves, readying for war.

He wandered not quite aimlessly. The blunt grey
dome of Holy Sepulcher drew him, ugly after the perfection of the Dome of the Rock, ugly and holy. Pilgrims
called it beautiful because it was what it was; not
through any distinction of its own.

He was like a ghost returning to the scene of its
death, probing again and again into the mortal wound.
At the foot of Calvary he hesitated. Almost he went up,
riding the current of pilgrims. But he could not. He
turned instead, and took a way he knew well.

The Mortmains lived their lives in a state of happy
chaos. Today it was chaos tenfold, but happy, it was not.
It had nothing to do with Aidan, except indirectly, in
that he had begotten the object of it.

Ysabel, it seemed, had taken it into her head to run
away. Again, and rather more successfully than she had
before. Now she was found. She had Simeon's whelp
with her, and Simeon adding his voice to the din, and
Ranulf looking bone-weary and saying nothing. "You
could have been killed!" her mother screamed at her, not
for the first time from the looks of it. "You could have
been kidnapped, taken by slavers, dragged away in
chains. Anything at all could have happened to you!"

"But it didn't," Ysabel said with that perfect confidence in her own righteousness which could drive any
self-respecting adult wild. "I was with Akiva. We prayed
at the Wailing Wall, and then we went to the Temple,
and then we went to the Mount of Olives. They shut the

gates while we were there. We found a place to sleep, and stayed there till Aimery found us. No one ever laid a hand on us."

"I'll lay a hand on you," her mother said grimly. "Right where it will do the most good."

Simeon's agreement was palpable. He had Akiva by the ear. The boy wore an expression of resignation, and even a glimmer of repentance. "Father, you did give me leave."

"I gave you leave? To stay out all night and make me tear my hair with worry, I gave you leave?" Simeon shook him till he yelped. "And you almost a man. A girlchild, nine summers old, running away like a whipped puppy, I can see that. But a boy almost a man—"

"I made him do it," Ysabel said staunchly, if not wisely. "He only went to look after me, because I wouldn't go back."

"All the worse," said Simeon. "A man should know when to disregard a child's whim."

"A child," gritted Joanna, "even a girlchild, ought to know better than to do such a thing to begin with."

"Just so," said Simeon. "And for that shall you be punished. Come, sir. We have presumed on these people's kindness long enough."

Akiva came with a fair semblance of meekness, but Aidan, unnoticed in the doorway, marked the flash of his eyes. There would be trouble later. Witchfolk trouble.

Oh, no, there won't.

Akiva went green. Aidan smiled amiably at him and went on in his mind, *Yes, I'm here, and I've heard as much as I need to hear. Shall we discuss it with my brother, or would you prefer to suffer your punishment— your well-earned punishment—in silence?*

That cowed him, though there was spirit enough in him to make him grin when his father, dragging him through the door, saw who moved aside to let him pass. Simeon was quite as startled as Akiva had been. Aidan laid a finger on his lips. Simeon ducked his head, muttered a reverence, and departed, with his son half running to keep pace.

Joanna had started on Ysabel again. Ranulf sat in a chair and lowered his head into his hands. Aidan knew the look of a night's hard hunting and a morning's hard fretting. And none of them had sent word to him.

Of course not. They were like everyone else: careful of his grief, sparing his temper.

That was cooling at last in this blessed human uproar. Aidan left the concealment of the doorway and came into the solar. Joanna's tirade wound down. Ysabel stared wide-eyed, with the first sign of apprehension which she had deigned to show. She had not heard what he said to Akiva, because he did not wish her to; nor known that he was there. Ranulf raised his head and put on a smile of welcome. It was not too ill done, all things considered. "My lord. Aidan?"

"Aidan," he said. He looked from one to another of them. "She did it again, did she? You should have told me. I could have found her for you."

Joanna shook her head. It was more tiredness than negation. "I suppose I should have. It didn't seem wise at the time. And, as you see, we found her. Or Aimery did. He kept his head when all the rest of us lost ours, and tracked her down."

Ysabel opened her mouth, but shut it again. Aidan looked her up and down. "What did I tell you the last time you did this to your mother?"

She hung her head. She did it, he well knew, to hide the rebellion in her eyes.

"Well?" he prompted her.

She mumbled something.

"Louder," he said, relentless.

"You said you'd give me a hiding I'd never forget!"

He winced at the volume of it. "So I did. So I shall. If you wanted to stay the night with me, you should have asked."

"I couldn't. They would have said no. You would, too. I had to get away from all of you."

Just as he had fled his own house, not two hours before. She saw that; she put edges in it and turned it to stab.

He caught her power's hand, lightly but inescapably.

"I am grown," he said, soft, for her and her alone to hear, "and I have gone where any of my kin may know to find me. Nor do I grieve my mother for doing it."

"It's not fair!"

"Life isn't," he said, still softly, still holding her power at bay. "Come here, Ysabel."

She did not want to, but there was no escaping the bond he set on her. She dragged her feet, she would not look at him, she came at last within his arm's reach. His hand flicked out. She gasped at the sting on her cheek. "That," he said, "is the merest prick of nothing next to the pain you gave your mother. And it is to remember by."

He had never struck her before, though she had had her share of spankings at home. She was as appalled as if he had taken a whip to her. He would not let her know that he was almost as shocked. His temper was never as cool as he had thought.

She stood with her hand to her cheek, too stunned even for tears. He quelled the stab of pity. He pitied her too often, indulged her too shamelessly. And this was how she paid him.

"Remember," he said. "Any wound you deal for failing to think, or for thinking only of yourself, harms far more than you alone. If you cannot think of others when you act, then you should not act at all."

She shrank under his words. When he stopped, she asked faintly, "Are you going to tan my hide?"

"Do I need to?"

She drew a shuddering breath, choking on the tears she would not shed. "It wouldn't hurt as much as this."

"Then this should be sufficient, shouldn't it?"

She sniffed loudly, but she nodded. There was no deception in it. Ysabel was a canny little witch, but she was honest.

"Now," Aidan said. "Apologize to your mother and your father, and promise us all that you'll behave yourself hereafter. Beginning by doing whatever your mother tells you to do, and not arguing."

*　　*　　*

Ysabel went to take a bath and put on a clean kirtle, and to be obedient to her nurse. Ranulf had fallen asleep with his head on the table, pillowed on his folded arms. Joanna regarded him with slightly exasperated affection. "He'll be the very devil to rouse," she said, "and worse if I let him sleep there and get a crick in his neck."

"I'll carry him to bed," Aidan said.

Her incredulity only lasted for an instant, before she remembered. Even then she widened her eyes at the sight of Aidan, barely taller than Ranulf and half as broad, taking him up as easily as if he had been a child.

"Almost," Aidan grunted, steadying that solid bulk, adding a touch of power to make it light. Then indeed he was easy to carry, hardly heavier than Ysabel. Aidan laid him in his bed, and with Joanna helping, eased him out of boots and cotte. He never stirred except to bury his face in the pillow and sink deeper into sleep.

Joanna drew the coverlet over him and smoothed his hair as if he had been one of her sons. "Poor man, he tramped the city all night, worried sick and doing his best to pretend he wasn't. I thought he was going to cry when Aimery brought the little beast back."

"She won't do it again," Aidan said, "for a day or three."

"Haven't I heard you say that before?" Joanna herded him out of the bedchamber and eased the door shut, leaning against it, pushing her hair out of her face. "God. Six of them. Seven now. Why haven't I gone insane?"

"You ask me?"

She met his smile with a weary grin. "That one is the worst, I have to confess. When the others get into trouble, it's journeyman-class trouble. She is a master."

"I'm sorry."

"Why? It's not your fault."

But it was. Her eyes met his. Human eyes, but otherwise exactly like her daughter's. The same bright impulsive spirit. The same suggestion of summer thunder.

He was not supposed to love her. He was Morgiana's now, and that bond would endure past the world's end. But before Morgiana won him, there was Joanna. She had borne the only child he had yet begotten, the only one he might ever beget. That she was well and contentedly married, that she had borne numerous children since, mattered not at all. Age and childbearing and the duties of a baroness in Outremer had not changed her. She was still Joanna; still the sullen-sweet, impetuous, headstrong child who ran away from her husband and loved a witchborn prince.

She shook her head, reading him as effortlessly as if she had power. "We can't," she said. "It's too long past. There's too much world between."

"And time."

She smiled, half sad, half tender. "I suppose I'll envy you someday. When I feel the years creeping up on me. When I see the dark at the end of them."

"Don't," he said.

She reached as if to touch him, but let her hand fall short. "I didn't mean to hurt you."

"I know."

"But I did." She pulled herself up, bracing her sorely taxed back. He did not even think. He set his hand on it. He took the pain, as much of it as his poor talent could take.

She was warm, human-warm, cooler than he, both more solid and more fragile. His fingers flexed against the solidity of her.

She eased away from him, carefully, with rigid control. "Thank you," she said.

That was not what he wanted to hear. What he wanted, she could not say, nor should he try to make her. It was past, as she said. Cruel to linger; cruel to force her to remember.

Cruel also to run away as her daughter had, because he could not bear it. She wanted him there, for all the pain it cost her. He wanted to be there. He stayed for that, longer than he should; taking strength from her, and giving it, in equal measure. Even yet, with all that was between them, they could heal one another.

14

It was late when Aidan came back to his own house, later than he had intended. His people went about their business with laudable industry. The message had gone to Millefleurs to summon the levies from the demesne and bid them meet their lord in Acre. Those who were in Jerusalem did what they might to prepare for the march. It was all in perfect and impeccable order.

Gwydion's doing, and Morgiana's. Aidan found them in the court of the fountain, sitting together, doing nothing that was not proper between brother and sister. And yet at the sight of them his heart twisted.

Gwydion reached out with more than hands, enfolding him in a warm, invisible embrace. Morgiana came more tangibly, as if they had never parted in a quarrel and then spent the night and the day apart. Her mouth was sweet; sweeter than he remembered.

He came up from the kiss, dizzy and dazzled. She laughed and drew him to the fountain's rim, set him down by his brother, sat on his other side with her arm about him. There between the two of them, he should have rested.

But he could not. He tried to hide it; to hear what they said. Nothing of great consequence. Gwydion had been in the city, had gone to the Temple and spoken with the knights who ruled it, and then, to be courteous, had spoken also with the Knights of the Hospital in their great house and hospital near the Holy Sepulcher, where they had gathered to mourn their Grand Master. "The Hospitallers speak well of you," he said.

"The Templars less well, I'm sure," said Aidan somewhat dryly.

"Well enough," said Gwydion, amused, "though you have been known to refer to them as 'those hotheads in bloody crosses.' "

"They are," Morgiana said. "That Master of theirs,

and that idiot who calls himself king—they are a pair, and no mistake. Allah could hardly have done a greater favor to my lord Salah al-Din than He has done in giving him such a pair of enemies."

"Fortunately they are not all he has to face." Gwydion leaned lightly against his brother, comfortably, as one who knows where his proper place is. "I told the knights of both Temple and Hospital that I would be fighting in the army of Outremer, if its king will have me."

"You know he wants you," said Morgiana.

"He does," Gwydion said, "when he's not being persuaded that I'm after his crown. If he requires an oath to that effect, then he shall receive one. I can hardly refuse to defend the Holy Sepulcher while I am here and it is in danger, even if my knights would allow it. But I will never undertake to be made its chief Defender."

She regarded him past Aidan's silence, not surprised, never that, but somewhat awed. "You are as zealous in the Crusade as any mortal fool."

"How can I not be? It's my Crusade as much as theirs; my holy places which are about to be overrun."

She frowned, troubled. "That is the heart of it, isn't it? Whose holy places, and how they shall be taken or held. I thought better of you. I thought you would see sense, and leave while you could."

"Why? Because I never in my life began a war, and never sought one out that did not come to me?"

"I never called you a coward."

"I never thought you did. But this is a war which has come to me, above all that I have ever fought. How can I turn my back on it?"

"It's a mortal war."

"It is holy war."

That silenced her. In the silence, Aidan rose from between them. Her body against his, Gwydion's body bracing it on the other side, were a white pain. They never noticed. He hid it too well; they cared too little to see. He said something of going to look in on his mamluks. They nodded, already dismissing him, moving back together to continue their colloquy.

*   *   *

His mamluks were in order as they always were, lodging cheerfully on top of one another in the guardroom. Some were at drill in the courtyard where, earlier, Aidan had crossed swords with Gwydion. The rest tended their arms and armor, or played at backgammon in a slant of sunlight. Arslan was winning, as usual. Timur, who was losing hopelessly, grinned at his master. "I'll win the next," he said.

"Optimist," said Ilkhan.

Timur rolled his eyes. "Such loyalty. Such confidence in one's own blood kin."

Aidan turned on his heel, not even thinking. He was in his own chamber before he knew what he had done.

He lay on the great bed, on his face, shoulders shaking. Not with sobbing. Not precisely with laughter. He knew it was a lie. He *knew.* Yet it poisoned every word they spoke, every move they made. It could have been true. It could, so very easily, have been so.

He should get up, ready himself to preside at dinner. It was his duty as lord of the house. He would go, face them both, be an innocent. Then when they could be alone together, he would tell them what nonsense had beset them. They would laugh, all three of them, at the lies and follies of human men.

A light hand smoothed his hair, ran down his back. He tensed against it. Morgiana stretched beside him, kissed his ear, nipped it lightly. It was all he could do not to fling himself away from her.

"We'll find the pope's letter," she said. "We'll exact the price for it. We only need time."

He thrust himself up on his hands. "Time? How much time will it take to seduce my brother as you seduced me?"

She was not even angry. She was too shocked. "What in the world— My beloved idiot, what ever put that in your head?"

"It's true, isn't it? While you were denying me, telling me that it was to keep yourself pure for the wedding, you were assuaging your lust with him."

He could not believe that he was saying it. No more, yet, could she. "Why would I want to bed him when I can have you?"

"For the difference. For the likeness. Because it takes your fancy."

"I am hardly as wanton as that."

"No? Tell that to the people who've seen you with him."

"You've gone mad," she said.

"What's mad? The instant I leave you, you're in his lap."

She drew her breath in sharply. "What are you trying to do?"

"Maybe I want to hear the truth."

"The truth," she said with careful, icy precision, "is that I am yours and yours alone. I like your brother very much, I can't lie about that. But not for my bed."

He shook his aching, throbbing head. "I know that! I know—but—I can't—I saw you there, just exactly where they said you were, just as close as they said you had been, and I wasn't—I couldn't—"

She reached out and pulled him to her, cradling his head on her breast. "Hush, love. They've done something to you; broken you. Iblis torment them with scorpions!"

He pulled away with violence enough to overset her. He rose above her. She was stark with shock; her eyes were more like a cat's than ever, stretched wide, rimmed with white. "Swear it," he said. "Swear that you have done nothing to shame me."

"I have not."

"Swear!"

His voice lashed her to the bone. She had held her temper in check, between shock and startlement; but she was no gentle creature, and, beyond a certain limit, no forgiving one. He had gone well past that limit.

It was what he wanted. He was almost glad to see the anger kindle in her eyes; to see how her nostrils thinned, her lips tightened. "What oath can I swear to you, that in this mood you will accept? Why should I swear it at all?"

"Because I ask it."

"If you asked," she said. "If you did that, yes, I would swear. But this— I will not be forced. Not even by you, my lord."

"Why? Because you can't honestly swear that you have been faithful to me?"

"Faithful?" She laughed, high and light and merciless. "That you should demand that. You, of all men. You with your bastard, with your doxy in her husband's house, with all the lies that blacken your soul."

"I have not—"

"Don't lie to me," she said. "Don't even try. I know where you were today. You reek of her."

"I did nothing," he said through clenched teeth. "No more than—"

"No more than I with Gwydion? Is that what you would say, my lord? And if that is true, then was it any mortal man who sired yon witchling?"

"That was eleven years ago."

"Surely," she said. "And again not three hours since. While I was—purportedly—disporting myself with your image and likeness."

"I have not touched her carnally since I became your lover."

"No? And have you not desired her?"

The devil that was in him made him lift his chin and say, "And what if I have?"

"Then you admit it?"

"I do not. No more do I suffer you to speak so of her. I hear what you think of her. *Cow,* you think. *Whore.* She is neither. She is a lady and a gentlewoman."

"And what am I?"

"You know what you are."

"I know what I am not."

"Faithful."

She bared her white sharp teeth. "Don't you wish that I were as she is. Wanton and wicked. Wedded to a horn-browed fool. Mother of your whelp."

He struck her. As he had Ysabel. Just exactly as he had struck Ysabel.

Morgiana did not raise her hand to her cheek as

Ysabel had. The bruise was already beginning on the ivory skin. Her eyes above it were as pale as beryls, and as hard. "You should not have done that," she said.

"Morgiana—"

"No," she said. She spoke slowly, as if to measure each word. "I understand now. This is not the old battle over your Frankish woman, or the new one over your brother. They are but pretexts. This is the oldest of all our battles. You are a Frank. I am a Saracen. If I will not yield to your world and your ways, if I will not fight with you in your war, then you will drive me away. It must be I who go: I who am the alien in this country, the infidel, the interloper. Less pain to you then that I remove myself from your heart and your presence. Less division in your soul, that you must go to war against my people."

She was calm, quiet, utterly reasonable. It seemed perfect sense, as she said it. And yet—dear God—

She rose to her knees in the billowing feather-softness of the bed, and went down in Muslim obeisance. "I swear by Allah and by His Prophet, by the words of holy Koran and by the black stone of the Qaabah: I have never been aught but faithful to you in thought and in deed, in body and in heart. I have never been aught but yours."

It was what he had asked of her; what he had thought he wanted. It blew black in him, like a wind off the northern sea. He wanted to weep; he wanted to howl aloud. He reached for her, to draw her to him, to break down the wall that his madness had raised between them.

She was not there. She stood on the floor in her Muslim garb with the turban wound about her head: all alien, and all apart. "You have your oath. I shall not again trouble your peace. Not while this kingdom stands. Not while you do battle for it and for the mother of your daughter."

"I have not touched her!" he cried in pain.

"So? And now you may. I promised you that I would never harm her again. I keep my promises."

"Morgiana," he said. "Sweet saints in heaven, I never meant—"

"Didn't you?" She stood in front of him, and there was no reaching her. No warming; no touching.

He fought his way out of bed and coverlets. He opened his mind wide, all defenseless. "Morgiana. It was a devil in me; it was a madness. Whatever price you ask, whatever atonement you seek—"

"And you call us merchants." There was no contempt in it. Only weariness, and implacable will. "I am not to be bought, sir Frank. Not with anything you can pay."

"Morgiana—"

He clutched at air. She was gone. Truly, utterly gone. Where she had been in the heart of him was only emptiness, and four stark words.

I keep my promises.

15

It was like her fortune, Elen reflected, that in others' joy she should be grieving, and now that their joy was broken, her grief escaped and would not come back. It started before the outrage at the gate of Holy Sepulcher, but like a candle it needed the dark to be seen for what it was.

The day the forged letter was read, when the wedding was disbanded and its principals led away to vent their outrage in privacy, Elen took it on herself to see to the ordering of Aidan's house. He was in no condition to think of it, and Morgiana was nowhere to be found; Gwydion was needed where his brother was. She would have been content with her maid for escort, but the king would not have that. Because she had no wish to darken the air with further contention, she acquiesced.

The guard who fell in beside her was one whom she knew. His blue eyes were less obvious under the shadow of his turban-wrapped helmet. He looked all Saracen, and all business, in his scarlet coat with mail sewn in it, and his high soft boots with the chased silver spurs, and his weapons hung about his saddle and his person. Her maid found him deliciously frightening. "So exotic," Gwenneth said. "So wild."

Elen slanted her eyes at him, and found him doing the same. His glance was bright with mirth. Clearly he liked the way people, and especially women, reacted to his foreignness; quite as much as he liked it when they thought him one of them. He was like Aidan, that way. He moved easily between the worlds, and made himself a part of both.

She said so, to see what he would say. He obliged her handsomely. "Better a part of both than a part of neither," he said in his accented Frankish. "My lord taught me that."

"I should think you'd have learned it when you were young," she said. "Islam being as it is, accepting of any who accepts its faith."

"So it is, and so it does. But Franks dwell outside of that pale. I could have forgotten what half of me is, and so I would have, if any other master had been granted me."

"Do you wish he hadn't?"

He faced her fully, not easy in that narrow crowded street, with his horse jostling hers, shouldering its way ahead. "Never," he said.

Their eyes held for an instant before movement and shyness drew them apart. She was purely amazed by what she saw there, under the Saracen helmet, in the Saracen face.

Amazed, but not displeased. Oh, no. Not at all.

She never knew precisely who named Raihan her guardsman. He stayed with her after that, accompanied her where she chose to go, stood guard at her door when she was in Aidan's house. At night he kept to his own place, which she told herself she was glad of. Certainly there was no need of him then, as well watched as that house was, and by more than human senses.

By daylight he was her shadow. He was impeccably trained. He could be invisible if she needed him to be, and visible likewise, and when she wanted to talk, he was ready and willing. He should not have surprised her, knowing what she knew of Aidan and the knights he trained, but he did that: he read widely and deeply, whenever he could, and he knew Latin and Greek as well as Arabic and the dialects of Francia. He was a fair hand at field surgery, a skilled hunter and falconer, a master archer with the Turkish bow, as well as a soldier and captain.

"We all are that," he said the second day after the wedding, as Elen rode to the palace to answer the queen's summons. "My lord knighted us all in a pack, and a fine scandal it was, but after all, he said, we'd done squire service to the best of our several abilities; shouldn't we reap the reward? We've all got holdings round about Millefleurs, and for a knighting gift he gave each of us sufficient funds to equip us and to have some over for our own pleasure. I put some of mine on a trading venture to Ch'in, which prospered well, and put the rest into my holding. I'm his horsemaster, you see; and I've got a herd of my own growing." He ran a loving hand down the neck of his mare. "This is one of my queens."

"She's beautiful," Elen said. It was true, but it was meant mostly to make him smile. His pleasure was as open as a child's. She wished sometimes that she could know what was under the heavy curling beard. What she could see of his face was very good to look at; it would be a bitter disappointment if he proved to be rabbit-chinned.

Not for the first time, she was glad that he was no enchanter, to know what she was thinking. She fixed her eyes on the lovely, haughty mare, and did her best to listen to him sing the beast's praises. When she undressed now, or when she slept and dreamed, it was not Riquier's body she longed for.

Queen Sybilla did nothing and everything to put Elen's heart at rest. She was full of half-truthful regrets for Prince Aidan's misfortune, and not averse to saying what Elen had heard elsewhere: "But then, perhaps it's as well that he is forbidden to consort with her. Infidel that she is, and Saracen; this is no time to nurture such a viper at our breast. When the war is won, we shall have to find him a lady to console him."

Elen kept her thoughts to herself, said what courtesy bade her say, escaped before she could be subjected to the same voracious matchmaking. That Sybilla had just that in mind was readily apparent. As Elen left, the queen said, "You will of course accompany your kinsmen to Acre. I shall be going to aid my lord husband as he musters his army; I would welcome your company."

A queen's request was a lady's command. Elen could only bow to it.

And, as she rode home, fight to keep the grin off her face. She knew what her kinsmen wanted her to do: stay in Jerusalem as Lady Joanna was doing, and Lady Margaret, looking after their households and their children, and keeping safe, well away from the war. She would have been pleased enough to do that, as fond as she was becoming of the Mortmains and their kin, but none of the knights who stayed behind to guard the women would be Raihan.

"You'll fight your own people?" she asked him when they were back under Aidan's roof, or rather on it, where there was a garden and a spectacle to rival any in the world: the great court of the *Templum Domini* under the Dome of the Rock. Her maid was near, sweet-natured Gwenneth who was half deaf and all discreet, engrossed in a bit of needlework.

Raihan leaned at ease against the parapet, but his eyes were narrowed slightly, fixed on the great golden dome. "I am my lord's man. Whom he chooses to fight, is mine to fight also."

"Even in the name of Christ and the Holy Sepulcher?"

"I fight in my lord's name."

She did not know what was in her that she should press him so, but she could not help herself. "You haven't thought of converting to Christianity?"

"No."

He said it quietly, but there was a snap in it.

"Not for any reason?" she asked him.

"What reason can there ever be for apostasy?"

She looked down abashed. "I—pardon me, I beg you. I shouldn't have addressed you so."

"My lady may address me in any way she pleases."

Her eyes flashed up. "Even if I excoriate you for a heathen and a turncoat?"

He straightened. His hand dropped to his swordhilt. But he said, "My lady may be the best judge of that."

"You are a perfect knight." She meant it truly. He did not think so at first, but under her gaze the blue fire faded from his eyes. She smiled to see it. "I can see who trained you, sir mamluk."

"To be a heathen and a turncoat?"

Her smile widened almost into laughter. "My knight may be the best judge of that."

"Your—" He blushed crimson. "My lady!"

"So I am," she said with rich contentment. "And so you certainly intended, or you would never have let yourself be made my nursemaid."

"Is that what you think I am?"

"I think that you are my knight. I hear what the others say. They twit you, don't they?"

He turned away from her, which was rude, but she forgave it. His fingers fretted the hilt of his sword. After a moment his shoulders went back; he drew a deep breath and turned again to face her. "My brothers in the sword are jealous to a man."

"They are? What of their wives? What," she asked with beating heart, "of yours?"

"I have no wife," he said.

She looked at him in silence.

"I do not," he said, not to defend himself, simply to make it clear to her. "There never seemed to be time; and no one suitable presented herself."

"Not even someone unsuitable?"

"I'm not an anchorite."

That was an unguarded utterance. Elen watched him regret it. She said, "I never thought you were."

He was like a cat in the way he kept recovering his balance, no matter how she upset it. "My lady can never be unsuitable," he said. "I, however, am that a thousand-fold."

"I made a suitable match," she said. "Once, and he is dead. Perhaps now I may choose to please myself."

She kept her eyes on his face while she spoke. It was still, expressionless, but she could not mistake the spark that kindled in it. As she had hardly dared to hope. As she had feared not to see. She was bold beyond believing, and he would be well within his rights to rebuke her for it; or simply to refuse to understand.

He did neither. He said, "Your kinsmen might have somewhat to say in the matter."

"A lady's hand is her family's to bestow to its best advantage. Her heart," said Elen, "is her own."

"And her body?"

She blushed. "My body is his who holds my heart in his hand. If I may hold his in my own."

"You are beautiful," said Raihan, and it was not an answer, but then again it was. "You are the falcon stooping out of the sun; the moon descending upon the water. You are as far above a simple soldier-slave as that soldier-slave is above the beggar in the bazaar."

"Does it matter?"

He bit his lip. She saw how young he was, after all, under the trappings of the warrior. "No," he said. "Before God, it should. But it matters not at all."

16

Morgiana was gone.

Aidan hunted her down all the ways of the mind, into all the places he knew, where she might be. A cavern in the desert of Persia. Masyaf of the Assassins, where the Old Man of the Mountain was lord. A swordsmith's house in Damascus, where was the one woman in the world whom Morgiana would call friend. Even, desperately, in their own castle of Millefleurs. Empty, all empty. She was gone, cut off from him, in a world that was too wide for his little power, too empty for his soul to bear.

He did not go mad, or run wild, or shatter into a million shards. He had already done all of that, and it had cost him Morgiana. He sat in his chamber in a dawn as bleak as his heart, and knew beyond hope of argument what he had done.

She was older than he, and stronger in power, and better by far at holding a grudge. While she did not wish to be found, he would not find her. And that could be never.

There were no tears in him. There was nothing at all but emptiness.

He lay, first on his face, then on his back, and watched the light grow in the room. He heard the house rising about him: the cooks to their cooking, the mamluks to their prayers and then to their exercises in the practice-court, the Rhiyanans to prepare for Mass. He was on all their minds in greater or lesser degree. They did not know, yet, how utterly Morgiana was gone.

"She is gone." Saying it aloud lent it solidity. He covered his face with his hands. His fingers tensed to claw; with an effort he relaxed them. He made himself rise, put off his sorely rumpled garments, wrap himself in the robe which he always wore to bathe. It was silk, and scarlet, embroidered with dragons. She had given it to him.

He flung it away from him. Everything in that room was her gift, or whispered of her presence. He snatched a cloak that reeked more of horses than of her, and went blindly where he had meant to go.

Gwydion was in the bath before him, alone without servants amid the sea-colored tiles, pouring his own water into the basin. Aidan almost turned on his heel and fled. He caught himself against the doorframe, clung to it as if without it he would fall.

Gwydion glanced over his shoulder, a flash of cat-green in the light that was, Aidan realized, witchlight. "Your bath is almost ready," he said.

Aidan hated him with sudden passion. If not for him —if not for that he had warmed so fully to Morgiana—

No. That was the madness speaking, and the devil behind the madness. Aidan was sane now, because Gwydion was here, with his calm, with his strength, with all that he was, that was the other half of Aidan.

The water was exactly as he liked it: hot almost to burning, and scented with green herbs. Aidan sank slowly into it. Gwydion knelt by the basin and began to wash him. At first he only allowed it because he would not quarrel again while he could help it. But those fingers, of all there were in the world, knew where to find the knots, and how to loosen them.

"She is gone," Aidan said when the water began to cool, when he was clean but unable to move, to rise and face the world.

"I felt her go," said Gwydion.

"Do you know why she went?"

"I know what the king's knights wanted with you yesterday."

"It's not true. Is it?"

"No."

Aidan sank down until the water covered him. He could breathe in it if he wished to. Or drown, if his will allowed it.

He rose out of it. Gwydion was there with the cloth, wrapping it about him, rubbing away the wet and the tautness and perhaps something more than that. "I never thought that it was true," Aidan said. "And I acted as if it were. She repaid me exactly as I deserved."

Gwydion did not offer empty comfort. He held out a clean shirt. Aidan struggled into it. "I won't let them break me," he said. "I won't give them the satisfaction."

"I never thought you would."

Aidan stood, swaying a little. Half of him was an open wound. The other half stood in front of him. He laid hands on his brother's shoulders, perhaps to embrace him, perhaps to fling him away. "But for you," said Aidan, "they would have had no power against me.

But for you I would be wholly in their power. You were the flaw in my armor. You are all that arms me now against the dark."

"So have you always been to me," said the voice that was the echo of his own, out of the face that was the image of his own.

Aidan drew a shuddering breath. He would not break. He would be strong, though half his strength was gone and half was not his own. And one day—one day soon, by God, he would win her back.

He reached for braies and hose, pulled them on. With them he put on a semblance of his wonted self. The world had not ended because he had lost his lover. He tied the lacings with meticulous care, as if to bind the cords of mind and will, and found the words with which he must go on. "We've much to do if we're to be ready for the muster." He looked up. "You are fighting, aren't you?"

Gwydion could not but see through Aidan's seeming. His brow went up, but his voice was cool, light, accepting what his brother had chosen. "I shall fight," he said. "How could I not?"

Aidan shrugged. "It's not your kingdom, and it's not your quarrel."

Gwydion cuffed him, spilling him into the tangle of his discarded robe. "Don't you start on me, too," he said. "I'll fight because I choose to fight. And," he said, "because there's no keeping you from it, and someone should be there to keep an eye on you."

Aidan struggled up on his elbows, glaring through a tangle of hair. "An eye, you say? And which of us is the known and notorious glutton for battles?"

"That's why," said Gwydion, reaching to draw him up. Aidan got a solid grip on his brother's hand, and pulled. Gwydion toppled as ignominiously as he had, but rather less painfully: he made certain to fall on top of Aidan.

They rolled and tumbled like lion cubs, until they fetched up, abruptly, at someone's feet.

Aidan, on the bottom, recognized the captain of his mamluks. Arslan was properly appalled. Aidan bared his teeth at him. But a little longer, and it might have been an honest grin. "Am I wanted for something?" he asked.

Arslan swallowed hard. He took a fair bit of time about it. "No," he said, "my lord. Nothing. I heard—that is—"

"You thought we were killing one another." Gwydion rose with impressive dignity, shaking his hair out of his face. This time Aidan let him draw him up.

Aidan laid his arm about his brother's shoulders. "It was a massacre," he said. "Go, we'll clear away the bodies. I'll be with you directly."

Arslan obeyed. He was, in spite of himself, amused. *Just like a brace of wild boys,* he thought indulgently as he went to his duties.

The brothers heard the thought, as they were meant to. They looked at one another. Suddenly, out of nowhere that he could name, Aidan began to laugh.

Aidan made a tendril of power, divided it, set it like a snare in the places to which Morgiana would most likely return. He would not weep or rage. His pride would not allow it. He sent his call echoing through the mindworld, a great ringing cry that surely she must hear; that surely she would answer. Yet there was only silence. She might never have been. He was all hollow; all empty. All forsaken.

People knew soon enough that she was gone. Why she had gone, they did not dare to ask. Most supposed that she had withdrawn to Millefleurs. A few suspected that she had returned to her own people. A fair faction hoped that Aidan himself had put her away. He did not speak to them nor they to him, nor did they venture to look on him with either pity or vindication.

It mattered little to a kingdom readying for war. She was a woman, and women were only to be thought of when there were walls to guard.

Ysabel was harder to deceive. She wanted explanations. Aidan gave her what he could, but lovers' wars were as far beyond her as the moon. She understood only that Morgiana was gone, and that Aidan grieved, and that it should not be so. She decided that he needed her; that, in short, she must go with him to Acre.

"I want to go," she said. She had come to Lady Margaret's house with one of her mother's women scowling in her wake, ostensibly to see her grandmother, actually to catch Aidan as he settled matters that needed settling if his holdings were to be secure in the midst of the war. "Lady Elen is going. So is Aimery. They can take care of me."

Aidan regarded her narrowly. The little minx had it all plotted, that was clear to see. "I would rather that your mother looked after you," he said, "here where it's safest."

"Jerusalem isn't safe," said Ysabel. "Not if the sultan beats you on the field. This is the first place he'll aim for, and the first place he'll want to take."

"Who has been telling you that?" Aidan asked her with a touch of sharpness.

"People are talking," she said, "all over the city. The pilgrims are scared."

"The pilgrims are wise," said Aidan. "But not as wise as they might be. Jerusalem won't be the first to fall. It's too deep in the kingdom, and too well defended, even if we strip every other place bare to make up the army. Acre is much more likely to be a target, because it faces on the sea, and the pilgrims' ships are there, and the king's winter palace, and the cream of the trade. What would you do there? There won't be any children to play with. Simeon is staying here to look after the women; Akiva will stay with him."

He had scored a hit there, but she was well dug in and determined to fight. "If you mean Mother and Grandmother, it's not Rabbi Simeon who will be doing the looking after, but the other way round. Akiva can't even fight." She did not say it with contempt, he was glad to notice. It was a fact, that was all. "Mother says she's staying here because she's so big with the baby, but it's really because Grandmother is here and doesn't want to leave. Mother will go to Acre later if she can, you wait and see. She hates to stay in one place when her men are out fighting wars."

"Your mother can wield a sword if she has to."

"So can I." Ysabel took his hand. "Why can't I go to Acre with Lady Elen? She's coming back here afterward, isn't she? She said she would. She doesn't like the queen much; she thinks she's too empty-headed. She'd rather be friends with Mother."

"What if you get killed trying to come back, or killed in the city's fall? What do you think that will do to your mother?"

"I'm a trial to her soul. She'll be glad to get rid of me."

Aidan let her know the full force of his disapproval. She lowered her eyes, sullen. "You care more about my mother than you do about me," she muttered.

"She needs more caring," Aidan said coldly. "And deserves more."

Ysabel looked up. She was hurt. He hardened his heart against her. "Don't you love me?"

"Not when you act like this." He relented a little. "Yes, I love you. That's why I want you to stay. And . . . you might be able to do something. Being what you are, and knowing what you know."

"You mean, witchery?"

He set a finger to his lips. "Hush the word, catling. I mean the power you and Akiva share, that can be a defense, if it's needed. But it should be the two of you together, learning from one another and making one another stronger. You can't do that if you're in Acre and he's in Jerusalem."

She understood a fine manipulating hand when she saw one, but he tempted her sorely. Power was a greater adventure even than riding with the army.

He waited, not pressing, lest he lose her. She frowned at him. "What will you do if I say no?"

"Put a binding on you," he answered. "I don't want to. I'd rather you stayed of your own free will."

That he could bind her, she knew very well. He had done it to her once; she had hated it. She chewed her lip, remembering that, and hunting for an escape, and finding none. "If I stay here, will you let me stay in your house until you go?"

"What do you think you can do there?"

"Keep you company," she said.

"That's for your mother to say."

She knew the taste of capitulation. She grinned at him. "May we have roast capon for dinner tonight?"

He shook his head at her impudence, but he had to laugh. "Roast capon with dates and nuts and cinnamon? Is that what you're asking for?"

"And rice," she said, "and honey sweets, and oranges from your tree."

"You shall have them. If," he said, "your mother gives you leave."

She pulled him down to kiss him, and danced away. "She will. You'll see. May I borrow Conrad to take me back? Mother likes Conrad. She'll let me do anything if she knows he'll be there."

"You may borrow Conrad," Aidan said, resigned. "Tyrant."

Her grin was the last he saw of her, seeming to hang in the air after she was gone.

She meant to work on Elen. Aidan wished her luck of it. Elen had the queen's command behind her, and something else in train that was not as well hidden as she hoped it was. She would not be wanting a bright-eyed small witchling about while she pursued it.

Elen and Raihan. They were a handsome pairing, whatever else was wrong with it. Aidan could not find it in himself to object, as long as nothing came of it but an exchange of glances and perhaps now and then a touching of hands. If it went beyond that, then Aidan would have to consider what he would do; unless Gwydion did it first. Gwydion, as a man, might be indulgent. As a king, and as her grandmother's brother, he would have to disapprove. A princess of Rhiyana should not take as lover an infidel, still less an infidel who had been a slave.

Aidan's heart twisted. And what of a prince of Rhiyana?

That was settled. He had done it himself, with his own flapping tongue.

*   *   *

When he came to his house by the Dome of the Rock, Ysabel was not there yet. She had her mother's leave—she had made sure he knew it the instant it was given—but its price was an hour's lesson in Latin, and after that the careful setting in order of her possessions. She was not happy to pay so high, but she did it, and well, as she could do when she was minded to.

Ysabel was not in the house, but another guest was, and one far less welcome. Messire Amalric had just arrived, he gave Aidan to know; he was still paying his respects to Gwydion, whose face wore its royal expression: blandly unreadable. Gwydion had received him in the solar rather than in one of the gardens, a double-edged courtesy. It was cool within, but dim, and there was ample evidence of duties interrupted and preparations deferred.

Aidan was glad of the sherbet that was waiting for him: it was hot in the city. He took a chair near his brother, but just far enough away that Amalric must turn his head in order to see both at once. Amalric, unperturbed, greeted Aidan with brusque courtesy, then returned his focus to Gwydion.

Aidan minded not at all. It gave him time to settle in, to drink his sherbet, to test the currents that ran beneath the surface. It was a courtesy of his kin that they did not read thoughts unless invited, or unless there was need; but Amalric's were not easy to make sense of even then. He thought around corners. Not as a Byzantine would, with serpentine subtlety. It was more that he could not, or would not, think in a straight line. He leaped from thought to thought even more than most humans did, and even within each single thought he buzzed and shifted like a fly on a carcass. It was easier to avoid him altogether, and to winnow truth and falsehood from his words and his body's signals, as any mortal could do.

"We have somewhat in common, sire," Amalric said. "Did you know that? The Lusignans are as proud of their descent from the fay Melusine as the Rhiyanan kings are of theirs from the goddess Rhiannon. And of course you are the son of the enchantress from Broce-liande."

He paused, hoping clearly for her name. Gwydion did not give it, nor would Aidan offer it. When she was queen she was called Elen, but the name she lived by was older than that by far. She said that she was no goddess; but she was, indubitably, Rhiannon.

Amalric went on after a moment, little deterred by the king's silence. "And of course you know that the kings of Anglia, through their Angevin forebears, are known as the devil's brood, because of their foremother who was a demon's daughter." He drank deep from his cup and smiled at Gwydion, well pleased with himself. "We demonseed are a breed apart, wouldn't you agree?"

"There is more than one kind of demon," Gwydion said.

"Yes," said Amalric. "Not many of us have the fortune to take after our foremothers. Is a demon's child a demon himself if he inherits his mother's powers?"

"That is a question for the philosophers, is it not?"

"They call you a philosopher king, sire," Amalric said.

"They call me many things. Some of them are true. Many of them are not. That is a king's lot, to be talked of endlessly."

"You more than some, maybe, sire. I've heard you called the Elvenking."

Gwydion raised a brow.

"I may choose to believe what it implies," Amalric said. "I'm less likely to join the mob that calls you witch and hellspawn. Fifty years of ruling as well as any king in Christendom surely counts for something. Or have you been preparing some last, awful stroke against us all?"

"Would I tell you if I were?"

Amalric laughed. "Of course you wouldn't. No more than I would speak of it if I suspected you of dark designs. You haven't even laid claim to the throne of Jerusalem."

"There's time yet."

"Which you won't use," Amalric said. "You're much

admired in certain circles, you know. Interesting circles. The Temple; the Hospital. Certain factions of the papal curia, and certain connections of the royal houses of the west. You have strong allies in a number of highly useful places."

"I call them friends," said Gwydion.

"Then you're fortunate," Amalric said. His cup was empty. There was no servant to refill it. He set it down on the table and leaned forward. "I should like, sire, to number myself among those allies. Would you consider it?"

"I give every man a fair hearing," said the king.

Amalric could not but notice the transformation from quiet, rather diffident, young-seeming man to royal judge. He did not flinch before it. "Our family is not in itself of great note, but it is an old one, and it has its share of honor; and it's rising in the world. My brother is proof of it. His line will last, I think. I'd like to hope that mine will do the same."

"May God grant you good fortune," Gwydion said.

"God well may, sire," said Amalric. "Your niece is widowed, I understand, and dowered well. I can offer a royal connection, ample lands and more to be gained, and the splendor that is on this kingdom of Jerusalem. My position in it is hardly to be scorned: lord commander of its armies, Constable of the kingdom, and regent by right should my lord brother be indisposed, which God forfend. Our line tends toward sons, and plenty of them. We have the blood of Melusine to make us stronger than the run of young cubs, and maybe a little magic in it, too. I have no objection to a lady from the line of Rhiannon."

Gwydion steepled his fingers, regarding Amalric over them, cool and steady. "Do you not, my lord Constable?"

"Not at all, majesty." Amalric smiled. "I admit, I'm smitten with her. She has her family's beauty; and she's quite as bewitching as one would expect of the kin of the Elvenking. I don't either ask or expect that you accept my suit all at once. She'll be riding to Acre with you, my

lady the queen tells me. Would you allow me to ride with
you and keep her company?"

If it had been Aidan's lot to choose, he would have
refused. But Gwydion was king, and wise with all the
years of it. "Have you no duties?" he inquired.

Amalric's smile widened slightly. "They're well in
hand, sire; and shall be better when we come to Acre."

Gwydion inclined his head. "You may ride with us,
messire. You will understand if I grant you no more than
that. If after the war is ended you wish still to sue for her
hand, then you may come to me and we shall speak
again." Gwydion rose and inclined his head. "Good day,
messire."

Amalric had no choice but to accept the dismissal.
He was not greatly pleased, but he suffered it calmly
enough. It was a beginning, his expression said. There
was time yet, and he would make good use of it.

"Elen can't abide him," Aidan said when the man
was gone.

"I know." Gwydion stretched and yawned. His teeth
gleamed, the long pointed canines looking as sharp as a
panther's. His mouth shut with a snap; he faced his
brother. "Messire Amalric doesn't need to know quite
yet what we think of his suit. There's something in him
that raises my hackles; it intrigues me that I can't name
it. He may be telling the truth when he speaks of Melusine. I should like to know."

"I'd think our catling's peace would be a high price
to pay for your curiosity."

"Our catling is as fragile as pressed steel. And," said
Gwydion, "she can take care of herself better than you
might imagine."

"I can imagine. I know her grandmother." Aidan
frowned at his feet. "We should warn her. If she can get
him to talk . . ."

"I'll warn her," Gwydion said.

Aidan paused. Was there more in that than there
seemed to be?

He held his tongue, not easily, but with late-dawning
wisdom. If there was, there was little he could do about
it, except start a quarrel. Then he would lose his brother;
and there would be nothing at all between himself and
the dark.

17

Elen paced restlessly, swirling her skirts with each sharp,
abrupt turn. There were many of them: the room was
small, and she was moving quickly. Her maid had long
since retreated. She could hear the woman chattering in
the garden just outside, and now and then a deep voice
that was Raihan's.

It made her shiver, but it also made her growl to
herself. The ride to Acre had never been the idyll she
had hoped for: out on the open road, free to ride up and
down the column or to spur off on a whim or a fancy.
Even if the road had not been choked with pilgrims and
with soldiers riding or marching to the muster, it was not
safe to ride in the hills. There were Bedouin, she was
told, and perhaps even true Saracens, raiders from the
sultan's armies, creeping like worms into the kingdom's
heart.

She could have endured that. Raihan was with her,
and nothing should have kept them from talking, or
even, under cover of various ruses, from touching hand
to hand or knee to knee. But Messire Amalric had at-
tached himself to their party as Gwydion had warned,
and what he wanted was transparent. He haunted her
shadow. She could not, would not, seem to favor one of
her uncle's mamluks under those sharp snake-eyes. She
had to speak to him, be civil, not drive him off, because
her king had asked it. "He has a secret," Gwydion said,
"which he is not unveiling to the likes of us. He may
betray it to a lovely woman."

If he had a secret, he had not given it away to her.
He had merely driven her half mad with hours of point-

less chatter. Now they were in Acre, and Amalric had perforce to forsake her for the duties of his office.

And so, inevitably, had Raihan. The mamluk was away more often than he was with her, readying himself and his people for the war. Sometimes he let her come with him. Always it was to a place that was thronged to bursting—smith's forge, armorer's stall, saddler's shop—and the way to it was always inescapably public. She was tempted more than once to seize him right in front of all the staring eyes, and kiss him till he gasped.

She never did it. She was her king's loyal kinswoman, in body if not in heart, and he was his prince's faithful servant.

Tomorrow he would go away, and he might well be killed. Then she would not merely have lost him, she would never have had him at all.

She slowed her pacing by a fraction. She had eluded the farewell feast on the pretext of her courses. Her uncles, alas for their comfort, had no such escape. But for a guard or two and her maid, the house was empty. Everyone else was at the king's table.

All of which she knew very well, and had planned for. But she had not reckoned on Raihan's choosing rather to play the rake with her maid than to help her elude the woman. She had not even been able to exchange a whispered word with him. He was evading her.

"Damn him," she said. He was being honorable in the only way he knew, which was to drive her to distraction with wanting him. He would be her knight, all carefully circumspect, but he would not give her more than that. It was not fitting, he would say. That was how well she knew him. She knew why he would not touch her. Because they could never be more than lovers, and he wanted more, and he would not dishonor her with less.

She could do with a little more dishonor and a little less frustration.

She swept up a cushion and flung it with all her force.

He caught it neatly and held it like a shield. She saw his smile over the edge of it. "What would you, my lady? Target practice?"

She glared at him. "Don't I wish. With your grinning face for a bull's-eye."

"Why, my lady," he said, "what have I done to offend you?"

"You know," she said.

He sobered. "My lady, you know that that is mad."

"I don't care."

"I do." He let the cushion fall. "No, not for me. For you. Your king treasures you. He'll never let you sully yourself with an infidel."

"He won't touch me. He might give me a royal tongue-lashing, but that's well worth the cost. And I won't let him touch a hair of your head."

"It's not my head I'm worried about," he said.

Her mouth was open. She shut it. "He wouldn't!"

"Maybe not that, either. But he could take you away from me and never let me see you again. I don't think I could bear it."

"What, you won't be going to the war?"

"Oh," he said. "The war. That's what I was born and trained for; it's in my blood. But to come back and not find you there . . . that would break my heart."

"Is that what you want, then? Chaste sighs and a touch of the hand now and then, and never anything more? Do you think I'm made of iron?"

"Ivory," he said, "and ebony, and grey glass. And warm heart. I'm not iron, either, but my honor is. I can't cause you grief."

"You don't call it grief that you're causing me now?"

"It will pass once I'm gone, and you find another who makes your heart sing."

She tossed her head, furious. "So that's all I am. A weathercock. Going all giddy whenever I see a handsome face." She had all she could do not to spit in his. "What do you take me for?"

She had wiped the smug self-sacrifice off his face, at least. He held out a hand. "Lady—"

She seized it. He stiffened, but he did not pull away. She pressed it to her breast over the beating heart. "Now tell me I'll trip daintily off into another man's arms. Tell me straightly, as if you believe it."

He shook his head, once, twice. "You shouldn't do this, my lady."

"What, love you? It is that, you know, and not just wanting. I'm no silly girl, that I can't tell the difference."

"You can't do that," he said. "There are too many obstacles. Too much—"

"You talk too much." That stopped him. She raised his hand from her breast to her cheek. It curved to fit, not meaning to, she could see that, but not able to help itself. His palm was hard, callused with fighting and with handling horses, a soldier's palm, but its touch was wonderfully gentle. "You are going to war, and I must stay behind, because my birth and my sex and my fortune tell me I must. You could die. Men do, in battle. Then what would I have of you?"

"Memory," he said. He made a warding gesture. "Which Allah avert. I don't intend to die."

"What soldier does? But it happens. And I want something more than remembrance. I want you. For this space only, these few hours until evening. How can you deny me that?"

Not easily; not at all. But he would, because he was what he was, great overgrown boy with a head full of songs and scripture.

"*Your* faith does not forbid you the body's joy," Elen said. "Why are you playing the Christian, and I the Saracen?"

"I am playing the soldier whose commander is your kin, and who will never allow what you are asking me to do."

She stamped her foot. "I don't *care* what my uncles think! I'm a grown woman. I'll protect you from them; stop fretting over that. They won't call what I do dishonor. How can they? They made love matches themselves, and far less suitably at that."

"They are men," Raihan said, as if that were an answer.

"So are you." She wound her fists in his shirt and glared into his face. "Are you my knight?"

"Always," he said.

"Then I command you."

He looked as if he could not decide whether to laugh or to hit her. Since he could do neither, he settled for a flat stare. "That is hardly fair, my lady."

"Love isn't," she said, unabashed. "My maid is going to go on an errand which will take her as long as it possibly can. You are going to stay here with me."

His brows knit. Handsome brows, strongly marked over those splendid eyes. "What if we're caught?"

Her heart leaped. That was assent, if not acceptance. She dazzled him with her smile. "If we are, then I'll do the talking."

"I—" He was caught. His eyes went wide as he realized it. "Witch!"

"I come by it honestly," she said. "Wait here. If you're gone when I come back, I'll give you cause to rue it. In the middle of the market. At the top of my lungs."

He blanched. She set a kiss on her fingertip and laid it lightly on his lips. "To hold you," she said.

Aidan took another sip of the king's wine. It was excellent. Whatever Guy's shortcomings, he had chosen well in his cellarer.

They were all together at last, all the lords and many of the knights of Outremer, gathered in the great hall of the winter palace. None but the king and a baron or two of Acre had brought his women to the feast; this was war, and the women were at home, looking after their lords' estates. The cities and the castles were stripped bare of fighting men. Guy was wagering all on this one great stroke, the full might of Outremer against the full might of Islam.

"We can't fight them on a dozen fronts," he had said in council that morning. "We can't lie down and let them trample us underfoot. We have to be a fist, one single knot of force, striking the enemy again and again until he breaks or gives way."

Aidan could not argue with the reasoning, whoever might have put it in Guy's head. Outremer was not a kingdom as other kingdoms were. It was an armed camp, a thin line spread over the hills of Palestine, a few

knights and men-at-arms holding their lands against half
a world. Saladin had twice a hundred thousand men, it
was said, from whom he could choose as many or as few
as he would, to ride to the war. Guy had scarce a tithe of
that, and less than a tithe of a tithe of knights.

He also had the cities, and the fortresses that were
the greatest in the world, and faith that was, when it
came to it, genuine. If he could drive the sultan and his
unruly hordes to a ground of his own choosing, then
force a battle, he could win his way far more easily, and
at far less cost, than if he settled for a siege.

And he would win. His numbers were small beside
the sultan's, but they were veterans every one, to the
sultan's raw levies; they had the best arms and armor to
be had, and means enough and to spare for aught that
they might need. The King of Anglia had rid himself of a
troublesome archbishop, and repented of it later. His repentance, being royal, took the form of gold, marked for
the defense of the Holy Sepulcher.

Aidan, sitting at Guy's feast, drinking Guy's wine,
reckoned that maybe, after all, Guy might be worth following. He could hardly go astray with Count Raymond
sitting next to him in determined amity, telling him what
to think. Master Gerard of the Temple, forced to a seat
some distance down the table, scowled to see them together, but could say nothing while there were witnesses.
He was wild to move, to fight, to kill Saracens. If it had
been left to him, he would have ridden out long ago with
whatever food and weapons he could snatch, and fallen
on the infidels. And died promptly, as he almost had in
his last mad foray against the Saracen.

Which would, Aidan reflected, have been a mercy.
Gerard was a hothead as well as a fool. Guy, at least,
was only a fool.

Gwydion, as Guy's equal in rank, sat near him at the
high table. He did his best to make it evident who was
king in this country: he had left the state crown in his
captain's keeping on his flagship before he sent his fleet
to harbor in Cyprus; all that he had now was a simple
silver fillet with a sapphire set in it, and the signet which
he did not relinquish even on his errantries. It was one

certain way, if people only knew, to tell which of the
brothers was the elder.

He had been quiet throughout the muster and silent
in the councils, except when he was called on to speak.
That was not often. For the most part he sat in a corner
and listened, like the young knight people could be
tricked into thinking him, even if they knew who he was.
Aidan was the one they turned to if they needed wisdom
from that quarter.

Aidan smiled behind his cup. He was quite willing
and able to be part of King Guy's councils, and it was an
old game to let people think that his brother was the
lesser of the two. Quiet, diffident Gwydion, who could
happily have been a monk, if God had not willed that he
be a king. In this place, under this king, it was more than
a game; it was pure prudence. Guy had decided, all by
himself, that Gwydion was harmless. He would not listen
to the few who preached distrust. No king lived so long,
in such evident tranquility, without there being more to
him than he was letting strangers see.

Guy was happy to let that be all there was. It reas-
sured him that he was a good king himself. Was he not
good to look at? Did he not listen well to everyone's
advice? Why then, there was the Elvenking with his fair
young face, as secure on his throne as any king alive, and
scarcely a word to say for himself.

There had, of course, to be an open affirmation of
Gwydion's place in the army. Two kings in an army,
however circumspect one of them might be, needed more
than a casual word to mark their amity.

It was almost time. The subtlety, the great *pièce de
résistance* of the feast, which had begun as an image in
spun sugar and marzipan of Jerusalem upon her hills, lay
in ruins. The wine was going round; heads would be
spinning soon, and then would be too late for matters of
state.

Aidan's eye caught his brother's. Gwydion nodded
very slightly. He leaned toward Queen Sybilla, who sat
on his left, and murmured in her ear. She smiled brilliantly. She thought him a poor shadow of his brother,
but he was too beautiful to despise; and she was always

at her best with beautiful men. She turned to her husband and whispered a word or two. He blinked, paused,
nodded. It took him a moment to gather his wits and
stand, while the steward struck a bell and the hall went
quiet.

"Tomorrow," he said, "we ride to war against the
Saracen."

He waited out the roar that went up, the clanging of
knife-hilts on goblets, the thudding of fists on tables and
feet on floor.

When it was quiet enough for him to be heard, he
went on. "We ride to war, all of us, the flower of the
kingdom and its strongest defense against the enemy.
There is no finer army in the world."

Again they whooped and cheered. Some bellowed
their own war-cries, or the war-cries of Outremer: *"Deus
lo volt!* Holy Sepulcher!"

Guy smiled, fidgeting with his dagger-hilt. "Yes," he
said. "We'll fight like champions, every one of us, in the
Lord Jesus' name. But before we go, there's something
that needs to be done. You know my royal brother of
Rhiyana."

They did indeed, loudly. There was more in it than
simple exuberance. Aidan was surprised to hear how
much more there was. The knights, unlike the council,
knew what they had in Gwydion, and were glad of it.

"My royal brother," Guy said, frowning as it sank in
on him what the uproar meant, "has given us the gift of
his person and his people, as many as there are here over
the sea. He is also determined that both should be entirely at our disposal. He will not be swearing fealty to
me—that would hardly be proper—but he will accede to
my authority in all that pertains to the ruling of my
kingdom and its army."

"That is," said Gwydion, rising, sliding smoothly
into the pause, "in all that pertains to the war against the
Saracen."

Guy nodded, still frowning. "Yes, precisely."

"I am a guest and a pilgrim," Gwydion said, "and a
royal ally. The war is yours, my brother of Jerusalem. I
shall aid you in all that I may."

Guy's frown faded. He liked the sound of that. So did almost everyone else.

Some, however, had heard what was behind it. Amalric's brows were knit. Lord Humphrey hid a smile behind his hand. Count Raymond seemed amused.

"As tidy a slither as I've ever had the pleasure to observe," the count said to Aidan when they could have a word together. Aidan had honestly needed the garderobe; Raymond, it was apparent, had followed him in order to speak with him.

Aidan flattened against the wall to let a burly knight go by. He cocked his head toward the stair. Raymond nodded, bowed, gestured him ahead.

The palace roof, like nearly every other in this country, was a garden and, in the summer, a sleeping place. There was no one there now. Aidan made his way to the side of it that looked on the harbor: dim now in the dusk, lit here and there by a flicker of torches. The sound of hammering and of drunken voices came up from the city. There was still a little to do among the smiths and the armorers. The rest of the army celebrated its last night before the march.

"I might not have allowed them to become quite so boisterous," Raymond observed, leaning on the parapet and taking a deep breath of air scented with smoke and dung and humanity and a tang of the sea.

"It can't harm them to run wild for one night before they come under discipline," said Aidan.

The Count of Tripoli cocked a brow at him. Raymond was a rarity in a lord: an intelligent man. Unlike Humphrey of Toron, whose intelligence made him no good in the field, Raymond was a thoroughly competent knight and general, seasoned in a lifetime of ruling and fighting in Outremer. He was not what Aidan would call a friend; that warmth was not in him, except for his lady and for King Baldwin who was dead. But they understood one another. "Your troops, no doubt," Raymond said, "are under discipline now, and have been since you rode up from Jerusalem."

"No more than yours."

Raymond smiled. "Some of us have odd views as to what constitutes proper behavior in an army." He rubbed an old scar along his jaw, which he disdained to hide behind a beard. "Your brother amazes me more every time I see him. Was he born knowing how to hoodwink kingdoms?"

"Every word he spoke was the truth."

Raymond laughed aloud. "The truth, and nothing but the truth. He'll fight because he wants to fight, but the war is Guy's. For better or for worse. And if it goes badly, he won't take it on himself to save it."

"I wouldn't go that far," Aidan said. "He'll do what he can, but he won't claim the crown to do it."

"Magnanimous of him," Raymond said dryly. "He must be the only man in the world who doesn't want the crown of Jerusalem; and he's in the best position to take it."

"I don't think the rest of the world would be delighted to see the Holy Sepulcher defended by the witch-king of Rhiyana."

"Ah, but how he would defend it! I'm rather sorry he won't. I'd happily relinquish my own claim in favor of his."

"No fear of that. I'll tell you a secret, messire. My brother is king of Rhiyana and no other, and that he will always remain, because that earth and that alone is his."

"Ah, so he's bound to it, like the pagan kings?"

"Close enough," Aidan said. "He can leave it, obviously. But leave it to rule any other kingdom, no. The land would never allow it."

"Remarkable," said Raymond. "He won't tarry here, then, whether we win or we lose."

"Not past this season. When the ships go west at summer's end, he goes with them."

"And you?"

It was like Raymond to ask a question so difficult, and to expect an answer to it. Aidan wandered a little, down along the parapet, back. "I don't know. I'd thought I would go, before this war broke on us. When my lady was my wife, and my affairs were settled. Now

. . . I can only wait, and fight as I'm called to, and see what comes."

"It's all any of us can do," Raymond said. "I dare to have hopes, myself. We have a fool for a king, but a fool who can listen to reason. And we are as good an army as I've ever seen. We'll singe the sultan's beard for him."

"So we shall," Aidan said, taking his arm to go back down among the feasters.

Raihan was there when Elen came back, precisely as she had commanded. He seemed to have come to a decision while she sent her maid to scour the markets for a trinket which, if she was lucky, Gwenneth would never find. When she shut and barred the door, he said, "I should take a proper revenge. I should call for a *qadi* and have this registered as a marriage."

"Why don't you?"

He gaped at her. Suddenly he laughed. "Do you want me to?"

"If it will content you," she said. She was not chaffing him. It was nothing that the Church would acknowledge, being an infidel rite, but in her present mood she would be pleased to call herself a Muslim's wife. It would give Messire Amalric pause. It might even drive him off.

Raihan shook his head. "I don't need a judge to tell me what you are to me."

"And what is that?"

"The world," he said.

Elen could not move. It was not enough, this meeting of mind and wit, but it was most of why she loved him. He faced her as an equal, and expected her to do the same. Maybe it came of growing to manhood where Morgiana was. Morgiana was a powerful argument for the capacities of women.

He moved in the stillness, not to touch her, not yet, but to take off his coat. He laid it carefully on the clothes-stool, and slipped off his boots with their silver spurs. He might have been alone, for all the self-consciousness he showed. When he was in his drawers, he sat cross-legged and began to unwind his turban.

Her heart was beating hard; her breath came short. He was no surprise to her as he was, since the day Lisabet's goat butted him into the fishpond. In this very house, in the kitchen garden. She could not have imagined then that he would be here, and about to be her lover.

He was as beautiful as she remembered. Not a big man, but not a small one either, built like a rider and a swordsman. The skin that seldom saw the sun was more olive than bronze, but still shades darker than her own. There were scars on his shoulder and down his side: marks of tooth and claw.

He marked her stare, read it easily. "Lion," he said, "when I was too young to have any sense."

"I wonder you survived it."

"I might not have, if it hadn't been for my lord and his lady. My lady killed the lion. My lord put me back together again, and between them they beat life into me. I had to live, they told me, to get the tanning I deserved."

"Did you?"

He grinned at her. "Twenty strokes with the strap when all my wounds were healed; and a wild foal to train, since it was so obvious that I needed to be kept out of mischief."

"It didn't do much good, did it?"

His turban was off, a long white ribbon, twisted in his hands. He set to work unplaiting his braids, but watching her, not quite smiling.

"Is that what half of you is?" she asked him. "A Turk?"

"No," he said. "I'm vain, that's all. And stubborn. I don't want to shave my head like an Arab."

And no wonder. A woman would have given her hope of salvation to have hair like that, thick and black and curling, growing of its own accord halfway down his back, and then obliging him by stopping. The three Turkish braids straightened it a little, but it found its measure soon enough.

She had nothing so marvelous. It was black enough, and it was nigh as long as she was, but it was almost straight except for the plait she kept it in. She moved slowly, sliding out of girdle and cotte, ridding herself of her veil and the elegant new fashion of the wimple. It was strange to breathe unconstrained under a man's eyes.

She almost ordered him out then. He would no doubt have gone, and even been glad that she had come to her senses. But she had not labored this long, to turn craven at the end. Barefoot in her shift, with her hair loose about her, she knelt in front of him and gently, almost fearfully, laid her hand on his cheek.

She laughed suddenly, startling him.

He had to know. "I thought you might be rabbit-chinned," she said.

He was offended, but he was keeping it in hand. She traced the firm line of his chin under the surprising silkiness of his beard. "It is an advantage," she pointed out, "which a woman can't share. Though it's a shame, too, when a man is beautiful under it."

"That's boy's beauty," he said, a little stiff still. "Or woman's. I am neither."

"That is obvious," she said. She measured the width of his shoulders, laid her palms flat on his breast. The black curling hair was as soft as it was thick. It grew like a tree: rising narrow out of his navel and spreading wide over his chest. It was not time, yet, to think about its root. His shoulders were smooth and silken-skinned, and his back.

He seemed as intrigued by her body as she was by his. He was not a virgin, she could tell from the way he touched her: light, deft, sure of his craft here as with his beloved horses. But as with a new mount, he was careful how he proceeded, asking nothing that she would not willingly give. His dark hands on her white flesh made her shiver. Not but that Riquier had burned nigh as black in the summer, but Raihan was gloriously foreign, with the scent of musk and rosewater that lay on him, and the lilt on his tongue when he spoke to her, and the cast of his face beneath its beautiful beard.

Her shift was lost somewhere, but he still had his drawers. Muslims were modest that way. Someone had told her that. Sybilla? They must be covered always from the navel to the knee. "But how do they—?" she had asked. Sybilla had laughed and said something silly about drawers big enough for two.

She was slender enough and he was enchantingly lean in the flanks, but she did not think that there was room enough for them both. The cord was just where she could reach it without alarming him. She slipped it free. For a moment she feared that she had failed. Then he laughed and stepped out of them.

A root, indeed. "So that is what a Muslim looks like," she said.

His cheeks were crimson, but he grinned at her, cocky as a boy. "Some of us," he said.

"What, you aren't all lions, bulls, stallions—"

He smothered the rest with kisses, laughing round them. He had not asked for this, except maybe in his prayers, but he did nothing by halves, did Raihan. He carried her to the bed and laid her in it. His face was the face of a warrior and a lover, both fierce and tender.

Her heart swelled. He was beautiful, and it was all she could do not to weep. He was going away to war, and he might not come back; and if he did, what place could there be in a princess' world, for a Saracen who had been a slave?

They had until the evening. After that, God would provide.

Part Three

THE HORNS
OF HATTIN

2–6 July 1187

18

Tiberias had fallen.

The army of Jerusalem camped about the springs of Cresson beside the cool and living waters, in green seared by the furnace heat of summer; where not long ago seven thousand Saracens had paused to water their horses, and the Grand Master of the Templars with his hundred-fifty knights, riding to Tiberias, had given way to temptation. Now the Franks had come back to take their revenge, thirty thousand of them, knights and fighting men, with their horses and their baggage. It was, for that country, a rich pasture, and a strong position from which to fight: a hill rising out of a barren and tumbled upland, with mountains to the east of it, and beyond the mountains the Sea of Galilee and the city of Tiberias. They were prepared to settle there, to bar the way to their kingdom, to wear the enemy down with their motionless, inescapable presence.

But Tiberias had fallen, and the great lords of the kingdom gathered in the king's tent, wrangling over the news. Scouts had brought it before sundown; a messenger had come just now, as the darkness fell, bearing word from the Countess Eschiva. *The citadel is ours still, my lord king, but the city and the lands about it are overrun. I beg you, my lord, come to our aid, or all of us are lost.*

The one to whom that message was greatest grief, Count Raymond whose wife the countess was, had said nothing at all. He left it to his fellows to cry their outrage and to consider what they had to face.

"Saladin has divided his army," mused Reynaud de Châtillon. "He attacked Tiberias with a force of picked men, laughed at the garrison when it tried to buy him off, sacked the city and camped amid the ruins. But the greater part of his force sits idle two leagues south of the city, barring the road and the main approaches. No doubt he thinks us nicely cut off."

"No doubt he wants us to think so," said Humphrey of Toron. In this rough camp, after a month and more in the field, with every man living in armor and with little water to spare for cleanliness, he still managed to look as if he were about to ride in a tournament. "He's trying to lure us out, to fight on ground of his choosing. He'll know what we've been doing: trying to wear him down, avoiding a pitched battle, trusting to his levies and his sadly straitened purse to lessen his army for us."

"And where has it got us?" Gerard de Rideford demanded. The Master of the Templars was on his feet, as restless as Aidan could be, and much less circumspect. "We knew that he would strike for Tiberias. Did we do anything about it? We did not. We sat by the water, dabbling our toes and singing to the birds."

Raymond regarded him in sour dislike. "Singing, maybe, but singing war-songs. Yes, he wants to lure us out. He knows that our position here is strong enough, with water for the taking, and ample pasture for our horses. We bar his way into the kingdom. He'll do nothing while we hold fast here; and if he does nothing, he'll lose his army. Half-trained levies, most of those, raiders from the desert and farmers from the fields, apt enough for a bit of fighting, but now they've had it, they'll reckon it enough."

"You know him well," Reynaud drawled. "But no, I'm forgetting. You were his friend until he broke your truce for you."

"This is more than a broken truce," Raymond said with careful calm. "Tiberias, after all, is my city. My wife holds it in peril of her life. My children will be meat for Saracen dogs, if the citadel falls."

"So, then," Amalric said. "You counsel that we bring the battle to it."

"No!" Raymond's vehemence brought them all upright. "*No*, my lords. It is my city, yes, my wife and my children. But this is my army and my kingdom. The plain of Sepphoris lies between us and the city. There is no water on it before the village of Hattin; none at all, but for one small spring, which is never enough for an army. If the enemy harries us, if he holds the wells of Hattin, if we cannot reach Tiberias before we run dry, then we shall be lost. We cannot fight in summer's heat, in our armor, with our horses, without water. That, we have here. It would be mad for us to leave it."

"But the city," said Guy. "Your city—how can you let it fall?"

"It may fall," said Raymond, "and that is bitter. But walls can be built again. My lady and my children are not so easily restored; but the enemy is a knight and a gentleman, though he be an infidel. I shall trust to that and to him. He will not have such mercy on this kingdom. You know what he has sworn: to break the back of every man of us, and to drive our folk into the sea. And that, as God is my witness, he shall do if we march on Tiberias."

"That is cowardice!" cried the Master of the Templars. "We must march; we must take the city back. Else the infidel will overrun us as he overran Tiberias, and our kingdom is lost." He turned to the king. "My lord. Remember how you held back from just such a fight four years ago, at Goliath's Well, and the Saracen drove you ignominiously from the field? That is what you are about to do now. As for my lord count"—his voice dripped with malice—"we all know whose fault it was that I lost my knights and well-nigh my life, here in this very place. He let the Saracen over our borders then. Now he would do it again, and destroy us all."

Guy looked from one to the other of them, pulling nervously at his beard. "We were going to stay here and let Saladin wear himself out trying to get past us. But if he has one of our greatest cities, right on the Sea of Galilee . . . we can hardly let him keep it."

"His army will settle it for us," Raymond said. "My lord, believe me. They are as innumerable as the sands of the sea, but unlike the sand they need to be fed and paid and given fighting to do, or they scatter back to their own places. Saladin knows it very well. He wants us to come to him; he wants us to fall into his trap. He knows that we are the full strength of our kingdom. He prays that we may all come into his hands at once, and be destroyed. We must not do it, my lord. We must not march on Tiberias."

Raymond leaned forward as he spoke. His voice was low, but it shook with the intensity of his pleading. Guy, rapt, lowered his hand from his beard. He drew a breath; he pulled himself erect. "Yes," he said. "Yes. We must not march."

Gerard let out a wordless cry of protest. Reynaud scowled but said nothing. The others were silent.

Guy nodded firmly. "We stay. We let the Saracen dig his own grave."

It was nigh on midnight when the lords went to their own places. Gerard cursed Raymond in no uncertain terms, all the way to his tent and his Templars.

Aidan, camped on the other side of the army near Raymond's own troops, did not need to hear Gerard in order to know what fury was on him. Most of the army slept, now that the word had gone out that they were not to march in the morning. Even the newest recruits had picked up a little seasoning in a month and more of playing cat-and-mouse with the infidel, and had learned to sleep when they could.

Gwydion appeared out of the darkness and sat by Aidan under the roof of the tent, with its walls rolled up to take what breezes there were. Aidan shifted slightly to make room for him. He was still in armor, his blue surcoat black in the starlight, the silver seabird of his blazon glinting as he moved. He crouched down in a clinking of mail-rings, raising a brow at Aidan's own armored discomfort. "You, too, brother?"

Aidan shrugged. "It's something in the air. Raymond

is right. Guy seems to understand it, for once. But somehow I can't stop twitching."

"Nor I." Gwydion, who never twitched, frowned at the carpet in front of him. "This is no kind of warfare for the impetuous."

"Gerard de Ridefort goes beyond impetuous. He's obsessed."

Gwydion seemed hardly to have heard. "I swore that I would not interfere. I've kept that oath. I've marched as the army marched, commanded my men as my brother king commanded, waged this war as the council of the kingdom wished it. I have done nothing that any man can question. And they've forgotten what I am. Have you noticed that? They don't stop and stare any longer. Their eyes don't roll white when I pass them."

"Some remember," Aidan said. "Just this morning someone asked me if I knew any spells to drive back the Saracen."

"Do you?"

"Of course I do," said Aidan. "But I'm not about to use them. Human will is doing well enough without help from me."

"Human will often does." Gwydion sighed. "I could wish that I were one of them. Then I could sleep."

"Even in the heat?"

Gwydion did not rise to the bait. "I pity my poor Rhiyanans. They never bargained for this when they asked to come to your wedding."

"Nor did I," Aidan said. He did not speak of it often. He did not want to speak of it now. She was still gone, still lost, still cut off from him as if she had never been. His fault purely for listening to ill counsel, and worse by far, for letting it rule him.

Messire Evrard was with the army. Likewise the men who had made him their messenger. They did not speak to Aidan, and Aidan did not speak to them. They reckoned the deed well done; some, even, that they had done him a kindness. Surely now he was one of them, heartwhole and undivided.

Surely, he thought. The thought was bitter. But there

was no anger in it. Not any longer. That, he kept for himself.

He levered himself up, stiff in chausses and hauberk, walking out under the bitter-bright stars of the desert. He was aware as a man is of his own body, of his men about him: his mamluks asleep or on guard, his sergeants amid their troops of infantry, his irregulars about the edges, the horse-archers whom his Turks had trained. Close by them were his brother's Rhiyanans, his own people, knights and men-at-arms tossing restlessly in the heat and the buzzing of flies. Flies were no great torment in the Elvenking's presence, or in Aidan's either, but there was no escaping their endless, maddening song, as they lived and bred and thrived in Cresson's pools.

The army was quiet, the enemy out of reach, waiting for a march that would not, God and King Guy willing, be undertaken. Aidan yawned, but there was no sleep in him. There seldom was when he was on campaign; and the more so now. He needed a fight. They had had none yet, simply a game of hide-and-seek, a pattern of marches and pauses, feints and counterfeints. Mostly they had waited, and seen their army grow to half again what had mustered in Acre.

It was still no match for Saladin's. Nor need it be, if it kept the high ground and ruled the battle from it.

Gwydion came out beside his brother. Aidan glanced at him, sensing the darkness that was on him, no closer to naming it than Gwydion himself was. It was nothing as distinct as foreseeing. Gwydion had had no more visions since he stood on the Mount of Olives and saw Jerusalem fall. But he was uneasy.

Neither needed to speak, to agree to walk the lines. But for the sentries, no one else was abroad.

No one but Raymond. He stood stone-still on the camp's eastern edge, face turned toward the shadow on shadow that was Mount Turan. There was a light low in the sky beyond it, a ruddiness like dawn, but that was an hour away still.

"They burn Tiberias," he said as the brothers came up beside him. Even in his grief, he could smile to see them, tall in firelight and starlight, and the same face on either side of him.

Aidan laid a hand on his shoulder. He did not shake it off: rare concession for a man as reserved as he was. "My stepsons are cursing me," he said, "as spiritedly as ever that madman from Ridefort. Their mother is in the city, they cry to me. My wife; my children, their half-kin. How can I be so cold as to forsake them?" He laughed, brief and bitter. "How indeed? What is this kingdom to me, or its upstart king? They say of me that I would have turned Muslim and sworn fealty to Saladin, for rage that I should be cheated of the crown."

"They say it of me, and no one ever accused me of wanting to be king." Aidan shook him lightly. "Raymond, you chose as you could hardly help but choose. Eschiva will hold the citadel until you can come to it; or if she has to surrender it, she'll win terms that honor you both. Saladin won't touch her or the children. It hasn't come to that kind of war. Not yet."

"I know that," Raymond said with a touch of sharpness. "But it's my city and my wife, and I stand here because I convinced our witless beauty of a king that we should abandon them. She may understand it, but she won't be quick to forgive."

"She'll be less forgiving if you die of thirst trying to ride to her rescue."

"There is that," Raymond admitted. He glanced at Gwydion. "You've been silent, my lord king. Is there something we haven't thought of?"

"Nothing," Gwydion said. He walked a little away from them, almost to the sentry's line.

"Nothing?" Raymond paused. "Nothing human, do you mean?"

Gwydion would not answer. Aidan almost did not, but the devil of restlessness in him made him say, "Nothing unhuman, either, that we can see. I wish we hadn't stripped the castles and the cities so bare to make up our army. But it makes us strong here; and it's here that Saladin will come, if he's to fight us."

"Or from here that he will retreat, if his army bleeds away through our inaction." Gwydion turned to face them. "Did anyone think to keep a watch on the Master of the Templars?"

Aidan went cold. Raymond, without power to guide him, said irritably, "When have we started spying on our own commanders? Ridefort is a damned bloody fool, but he's not a traitor. If anything, he's too fervent in defense of the kingdom."

"Fervor can kill," Gwydion said, "as easily as its opposite."

Aidan shook his head, not at Gwydion's words but at what they implied. "He can't get at Guy now. Raymond made up his mind for him."

"Can you be sure of that?"

Gwydion spoke with more than simple apprehension. Aidan, cursing himself for an idiot, unfolded his power as Gwydion already had, and spat a curse.

Before Raymond could open his mouth to ask, a trumpet brayed from the king's tent. One long, brazen peal; then a pattern of notes they all knew. *Rise and arm. Prepare to march.*

The Templar had had the last word. They were marching on Tiberias.

19

The king's tent was in uproar. The king would not come out of it. His mind, at last and immovably, was made up. The barons, kept out by a determined wall of guards, had begun to howl like dogs. "This is mad!" roared the strongest-lunged of them. *"Mad!"*

As the tumult wavered on the edge of violence, Guy came out. He was in full armor, his white surcoat embroidered with the golden crosses of the kingdom, his head bare and impeccably barbered. The torchlight made him seem made all of gold and silver. The clamor died to a growling mutter.

Guy ran his eyes over the lot of them. His mouth was

set; his glance was fierce. "Do you argue with your king?"

Only if the king was mad. That thought was as loud as a shout, but no one dared, quite, to utter it.

The king raised his chin. "This is the course on which I have decided. On my head, and mine alone, be it. My duty is to command; yours is to obey. Go then and do it."

There was nothing that anyone could say. None but Raymond had the power or the courage, and he was not there. When he heard the trumpets, he had thrown up his hands and said what they all said in extremity; what the Muslims themselves said. "God wills it."

As the barons retreated, cursing the world and its laws that made them subject to such a king, some of them saw who stood on the edge of the torchlight, one shape twice over, one in blue and silver, one in scarlet. Lord Humphrey, Lord Balian, a handful of lesser luminaries, turned toward them.

Humphrey spoke for them all. "My lords. Is there nothing you can do?"

Gwydion shook his head.

But Humphrey was not prepared to accept that. "My lord, you're his equal in rank. He has to listen to you."

"No," Gwydion said. "Not in his own kingdom. Not by the oath I swore. This is his war, as he himself says. I have no power to command him."

"You can persuade him," Humphrey said. "You can talk to him, my lord. For the kingdom's sake, we beg you."

Gwydion looked toward the tent. The barons were nearly all gone from it. The king had gone back within with the Templar and the Constable. *They* were well content. They reckoned this a bold stroke, and a necessity; they hated to sit still while the Saracen ravaged their lands. Better to force a battle now and end it, than to wear themselves away with doing nothing.

Suddenly there were no minds to read; only a buzzing emptiness. Gwydion swayed, shocked. It was as if there had been a power in the tent, and it had roused to his presence. But he had sensed nothing at all. Only human minds turning over human thoughts, planning a battle. Then a hum of silence.

His temper, never as thoroughly mastered as people liked to think, pricked him to say, "I shall do what I can. Come, brother."

The guards closed up as he approached with his brother just behind him and the barons hovering within earshot. He halted. Their uneasiness was palpable even over the power, or lack thereof, that walled the tent. "May I pass?" he asked, courteous, but not as one who expects to be refused.

The guards did not move.

Gwydion raised his voice slightly. "My lord king. May I come in?"

It was not an answer that came back. The king's voice was low, but audible to such ears as his. "Don't let him cast a spell on me." Then the Templar spoke in Latin. A prayer against evil.

Gwydion's back went stiff. Almost he raised his hand. Almost he struck the guards aside.

Almost he did more than that.

No. He mastered himself. He met the eyes of each guard in turn, setting no power in it but what was in his kingship.

They gave way. He allowed himself the fleeting warmth of a smile. With Aidan for his shadow, he entered the king's tent.

The king was no coward, however much he feared ensorcelment. He remained where he was, sitting in his carven chair, and his eye on the brothers was cold. "Majesty," he said. "Highness."

Gwydion inclined his head. He did not sit. The silence hummed and sang; then, abruptly, stilled. It was only silence. No maddening, buzzing wall. Nothing but what it ought to be, human silence, full of the babble of human minds.

Gwydion, braced for an assault, gasped in its absence and nearly fell. His brother steadied him. The eyes on them were human all, no power in them.

There was fear enough. There was always fear, soon
or late.

Gwydion was out of charity, if not quite of prudence.
He did not say the words that were on his tongue. He
stood before the king and let his shadow stretch behind
him, and a glimmer in it that might have been eyes.
"Messire," he said, soft and almost gentle. "What is this
that you would do?"

Guy sat straighter in his chair. "I do what I must,"
he said. He sounded quite properly a king.

"What you must do," said Gwydion, "is to forbear to
march."

Guy's jaw set. "Are you commanding me?"

"You know that I am not." Gwydion was quiet still.
"Nor shall I lay a spell on you."

"You would not dare," said the Master of the Templars.

"And who are you," Gwydion asked of him, "to say
what I would and would not venture?" He spread his
hands. The lamplight gathered in them, spilled over his
fingers. "My lord of Jerusalem, what you propose to do
is rash and far from wise. Will you not heed your brother
king? Will you not return to the wisdom of yestereve?"

Guy tugged at his beard. His eyes were fixed on
Gwydion's hands. His mind was nothing that Gwydion
could grasp.

"My lord!" The Templar's voice was harsh, peremp-
tory. "Will you listen to him? Will you let him bewitch
you? You heard them all without. He is their weapon.
Who is to tell why he yields to their commands?"

"Perhaps," said Gwydion, softer than ever, "I am
your equal and a king, and I have erred even as you
propose to do, and suffered for it."

"Indeed," said the Templar. "Remember, sire, what
he is. Remember how long he has been a king. Has he
gained wisdom from it? Or only damnation?"

That was too subtle for Guy's intelligence. He looked
at Gwydion, and Gwydion saw himself reflected in those
eyes, tall and fair and terrible. There was nothing in
Gwydion that Guy could understand.

Gwydion's power waited for him to gather it. He

could bend that mind, weak as it was, the mind of a mortal and a fool. A touch only, and it could be done. The march halted, the battle averted, all this madness turned to sanity.

Guy thrust himself to his feet. His voice came high and quick. "Swear," he said. "Swear that you'll work no sorceries."

Even the blind, on occasion, could seem to see. Gwydion stood face to face with Jerusalem's king and raised his hands. Guy flinched. But there was no light in them, no glimmer of magic. Gwydion let him see it; then, slowly, let them fall. "Will you swear to remain at Cresson?"

"I will do what I will do," Guy said.

"Then I will not swear to trammel my power."

"Not even for your life's sake?" asked the Master of the Templars.

Gwydion kept his eyes on the king, his temper rigidly in hand. "Even if you will not stay, there is much that I can do. You have but to ask."

"Yes," said the Templar. "He will ask, and you will take. All; all that is his and ours and the enemy's. Do you take us for fools, my lord of Rhiyana? Do you think that we cannot see?"

"I see that you have chosen the counsel of a fool," said Gwydion to the king. "So be it. But there may be hope, if you will take what I will give."

Guy looked away from him, biting his lip, worrying at his beard. But not, dear God, in indecision. He was more set than ever upon his course. It was fear that swayed him; and temptation.

"Hear the voice of God's Adversary," said the Templar, buzzing in his ear as the strangeness, rising anew, buzzed in Gwydion's mind. Yet it was not from the Templar that it came. It was all about them, throbbing in them, robbing him of wits and will.

"No!" said Guy. "No. I will take nothing from you except your oath. There will be no magic in this fight."

Gwydion's hands ached. They were knotted, clenched tight. "My lord. Will you not reconsider?"

"You won't witch me into it," said Guy. "I won't let you. I need you and your men, but not as much as that."

"Are you asking me to leave you?"

Guy blinked rapidly. "You said you'd fight for me. But not with sorcery. I won't endanger our immortal souls."

"Even to save your lives?"

"Damnation is eternal," said the Templar.

"Fight for me," said Guy. "But not as—your kind—fight."

"Our kind." Gwydion's mouth was bitter. "I gave you my word that I would not enchant you. I swore before your court that this is your war; that I will aid but never seek to command. Both oath and promise have force to bind me. And yet, my lord—"

Guy had heard all that he wished to hear. "Good, then. We need you, you know that. As long as our souls are safe . . ." He stopped, shook his head. "Of course they are. You aren't a devil. Will you excuse us now? There's more to do if we're to march by morning."

Gwydion stood still. There was no yielding in the man; no hope of it. Gwydion's own word had bound him, his honor and his temper between them, colluding in this folly.

Aidan was a banked fire behind him. What Aidan would do, he knew too well. Loose the flame of his anger. Blaze up in white light. Show them truly what it was that they feared, and what they had renounced, and what they would gain from it.

That was Aidan's way. Gwydion could not follow it. If that made him a weakling, then so be it.

He turned on his heel. In one long stride he was out of the tent.

Aidan was face to face with him. His expression must have been appalling: even Aidan checked a little at the sight of it.

"The king has spoken," Aidan said with bitter irony. "Our task is simply to obey."

"And to do what we may to head disaster aside." Gwydion had his temper in hand at last. The barons were waiting, knowing from his face that he had failed, but in their human fashion insisting that he set it in words. "I can do nothing," he said. "The king refuses to hear me. Even I can do no other than he commands."

"Then God help us all," said Humphrey of Toron.

God seemed far away from that bitter march. The heat of the night gave way to the furnace heat of the day. They had taken all the water that they might, but thirty thousand of them, in high summer, under the hammer that was the sun, needed an ocean to keep themselves and their horses from thirst. They had nothing approaching an ocean; no wagons, no barrels to carry water in. Only flasks for the men and skins for the horses, barely enough for a day's march.

It was bad, Aidan thought, but not quite intolerable. Not yet. He had his men on strict orders to waste no water; to drink only when he commanded. They marched in silence, with none of the joyful clamor that usually hung about an army on its way to a battle. No one sang to set the pace; the trumpets were silent, the drums mute. When a stallion screamed, down the line, some of the men started, and one fell out of formation.

He scrambled back in again before Aidan could do more than glance at him. At least they did not have to breathe the army's dust: they were in the van, just behind Count Raymond. The king was farther back, in the center; the rearguard was the Templar's.

They crossed the plain of Sepphoris with its dry scrub and its sere grasses, no tree, no water, not even a stone to cast a patch of shade. The ground was rough, treacherous with stones and hollows. They scrambled and stumbled more than they marched; the horses were hard put to keep their footing. It was like a passage in hell: for every step forward, two steps round or about an obstacle, and the devil's own task to keep the line steady.

The infantry were wretched enough without horses to carry them, in their iron helmets and their heavy coats, some of mail, some of leather, most of felt so thick that arrows could not pierce it. But the knights were in torment. Shirt under padded gambeson under ringmail;

breeches of leather, chausses of mail from loin to toe, padded caps and coifs of mail on their heads, and helmets over that. Surcoats kept off the worst of the sun, but there was no escaping the heat; and with the heat, the burning, maddening thirst.

Aidan was stronger than most. That was part of what he was; and he could do somewhat to cool himself, even to spare his men the torment at least of flies, and to make a breeze for them. But he had no power to veil the sun, or to conjure water where there was none.

He kept a careful eye on Gwydion. His brother was doing the same for his own men, young knights of Rhiyana where the sun was never so strong, the land never so appallingly dry, who had never imagined such a horror of heat. Within an hour of sunrise, some of them were near to fainting. One had to be held back by main force from draining his flask dry and falling on the skin of water that was meant for the horses. Gwydion dealt him summary justice: put him down off his horse and set him to walking with the footsoldiers. It was not as cruel as it seemed. He was rid of his chausses, and he could hold to a comrade's stirrup, and the horse did most of the walking; and it kept his mind off his torment in raging at the king.

The enemy came out soon after Gofannwy became an infantryman: small bands of skirmishers on light swift horses, armed with bows, shooting from just within the limit of their range, and galloping away when their arrows were exhausted. They did no great damage, but they were a hindrance, like stinging flies. And they were aiming at the horses.

A knight without a horse, as Gofannwy well knew, was like a turtle without its shell: soft, slow, and helpless. To protect their mounts, they had to move more slowly, watch more warily, hold the line more firmly.

Aidan's Turks would happily have done something about the skirmishers. But the order had gone out. No return of fire. No pauses to fight. The army must move, must escape this waterless wasteland, must cross the five leagues to Tiberias.

"Five leagues as the eagle flies," Aidan said between

harryings, when he had allowed himself a sip of water. "We'll be lucky if we make two in the straight line, at this pace, and by the road we're taking."

Gwydion had his helmet off but his coif up. His face was a mask of dust and sweat, but his eyes were clear in it, the color of flint. He nodded at Aidan's words, looked ahead through the column. They were not aiming straight for Tiberias: there was an army in the way, on the other side of the ridge. The northern road was open, scouts said, and there was water to be had at the end of it, in the village of Hattin.

Aidan did not want to think about water. There was a whole sea of it over the hill, with the whole army of Islam between.

He could have been on their side. He had been asked, and more than once. Saladin, when he was not being sultan, was a friend. Aidan had more friends than that in the sultan's army, men with whom he had ridden and hunted, even shared bread and salt, and been a guest in their houses.

Now he was here, under the hammer of the sun, bound to follow an idiot king. His men were hardly pleased to obey Guy's commands, but their loyalty to Aidan was unshaken. His Saracens looked to him for their protection. He would keep them safe, their eyes said. He would give them a good fight, and if any was hurt, he would protect that one from the Angel of Death. It was an article of their doctrine. Had they not fought on a hundred battlefields in the years since he came to Outremer? Had he not brought them all out alive, and most of them unscathed?

He ran his tongue over dry and cracking lips. It was well that they could have such faith in him, when he did not. He could raise fire, bring down the lightnings, shake the earth under their feet. And what, after that? There would still be the war, still the enmity of Christian and Muslim, Frank and Saracen, as old as Muhammad and as implacable as the sun that beat down upon them. Saladin would have Jerusalem, or die in the trying. Guy would keep it or perish. There was no middle ground.

Magic is a little thing beside human will, Gwydion

said in Aidan's mind, sparing their parched throats and swollen tongues.

Aidan smiled thinly. *We could do it, you know. If you would break your word. Drive the army back with a storm of fire, hold it at Cresson, herd the enemy back into his own country.*

From which he would promptly return, thrice as furious as before. Gwydion shook his head. *No. Even were I not a man of my word, I would not do it. If we were to rule this country with power, we would have to rule it absolutely, and never leave it. Then all of Christendom would rise up against us, as well as all of Islam. There are too few of us; our strength is too little. We can't hold humanity's most holy places, not against the full tide of them.*

We're too long-sighted, Aidan said.

So we are. Gwydion threw up a hand. An arrow shot by a shrilling Turk rebounded as from a wall. A thin hail of them fell about the column. One of the horses squealed and bucked, stung in the flank.

With sudden fury Gwydion lashed out. The second flight of arrows arced high over them and shattered, falling in a rain of dust and splinters.

A cheer went up. Count Raymond's rearguard, looking back, gaped at the spectacle. The Turks shrieked and bolted.

Gwydion clenched his fists on the high pommel of his saddle, head bent, shoulders hunched. It was no great cost to his strength, but he had lost his temper. Again. That was why he avoided battles. He was wilder in them than his brother, a white, singing madness that was to Aidan's fierce joy as the hawk's stoop to the lark's descent. That was why Aidan was his commander of armies; why he never went to war alone, and seldom to a tournament. The king's dignity was his refuge. He could not, for his life's sake, keep his head in a fight.

"Nonsense," Aidan said, rough with more than the dryness in his mouth. "You just won us a respite. That lot won't be troubling us again, I don't think."

There were more where they came from, though few of them, to be sure, went near Gwydion's portion of the

column. They harried the very front of the van, and the
center somewhat, but they were fiercest against the
rearguard: a flurry of men and horses, dust and arrows
and outcry.

They're driving us, Aidan said in his mind. He had
hoped that he was wrong. He turned his sweating horse,
rode back along the line. Here and there a grin flashed
white in a dust-smeared face. No one wasted breath in
cheering him.

They were ascending now, and he could see the army
advancing behind, straggling over the rough ground. The
center was reasonably well in order, but the rear was
sore beset. It had had to halt and fight or be overrun.
Templars in dust-stained white surcoats, the red cross
bloody on their breasts, spread ever wider, some darting
in reckless charges, called back by their commanders'
bellows or by the braying of trumpets. A space opened
between rear and center. If it grew too wide, the
rearguard would be cut off.

Guy, or Amalric his Constable, seemed to be aware
of the threat: a rider went back at a scrambling run,
dodging arrows, and plunged toward the Templars' command. The horncall sharpened; men went out to herd the
stragglers in. With maddening slowness the line straightened; the knights came to order. They began to move.
But the gap did not narrow. The enemy, having found an
advantage, was not about to let it go.

Aidan could not, though it tore at him, ride down the
length of the army and abandon his own people to tell
Gerard de Ridefort how to command a company. He
rode back to his place, pausing to say a word here and
there, to lighten spirits where he could, to allow another
sip of water.

The slope steepened. The horses strained. One went
down. Its rider struggled to pull it up again. He was
Rhiyanan, the horse likewise, a great slow mountain of a
beast, never bred for such a country as this. Before
Aidan could move, Gwydion was there, off his own east-
ern-bred mount, cutting the beast's throat. Its rider wept
and cursed. Gwydion shook him into silence. "I'll buy
you a new horse," he said. "Hush now, and march. We

have a war to fight." He called to his horsemaster, who
came promptly, leading a smaller, lighter, tougher
mount. The young knight regarded it in distaste, the
more for that it was a gelding; but he let his gear be
shifted to it, and heaved himself onto its back.

He would keep the beast, Gwydion said when he
came back to Aidan's side, *and he would ride it on the
march, when it was never good for anything but a charge,
and a short one at that.*

He's young, Aidan said. *Give him time. He'll learn.*

Not that lad, said Gwydion sourly.

A cry went up ahead. The first riders had reached the
top of their ascent. It was in truth a pass between two
hills, paved with stones and scree, rough with sun-seared
grass.

"The Horns of Hattin," Aidan named the hills, as he
himself came to the height between them. The ridge
broke like a wave, and the Sea of Galilee shining blue
below, and Tiberias on the shores of it, and the Saracens
as thick as flies about it.

Raymond's column descended slowly. There was a
village on the valley's floor, the village of Hattin, where
were wells enough to sate the army's thirst.

And there were Saracens. They held the way to the
wells; they were ready, it was clear, to fight.

The vanguard halted. A messenger rode back toward
the king in the center. He spared a word for the king in
the van: "There's water at Marescallia, under Turan. My
lord Raymond says go there."

And when, after an endless while, he came back:
"The Templars can't advance. The king says head for
Marescallia."

Aidan shook his head at that. They were only halfway to Tiberias. It was hardly yet noon, but the enemy
knew where they were, and they had to have water to go
on. There was water at Marescallia, but never enough for
thirty thousand men: one small spring and a bit of a
pool. They would drink it dry and still be thirsty.

What choice did they have? He dismounted to spare
his horse, passing the order down the line, not to descend
in a straight line but to make their way along the ridge to

the mountain's knees. The ground was even more treacherous here than on the other side of the ridge: a field of dry grass, it seemed to be, but under the grass were sharp-edged stones, the black eggs of mountains, where the earth had spewed forth fire long ago. Every step threatened misstep; and worse for horses with their rigid hoofs than for men with armored or booted feet. A charge here would be madness, a battle suicidal.

Marescallia was smaller than he remembered, the trickle of water thinner. Raymond's men had already muddied it, for all their efforts not to. The horses strained desperately to drink; it was white pain to pull them back after a swallow or two and make way for the rest.

At least there was fodder for them, though they were not delighted to find it so dry. Aidan found a place to rest his men and his horses, near the spring but out of the way of the army. Some, his mamluks among them, made tents of their cloaks and settled down in the small shade.

The rearguard was still fighting. The king came up under his banner, took his share of water—and no more, Aidan noted—and made way for the men behind him.

Gwydion, who had been walking among his men, giving what comfort he could, slanted off toward the king. Aidan called Arslan to look after the two companies, and set out in his brother's wake.

Others had the same impulse. Raymond was there already, and Humphrey for once looking less than impeccable, and Reynaud with much of his arrogance muted. Guy looked haggard but not yet disheartened. "We've got to move on," he said. "We'll take Hattin if we have to, but Tiberias is burning."

"Tiberias is surrounded by a hundred thousand Saracens," Raymond snapped. "For God's sake, my lord, look about you. This is a pitiful place to make a stand, but it's better than anything near it. We've got the mountain behind us, we've got what water there is, we can lure Saladin to a fight here and maybe win it."

"Just like Goliath's Well," Reynaud said, not quite sneering. "We sat there, and what did it get us? Nothing but defeat and the king's disgrace, Count of Jaffa that he was then. The Saracen is too canny a fox. He won't come to us when he knows we have an advantage. We have to go to him."

"What, take the fight to his own ground, and let him trample us?" Raymond was incredulous. "Where did you study warfare? In a pig-farmer's hut?"

Reynaud growled and would have sprung, but Amalric pulled him back. "Stop it, both of you. I say we move on. They've got the high ground as it is. If we can lure them down, we can charge, and pin them against the ridge, and hack them down at our leisure. If they don't move, we can come back here and go out again later, till they give in to the temptation."

Raymond nodded unwillingly. "That might work. Give ourselves a base here, with water in it; keep challenging them to come out and fight us."

Guy nodded, chewing his lip. "We'll march, but slowly, till the Templars catch up."

They marched, slowly. The brief respite, the bit of water, soon wore off. The enemy kept harrying them. It was worse now that they could see what was before them: how very many of the enemy there were, and how utterly they had sacked Tiberias.

As the army struggled down from Marescallia, a horde of shrilling Saracens poured out of the hills, streamed around them, overran the spring. Saladin had foreseen even that bit of cleverness.

The rear of Guy's column wavered and almost broke, straining toward the enemy and the water that should have been their lifeblood. Their commanders beat them back. There were too many of the enemy, and more coming from all sides, endless ranks of them, closing in as inexorably as wolves about a flock.

There was no way now but forward. No hope but in Hattin, or in Tiberias. Saladin did not take their challenge. Nor would he. He nipped at their flanks. He brought down their stragglers. When they would have resisted, his men melted away, only to come back four-fold in another place, laughing and jeering. They were all that there was of the army of Outremer. Their attackers were an endless river, never weary, always fresh, on fresh horses, fat and sleek with good food and clean water.

The advance slowed to a standstill. They could not keep their ranks against the pressing of the enemy. The bleak dun plain spread about them. The Templars were over the ridge, past Marescallia, fighting as only Templars could fight. But it was like fighting sand. The more they battled against it, the more it eluded them.

The infantry had had enough. They stopped and would not go on, even for their commanders' curses, even under the flats of blades. "No water," they said, "no march."

"You won't *get* any water if you stay here!" Amalric raged at them. But they were adamant.

His brother had reached his own limit of endurance. "We camp," Guy said, "and hold on till the Templars can win through to us."

"Mad." Even Amalric said it, but Guy was as obdurate as his footsoldiers.

Although it was barely midday, they pitched camp amid the stones near the upland of Hattin. The Saracens were all about them now, making small sallies, shooting flights of arrows, simply sitting their horses and grinning at the tired, dusty, bone-dry Franks.

Saladin himself was on the ridge. They saw him up there under his banners, the caliph's black standard and his own golden eagle: the golden gleam of his corselet and the whiteness of the shawl that he wore to shield his head from the sun, and the yellow coats of the mamluks who were his personal guard.

It was a hot, dry, hungry camp. The blue water of Galilee sparkled in the sun, taunting them more bitterly than any of their enemies. Tiberias, burning, offered neither hope nor help. Reinforcements could not come, even if a messenger could pass the infidels' lines. Worse than that, neither food nor water could be had. They had no wagons, only what each man and horse could carry. They had been depending on the stores at Cresson, or failing that, at Tiberias.

"I may have been in more desperate straits," Raymond said. "If so, I don't recall it."

His tent was pitched in sight of the Sea of Galilee, as if he wanted to remind himself of his lost demesne. The air was still, and breathing it was cruel, parching the nose as well as the mouth. His page offered wine. It was thick sweet wine of Bethlehem, meant to be well weakened with water; it fed the thirst almost more than it quenched it. But it was wet, and it filled the stomach. The page stood near with the bottle, in part to be of service but in part to seek comfort in the others' presence.

Aidan caught the boy's eye and smiled. Aimery looked down, pricking Aidan's senses with embarrassment. His mother had not wanted him to go, but Count Raymond had settled it by asking for him. It was time, the count said, that the boy acquired some seasoning in war.

Even Raymond could not have expected such seasoning as this. The count had wiped off some of the dirt and sweat, but had kept on full mail except for the coif, as had they all. He gestured toward the ridge and the figures on it. They were out of bowshot: that had already been tested. "Rats in a trap," he said. "We should have known what would happen with so many of them to hem us in. They can fall on us in waves, each fresher than the last."

"We might break through," Aidan said. "A miracle might save us. Who knows, until we've seen the end of this?"

"A miracle?" Raymond's brows went up. "Have you one to offer?"

"Not we," said Gwydion.

Raymond might have said more, but chose instead to beckon to Aimery. The boy came willingly enough, and lively enough still, though he was filthy and his leather coat must have itched abominably. He bowed politely and waited for his lord to speak.

Raymond smiled. "I've trained you well, I think, messire. Will you do something for me?"

Aimery's eyes were full of worship for his lord and

teacher. *Anything!* they cried. Aloud he said, "Surely, my lord."

"I am not sending you away," Raymond said, "even if that were possible now. But I would like you to go where you may be safer than with me. If your kinsmen will agree to it, will you enter their service until this battle is over?"

Aimery's face was a study in ambivalence. He looked from his kinsmen to his lord and back again. "There will be a battle, my lord?"

"You can be sure of it." Raymond tilted his shaggy grey-gold head. "Well?"

"My lord—" Aimery looked again at Gwydion, and at Aidan. "My lord, what would they do with me?"

Aidan bit back a smile. Raymond made no such effort. "Guard you," he answered, "as they always guard their own. I may not be able to do it; and I should hate to have to tell your mother that I lost you."

"I'm not a child, my lord," Aimery said, stung.

"Surely not," said Aidan. "I could do with a squire, at that. I've been sharing Gwydion's Urien, and it's hard on the poor lad, looking after two of us."

Aimery sucked in a breath. "You *want* me, my lord?" He caught himself. "I mean—my lord Raymond, I don't want to leave you, but if I have to—"

"But if you have to," Raymond said, "you're more than happy to be squire to the prince." He smiled. "I don't blame you."

"After the battle," said Aimery, "my lord, I'll want to come back to you. If you'll have me."

"If I live, and if I can offer you anything to come back to, yes, I'll have you." Raymond inclined his head to Aidan. "I'm grateful, my lord. That's as good a page as I've had in long years; I'd not be pleased to lose him for a king's folly."

Aimery blushed and ducked his head. He was given to thinking too little of himself, Aidan noticed. That would have to be seen to.

He was also thinking, with no little malice, *Just let Ysabel do better than this!*

Aidan quelled a sigh. She at least was safe. He would

do what he could to protect her brother. As little love as
there had ever been between them, neither would forgive
him if he let the other be hurt. They reserved that privilege for themselves.

Aimery, as Prince Aidan's squire, had expected to
serve his new lord as he had Count Raymond: well out
of the way except when he was needed, well back in the
column when they marched, and quiet in the tent when
his lord attended councils or called on others of the great
ones of Outremer. But Aidan seemed to take it for
granted that Aimery should follow him wherever he
went. Aimery wondered at least once, who was guarding
whom.

Not that Aidan went anywhere at first except back to
the tent he shared with his brother. Urien was there already, a tall slender young man almost old enough to be
a knight, and like enough to the king to be one of his kin.
He was in fact a cousin, if a distant one. Rhiyanan
nobles, Aimery had heard someone say, all looked alike,
as if God had stamped them in the same mold.

"That's the mark of Rhiannon," Aidan said, startling
Aimery half out of his skin. He laid his hand easily on
Aimery's shoulder, though Aimery would have liked to
sink into the earth, so torn was he between joy and mor-
tification. "Urien, I've got myself a new squire. He's had
good training in Count Raymond's court, but there's a
thing or two he may need to know of how we do things
here. Will you teach him tonight, after I'm done with
him?"

He asked it as if the squire had a choice, and Urien
answered in the same vein. "Surely, my prince." He
looked Aimery over. "He looks like a good one. Is he a
Mortmain?"

"The eldest of them," Aidan said.

"Ah," said Urien. "I remember, from Acre." He be-
stowed a smile on Aimery. "Well met again, messire."

Aimery bowed, which felt like the proper thing to do,
and murmured an answer. Urien seemed pleased enough,
though Aidan was in one of his moods: bright, wicked,

and more than a little fey. He kept Aimery with him, not asking anything of him, while he inspected his portion of the camp.

Aimery had noticed before how Aidan's people loved him. It was palpable now, with the camp sunk in desperation and Saracens surrounding it and a skirmish apt to break out almost anywhere at all. Aidan's people were not as desperate as the rest. They were thirsty, but they bore up bravely, even showed their prince how they had kept a little water still, and wine in remarkable plenty. "Enough to get us through the night," one said proudly.

He did not say what everyone was thinking, that there would never be enough for the day that would follow the night, and that would be a day of battle.

Sensible soldiers kept their armor on but rested as much as they could. They did not talk much, or dice round the tents the way they usually did. Many looked after their gear. They expected to fight in the morning, if not sooner.

Aidan's mamluks kept a little apart. That was always so, but today more than ever. People did not forget that they were infidels, or that they looked and fought like the enemies who ringed the camp.

They were proud; they did not seem to think of themselves as turncoats. Saladin had given them to their prince, and they were loyal to a fault. If it dismayed them to find themselves pitted against the whole army of their people, they were not about to show it.

They would be useful when it came to a battle. Franks were strong beside the Saracens, whether mounted or afoot: bigger, better armed, often better trained. Nothing in the east could hold against a charge of full-armed knights on their great horses. But Saladin was a wily general, and wise in fighting Franks. He knew that their strength was of little use against his light swift cavalry with their bows and their slender lances, who could dart in and then out again like wolves harrying a bull. He had numbers to throw against them, numbers enough to surround them and pen them in, and still keep an army in reserve. And worst of all he had water, and clear lines of supply, so that his men fought with full bellies.

Aidan's mamluks were hungry and thirsty, but they were as tough as old leather; and they fought as the enemy fought. One of Aimery's favorite lessons in Count Raymond's house had been the one in which the pages learned how the lord of Millefleurs disposed his forces: infantry to anchor them, knights to strike the heaviest blows, and mamluk cavalry to dart in where they were needed, then out again before they could be trapped. Saracens were not great masters of formation or of discipline, but Aidan's Saracens knew both. Even Saladin was said to be, if not afraid of them, then justly wary.

Aimery, who had grown up with all twelve of them, found that he was glad to have them there. They would not turn traitor. Not Conrad who had taught him to sing, or Raihan who had set him on his first pony, or Arslan who had shown him how to shoot from that pony's back. They looked at the hordes of their fellow infidels and shrugged. "One of us is worth a dozen of them," said Timur.

"That about evens the odds," drawled Andronikos.

"It can't be more than five to one," Raihan said.

"Five well-fed, well-watered Muslims, to one of us." Andronikos covered his face with a corner of his sunshawl and seemed to go to sleep, until he said. "Even odds, children. My wager on it."

"Done!" said Raihan.

"What, you'll wager on our losing?"

"*We* won't lose," Raihan said. "I can't speak for the rest of the army. Or, Allah help us, for the king."

"No one speaks for the king," Andronikos said, muffled in the cloth. "Not even himself."

20

The Templars came in at sunset, haggard and limping and panting with thirst, but grinning through the dirt. They had beaten back the skirmishers: the rear was safe, for the moment.

The wail of the muezzin sounded high and eerie through the heavy air, sending that whole terrible army down abject in prayer. The army of Outremer had little strength to jeer at the spectacle of so many rumps upturned, so many turbaned heads bent toward Mecca. No one ventured a sortie during the prayer. It was all too brief, and the enemy all too adept at leaping up from rapt contemplation of the Infinite to blood-red battle.

Night brought no coolness, only a heavy dark and a redoubled buzzing of flies. The enemy's fires flickered all about the camp, innumerable as stars in the sky, but illuminating little. The Franks, huddled in their camp, heard more than they saw: men speaking in the rhythms of Arabic or Turkish or Nubian or even once, to Aidan's ears, high-court Persian; horses whinnying, camels roaring, now and then a falcon's scream; bodies moving in the dark, the clink of metal on metal, the song of arrow shot from the bow.

What little water was left, the king ordered kept for the horses. Men lay gasping in the sultry night, trying to sleep.

The king's council met again in his tent. Again it was a great deal of sound and fury, and all for very little. Guy could not have moved now if he had wanted to. Ridefort was all for a forced march to Tiberias, but even Guy laughed at him. "March? How? Through the whole army of Islam?"

"Yes!" Ridefort shot back.

"Suicide is against canon law," Raymond said mildly. "My lord, we have no choice but to fight. If I may offer any advice at all, it is this: Keep the knights in hand. Don't let them charge at will, and don't use them up too soon. The horses are the greatest resource we have, and the most fragile. If we lose them, we lose the war."

"We'll have to charge," said Amalric. "It's our strongest weapon."

"But not too often; not too soon." Raymond rubbed his jaw. The rasp of callused fingers on stubble set Aidan's teeth on edge. Mercifully, he did not do it long. "We may yet get out of this. If we can break their line. If we can make Tiberias, or failing that, win back to Marescallia, or even Cresson."

"Retreat?" Ridefort was outraged. "Not I. I'll break through to Tiberias, or die trying."

"You well may," Aidan said. He was running out of patience. "You ran soon enough the last time you faced an army of infidels. Do you have anything useful to say? Or will you hold your peace?"

"We all know what you are," Ridefort said through clenched teeth. "How do we know that it wasn't you who told the infidel where to find us?"

Aidan smiled. "You don't." Their faces were shocked; he laughed, though it made him cough. "I didn't need to tell him. He has scouts enough, and he has a brain in his head. Nor were we exactly quiet about coming here."

"We weren't," said Guy, rather surprisingly. He fretted in his seat, worrying at his beard. His eyes kept darting from Gwydion to Aidan. Suddenly he said it. "Can you do anything?"

Gwydion said nothing. Whatsoever. It was Aidan who spoke in the sudden and profound silence. "What would you have us do?"

Guy gnawed his mustache. This was ghastly hard for him, and Aidan did not intend to make it easier. "You know," the king said. "Get us out of this. Call up a devil, or something."

The priests were properly horrified. The barons either pretended to be, or were honest: narrowed their eyes and considered the usefulness of sorcery.

Aidan was almost sorry to disillusion them. "We're

not black enchanters. What we could have done, should have been accomplished before we fell into this trap."

Guy barely flinched. He never troubled to remember what was inconvenient. "But you can do something. You —your brother—told us—there are tricks, magics—"

"We can't drive away the whole army," Aidan said. "Still less smite it dead where it stands."

"A murrain on the camels?" Amalric suggested. "A fright among the horses?"

Aidan stilled. There was something in the Constable's expression . . .

It passed. Aidan put it out of mind. "Nothing that will last."

"You're not much good, are you?"

Guy's bluntness made Aidan laugh aloud, though it was laughter without mirth. "No, we're not. Not this late in the race. Not against a hundred thousand Saracens."

"What of one?" Amalric asked. "What of the sultan? If he's killed or disabled, his army will fall to pieces."

"This is appalling," said the Bishop of Acre, who was a good enough knight when he was not being a man of the Church.

"Yes, it is." Gwydion's voice was soft. "So is all this war, and this place in which we find ourselves. I might be willing to consider something of the sort, though not perhaps as you would wish: a sortie into the sultan's camp, a swift stroke of the dagger, and what matter whether the assassin escapes or is killed? But that is not possible. He has his own protection, my lords. We have no power against it."

"Not even you?" Amalric demanded.

"We are not gods," Gwydion said. "We are not even lesser demons."

"I think," said Amalric, "that it's less a case of *can't* than of *won't*. For God and Jerusalem's sake, can't you stop being a good Christian long enough to save this kingdom from the infidel?"

The bishop gasped. One or two of the barons hid smiles behind their hands.

"And if I stop being a good Christian," Gwydion

said, "then I become a witch for burning. I see your
logic, my lord Constable. Yet I would do what you ask, if
there were any way to do it. Unfortunately there is not.
The enemy is protected against me. I cannot even turn
spy for you and let you know his mind."

"You've tried," Raymond said. He was considerably
less perturbed than most of them were to have it spoken
of openly at last. "Is there anything at all that you can
do?"

Gwydion sat still on his stool. He did not laugh in
the lords' faces, which was more than Aidan could have
done. His eyes were faintly blurred, with thought, with
testing the limits of his power. How sorely circumscribed
they were, Aidan knew all too well. "Very little," Gwydion answered the count. "Except fight as any man may,
and look after the wounded."

"The wounded?" Raymond asked. "You are a physician, then?"

"Of sorts," Gwydion said.

"He touches them," said one of the barons, "and they
heal." He blanched under the force of their eyes, and
Aidan's keener than any, but he went on boldly enough.
"I saw, on the march. One of my men was horse-kicked,
and my lord king was near, and touched him, and he
walked away whole."

"Miraculous," someone said.

"Useful," Raymond observed.

"Mad," the bishop protested. "We can't do this. We
can't call on witches; no matter how benign their powers
may seem. We'll damn ourselves."

"Would you rather we lost the battle?" Raymond
asked sweetly.

The bishop sputtered into silence. Aidan regarded
him almost with affection. "Excellency, you have every
reason to be afraid, but you must believe us when we say
that there's nothing of the devil in us. We don't work
black sorcery. We can't."

"Which is rather a pity," Amalric said. "If you were
evil enchanters, you could call up a horde of devils and
sweep the enemy away."

"Why not an army of angels?" asked Guy.

"We're hardly so well connected," Aidan said dryly. "Are you, your excellency? Maybe if you put in a word with the Almighty, Saint Michael would send a wing or two."

The bishop signed himself with the cross. Before he could burst out in rebuke, Gwydion said, "Peace, brother." And to the council at large, with great and kingly patience: "We will do what we can. I regret that it is so little. Your strength will decide the day; ours will but bolster it. If you will accept it."

Guy glanced about. Everyone was looking at him, waiting for him to decide. He shifted nervously. "No spells on any of us. Promise us that."

Gwydion's face was quiet, his voice touched with the merest whisper of stiffness. "None but what you yourselves ask for."

Guy was still not persuaded, even though he had been the one to do the asking. "You can fight, too? While you're doing—that?"

"My brother can," Gwydion said.

"Then do it," Guy said all at once, gasping as if he had run a race. "Do what you can. Help us get out of this trap."

This trap into which he had led them. Gwydion bowed his head a fraction and rose to go. No one ventured to stop him.

Aidan stayed until the council wound down. He found Gwydion in front of their tent, lying on a pallet, staring sleepless at the stars. He did not turn when Aidan hunkered down beside him, but said, "They didn't decide much."

"They never do." Aidan wriggled. He had been in mail for two nights now; it was past being uncomfortable and into excruciating. Gwydion, reckless, was down to his shirt and braies. He looked cool and comfortable and almost clean.

Aidan decided abruptly. He shed his chausses and his coif, and after a moment the mail-coat and the sweat-sodden gambeson. The air was heaven on his skin. He wished futilely and desperately for a bath; though if he had had one he would have drunk it dry. He settled for a scrubbing with a twist of grass, and the clean shirt and breeches which Aimery, owl-eyed but wide awake, brought him. The boy stayed when Aidan lay down, crouched by the tent pole with his chin on his knees. Aidan let him be. He would sleep soon enough.

"If your patience weren't a legend already," Aidan said, "tonight it would be. What kept you from blasting that idiot where he sat?"

"Nothing," said Gwydion. "That's why I left. Am I a fool, do you think? Should I have stayed and given my temper its head?"

"No," Aidan said after a moment. "No, you were wise, as you always are. And clear-sighted. There really is a warding on the enemy: I searched it out while the barons wrangled. It's subtle. How did you find it?"

"By being a witch," Gwydion answered. "Hunting for ways to win us free of this. The sultan is better warded than Guy ever was."

"Yes," Aidan said. He was silent for a while. Stretching his power; touching the edge of a ban, a dome of air and darkness over the armies of the enemy. Then at last he said it. "I know who it is."

"So do I."

Aidan rubbed his hand over his face, tugging viciously at his beard. "Of course she would be there. I'm here, aren't I? She was fighting for Islam before we were even born."

His eyes blurred. He blinked, furious. He had no water to spare for tears. "And I didn't know. I didn't—even —know."

Gwydion held him till he finished shaking. It was more shock than grief. And joy, though that was mad. She was there. Fighting for the enemy, hating him, but there. Maybe he would die; maybe she would kill him. But he would see her again.

"God," Aidan said. "God, God, God." He pulled out of his brother's arms. "I wish we hadn't gone prowling. Then we'd still be merely desperate, instead of hopeless."

"There is hope," said Gwydion.

"I don't know if I want any." Aidan flung back his head. The stars stared down. He glared back. "Damn her. Damn both of us."

Around midnight, as the camp lay in uneasy sleep, the enemy moved. More sorties; more flights of arrows. None found a target. None was meant to. For with them came a clamor to wake the dead. Trumpets; kettledrums; the clatter of the nakers that were the sultan's alone; the blare of brass and the shrilling of pipes, and all the hideous tumult of the Saracens' battle music. And voices with it, war-cries, shouts and mockery and the ululation of the faithful: *Allah-il-allah! Allahu akbar!*

They swept in upon the camp; they brought the Christians to their feet, swords in hand, braced for battle. And then abruptly they stopped. No attack came. The camp subsided slowly, shaking with reaction. Horses needed to be soothed, men to be bullied back to what rest they could muster.

Just as they settled, it came again. Again they were beaten out of sleep; again they braced for an assault that never came. Again the enemy ended it and withdrew.

And so it went, all night long. Aidan's senses, keen as they were, were in torment. After the third feint he gave up any hope of sleep and struggled into his armor again, hating the way it weighed upon him. It did not stink as a human man's would; but that was little comfort when everyone about him, except for Gwydion, was human and filthy and reeking to high heaven.

By the dark before dawn, the Franks were too exhausted even to stir when the enemy burst shrilling out of the night. Saladin let them be after that. He had gained what he wanted, which was to add sleeplessness to thirst and hunger. What little rest they could manage between the end of his last sortie and sunrise was hardly enough to go to battle on.

When the sun was full up, promising a day as scorchingly hot as the one before it, the trumpets roused the Franks to choke down what they could of dry rations, and to arm and break camp. Word went among the commanders: They would try again for the wells at Hattin.

The army gathered together as well as it might on the broken ground. The ridge was empty of Saracens. The plain was ringed with them, camped at their ease in their bright tents, idling about and, no doubt, laughing at the poor driven sheep of unbelievers.

The trumpets sang the command to march. The army seemed to take life and strength from the sound and from the prospect of battle, with water to be won at the end of it. They took the formation which was most deadly to the enemy: a shield-circle of infantry, bristling with spears, and the cavalry within, to be flung like a dart when it was most needed. Like one great, deadly creature, they began to move.

Saladin was waiting for them, a wall of men and horses athwart the way to the wells. The Franks barely paused. They came on at a steady pace, step by step.

The clamor that had driven them mad all night, began again under the sun: a booming of drums, a braying of trumpets, a skirling of pipes. The great line of Islam began to move. The center held its place with the sultan in the back of it, settled on an eminence with a canopy over him, ruling the battle. The wings closed upon the Franks, with a hail of arrows before it and a thunder of hoofs and the cries of men and horses.

The Franks ground to a halt. Arrows gave way to flung spears and then to swords, as the Saracens closed in. The infantry dug in their heels, standing like stones in the millrace of Islam.

The first to reach them was one from the very center: a man alone, all undefended, in the yellow coat of the sultan's mamluks. He came singing, gloriously reft of his senses, emptying his quiver and then flinging his spears and then, with a clear cry to his God, drawing his sword and falling on the line. A spear spitted his horse. A Christian sword hewed him down.

His army descended, howling for revenge.

The knights, penned in, broiling slowly in the sun, were like to go mad with idleness. The Master of the Templars sent again and again to the king. *A charge,* he

begged. *Let us make a charge.* Again and again the king
sent back: *No. Wait. You'll have your time.*

The sun crawled up the sky. The footsoldiers fought
against wave after wave of Saracens. Each broke, poured
round the army's flanks, sought gaps and hollows,
flooded past the rear and then away, back to their sultan
on his hill. A full third of his army, his own picked men,
had not fought at all. They rode their horses up and
down, easily, or leaned on their spears, or drank often
and deeply from flasks which were refilled as often as
they emptied.

Some of the Franks had hoarded wine from God
knew where. It was potent without water to thin it, and
the more so for that they were so dry, but those who had
it were stronger than those who did not.

Horses could not drink wine. Aidan feared for his
mounts: the grey that carried him on the march, the bay
that was his battle charger, the remounts in their herd
with the others under the heaviest guard. He held the
grey's bridle himself, waiting out the battle, while
Aimery stood with the bay. Both were livelier than some:
they nosed at the sere brown grass, and nibbled at it
without pleasure.

His men were in good order. None of his foot had
gone down, though there were wounds. Gwydion tended
those under a tent made of spears and someone's cloak.
The field surgeon, passing by, had taken a long look at
the king's ministrations, crossed himself, and gone away
muttering. Men who came under the Elvenking's hand
did not come away simply dosed or bandaged. They
came away healed, able to fight unless the wound had
been very bad, and then all they needed was sleep and—
worse—water. Gwydion had a skin of wine for those,
which he was rationing out as tenderly as if it had been
the elixir of life.

Someone tried to steal it. Once. Gwydion looked at
him. Simply looked. He fled empty-handed.

Aidan glanced back. Aimery's face was white under
the dirt, but he was steady. This was his first battle. He
shied a little when a stray arrow went over; more than

that, he did not do. Aidan smiled at him. His answering smile was more a grimace, but brave enough.

There was little enough to smile at. The infantry, driven mad with thirst and beaten down by wave on wave of fighting, broke at last and ran. The cavalry stood alone, stripped bare. Knights and mounted sergeants scrambled together, snatching horses, goaded by drum and trumpet. *Form ranks. Hold the line.*

It was meant for the foot as for the horse; but the foot had reached their limit. They would die if they had no water. Water was before them, a whole blue sea of it. They clumped together at the run, heedless of rank or file, scrambling and struggling up one of the Horns of Hattin. The king's trumpets bellowed at them, commanding them to come back, form ranks, defend the horsemen. There on the hill, ringed in Saracens, they threw down their weapons and would not fight.

Still the king would not allow a charge. The lion of battle was become a hedgehog, a tight, bristling circle. Aidan worked his way to the outside of it, though the knights were bidden to hold back, to let the Turcopoles and the light horsemen defend them as the infantry had refused to do. He had had enough of waiting. His foot-soldiers had held, but they were pitifully few; he ordered them back to guard the remounts. They went none too reluctantly, but keeping their heads up, for they were no cowards and now the world knew it.

Aidan's mamluks, set on guard where the foot-soldiers had been, were hardly delighted to spend their arrows from a standstill, but it was better than nothing. At Aidan's command they took turn and turn about: one of a pair on guard with lance couched against the onrush of the enemy, the other sending forth a volley of arrows; then the lancer would reach for his bow and the archer lower his lance, and so they spelled one another, sparing their strength as best they could.

The sun touched the summit of noon. The enemy stopped, every man of them, and drew back, and bowed to pray. The latest of Ridefort's messengers went past, looking heartily sick of his round. Even before he reached the king's banner where it was set in the center, a trumpet rang.

Raymond already had his command. He had not passed it to the Rhiyanans, or to the lord of Millefleurs. Even without them he had tenscore knights, and among them Balian of Ibelin and Reynaud Prince of Sidon, who shared his name if not his spirit with the lord of Kerak. They were ahorse already, straining at the leash. The trumpet's note had hardly begun when they moved. The infantry who guarded the van folded back with an audible sigh. The knights sent up a shout. "Holy Sepulcher!"

The charge was always slow at first, as the horses found their feet, as the men fell into place, as the sheer weight of them transmuted from hindrance into unstoppable force. The enemy knotted and tangled before them, scrambling up from prayer, snatching at bridles, sweeping out swords. Their commander's banner was one which Aidan knew well: a pair of trousers, gold on white. It was nothing to smile at. Taqi al-Din, brother's son to Saladin, was a great lord of Islam, a king indeed, and high in the sultan's counsels. His troops were mamluks of his royal uncle, nigh a thousand strong under yellow banners, and for each company its own pennant: scarlet, blue, green, black, white, russet.

Proud though they were in their golden coats, they folded back before the power of the charge. But they took toll with their archery, and it was high. Aidan saw knight after knight go down, killed or taken.

Raymond, under the banner of Galilee, broke free. A bare handful of men rode with him.

He reined in his horse. There was no telling his expression behind coif and helmet; no reading his mind through the wards that were on the infidels.

He sat for a long moment while the enemy gathered to strike. He spurred forward. But they were too many. They drove him back with the sheer weight of their numbers.

His horse stumbled and nearly fell. He hauled it up. That, it seemed, was omen enough, and warning. With the last remnant of his knights, he spurred north and west, away to water and safety, out of the battle and the defeat.

For it was that. The infantry was gone beyond re-trieving: the enemy had mounted their hill and slain or taken them as effortlessly as a child herds geese in a meadow. Tenscore knights were lost or fled; and more from the rear, Templars who, under cover of Raymond's diversion, broke for freedom. Of an army of thirty thou-sand, a bare two thousand were left: knights and light horses and a dozen mamluks against a hundred thousand infidels.

That was no wind to yield to any enchanter's asking. Aidan tried with all the power that was left in him. The wind only laughed. It was at the enemy's backs, blowing out of the west, a hot blast in the Christians' faces. Now the Saracens made it hot indeed: they kindled torches, and as the Franks looked on appalled, set fire to the grass.

The wind seized the flames and drove them toward the ranks. But worse than the flames were the clouds of bitter smoke. Sun, fire, smoke, battle, wrung every drop of water from them. Their eyes could not even weep. They coughed, convulsing in pain, trying still to fight, to keep their horses from running mad with terror of the fire, to hold the line their king had set for them. He was in the heart of it, fighting as valiantly as they: never for him the lordly isolation of the sultan, to stand above the battle and rule it as one who did not himself take part in it, save when his position itself was attacked.

The fire broke the strength of all too many men. A handful of them abandoned the ranks and rode toward the Saracens, gasping out the words of faith: " 'There is no god but God, and Muhammad is the Prophet of God!' "

Even Aidan was appalled. It was one thing to accept Muslims in one's army. It was another altogether to des-ert in the middle of a battle and turn apostate.

"Cowards," said Conrad, his sweet singer's voice thinned to a dry rasp. His quiver was empty, his spears all cast and lost. He was down to his sword, and giving a good account of himself. They all were, all Aidan's faithful infidels.

The Saracens did not take so dim a view of converts. They took in the deserters, clear for the Christians to see, and gave them water, poured it over them if they wanted it, and led them away to shade and food and blessed rest.

No one weakened so far as to follow them. Guy had them moving at last, step by bitterly contested step, up the double-horned hill of Hattin. There, with the fire still burning its way toward them and the wind blowing the smoke in their faces, but the enemy stymied for the nonce by the steepness of the hill, they made their stand. Guy was in their center among the Templars and the Hospitallers. The knights spread out on either side. The order was out: *Charge at will. Fight as you may.*

They charged. Out, down the hill with its slope lending them weight and speed, into the horde of the enemy, hewing, straining, pelted with arrows. Driving them back clear to the sultan under his canopy, close enough to see him standing under it with a youth beside him, his son in a golden coat, and to see how he was ashen pale with fear for his victory, his hand a fist in his beard; but never quite breaking through the guard about him. Losing the horse more often than the man, as often to the treacherous, knife-edged, hoof-rending stones beneath the grass as to the Saracens; but once the man was down, he was lost, inundated with infidels, however hard he fought, however bitterly he cursed his enemies. But if he could escape, if his horse took a small wound or none, or if he could seize another before the enemy pulled him down, he spurred away, hacking through an ever-growing thicket of swords, spears, yelling faces, back to the hill and almost-quiet and vanishingly brief safety.

Aidan's bay went down in the second charge, but Aimery was there—God love the boy, was he mad?— and he was on a leggy roan and leading a bow-nosed chestnut that Aidan had never seen before. God still had a soft heart for fools: the child had a sword but no hand free to wield it, yet no one had touched him or so much as threatened him.

Aidan blew the hunting horn that he resorted to in

battles, the quick scatter of notes that cried, *To me! To me!*

They came as they could, the Kipchaks both on one staggering pony, Conrad clinging to Raihan's stirrup, Arslan bloody to the elbows but never a scratch on him, and after him the others.

Three only. Dildirim, Andronikos, Janek the Circassian with his ruddy beard. Four were dead. Shadhi, Tuman, Zangi, Bahram. Janek was badly hurt: he swayed in the saddle and would have fallen, had not Conrad come round to hold him.

They struggled back up the hill. The king, between his own charges, had ordered tents pitched: his great scarlet pavilion and two others close by it. One was full of wounded, and Gwydion was in it, spending his strength in a battle no less potent than that with swords and bows, though far more to his liking.

In the third charge Aidan kept his horse and drove clear up to the guard about the sultan. For a moment, as he locked in fierce combat with a pair of mamluks, his eyes met the sultan's. Saladin's widened more in surprise than in fear; then, with a start, in recognition. Then the tide of the army rolled in, roaring, and flung Aidan back. Dildirim was fallen and trampled, and Andronikos hewn by a mamluk's axe, and Janek who had broken Aidan's command to ride again after Gwydion nigh spent himself to heal the spear-thrust in his side, this time took a lance in the heart, and there was no healing that.

They brought the bodies back, high though it cost them, and counted who was left. Five mamluks, none with a whole skin. Aidan, looking as if he had washed in blood, but only a little of it was his own. Of thirty Rhiyanan knights, a mere dozen lived to half-fall from their spent and staggering horses.

This, Aidan knew, was how the damned dwelt in hell. The sun a hammer on the anvil of their heads. Thirst a fire in their throats. Smoke a dagger in their lungs. A sea of screaming infidels, inexhaustible, and they dwindling one by one. He could not even weep for his dead. All the tears were burned out of him.

The Bishop of Acre was dead. With him had fallen

the soul of the kingdom: the True Cross in its casing of gold and pearls and jewels, bound about with silver. The infidels took it and hacked at it, until the sultan sent his guards to rescue it. They nailed it to a lance and set it up by the sultan's post. There it glittered, broken and dishonored, while the Saracens hounded the knights to their deaths.

A scarce tithe of them were left, of all who had ridden to the battle: sevenscore and ten about the king's tent on the height, fighting like men in a trance. The enemy pressed them harder, harder, harder.

The smaller tents fell. Gwydion escaped the one which held the wounded, afoot and raging, shieldless, helmetless, whirling his sword about his head. His fury drove the enemy back, but they were too many. They simply evaded him and turned on the knights about the king. Gwydion hacked his way through them to Aidan's side, wound his hand in his brother's stirrup, and there took his stand. His mind was pure white, like the sun on snow. Whatever he struck, he killed.

But he was fresh only to this battle, and he was living flesh, though never human. His fury alone could not make his arm wield the sword again and again against an enemy who never tired, never paused, never granted him respite. They wanted the king's tent. They wanted the King of Jerusalem. They were victorious, and they wanted to end it, but these madmen of Franks would not, could not know when they were beaten.

There was no room for a last charge. They tried. They bunched together with their backs to the tent. Aidan was knee to knee with the king himself. Their eyes met, blind alike, stunned alike; then parted. They set spurs to their horses' sides.

But the enemy was too thick, the press too heavy. They were hemmed in.

A shrilling horde broke past them and toppled the tent. Now even their backs were beset.

They stopped in the circle of infidels. Their horses' heads hung low; the beasts' knees trembled with exhaustion. Their own heads were no higher, their knees no stronger. Without word or signal, but raggedly together, they slid to the ground. Most of them could not even stand. They sank down, swords still in hands, and lay there, not caring if they lived or died.

The battle was ended. The Kingdom of Jerusalem was lost. Salah al-Din Yusuf, al-Malik al-Nasir, the king and the defender, the rectifier of the Faith in the House of Islam, was victorious.

21

The sultan pitched his tent on the hill which he had taken, and ordered his army to make camp, as any good general should do after a battle. Then he had Guy de Lusignan and Reynaud de Châtillon brought to him in his pavilion. He spoke first to Reynaud, through his interpreter for Reynaud knew no Arabic. "So, sir. Do you repent now of your treachery against us?"

Reynaud was exhausted almost beyond endurance, filthy, blood-stained, and bone-dry, but he had lost none of his bandit arrogance. "If what I have done is treachery, then what is that but the practice of kings?"

Saladin's eyes glittered, but he made no response. He called instead for his servant, who brought a cup of water cooled with snow and offered it to Guy. The king stared at it blankly for a stretching moment, as if at a dream of paradise. Then, trembling, he took it. He tried to drink slowly, but he was human and no saint, and he had had no water since the morning before. When half the cup's contents had flowed deliriously down his throat, he caught himself with a start. His eyes met Reynaud's. The lord of Kerak watched him as a starving man watches a king at the feast. Guy passed him the cup.

The sultan smiled. It was not an expression to set any man's mind at rest, still less a king whom he had vanquished. He spoke in Arabic. The interpreter said, "My sultan says, 'Say to the king: You, not I, have given him to drink.' "

That was to say, once a captor had fed his captive and given him to drink, that captive would be allowed to live. But Saladin would grant Reynaud no such grace.

There was a silence. Neither Frank moved to break it. The sultan gestured. His mamluks beckoned to the king. He hesitated, eyes on Reynaud, but the soldier-slaves were firm, if not disrespectful. Guy had no choice but to let them lead him to the outer chamber.

When he was gone, the sultan faced Reynaud. "You may still live," said Saladin, "treacherous dog though you be. You have but to accept Islam."

Reynaud laughed, and spat in the sultan's face.

Saladin's smile was even more terrible than before. He drew his sword. Reynaud did not, even yet, believe that he was in danger. It had always been his failing, to know that he was invincible. The fine Indian steel pierced him where he stood.

Saladin stood over the body. His face was calm, at rest. "Kings are not wont to murder one another," he said to the dead man. The eyes stared up at him, wide and astonished. "But you," said Saladin, "went beyond any king's endurance. I swore a sacred oath that I would slay you. I, at least, am a man of my word."

Aidan knew nothing of any of that. He had never lost a battle in his life, never been taken captive by any mortal man, never known what it was to be stripped of his weapons and driven stumbling through the camp of the enemy. He fought to stay near to his own people: his brother, his mamluks, the pitiful handful of Rhiyanans who yet lived. He could not see Aimery anywhere, nor Ranulf, who should have been in the center with the king. But Guy was gone, and Reynaud, taken away God and the sultan knew where; and in this camp under the bright shield of the wards his power was the faintest of flickers.

They were herded to an open space where the grass was burned but had stopped smoldering. Saracens ringed it, making a great deal of noise. All of them jeered. Some kicked or spat as the Franks were driven past.

There in the open they were made to stand. They were not allowed to lie down. Any who tried was kicked and bullied up again. Their guards did not keep the weaker from leaning on the stronger.

Aidan held to his brother, who seemed like one in a trance. He looked quite sane if utterly worn, but his mind was still a white absence. He had gone very far to heal those who could be healed, then fought with all that was in him. There was too little of him left to do more than go where he was made to go, and stand where he was told to stand.

Aidan's mamluks had had the sense to rid themselves of their turbans. With all the stains and ravages of battle and thirst that were on them, and in the company of battle-wearied knights, even Arslan's indubitably Seljuk face was hard to distinguish; and that might well have saved him. He, like Raihan, could have been a Turcopole, and Conrad looked pure Norman, and the Kipchaks had little enough beard and little enough stature to be taken for boys, if no one looked too closely at their faces.

No one came close at all. They were to be forgotten, it seemed, left in the sun until it killed them. It would not take much longer. Aidan was dimly surprised to see how much daylight was still left. Two hours, or three. This day had already been years long.

At the end of the line one of the knights went down and lay unmoving. Another dropped beside him. The guards closed in, spearbutts raised to goad or strike.

Gwydion was gone from Aidan's side. That was the blur of him, leaping toward the fallen man, the kneeling boy, the guards with their spears and their cold eyes. Aidan sprang after him.

It was Ranulf down, Aimery with him. The boy tried to shield his father from the guards' spears. Gwydion fell on the foremost. The snap of the man's neck was hideously distinct.

Spears whipped round. Gwydion laughed, light and mad. The guards cried out. Their weapons writhed in their hands, raising fanged heads to strike. The Saracens

flung them away in horror. They fell as plain lifeless
wood, but their heads were gone.

Gwydion left the dead guardsman and turned back to
Ranulf. Aimery's face turned up toward him, white under dirt and blood and soot. It was not grief, not horror,
not even fear. It was rage as pure as Gwydion's own.
"They killed him," the boy said. His voice was perfectly
calm.

Ranulf was not quite dead. But he was beyond Gwydion's strength to heal. A great torn wound in his thigh
had drained his life away; there were other wounds on
him, and ribs broken where a mace had caught him.
How he had lived this long, walked this far, only God
knew. That Aimery had done his best to carry him was
clear to see.

Gwydion could do no more than ease his pain, give
him the illusion of water in his burning throat, let him
see that his son was with him. He could not speak, but
he smiled at the boy. He had fought well; he had seen
that his son was brave, and would make a man. He was
content. He went softly into the great dark, with no fear
at all.

Aidan stood guard over them, little need though
there was of that. Even Saladin's warriors were not about
to pick a quarrel with a lord of the afarit.

Aidan's mamluks had followed him, unmolested for a
miracle, and the Rhiyanans stumbling after. They made
an honor guard for Ranulf's body. The one who still had
a whole cloak, Gwydion's squire Urien, spread it over
the knight. Aimery raised a hand as if to protest, but
then he stilled.

Aidan did not like the look of him. But there was
nothing in this place or this circumstance to like. The
boy was quiet, at least, and stood by Aidan when he was
bidden, even let Aidan rest an arm about his shoulders.

It was not long after that, that the sultan came out of
his tent. A mamluk went before him with a spear, and on
it a head which all of them knew. Reynaud de Châtillon,
the reiver of Kerak, had broken his last compact with
the infidel. King Guy followed, head up, walking free,
but his eyes were haunted.

The line of knights stiffened as the sultan approached. The warrior monks, Templars and Hospitallers, glanced at one another and, in one concerted motion, turned their backs on him. The guards would have forced them about, but Saladin shook his head. Aidan heard him in strangely doubled fashion: first in Arabic, then in the interpreter's *langue d'oeil.* "They know what hope they have here." He raised his voice slightly. "Any of you who wishes to accept Islam, may do so and live."

None of them moved. Someone near Aidan was trying not to laugh. It was one of the Kipchaks. Aidan hissed at him to be still.

The sultan was too far away to hear. He called out his sufis and his men of religion, one for each Templar and Hospitaller, each armed with a sword. Some of them looked as if they hardly knew which end to hold, but they were all alight with holy zeal.

"Now," the sultan said.

The warrior monks fell. Some did not fall easily: poorly or weakly smitten, or roused to resistance at the end. Those the guards finished off, as one gives the grace-stroke to a fallen animal. Only the Grand Master of the Temple was spared at the sultan's command, with two hulking Nubians holding him in his place while his brothers in the cross died. His curses were inventive, and quite surprising in a man of God. The interpreter conveyed some of them to Saladin, who was grimly amused. "Take that one away," he said to the Nubians, "and see that he is kept from mischief. He is a fouler dog than any of those who followed him, but he is a prince of his people; and a prince owes courtesy to a prince."

Gerard de Ridefort clearly did not think so, but he was not strong enough to escape his captors, still less to tear out the sultan's throat. He was still roaring maledictions as they carried him off.

That left the knights of Outremer, a pitiful straggling few, too worn with exhaustion even to beg for mercy. They could only stand, and wait mute for what would come.

Saladin bade the great lords be led forward. It was

shocking to see how few they were. Besides King Guy, there were only Amalric his brother, and Humphrey of Toron, and the Marquis of Montferrat, and Joscelin de Courtenay, Count of fallen Edessa, and a bare handful of lesser lords. Gwydion would not go; Aidan would not go without him. Their knights and their mamluks stirred, growling softly. One of the guards, his patience exhausted, raised his fist.

"No."

Clear, that voice, and oddly sexless. It was not deep enough for a man's, but for a woman's it was very low. The one who owned it came from behind the sultan. A young emir, it seemed, in a coat of amber silk over mail, and a helmet with a turban wound about it, and long Turkish braids; but that face was never a Turk's, white as ivory and carved as pure as any face in Persia. There was no beard on it, nor would one ever grow there. Though not, as the army might think, because the warrior was a eunuch.

Aidan had been strong enough until then. Numb, yes, and powerless, and worn to a rag, and desperate for water; but he could keep his feet, he could do what he must, he could will himself not to think.

Now he felt all the strength drain out of him. Only Gwydion's arm kept him from falling.

"No," said Morgiana. "Let them be."

She had some power here, and ample presence. She was obeyed. The sultan, occupied in winnowing barons from plain knights, paused to glance down the line. What he saw made him hand the task to his son, who was close by him and more than pleased to take it, and with but a pair of mamluks, stride toward the knot of Franks and Saracens.

Saladin looked well, Aidan thought distantly. Older, yes; that was inevitable. He was nigh fifty years old. His beard was still black, still trimmed neatly, close to his jaw. He was still slender, still quick on his feet, with fine eyes in a face somewhat thickened with age. The scar of an Assassin's blade seamed one cheek; the years marked it more deeply, and the asceticism to which he was given, king of kings though he was. He was not in the plain black robes he preferred, but then this was war, and he had, for that, to look a king.

What Saladin saw could hardly be as pleasant: two battered and filthy knights with the same face, a boy whose eyes on him flashed hate, a bare handful of warriors who tried, even weaponless, to guard them.

Five of those warriors made the sultan's eyes narrow. "So, sirs. You're still with him."

Aidan spoke before one of them could do it and earn a spear in the vitals. "They're still with me," he said. "A better gift I've seldom had, nor ever one more faithful."

"Faith," said Saladin. "Yes. They are Muslims. How came they to fight against their own people?"

"We fought for our prince," said Timur, always the one to open his mouth when anyone else would have known better. "You gave us to him, my lord. You must have known what would come of it."

"As you must have known what the price would be," Saladin said.

Timur nodded, but his eyes were fearless. "We're glad you won, my lord. We're good Muslims, after all. But we had to fight for the master you gave us."

Saladin looked him up and down, then each of the others in turn. "Five of you," he said. "Seven dead. That must be grievous to bear."

"They are in Paradise," Timur said steadily.

"For fighting Muslims?"

"For fighting for their prince."

Saladin almost smiled. "You haven't lost your impudence," he said. He paused. "Your prince is beaten now and in my power. Will you come back to serve me?"

They glanced at one another. Timur, for once, gave precedence to Arslan. The captain said, "With all respect, my sultan, no. We belong to our prince. We can serve no other master."

"I was your master once," Saladin said, dangerously soft.

"We are his now," said Arslan.

Saladin turned the fire of his glance on Aidan. "You would have refused them once. Will you relinquish them?"

"Will it save their lives?" Aidan asked.

Saladin nodded.

"We won't go," Timur said.

It was Conrad who added, "We'd rather be dead and yours, my lord, than alive and any other man's. Not to insult my lord sultan. If we could serve any other master, it would be he. But we cannot."

"Loyal servants indeed," said Saladin. He seemed torn between anger and admiration. "Your master will have to ransom you if he wishes you to live."

"I shall ransom them," Morgiana said. "All of them."

Saladin turned to her, not startled, not entirely, but somewhat disconcerted. "All? I count a dozen here, drawn together like an army in ambush. One of them is a royal prince. Another, if I am not mistaken, is a king. Can you pay a king's ransom, my lady of the afarit?"

"Set it, and I shall pay it," she said calmly. "The only grudge you bear them is that they fought under an idiot. They could hardly do otherwise, being idiots themselves when it comes to the swearing of oaths."

"I won't have you—" Aidan began hotly.

A force like a hand stopped his tongue. He was in no state to defeat it, although he raged against it. Morgiana never spared him a glance. "I stand hostage for their honor," she went on, placidly giving her wealth and her life away. "I will answer for them, and pay the ransom you require."

Amusement conquered anger in the sultan's face. He had always found the afarit highly entertaining, even when they terrified him. "I give you their lives," he said, "to do with as you will. Of ransom I ask but a token. Their oaths, given singly and sincerely, that they will not again take up arms against me."

He was smiling as he said it, but there was no laughter in his eyes. If they refused, they would very likely die. Saladin was a knight and a gentleman, but he was also a Muslim and a king. He had sworn holy war against all of Christendom.

"I can swear that oath," Gwydion said, startling them. His voice was low, as if he spoke in a dream. "You will live to take Jerusalem. You will even hold it, and face the Crusade that will come. But you are a mortal man, and when your days are done you will die. I will swear never to fight against you. I will not swear never again to raise my sword against Islam."

Saladin paled a little under the bronze of sun and wind and years of war. "You are a seer, then, lord king."

Gwydion's eyes turned to the sultan. They were the color of steel in the sun, seeing clear through him, to what, only Gwydion knew. "I am nothing but what God has made me. I will not again take arms against you, though all the kings of Europe shall raise the Crusade."

It was not an oath to comfort any man, even with his victory promised him. Saladin took no joy in it. But he accepted it as graciously as he might, as years of kingship had taught him.

The Rhiyanans followed their king, not liking it, but loyal enough, and well tamed by the battle and the defeat. Aidan was slower. It was not that he feared to be called a coward, or that he had ever intended to stay in Outremer past Michaelmas. But he did not like, ever, to be told whom he could not fight.

His mamluks would do as he did. They were no happier than he to have their sword-hands trammeled, but they were Muslims, and they had been Saladin's. It would save them grief to be forbidden to fight him or his armies.

But to take such an oath. To bind himself to what the world would perceive as cowardice. To break his given word, that he would defend the Holy Sepulcher . . .

He opened his mouth to refuse. What held his tongue, he hardly knew. Conrad's face, perhaps, bruised and bloodied. Gwydion's steel-cold eyes. Morgiana's white face, half-turned away from him.

It was for his mamluks, and for Gwydion, and—yes —for Morgiana, that Aidan bent his head and swore. He felt the lighter for it, though never the more joyful. Defeat could not be aught but bitter, however swiftly he drank it down.

Then there was only Aimery. He would not swear. "I can't," he said, though it shook him almost to the

ground. "I am of Outremer. I can't swear never to defend it again. I *can't.*"

Aidan could not be the one to break the impasse, to
compel him to swear the oath. Gwydion would not. Saladin looked at the boy and frowned. "The lion's cub
grows into a lion. Would you die, then, for the threat
that you will be when you are grown?"

Aimery swallowed hard. "Yes. Yes, I'll die. You
killed my father. You can kill me, or sell me for a slave. I
don't care. I won't unman myself to save my skin."

"You intend, my lord," said Morgiana quietly, "to
ransom the king and his barons, and such knights as
have the wherewithal. None of them will be bound to
keep his sword sheathed against you. I allow that binding for my kin and for their following, because it can do
them no harm and may teach them sense. But this will
be a knight of Jerusalem. You can kill him, or you can
ask his kin to ransom him. They will do that, my lord.
You have my word on it."

Saladin had never had much stomach for murdering
children, though men who opposed him did well to be
afraid. He looked long at Aimery, as if he would remember that tired young face. In the end he said, "I give you
into the lady's governance. Will you, in return, give me
your word of honor that you will purchase your life as I
shall determine?"

Aimery stood stiff. Clearly he thought of refusing,
but he was too sensible to do more than think it. Nor
was he so blind that he could not see how Morgiana had
won him the advantage. He was almost able to smile as
he said, "You have my word."

22

Morgiana had a tent of her own, and a handsome one it was, grand enough for an emir and looked after by servants of impeccable manners. They were not at all dismayed to be presented with a dozen Frankish captives, all of whom needed water first and urgently on the inside and then, at length, on the outside. Most of them by then were dead on their feet. They had refused to leave Ranulf lying on the field to the mercy of jackals and Saracens. With their own hands, under the eyes but not the hindrance of their captors, they had dug a grave for him. It nearly finished them. Once they had drunk all that the servants would allow, lest they sicken with too much too soon, they wanted only sleep. They were undressed and bathed like infants and laid on pallets, and left there to heal.

Gwydion was one of them. Aidan would not have taken even water until he saw his brother tended, but the servants were firm, and numerous enough to persuade him. He did not, when it came to it, need much persuasion.

Morgiana did not linger to watch. She had duties, and those were pressing: as envoy and messenger and gatherer of forces, and, even now, as guardian of the camp. She had not fought in the battle. Aidan did not know if he should take comfort from that. It might only have been that Saladin would not waste her power in mere bodily combat.

She had said no word to Aidan. Not one. He might have been but one of the dozen whom she had bargained for and won, worth no more and no less than the others. Was that what he had become to her? An enemy only, to be ransomed because it pleased her fancy? It must have made her laugh behind the walls of her mind, to hear him renounce all right to avenge the slaughter of Hattin.

Clean, fed, with a jar of water within his reach if he

should want it, he should have been in bliss. His bones ached, but that would pass. He had a wound or two, none more than a scratch, and a multitude of handsome bruises. None of that should have kept him from sleep.

He tossed on the pallet. The tent was as cool as anything could be on that furnace of a hill, with a servant swaying a fan over the sleepers, the great blade wetted down with water to cool the air—such prodigality as Aidan could not have imagined while he fought the hopeless fight. It was not shame that kept him awake, nor grief for the fall of the kingdom. That was on Guy's head; Aidan had done all that he could. The time to grieve in earnest would be later, when it would do the most good: in front of those who had stayed behind, and thereafter in the courts of Europe, when the pope preached the Crusade.

That was what Gwydion meant to do, Aidan knew. He would not break his oath, but he would not hide his head, either. What Gwydion could not do, the kings of the greater realms could. Henry of Anglia and Richard his turbulent heir and Eleanor his strong-willed queen, who for this might be willing to give up their warring against one another; Philip of Francia with his grand ambitions and his talent for intrigue; Barbarossa who was emperor of Germania and the Italies. They would avenge Hattin, if they could be persuaded to labor together. And there were few who could persuade as convincingly as Gwydion of Rhiyana.

Or, for the matter of that, as Aidan his brother. That was not why he could not sleep.

He rose. His legs cried pain; he cursed them until they muted it to a dull ache. Muslim modesty had clothed him in drawers to sleep and tried to make him take a light robe, but he would not. He brought it with him now, thought of dropping it again, put it on instead. It fit. As it ought: it was one of his own.

Night was well fallen. The camp rested, with little of the drunken revelry that would have marked a Frankish army after a great victory. Muslims on jihad, when Saladin was their commander, did not indulge in wine.

Aidan walked through the camp. He was barefoot,

but he did not care. He looked like a Saracen with his
black hair and his hawk-face, though he was taller than
most and paler than any; he was not stared at overmuch,
nor cursed for a Frank. He could very likely have taken a
horse and ridden away, and met no hindrance.

The sultan's tent stood under armed guard. Saladin
did not rest quite yet: there were wounded to see to, dead
to gather, prisoners still to dispose of. Most of the captive knights were dead. They would fetch no ransom,
and the sultan was in no merciful mood tonight. He had
commanded the slain Templars and Hospitallers to be
stripped and flung out for the jackals. It would seem fair
recompense for the trouble they had caused him, warrior
fanatics as dangerous as any *fidaï* of the Assassins.

Aidan paused in the shadow beyond the great golden
tent. Morgiana was there within, he knew as surely as
the wind in his face. Not many in the army knew what
she was. She was the sultan's servant, the eunuch from
Persia who ran his errands for him.

Aidan's power was recovering as his body rested
from fighting, or she had lowered the wards, or both. He
was aware of the camp as a presence in his mind, a hum
of human minds, the mingling of overriding instinct and
surprising intelligence that was horses, the haughty indifference of camels. The prisoners were nearly all asleep,
King Guy most deeply of all, burying grief and shame in
oblivion. Lucky man. All he had to do was beggar his
kingdom of wealth as he had of soldiery, and he was free
to fight again.

This much at least Aidan could be grateful for. He
would never again be forced to follow such an idiot of a
king.

"Baldwin," he said, soft in the dark. "Baldwin my
dear lord, thank God you never lived to see what your
sister's fancy man has done to your kingdom."

"If Baldwin had lived, this battle would never have
been fought at all."

Aidan quelled a start. Morgiana never came any
other way but out of thin air; and she always listened for
a prudent while before she showed herself.

"If Baldwin were alive," she said, "Reynaud the fox

would likely have been hunted to earth before he attacked the sultan's caravan, Count Raymond would
never have let our people over the border, and you would
never have come to Hattin."

"There would still have been a war," Aidan said.
"Who knows who would have won it? Baldwin was a
good general, but so is Saladin; and Saladin is older." He
shrugged irritably. "What use is there in what-ifs? This is
what is. You should be happy. Your side has won."

"I'm sorry it cost you so much."

Her voice was soft. It woke memories. Too many; too
painful. How very fierce she was, but how gentle she
could be.

He could see her in the gloom, a slender figure in a
turban, a pale oval of face, a green gleam of eyes. She
was not quite close enough to touch.

"What do you care what it cost me?" he demanded
roughly. "I'm alive, aren't I? You've had your chance to
gloat over me. Now I owe you another debt. How are
you going to make me pay it this time?"

"By loving me."

Her voice was hardly loud enough to hear. It stilled
him utterly.

But his anger ran deep, and it was master of his
tongue. "You left me for months without a word. You
fought in the army that defeated me. You bought my life
with an oath which will shame me for as long as men
remember it. And you expect me to fall straight into
your arms, as if none of it had happened?"

"I thought that you might try," she said. "For a beginning. To forgive me. Or is forgiveness not a Christian
virtue?"

"I'm not feeling very Christian tonight."

"No. You're not." Her tone was sharp. "It never oc-
curs to you that I might have something to forgive."

"What, that I fought against your sultan?"

She hissed as she always did when he exasperated
her. "Iblis crack your thick skull! Won't you even ask me
how many men I've bedded since I left you?"

He opened his mouth. No sound came out. He closed
it.

"The answer is none. Not one. Can you say the same?"

"My taste doesn't run to men."

She hit him. He caught her. She was warm in his grasp, snake-supple, and not fighting very hard. When Morgiana fought in earnest, she was too strong even for his strength. He drove his mind at hers. She hardened against him; then all at once she cast down the walls.

He gasped. He did not want it. But, ah God, he did. He had been a raw wound, roughly scabbed over. Now the wounds opened to the cleansing air. Now, painfully, he began to heal.

She went still in his arms. The struggle had unknotted his sash, opened his robe. She laid her head on his bare shoulder. Her heart beat hard against him. "I was deathly afraid that you would fall."

"I'm not easy to kill."

She nipped him, not gently. Her teeth were as sharp as a cat's. "Arrows don't care whose eye they pierce. Maces don't mind that the skull they split is one of ours. I couldn't guard you. Wards don't allow the warder out, any more than they allow the intruder in."

"Then why did you put them up?"

"To keep you from using power against my sultan."

"They did that."

"Of course they did. I raised them."

He shook his head ruefully. "I'd forgotten quite what you were like."

She glared from the hollow of his shoulder. "Your memory is short."

"I've been slightly distracted."

"And I haven't?" She drew back a little. Her eyes left his face, found the edge of the most impressive bruise, the one that stained his side from shoulder to hip. This hiss was one of fury. "Who did that to you?"

"We weren't introduced," Aidan said. "I killed him, I think."

"I should hope you did." She pulled his robe the rest of the way off and relieved him of his drawers. He tried to snatch at them, but her methods had nothing to do with hands. She examined every inch of him, there in the

shadow of the sultan's tent, with a council on the other
side of the wall, and a camp about them, and guards
making their rounds. He would have laughed if he had
dared.

"You have a cracked rib," she said.

"I do?"

"It's the one that stabs you every time you breathe."

"It didn't," he said. "Until you mentioned it."

"Idiot." She set her lips to his side. Warmth rayed
out from them, and pain that was almost pleasure. He
could feel the rib mending.

She straightened. Her eyes burned green in the
gloom. "Ya Allah! What would you be without me?"

"Peaceful."

"Dead of ennui." Her hand ran down his side. The
bruise ached appallingly, then warmed and flowed and
eased. Black-purple paled to sick green to yellow to his
own bloodless white. She caught her breath. She was not
the master of healing that Gwydion was, no more than
he was a master of passing from place to place in a
breath. This twofold mending taxed the limit of her gift.

Aidan caught her before she could spend it wholly,
and held her until she could stand again by herself. He
was keenly aware of her body in all its garments, and his
in none at all.

"I haven't bedded a woman since you left," he said.
"Not one."

"What, not even your Frank?"

"She's eight months pregnant," he said.

"Yes. Of course. She would not want you then.
Would she?"

He cursed himself for a tactless fool. All the warmth
that had been between them was gone. For a few words;
a jest that had cut her to the bone.

He took her hands and kissed them, cold though they
were, neither resisting nor responding. "I love you, Morgiana." He said it as if he had never known it before. "I
love no one else as I love you."

"*She* gave you a child."

"You gave me yourself."

"Her husband is dead. You can marry her now. No

one will object. She is Christian. She has lands and castles to give you. She can give you children, as I cannot."

"You don't know that!" he snapped. "Gwydion says you're like a maid just grown. You aren't ready to bear children yet. But you will be. Even I can see it in you."

But she was shaking her head, refusing to listen. "Now you resent me for buying you out of captivity yet again. I'll never be or do what you need. I'll always do the wrong thing, say the wrong words, spare nothing of your pride or your manhood. I don't know how to be a woman."

"Why would you want to be?" He tried to grip her shoulders, but she slid away. "Morgiana, stop it. If I wanted a simpering coquette I'd find myself one."

"What if you wanted a woman who is not barren?"

"You aren't."

"Then why can't I make you a child?"

"Maybe you want it too much."

She stared at him, all wide eyes and wicked temper, like a cat. A moment more, a breath drawn awry, and he would lose her.

"If you go away," he said, "I'll follow."

"You know what that does to you."

"I don't care."

"You will if you lose your dinner all over my cave in Persia."

"So don't run away to it."

"You have got to learn not to get sick when you go otherwhere. It's purely your panic that does it."

"Stay and teach me not to panic."

Her eyes narrowed. He stifled a sigh. She was solidly there again, not braced to flick herself to the other side of the world. "What makes you think I ever meant to go away?"

That was not anything he cared to answer. He said instead, "I'll forgive you. If you'll forgive me."

"Even for Hattin?"

Aidan willed his teeth to unclench. She never bought her truces cheaply, did Morgiana. "Hattin was none of your doing."

"I prevented you from preventing it."

"Out of hate for me?"

"Out of love for my Faith."

The wall of it rose between them, higher than any she could raise with power. Too high by far to leap, too sheer to scale.

But a gate—that, God willing, they could build. If she could learn to trust him again. If he could learn to rule his temper.

He held out his hand. She looked at it. Her eyes were wary: wild-beast eyes, hunting-cat eyes. Just as his hand began to fall, she caught it. "I love you," she said.

"And forgive?"

She did not answer that. But his hand was still in hers, and she had not vanished otherwhere. Forgiven, unforgiven, still he had her back. He could, for the moment, be content.

Part Four

ACRE

June–July 1187

23

Jerusalem was empty with its fighting men gone from it. There were pilgrims in plenty and townspeople as there always were, tradesmen and artisans, women and children, the old and the halt, and the lepers on the dunghills by the north gate. But there was almost no one to protect them. A few knights in the Tower of David, a company or two of guardsmen, and that was all. The rest had gone to war with the king.

The Patriarch was still there, and the pope's legate, and priests enough and to spare. The Holy City was still holy, even without swords to defend it.

Ysabel would have been happier if Aidan had been there. She hated it when he was away fighting. He might be hurt. He might even die. Then what would she do?

Akiva never admitted to worrying about his king. He spent most of his days studying, sometimes with his father to teach him, but mostly by himself. He and his father were living in the Mortmains' house: Joanna had pointed out that otherwise they would be all alone by the Dome of the Rock, with only Aidan's servants to look after them. That would not have swayed Simeon, but he looked at Joanna and decided that she needed protecting. Joanna, who knew very well what he was thinking, was careful to keep her smile behind her eyes. He took his son and moved into the room by the library and made

himself useful with the accounts, when he was not studying or praying or talking to people in the city.

Ysabel was supposed to let them be. She had lessons
of her own, and duties, and more of both since her
mother had decided that she needed reining in. But neither lessons nor duties could keep Ysabel occupied for
every moment of every day.

She liked to watch Akiva study. He would let her
into his mind and take her with him where the words
went. Strange places, sometimes. He had a secret, and a
gift. He could think of something that he had read, make
a picture of it, and it would grow out of air in front of
him. It was like Ysabel's mirror, but it was not solid.
Hands passed clear through it.

He made animals that way one day, out of a bestiary,
and Ysabel found that she could make them move. The
lion was a fine golden beast, but the unicorn had come
out wrong: a great, lumbering, armored creature the
color of a thundercloud, with a small mean eye and a
fondness for charging blindly at anything that moved.
Ysabel scowled at it where it grazed on the meadow that
was really a tabletop. "It's ugly," she said.

"It's what it wants to be." Akiva propped his elbows
on the table and set his chin in his hands. "You should
see the cameleopard. It's preposterous. All those spots,
and a neck as long as my king is tall, and the head on top
like a flower on a stalk."

She eyed him dubiously. "You're chaffing me."

"I'm not."

She was hardly convinced, but the picture was in his
mind, and it was hard to argue with that. She thought of
an animal she would much rather see; surely it was much
more probable. "Do me a gryphon," she said.

But he would not. "All I ever get is eagles," he said.

She was disappointed. He flicked his power just so;
beasts and meadow melted, and there was only the table
with its heaps of books and parchments. He closed his
eyes and sighed. "Do you know what I think? I think the
only magic there is, is ours."

She could not say that she was shocked. She had had
thoughts like that herself. But he said it, not she, and she

was nothing if not contrary. "There's the pope's letter that was what it was, and then it wasn't. What do you call that?"

"Human trickery," he said.

"Then why can't we find the humans who did it?"

"They know how to hide."

She narrowed her eyes. "Well? So how do they know?"

He shrugged.

It was a victory, but small. "We can find out," she said. "We can hunt. People don't know what we are. If the ones they do know are gone, maybe they'll stop hiding and let us see them."

"What makes you think we can see them, when Morgiana couldn't?"

Ysabel hissed, just like Morgiana, and for much the same reason. "They *knew* Morgiana would hunt them. We're nothing and nobody. All we have to do is make a snare and wait. Then if anyone thinks about the pope's letter, he'll be caught."

"Is that what Morgiana did?"

"No," said Ysabel. "She was too angry. She wanted to prowl and growl and flex her claws. But she's done it before. I watched her; I know how."

Akiva was skeptical. His king had never done anything quite so underhanded.

"Does he know how?" Ysabel wanted to know. Akiva had no answer for that.

She was not about to waste time. She took a deep breath, and emptied her mind as she had been taught. It was getting easier; or maybe need made a better pupil of her than when she did it just to please her father. She put even that thought aside and paused for a moment, clean and empty and waiting, like a bit of fresh vellum before the scribe wrote on it. In that emptiness she gathered her power. It came as her breath had a moment before, and filled her in much the same fashion, but breath was cool, and this was fire.

When she was as full as she needed to be, she made the snare. She saw it in her mind as a loop of fire-colored

cord hidden in a thicket that was this part of the mindworld, marked and baited for the pope's letter.

Someone seemed to be standing behind her. Here she
was eyes all round; she saw but did not say anything to
Akiva. She felt his interest and his unwilling admiration.
It stung him that she should be able to do something that
he could not, and she a full three years younger.

Girls learn better, she said, *and grow up faster.*

That was nothing more than the truth, but the truth
was not always what a person wanted to hear. Akiva
flicked her with an edge of his temper, just hard enough
to sting. She would have liked to sting him back, but she
had already done that just by being herself. She laughed
instead and set her snare solid, where it would stay until
it was sprung, and opened her eyes on the world that
humans called real.

Akiva looked ready to hit her. It was interesting to
watch him master himself. Obviously he had learned that
from Gwydion; just as obviously he had somewhat more
to learn. He did not mind an equal, but he hated to be
bested.

He was disgustingly glad that Nurse came just then
and dragged Ysabel away to her hour of Latin. *But,*
Ysabel said sweetly where only he could hear, *I like
Latin. It's better than being pricked at by jealous little
boys.*

"Little" was what did it. She left him speechless and
simmering and threatening revenge.

He punished her by not speaking to her for three
days, though she came every day and watched him
study. His mind was shut tight. He was better at that
than she was, which she knew already; she tried to find a
chink in the wall, but mostly she sat still and watched
him. She could read Greek or Hebrew over his shoulder
or reflected in his eyes, or however she pleased. Her father had that gift: to know any language once he saw it
written or heard it spoken. She was not as good at it as
he was, but days of sitting with Akiva had given her as
much Greek and Hebrew as she was likely ever to need.

Akiva did not know it. She was not about to tell him. He might stop reading interesting things and choose the dullest tomes he could find, just to spite her.

On the third day, when she was just about to have mercy on him and go to her Latin, something stopped her. A tugging. A tickle on the edge of her thinking. A cord closing about the leg of a small startled creature: a thought of the pope's letter.

She must have said something aloud. That was a bad habit, Aidan said; it could be dangerous where humans were. But here was only Akiva, and he stopped punishing her and shouldered in beside her, standing over the trapped thought. It had a collar about its neck, and a cord as thin as a spider's thread leading from it.

Akiva was with her, his power like a hand clasping hers. Two together were a hundred times stronger than two apart: Aidan's arithmetic, and he would know, being half of his brother. Ysabel was leader here, which was part courtesy and part necessity, since the snare was hers. She took time to firm her power, and set herself to follow the thread.

It was very thin. It wavered, sometimes almost to vanishing. It was unsteady even for a human thought, as if it tried still to hide itself; but it kept deciding that hiding was too hard, and the witches were gone, and what harm could there be in letting down its guard?

Ysabel had no name for it yet. But it had a scent, even a taste. A little too sour, a little too sweet, with a human reek on it, and the cloying stink that was greed. It hated Aidan. It wanted what he had, or what it thought he had. Riches, mostly. Power in the world. A beautiful woman. Beauty of its own, and a body that would never age or sicken or die.

The fear of death was always there in human awarenesses, even humans who were saints. In this one it was chokingly strong. It filled Ysabel; it took her breath from her. She fled it blindly, sickened, gagging on its stench.

Akiva was there, strong and clean. No fear in him. Only strength, and the scent and taste that were her own kind.

"We have him," Akiva said. "We marked him. We can find him now."

She forgot anger, fear, even disgust of the mind they had touched. "Why," she said, wondering. "We can. Morgiana couldn't do it, but we did."

"Only because Morgiana was gone," Akiva reminded her. "We still don't know who he is. Just where. What if he goes away?"

"We'll find him now, of course."

He knew she did not mean with her mind. He wavered transparently between grown prudence and young eagerness to do something solid. She settled it for herself by starting for the door. He was quick in her wake, still half minded to stop her, but she was not having any of that. What she did was her own business. He could follow or he could stay.

He followed. It took a little stealth to get out of the house: Nurse was getting ready to come in pursuit of Ysabel, and Mother was somewhat too close to the gate for comfort, going over something tedious with the porter. But the garden was empty in the heat of noon, and the garden gate was no match for a pair of witch-children.

Akiva had a hat: Jews never went anywhere without one. It was part of their religion. Ysabel did not even have a scarf to cover her hair. She would not have minded, but Akiva bought her a bit of veil in the market, that matched her dress. He would have put it on her, but she was having none of that.

She put on the veil herself, and kept her grip on the thread they were following. They were going in the right direction, toward the scents and savors of the Herb Market. It was a little slow: Jerusalem was crowded, and there was a procession in honor of a saint. Ysabel would have given much to be able to go straight, as Morgiana did, or even to fly, as Ysabel could do but dared not in front of so many humans.

While they were caught, the thread moved. Away from them; out of the Herb Market. Ysabel tried her tongue with a curse or two that she had heard from Aidan. She shocked a monk who was treading on her toes. She smiled cloyingly at him and eeled round him, back the way she had come.

Her quarry could move faster than she: he was on a clearer street, and he was in a hurry. He had an appointment with someone. There was another with him, a young person whose mind leaked like a sieve.

Ysabel almost whooped aloud. Here was just exactly what they had all been looking for. It was not the one who had stepped into her snare. It was better. Young. Disgruntled. No good at all at hiding what it was thinking.

His name was Marco. He was seventeen years old; he was from Genoa in the Italies. He remembered it very clearly indeed, having been brought to Outremer a bare year before; he pined to go back. He hated the heat and the flies; he hated the dust; he hated the constant threat of war. But worse than any of them, he hated what he did here. He was a merchant's son. He was supposed to be learning to be a merchant himself, and he loathed every part of it. He wanted to be a priest. That was all that made this country bearable: that it was so holy, and he was here, and every step was a prayer.

He was glad that they were going where they were going. His mind gave Ysabel a picture of a house near the Patriarch's, and a man in it, waiting. A monk with a thin and wizened face, grown old early even for a human man, but burning with a strong slow fire. Marco wanted that fire. He wanted the holiness he saw in this Brother Thomas, the purity of intent. *He* did not do what they all did for envy of a prince's wealth. He wanted that prince cleansed from the earth, and all his sorceries with him.

Marco was not so pure. He did not believe, quite, that those sorceries were as terrible as Brother Thomas thought them. That was Marco's failing, and not Thomas's; he was trying to overcome it. He made a picture in his mind, in blurry human fashion, of someone whom he called Prince Aidan. It was not Ysabel's father. It was too tall and too menacing and too much like a picture Ysabel had seen that came from Egypt, of a man with a falcon's head. The picture blurred and shifted. It had a sword in its hand and fire coming from its eyes, and a terrible, booming voice. It looked like a devil out of a monk's nightmare.

What Marco was trying not to remember was how the real Aidan had seemed to him. Frightening, yes, but as a stallion is, or a leopard: because he was so dangerous and so unpredictable, and so beautiful. Marco wanted to hate him. Marco also wanted to fall down and worship him.

They often hate what they long for most. Akiva was with her, watching as she watched, though keeping half of himself for walking through the human city.

Humans are strange, Ysabel said. Marco made her head ache. She clung to him out of sheer stubbornness. He was not thinking about the pope's letter, but even if he had been, he would not know where it was. No more would his father. He was very sure of that. But Brother Thomas knew. Brother Thomas was the one who had done it.

Ysabel had to stop and gather in her power, or it would flame itself all over Jerusalem. She was almost caught up with the ones she followed. They had gone into the house.

Into nothingness.

She reeled. They were gone utterly between one step and the next. There was not even a hint of them left.

"Wards," Akiva said in her ear. He looked as white and shaken as she felt. The street was crowded; they moved out of the jostling and cursing into the lee of a doorway.

"Wards," Akiva said again. "As strong as I've ever seen. But I've never seen wards quite like these. Can you hear the buzzing behind them?"

She could. It set her teeth on edge. She could almost have thought that the buzzing had words in it: a ceaseless, droning monotone, repeating nonsense over and over. *Hic haec hoc haec hoc haec hic haec. . . .*

She tore herself out of the trap. Her people's wards were like glass, or like walls of light. They repelled, gently but inexorably. A touch slid off them. These sucked one in, tried to make one think as they thought, round and round and round.

"I don't think we should stay here," Akiva said. His voice was faint. He was quite unabashedly afraid.

She set her chin and her will. "We have to. How can we know, otherwise?"

"We can tell Prince Aidan when he comes back. Or Lady Morgiana. They'll know what to do."

Ysabel shook her head stubbornly. "That's cowardice."

"You can call it that if you like. I don't want my mind undone. I'm too young, Ysabel. I haven't got all my strength yet."

He was talking about Ysabel, too; and not hiding it very well. That was how much these wards had shaken him: they had made him forget how to build the wall about his own mind. She was obstinate, he thought, just to be contrary.

Which was true, and which stung. "All right then," she said angrily. "Be a coward. I'm going into that house."

His breath caught. "You can't."

"I can."

He seized her, which he had never done before, and shook her so hard that her teeth rattled. Then he let her go. "You can be stupid," he said with temper to match hers, but bottled up, held down hard, until it was absolutely quiet. "You can be as much of an idiot as you could ever want to be. But not here. Not at your father's expense."

She stared at him. There were words in her, but they were too many. She could not find one that would do.

"Your father," he said, striking at her with it. "Think of him for a moment, if you can. Suppose you go to that house. Suppose, by the devil's luck, you get in. What do you do then? You won't be able to use your power. You can't hide for long. The one who raised the wards will catch you. He'll know what you are. He'll hold you just exactly the way he holds the pope's letter, where your father will never be able to find you. What will it do to him to lose you as well as his lady? Have you even stopped to think of that?"

She had not. "They're priests. They won't hurt me."

"Do they need to? They can hold you. They can snare you with their wards. Then they can use you against your father."

"They won't know. How can they? I'm just a girlchild, sneaking about where I shouldn't."

"All they have to do is look at your eyes."

That was brutal, and it stopped her cold. She looked at Akiva. His eyes were so dark that the difference did not show at all. Until he shifted, and they flared.

She could not hide even as well as that. Not without power to help her. They would see, no matter what she did, and know. Then they would have everything they needed to break the prince and his kin.

"But we have to do something!" she cried.

"We wait," Akiva said. "We watch. We know who they are now; we can tell our kin."

"No," she said. "Not them. Not yet. It's too much explaining, for nothing. When my father comes back . . ."

Akiva did not agree at first, but then he thought about it. "We can't do anything until he comes, after all," he said. "Our human kin will only fret, and want to know how we did it, and probably punish us." He nodded, deciding. "We wait and we watch, and we keep quiet."

"And if it turns out that we can do anything, we do it."

Akiva opened his mouth, closed it. "If it's sensible, and unavoidable. Only that."

"Of course," Ysabel said. She meant it. Mostly.

He looked hard at her. After a moment he shrugged and sighed. He was learning, was Akiva.

24

Joanna had had enough of Jerusalem. She liked it not too badly when everyone was there and court was in session and there was more to do than go over and over the same fruitless maunderings. Now there was not even a caravan to lighten the monotony. Every intelligent caravan master was avoiding the Kingdom of Jerusalem since Saladin had raised the jihad.

A woman as pregnant as she was should properly be so deep in herself and her baby that she hardly noticed the world at all. Joanna had never been a very proper woman. She was losing sleep, she was losing her desire to eat, she was losing her temper at anything and everything.

"Acre," she said in mid-pace, turning ponderously to face Simeon. "I'm going to Acre. Elen is there; there's still a bit of trade in and out; and I have Ranulf's estates to look after."

Simeon regarded her calmly. "Acre is rather less well defended than Jerusalem; and it's a surer target. The Saracen will strike for it if he breaks through the army."

"How can he? Saladin can't come any closer than Tiberias. They'll hold him there, or harry him up and down the border."

"One should allow for contingencies," Simeon said.

"So I shall. Acre has one escape that Jerusalem can never have: it faces on the sea."

Simeon sighed. "You will do what you will do. But if you go to Acre, the rest of us go with you."

"What if the Saracen attacks?"

"As you say. We turn to the sea."

Joanna was trapped in her own net. "So," she said. "Come with me. Show me how much trouble you'll all be. Delay me till I'm like to scream. It won't matter. I'm going to Acre."

Simeon said nothing. He had no need. Prudence was no part of Joanna's intention. All she wanted was escape.

At least it would be a different sky. And preparing for the exodus preoccupied her wonderfully. It even made her forget for whole minutes at a time that she was too heavy with pregnancy to be traveling. Not even her mother had reminded her of that. As Margaret knew all too well, Joanna would only have been the more determined to prove them wrong.

She would not try to ride. That much sense at least she had. She hated riding in a litter, but for the baby's sake she would suffer it. Lady Margaret had hired a midwife and named her Joanna's maid. Joanna, undeceived, let the woman be. It could not hurt to have her there, and it would keep people quiet. For herself, she intended to have her baby in her own house in Acre as she had had every one of the others, and at the hands of the one who had been with her for every child but Aimery: Zoe the Byzantine, whom she first met in Aleppo, and who had come back to Outremer with her and become friend as well as physician.

Zoe would have plenty to say to a woman who tramped the roads in the middle of a war, at eight months pregnant. She would have had more to say to one who trusted to any other power than her own, to bring that baby into the world.

Joanna would have reckoned that her own company of men-at-arms was enough to protect them even in as unsettled a country as this had become. Lady Margaret did not agree. She would not go; Jerusalem was her city, and she was not about to leave it. But neither would she leave her daughter to her folly. "I have found companions for you," she said the day before Joanna was to go—a good week later already than Joanna would have liked. "A small caravan from Jerusalem to Acre, with troops to guard it. Its master owes me a favor. This will be part payment of it."

Joanna could not find anything to say. Margaret was a daughter and an heir of the House of Ibrahim in

Aleppo, although her father had been a baron of Jerusalem; that, in the world of trade, made her a princess of a house of queens. She could outmaneuver and outbargain Joanna at every step of the way. That she had not offered more than token resistance to Joanna's idiocy, meant that she did not choose to; this doubled escort was small enough price to pay for her acquiescence.

Ysabel, having found her father's enemies, was hardly minded to leave them now. Who knew what they would do without anyone to watch them? But her mother was set on going to Acre. There was no budging her.

Ysabel did not learn what her grandmother was up to until the very last moment. Until, in fact, they were all together in their caravan, with Joanna in her hated litter in the middle of it and all their goodbyes said. As they began to move, a second, slightly larger caravan came up behind them. At first Ysabel knew simply that the two companies had decided to travel together as their like often did, for safety and for company. It was Akiva who pointed out the one who led the second caravan.

She did not know his face. An ordinary enough face, fleshy with prosperity, with a grizzled beard to give it authority. But his mind—she almost shouted aloud. No need after all to wish she had remained behind. Their enemy was riding with them to Acre.

She found his son near enough to him, dangling at the heel of a portly monk. Young Marco was not ill to look at, if somewhat weedy and awkward. His mind was as blurry as ever, and as weak in hiding what it thought. He was half excited, half afraid. He knew very well whose kin they were riding with. He shared his father's confidence that they could not know what part the Secos, father and son, had had in their kinsfolk's discomfiture, but he went in imminent, delicious dread of their finding it out.

Brother Thomas would be furious. He did not know. Neither of the Secos had told him, and Brother Richard said that he had not seen fit to.

Brother Richard warded himself better than either of the others, but it was not the wall Ysabel had run afoul of when she first found the conspiracy. That was still in Jerusalem. Maybe Brother Thomas; maybe someone else she had not learned of yet. Morgiana would be interested to know how many humans had escaped her hunt. She would want to kill them all.

Ysabel might be willing to let her. The merchant was a sly, smug, horrible creature. He actually smirked when he came to pay his respects to the ladies, though he did it where he thought no one could see. Guillermo, his name was. Guillermo Seco. Ysabel committed it and his face to memory beside her remembrance of his mind. It was shielding now, but haphazardly, and—that thought was as clear as if he had said it aloud—only because the damned fools of monks had made him swear to do it. He was ignorant. He thought Brother Richard might be able somehow to tell if he slacked off too badly.

Brother Richard could no more read another man's mind than he could fly. He could shield his own mind, to be sure, and do it well. There was no profit in trying to break the wall. It was not as strong as the one in Jerusalem, but it was quite as dangerous. Even being near it, taxed her will to stay away from it.

It was not so far to Acre, if one had a falcon's wings, or relays of fast horses. In a caravan, in summer's heat, with wagons, and women in litters, it took the better part of a week. They dawdled, for a fact. Every day they had news from here or there. Saladin was massing on the eastern borders. Guy was mustering his army near Nazareth. Castles and cities that had been scant enough on fighting men already, now stripped themselves to the bone. The whole country held its breath and waited for word to come that there had been a battle.

There was even, once, a message from their own kin, brought up from Jerusalem by a servant who had been left behind. No news in it to speak of. Just that they were well, and there had been no fighting, apart from a skirmish or two.

Joanna was not fit for human company for hours after that, between missing her husband and missing Aidan and fretting over the letter she had had from Aimery. There were no secrets in it; she read it to Ysabel. *Aimery de Mortmain to the Lady Joanna de Hautecourt. Lady mother, I am well, I hope you are well and the baby is well and the children are staying out of trouble. I am with Count Raymond every day, but he lets me ride sometimes with Father or Prince Aidan. They are well. Prince Aidan hasn't yelled at the king even once. He says that I shoot well. I shot a gazelle yesterday. We had it for dinner. Tomorrow, maybe, we hunt Saracens.*

That was all there was room for on the parchment. Aimery had written it with his own hand: it wobbled in places, and the spelling was, as Joanna thought and Ysabel heard, inventive. Joanna was proud that he could write at all. Most young lords could not, still less in decipherable Latin. Something of his lessons had stayed with him. Joanna glared at the letter, furious, because it made her want to weep.

A good part of that was pregnancy, but some was what she always felt when she thought of Aimery. He had been taken away from her when he was a baby and sent to be fostered where his father saw an advantage. Ranulf was young then; he never thought to ask his wife if she wanted to give up her baby. That was why Ysabel was born. Joanna left her husband, hating him for what he had done, and went first to her mother, then to her mother's kin in Aleppo. Aidan went with her, because there was an Assassin on her track, and he thought he could protect her. He did not do that very well—Morgiana caught her in Aleppo, and almost killed her—but he fell in love with Joanna, and Joanna with him. She chose Ranulf in the end, and Ranulf let her have Aimery, but by then she was carrying Ysabel. It was all tangled up in her, and Aimery most of all. He thought she did not love him. It was not that at all. She loved him too much. It made her do and say all the wrong things, at all the wrong times.

Ysabel left her to brood over the bit of parchment. Akiva had proved himself a surprisingly good horseman;

after a day on one of the servants' nags, he was given leave to ride Joanna's own tempestuous mare. She was one of Aidan's beauties; she had the fire of her Arab kin, and the size and strength of her Frankish sire. Akiva sat her easily, undaunted by her fits of temper.

Ysabel came up beside him, her own mare dancing and playing with the bit. Her eyes were on the ones who rode just ahead of him. Guillermo Seco would not condescend to notice a horseboy in the coat and cap of a Jew, still less a mere girl, but Messer Marco took time to be scornful.

"He shouldn't turn up his nose so high," Ysabel said, precise and clear. "It makes him sit his horse even worse than he would to begin with."

Akiva knew what she was doing. His eye sparked on her. "To be sure, my lady, we can't all be born to the saddle. I wonder, did he learn by riding camels in the caravans? They look just like that, rocking and swaying and flapping their reins."

"His poor horse," said Ysabel. "Tell me, who taught *you* to ride? Was it the King of Rhiyana?"

"His very own self," Akiva answered her. They were both gratified to see Marco's shoulders stiffen. "I'm to be a secretary, of course, and a scholar of the Torah, but my lord says that no man, even a scholar, ought to live forever within four walls. He taught me to ride, for that, and to shoot a little."

"Not to use a sword?"

"I've no art in that, and no time to learn. I'll have to trust to him if it comes down to bared steel."

"Or you can trust to his brother's lady. She was an Assassin, after all. She can hunt like a tigress in the night, and she never loses her quarry."

"Ah," said Akiva. "Yes. Is she hunting still, do you think? She wasn't happy at all to be cheated of her wedding. I'd not like to be the man who did it to her."

"Nor I," Ysabel said, and her shiver was real enough. If Marco had been a dog, he would have been prickeared and trembling and whining with anxiety. "Maybe she's found him, or is about to. He'd be distracted with the war; thinking he's safe. Ripe for her taking."

"God help him then," Akiva said.

Marco broke at that. He hauled his horse bodily out of the line and said something to his father about seeing to the camels. He had to ride past the children to do it. They were careful to be innocent, offering him smiles and lifted hands. He ducked his head and dug heels into his gelding's sides.

"That was cruel." Akiva spoke much softer now than he had a moment ago.

"He deserved it," said Ysabel. "He was worse than cruel to Morgiana and my uncle." She was careful to say it that way, here where people could listen if they were minded. No one seemed to be. The merchant would not stoop to, and the fat monk looked to be asleep on his mule.

She fixed her eyes on the monk's broad back. He knew what she needed to know. She was sure of it. But there was no getting into his mind. There might be ways of tricking him into dropping the wards; she could not think of any, though she tried. Her snare was still set, still waiting for the stray thought that would catch him.

She could be patient, if that was what she needed. She could hide herself down deep, be all human and all harmless, and let him betray himself. Men had trouble enough paying attention to women. To monks, women were not there at all, except as bodies to be preached against. And a small girlchild on a horse that seemed a bit too much for her, however noble her family, was the next thing to invisible.

Not if he paid any attention to what we were saying.

She glanced at Akiva. He was working a tangle out of his horse's mane. *He didn't,* she said. *His ears aren't as good as that. I don't think he has a guilty conscience, either.*

I don't think he has a conscience at all. Akiva frowned at the worst of the knot. *How can a horse get elflocks just walking on the road?*

Think about what's riding her. Ysabel swatted a fly on her mare's neck. Akiva had stopped being aware of her. He was trying what she had tried: to insinuate himself through a chink in the monk's wards. He had no more luck than she had, and came out rather less intact. His face was bloodless; his eyes were holes in it, with all the fire gone out of them.

She snatched in sudden fear, with mind and hand both. He was there to both, though he was cold and shaking. "No more," she said. *"No more."*

He nodded as if his head were too heavy, almost, to lift, but it was more assent than exhaustion. His eyes closed. *They're too strong for us. We need the grownfolk.*

We'll have them, Ysabel said. *Soon.*

After the war.

Soon, she said.

25

The arrival in Acre of the lady of Mortmain with her children and her guardsmen and all her attendants, took Elen somewhat by surprise. She had expected it; there had been messages, and she had seen that the house was in order for their coming. But there were so many of them, and they made such noise after the quiet of her solitude. She almost resented them. The queen was gone days since to Jerusalem and then to Nablus; she had not been able to persuade Elen to follow her. Elen had been content to be alone, to drift and to dream; to weep when her courses came in their due time, and she could not have told whether it was relief or regret. She was hopelessly besotted with a man who might be dead before the summer was out; and though she could pray that he would be safe, she knew all too well that he could not come back and be her lover.

All these noisy crowding people did their best to drive him out of her mind. The children needed chasing after, the servants needed watching over, the house needed these stores and that improvement in its furnishings, and someone had to mend the tiles on the roof over the gate. Joanna, grown enormous with the approach of her time, still seemed to be everywhere at once, even when she did not leave her chair in the solar. She was shameless in making Elen her hands and feet. "You can run," she said, "and I can't. And you're looking a little too pallid for my peace of mind. Your uncles will never forgive you if you pine away for their sakes."

"I'm not," Elen said, but she went where she was bidden and did as she was told. She felt as young as Ysabel, and fully as rebellious.

When she came back, Joanna let her sink into a chair. A servant brought her sherbet cooled with snow from Mount Hermon. Somehow, without her noticing it, high summer had come in: summer as high as the sun in this country, with a heavy, clinging heat. Elen had been persuaded to forsake western swathings for the thin silks of the east. She was all in eastern dress today, except for the veil. She let her mantle fall over the back of her chair and daringly enough, even with no one but Joanna and her maid and the single servant to see, sat bare-armed and silken-trousered and blessedly cool in the dim, airy room.

Joanna shifted in her chair, waving off the maid and the servant. She was in pain, Elen knew: her back was always troublesome, and the baby, growing large, kicked hard enough to bruise. But Joanna was never one to bow to any will but her own, even when that will was her body's, readying itself to give birth.

"Not quite yet," Joanna said, catching Elen's eyes on her mountainous middle. She sat up a little straighter, brushed a stray lock of hair out of her face. "What I wouldn't give for a good, hard gallop under an open sky . . ." She grimaced, shook her head. "I'll get one soon enough, once this little monster has got itself born."

"Maybe we'll ride together," said Elen.

Joanna's glance was sharp. "You've been keeping yourself mewed up like a nun. Why? Do you think the sacrifice will keep the army safe?"

"No." Elen tried to keep her voice light, to keep her temper out of it. "I haven't wanted to go out, that's all. There's always enough to do in the house or round about the market."

"The day's heat comes up fast, this time of year."

Joanna seemed almost to be thinking aloud. She shrugged. "It's your folly. If I were young and thin, I'd ride in the mornings and bring back meat for the pot."

"Do you want me to?"

Elen's sharpness ruffled Joanna not at all. "No. I'm just feeling sorry for myself. This is going to be the last, you know. Ranulf and I, we agreed. I've done my duty by him, and he's pleased with me. He won't ask me to go through this again."

Elen lowered her eyes, abashed. She had been too caught up in her troubles to notice that Joanna had troubles of her own. Elen did not think Joanna old, nor did she look it, even swollen with pregnancy; she had all her teeth, her hair was nigh as fine and fully as thick as Ysabel's, and the lines that marked her face were lines of laughter. But she was close to thirty; she had borne nine children. Even her husband could hardly fault her for wanting to end it.

"I'm sorry," Elen said, "that you have to—give up—"

"He's not the greatest lover in the world," Joanna said.

Elen blushed. It was like Joanna to go straight to the point.

"He won't suffer," said Joanna. "No more than he has when I've been pregnant and not wanting him. What we've had together, what's been most real, we'll still have that. The children. The lands and the people on them. The two of us working side by side. It took me a while and cost me a bit, but I've learned to understand him. We do well together."

"But," Elen said. "How can you let him go to another woman's bed?"

For a moment Joanna looked like another woman altogether: a woman of no age at all, wearing no expression. "How can I stop him? He takes pleasure where he pleases, but I'm the one he comes back to. I'm the one he calls lady and wife."

"Have you ever wondered," Elen said, "what it would be like if a woman were as free to choose her dalliance as a man is?"

Joanna's face did not change. "I've wondered. I've seen what comes of it." She spread her hands on the dome of her belly. "It's how I know that God is male. He would never have given His own sex so much of the burden."

"You mind so much?"

Joanna laughed, and suddenly she was herself again. "Of course I mind! I'm ready to kick this monster out the door. When I'm in my right mind, I'm more sensible. I wouldn't want to be a man. Poor half-baked things, they're terrified of us; of the power that's in us."

"Is that why they tell us we're so much less than they?"

"Why, aren't you feeling your feminine fragility these days?"

Elen's laughter was rusty with disuse. "I'm feeling ready to snatch up a sword and gallop off to join the army. That's the worst of being a woman. Having to sit at home and wait."

"And hold the world together while the men do their best to tear it apart. War," said Joanna, "is pure idiocy." She heaved herself up as if she could not bear to sit still. "Come out to the garden with me."

Elen went with her, offering an arm for her to take. She ignored it. Her gait was ungainly but oddly graceful. Without the weight of the child, she would walk like a lioness, in long powerful strides. Yet for all her size and evident strength, there was nothing masculine about her; she was strong and a woman and—yes—glad to be that, even at the worst of it.

They did not walk long in the garden. Even in the shade it was hot.

As they turned back to the house, Elen could not hold in any longer what she had heard in the market. "Tiberias has fallen," she said. "The army has left its camp at Cresson. They're going to try to win back the city."

Joanna stopped short. Her hands locked on Elen's arm. "Why didn't you tell me sooner?"

"I didn't want to upset you." Even as she said it, Elen hardly believed it. She did not want to face it herself. She had been a coward; she had let herself be distracted, away from fear, toward the little matters of women.

Carefully Joanna unlocked her fingers. Drew a breath. Made an effort to compose her face. "People always seem to think I'll drop the baby at a word. What else have you been keeping from me?"

"Nothing," said Elen. "That's the news that just came in. I had it from one of the Lord Marshal's servants, who heard it as he went out on his errand. Saladin has Tiberias; the countess is barricaded in the citadel; the army is going to win her free."

"From Cresson to Tiberias? At this time of year? Have they gone stark mad?"

Elen could not understand why she was so appalled. "It's only a few leagues, isn't it?"

"Five," said Joanna. "As the vulture flies. In July. In this heat. With no water for an army, anywhere on the plain. Why didn't they stay at Cresson like sane human beings, and wait for the sultan to come to them?"

"They couldn't just abandon Tiberias, could they?"

"If they had the wits of a gnat, they would. Sweet saints," said Joanna. "There's going to be a battle, and Saladin will choose the ground."

"I knew I shouldn't have told you," Elen said.

Joanna raised her clenched fists, but lowered them again, breathing deep, calming herself by effort of will. "If Saladin has Tiberias, and Guy is trying to fight on ground of Saladin's choosing, then the whole kingdom is in jeopardy. Has the marshal done anything about the defenses here?"

"As much as he can do, with almost no troops to man them."

"Then we had better pray," said Joanna, "that the army holds off the Saracen; because if it fails, every one of us is ripe for the plucking."

Elen's hands were cold. She knotted them at her sides and lifted her chin. "I'll pray. And I'll hope. They have my lord king, after all, and his brother beside him."

"They do," Joanna said. Elen could not tell from the tone of it whether it was agreement or irony.

* * *

By evening the whole city knew what the city's marshal had heard from the east; and that the king had, the night before, been forced to camp well short of Tiberias, without water, harried mercilessly by the enemy. The messenger who had broken through had been arrowshot for his insolence. He was expected to live, unless the wound went bad.

The churches were full of people praying for the army's victory. Elen went to the cathedral, where the pious and the frightened kept vigil—more of the latter, she would have wagered, than the former—but came back at dusk to give Joanna what news there was. The house, like the city, was unwontedly subdued. Today would have been the battle. The signals that had come from the long line of castles along the marches of Syria told only of Tiberias' burning, the enemy's massing about it, the army's halting to fight between the hills called the Horns of Hattin.

Joanna was not in the solar. Elen found her in the nursery, from which her younger children had been banished with loud and echoing protests, sitting by the bed on which lay her eldest daughter. Ysabel was coiled in a knot, as rigid as a stone and nearly as cold.

"Dear God," Elen said.

"She's alive."

Elen had not even seen the boy until he spoke. It was Simeon's son. He looked like a ghost in the lamp's shadow.

Clearly Joanna had not seen him, either: she jumped like a cat. She got hold of his coat and pulled him into the light. "What's wrong with her? Why is she like this?"

Joanna, it was evident, knew what Akiva was. He did not seem surprised. He looked down at Ysabel. His face was deathly white, his eyes huge in it, like holes in a skull. "She wore herself out," he said. "I didn't know until it was too late. I don't think she'll die. She may sleep for days, that's all."

"That's all?" Joanna's voice cracked with incredulity. "That's *all*? For God's sake, what was she doing?"

"Watching the battle."

Elen did not disbelieve it. That was the worst of it. She was kin to these people. This one, too. Now she understood much that she had not, of Joanna's troublesome eldest daughter; and of Aidan's patent preference for her over her siblings. She was of his own kind.

"The battle," Joanna prompted Akiva with conspicuous patience.

Before he spoke, they read it in his face. "Lost," he said, almost too faint to be heard. "All lost."

"No," Joanna said.

"All." He swayed as he stood, but he would not let them touch him. "The Saracen surrounded them on the field of Hattin and broke them with fire and no water and the summer's heat. The footsoldiers rebelled and would not fight. The knights fought as long as they could, but there were too few of them. They are all dead or taken."

Joanna's face was as bloodless now as his, but she stood erect, motionless. What came from her was not the name Elen had expected. "Prince Aidan?"

"Alive. And my king. And your son."

Her eyes closed briefly. She opened them. "My husband?"

He would not answer. Perhaps could not. All at once and all of a piece, he crumpled.

Elen caught him. He was not rigid as Ysabel was; he was as limp as a rag.

"Ranulf is dead," Joanna said. She said it quite calmly, as if it were nothing to her. "The kingdom is lost. The sultan will be wanting a sizeable ransom, I suspect; particularly for a king and a prince."

Elen's arms began to tremble. She laid Akiva on the bed beside Ysabel. Now that Elen knew, she could see the alienness in Ysabel's face, the whiteness that was not natural for this country, the awkwardness that would bloom into piercing, inhuman beauty.

Joanna laid her hand on the tousled curls. "Now he'll never know," she said.

Elen would not ask what she meant; did not want to know. "He may still be alive."

Joanna shook her head. "I'm none of their kind, but I can see the truth when it stares me in the face." She straightened painfully. "I could have done with a little more false hope."

So could they all. Elen looked down at the ones who had told them what the rest of the city would not hear for hours yet, and reflected on human envy, and unhuman power, and what it must be to be a child and to know that one's father was dead. To know it as only witchkind could, as one who had been at his side, and gone down with him into the dark.

There was little that they could do for either of them except make them comfortable and try to keep them warm, and watch over them. Joanna would not leave the room. Nor, when he had been sent for, would Simeon. Elen took on herself the ordering of the household. She did not tell the others what she knew. Let them discover it as the rest of the city did. Let them have this last glimmer of hope.

Not that she despaired. Not yet. She had no word that Raihan was dead. Would Saladin punish him for fighting against his own people? Or would he have made his choice before it was too late, and gone back to the sultan's service? That he could have been cut down in the battle, she would not think of. He could not have died. She would not allow it.

She watched with distant interest as the news reached the city. Saladin was the victor of Hattin. The king and his high lords were sent to prison in Damascus. The lesser knights, the Hospitallers, all the Templars but their Grand Master, were dead. The citadel of Tiberias had fallen; the Countess Eschiva was permitted to depart with her children and her possessions, and set free to join her husband where he nursed his shame in Tripoli. The Saracen was marching on Acre.

When Joanna was told, she laughed. She had not lost her wits, it was not in her, but grief made her angry, and when she was angry, she was dangerous.

Acre could have used that anger. For lack of a proper defending force—all that they had had, had gone to the defeat at Hattin—they could do nothing but seal the gates and wait. Someone had the wits to put all the men they did have, armed, on the walls, and to eke out the numbers with boys and old men and, here and there, a woman large enough to look daunting in a helmet. All together they seemed numerous enough; in war, where seeming could be everything, they might succeed in persuading the Saracen to draw off and choose another target.

It was down to that. Every city for itself, each castle to its own devices. "This isn't a kingdom anymore," Joanna said. "It's a henhouse full of foxes."

The witch-children slept for a night and a day, and woke ravenous and, to all appearances, healed of the blow that had felled them. But Akiva did not go back to his books. He stayed close to Ysabel, who would not leave her mother. Joanna tolerated them both. She used them as pages and errand-runners. She did not ask them to be messengers as only they could be.

Nor did she talk with her daughter of Ranulf's death. The household would know when it was humanly possible, when the full tally of the dead and captive came from Damascus. Joanna nursed her grief alone, and brooded on the child that would never know its father.

On the second night after the battle, Joanna sat up long after the others were asleep, with a book in front of her. She did not even remember which book it was. Her eyes on the page saw not the close, crabbed lines, but faces. Ranulf's. Aidan's. Her daughter's.

"I sinned once," she said. "The worse for that I never could repent it. But except for that one sin, I was all the wife a man could ask for. I learned to love him. Better than that: I liked him. We were friends."

There were no tears in her. Her grief was too deep for that. Aidan was alive and unwedded, and Ranulf was dead. Time was when she would have been glad of that; when she would have made something of it.

So she had. It slept in her bed, curled about one of the cats. Ranulf would never know, now, that Ysabel was not his daughter.

Joanna despised herself for being glad. She had meant to tell him, someday, when he would be able to understand, if not to forgive. Now she never would. God and the infidel had taken that burden from her; and with it any hope of absolution.

There were eyes on her. She turned slowly, willing herself to be calm. Ysabel came as she almost never had, even when she was small, and climbed into Joanna's lap, what there was of it with her soon-to-be-born brother or sister between. She laid her head on her mother's breast, careful as no ordinary child would know how to be, not to rouse the ache of the milk that had begun in it.

Joanna hesitated. Ysabel was silent. Joanna's arms closed about her daughter, uncertainly at first, unsure of their welcome. Ysabel was always a prickly creature, as fierce in her independence as a young cat. She was more like Morgiana, that way, than like her father. Aidan, twinborn, raised human, knew what it was to need the nearness of his kin.

A child was a wonderful, terrible thing. Born of one's blood and bone, but grown apart from them. This one, who should have been three parts human, was all strange. Her body that was warmer than a human child's, warm enough to be a constant source of alarm in nurses and servants; her heart that beat on the right side of her body; her skin that was clean even of child-scents, giving the nose only what was set on it from without. Soap from the evening's bath, scented with rosewater. New-washed linen. A suggestion of cat, from her erstwhile sleeping companion.

Joanna stroked the softness of her hair. She was not a human child, and yet she was Joanna's. Knowing that her mother grieved, grieving herself, she came to give and to receive what comfort she could. It was not, that Joanna could perceive, anything to do with witchery.

They never resorted to that if human means would suffice. It was a courtesy, and an economy, and perhaps a sacrifice, too; as saints gave up things of the flesh to make themselves more worthy of heaven. Odd as some might reckon it to think of these uncanny people in con-

nection with saints. The Church would not even give
them the courtesy of souls.

Her arms tightened on the thin child-body. No. That,
she would not believe; that her daughter was flesh without spirit. That lie was for the barren meditations of
priests. Priests were men, after all. What did men know
of the truth that was conceived and carried under a
woman's heart?

Ysabel sighed against her. Asleep, and at peace. That
should comfort her, surely; for if there was anything to
fear, Ysabel would know.

At the gate of a fallen kingdom, with war coming as
inexorably as tides in the sea, Joanna cradled her eldest
daughter and, however late, however fleetingly, let herself rest.

26

On the fourth day after the battle of Hattin, as the sun
descended to the hills of Carmel, what had seemed to be
a storm of dust and wind revealed itself for what it was:
the army of the infidel, marching swiftly on Acre. They
came in all their ranks with their banners flying, to the
beating of the kettledrums, chanting the praises of Allah.
Victory rode on them; they laughed as they came.

When they had a clear sight of the city, they slowed.
The walls were lined with armed figures, a flame of sunlight on helmet and spearpoint, a manifold glitter of eyes.
Acre, which they had thought bereft of defenders, was
guarded after all, and by a fair army.

Almost, the ruse succeeded. Elen, up on the wall in
helmet and mail, with a sword at her side, watched the
enemy come to a halt. There were not as many of them
as rumor had promised. But enough; and they were visibly deadly on their light Arab horses, with their lances
and their swords, their bows and their maces and their
fierce foreign eyes. Soldiers of Allah. It was more than a
word now. It was thousands strong.

She saw the sultan in the center behind a wall of steel: a doll-figure at this distance, splendid in his golden corselet, mounted on a white horse. There was a canopy over him, a guard about him in sun-colored coats. His mamluks, his soldier-slaves who would die for him.

As Raihan would die for his prince. As Raihan might well have done on the field of Hattin.

The wings of the army halted just out of arrow range. Some of them seemed to have come forward because of their keen sight; they peered under shading hands. One lowered his hand suddenly and wheeled his horse about. It was a handsome display of horsemanship. Elen watched him gallop headlong through the army, toward the sultan.

Well before the laughter began, it was evident that the enemy was undeceived. He had taken count of the faces under the helmets, and marked how many wore grey beards or none at all, nor could grow any. Acre had no defense that could match the army of Islam.

The enemy camped on the field outside the walls, conspicuously at their ease, laughing and singing. From within it sounded as if they were all drunk on wine, but Elen did not think that many of them were. Saladin was too devout, and too strong a commander. All that intoxicated them was victory won, and victory soon to be won. They had no doubt at all of it.

"The seneschal will give in," Joanna said. The children were fed and put fretfully to bed, even Akiva, who clearly reckoned himself more than a child.

"Not until Rosh Hashonah," his father told him, and that ended that.

The three of them sat on the roof: the two women and the Rhiyanan king's friend. They could not see the enemy's army even if they had been minded to; there was a church tower between. They looked seaward instead. The harbor had been emptying since word came from Hattin. Tonight there were almost no ships left in the outer harbor, and most of those in the inner readied for a swift departure in the morning. Some would go to Cyprus. Many meant to take refuge in Tyre, a short sail up the coast. The harbor there was less secure in a storm, but the city was strongly defended against attack by land; more strongly than Acre.

"The rats leave the ship," Joanna said. It was hard in lamplight to read her face. Her voice was flat. "My lord Joscelin will surrender. What else can he do? He can't put up anything resembling a decent fight. He's not mad like our noble king. He'll get what concessions he can, and hand over the city."

"I wish I could call that cowardice." Elen's head ached. She leaned it against her cup, letting the coolness give what comfort it could. "I've never been on the losing side of a war."

"None of us has." Joanna was a shadow in the gloom, massive and immobile. "We don't know how to act."

"With dignity," said Simeon. "That is how one acts."

They looked at him. The lamplight caught his coat, and the raven sheen of his beard, and half of his face: flat cheek, deep eye, broad uncompromising nose. His voice was as dry as the plain of Hattin.

He met their stares calmly, with a glint that might have been irony. "One acts with dignity," he said, "as much as one may. One compromises only as much as one must, and still remain oneself. And one keeps one's pride, even if one must keep it in secret, where only God can see."

"One doesn't fight?" Elen asked.

The narrow shoulders lifted in a shrug. "What good does it do?"

"It makes one feel better."

"And maybe one dies, and the enemy is still the victor." Simeon sat back in his chair, stroking his beard, more at ease than she had ever seen him outside of Gwydion's company. This, the edge of disaster, seemed to be his element. "What will you do, my ladies? Will you fight?"

Elen shook her head but did not answer. Joanna said, "I will do what I will do." She heaved herself up. "Which is, now, to get what sleep I can."

They watched her go. Elen was disinclined to move.

She did not like the taste that was in her mouth. It was defeat; it saw no escape.

"There is a way out of this, you know," Simeon said, as if like his son he could know what she thought.

"Death?" she asked.

Simeon's eyes glittered. "Of course not. That is final, and God forbids it. What He will allow . . . Who is to say that He wouldn't be as pleased to be addressed as Allah by a new-made Muslim?"

"Is that what you will do?"

He laughed, which both dismayed and comforted her. "I, no. I lacked the sense to turn Christian when the Anglian king's dogs hunted me out of the isles. What makes you think I'd turn Muslim now, with the Syrian sultan's dogs yapping at the gates?"

"Why didn't you?" she asked. "Turn Christian, that is."

"Why don't you turn Muslim?"

That was answer enough, if she thought about it. "Does God even care what name we call Him by?"

"He may not. We, being human and imperfect, do. And I have generations of pride to protect. We kept our faith when the whole world turned against it. How can I forsake it now?"

"What would your son say to that?"

"My son is as stubborn as I am." Simeon was proud of that and of him.

"It must be strange," Elen mused, "to know that one's child is of that blood. And he will carry it on through years out of count. Our Church is appalled. What do your people think of it?"

"My people accept what is. Maybe he is something out of the Enemy's kingdom: golem or dybbuk, or creature of a darker persuasion. I, and such of my people as know him, prefer to think him a new face of God's creation. He says that he is mine, and he was incontestably Rachel's. I know that I have no such blood as your family claims; Rachel saw farther and deeper than most women do, but she was human enough for all of that. So: God gave us a gift, and let Rachel live long enough to know it for what it was. She seemed glad. I know she

loved him. What could I do but love him enough for
both of us, once she was gone?"

"And now he sleeps on the edge of war."

The dark eyes closed; the face withdrew out of the
light. "I would have spared him that if I could. Or," said
Simeon, "no. He has to know what the world is. It will
betray him twice over, once for his faith and once for
what he is, unless he knows how to live in it."

"Then pray God the Saracen doesn't kill him."

"I am praying," said Simeon. "Every moment, I
pray. This country has suffered enough from rashness
and folly. It's time someone showed sense."

Joscelin, seneschal of Acre under the captive king,
seemed to have come to the same conclusion. In the cool
of morning, but with the sun threatening already to
scorch that little coolness out of the air, he sent his envoy to the sultan. His terms were simple. As the Muslims
had done fourscore years before when the Franks took
the city from them, he offered surrender. In return he
asked that the sultan spare the lives and the goods of the
city's people.

Saladin had had enough of summary justice after
Hattin. He accepted the terms.

But the city would not accept him. Some of the
wealthier merchants and one or two young sprigs of the
nobility and a remarkable number of plainer citizens saw
in surrender only shame. They rose in revolt.

Joanna barricaded her family in the house and would
not let any of them out. Even through the walls they
could hear sounds that were more like riot than proper
battle. Trumpets marked the seneschal's response. It was
swift, it was firm, and it was exactly as brutal as it
needed to be. Word of it came through the barred gate
from a crier who traversed the streets, relaying the seneschal's command for citizens to keep to their houses, master their tempers, and forbear from assaults on the new
masters of Acre. Merchants, the crier added, were be-
seeched to remain; the sultan was well disposed toward

them, and would welcome their presence and their commerce.

Those merchants who still lingered responded by departing in a caravan. As hastily as they did it, they had no time to gather their stores. When toward evening the sultan rode into the city he would find the warehouses filled to bursting with the wealth of an empire: silks and satins, gold and silver and copper, jewels and weapons and a myriad lesser riches. More than one trading enterprise would founder for its owners' cowardice.

Joanna, behind her walls, settled in to wait. Saladin was a clement conqueror: he did not set his troops free to sack and burn unless he was provoked. As here he seemed not to be, rebellion notwithstanding.

Her household could not understand what she meant by refusing to leave. Those who could think of it at all, thought that she was about to deliver herself of her baby. So she was, but she had more in mind than that. Which was why, when the hour drew near to sunset, she called for her litter.

Elen, God be thanked, did not seem to mark the signs; she simply insisted on being part of the deputation. So did the witch-children. What they knew, they were not telling, but they stayed closer even than they had been doing. Simeon she left to look after the house. He was not happy, but he was a practical man. He could see that one of them should stay, in case there should be looting after all. One wing of Saladin's army had escaped his vigilance, mercifully outside the walls, and plundered the sugar mill; God knew what the sultan's own troops might take it into their heads to do.

The city was full of them. Most quartered in merchants' abandoned houses. Some established themselves by the harbor, though they did not try to stop ships from leaving. A goodly number took the citadel and the surrender of its defenders, and set themselves on guard.

A lady's litter, with a second lady walking haughtily beside it and a pair of children flanking it and a pair of guards with swords carefully in sheaths, was startling enough that it passed unhindered even where the conquerors were thickest. No one offered them insult. Elen, wisely, had drawn her veil across her face. Joanna was borne in curtained propriety like a Muslim *khatun.*

Like a Muslim lady, she had learned the art of seeing the world from behind the veil. She saw what the infidel had made of the city: a shocked, silent place, with here and there a remnant of the rebellion. A stain of blood on a wall; a broken door. A dead man awaiting his turn for burial.

Then, as the shadows lengthened, it came: the sound that above all marked the triumph of Islam. From the summit of a tower, perhaps a church, perhaps a crumbling minaret, the muezzin's wail called the faithful to prayer. *God is great! God is great! There is no god but God, and Muhammad is the Prophet of God. Come to prayer, O ye Muslims, come to prayer. . . .*

Joanna shivered on the too-soft cushions, in the stifling confinement of the litter. Her throat was locked shut. She refused fiercely to burst into tears.

The wailing died away. The city's masters bowed down in prayer. Joanna's litter made its way through the silent, all-but-empty streets to the citadel and its turbaned guardians.

They were taken aback as their fellows had been in the city, by a Frankish lady who wished to speak with their sultan. Who expressed that wish, further, in Arabic somewhat purer than their own, with an accent that bespoke Aleppo, and noble Aleppo at that. That they were turning petitioners away, she could see for herself: a man with the look of a merchant left even as she arrived, clearly unsatisfied, and muttering what sounded like curses. What he had hoped to do, she could imagine. Make a profit from the invading army, then abscond with it. Clearly Saladin was having none of that.

She was not asking for profit, and she was anomalous enough to gain at least a promise that her message would be passed to the proper authorities. "To your sultan," she said firmly.

The captain of guards, who had come to his underlings' call, bowed and sent a guardsman inward. He promised nothing, she noticed, but she was prepared to wait, and if she must, to insist.

In good enough time, considering that they were kept
waiting at the gate, the guard returned and spoke to his
commander. His voice was too low for Joanna to catch.
She was admittedly somewhat distracted. Her belly had
tightened in a way she knew too well. Not painfully, not
quite, not yet, but its message was plain.

She would not need after all to test her willingness to
give birth on the sultan's doorstep. Saladin would speak
with her. She was to understand that propriety could
hardly be observed here in what was in essence a camp of
war. Would she be content with the presence of the seneschal?

She would. She would not, mercifully, be forced to
walk up from the gate. As far as the litter could go, it
was allowed: only into the courtyard, but even that was
something. She extricated herself from it, stiffly, struggling not to double up as the first honest pain lanced
through her center. The support she clung to resolved
itself into Akiva. Growing like a weed, the boy was: he
was as high as her shoulder already, and slender-strong
as all his people were.

The sultan's men were appalled to discover that not
only was she big with child, she was perilously close to
giving birth. She drew herself up under their darting,
half-frightened glances, and mustered strength to walk.

It was easier once she had begun. A woman should
walk when she was at her time; it made the baby come
more easily. She climbed the last flight of stairs almost
lightly, and entered the lamplit hall.

It was full. The seneschal clearly was an honored
captive; he sat near the sultan, and his men were not far
from him, though they carried no weapons. They seemed
to have decided to accept what they could not alter.
There was no open rebellion to be seen, and of sullenness
no more than there should be.

The sultan's men were jubilant, though they stilled
for Joanna's entrance. She must have been impressive.
She was taller than most of them, and she was dressed as
a Frank, scorning the veils and the modesty of Muslim
women. The boy who was her prop, so evidently a Jew,

and the lady and the maidchild behind her, made a most peculiar procession.

Saladin could not know Joanna's face, but she knew his well enough. She had been in Damascus once, when Ysabel was conceived, and she had known his Turkish wife, the Lady Ismat; from the sultan's harem, through secret lattices, she had been privileged to observe the sultan at his diwan, his time of open audience. Saladin was older, inevitably, but he had still the same fine, close-bearded, pleasing face, and the same air almost of diffidence, as if he could not believe that he of all men was the lord of both Egypt and Syria, a king of kings in Islam. His rank sat more easily on him now; he wore simple black as she remembered, but it was somewhat less threadbare than it had been, and his weapons were beautiful. The sword in its damascened sheath reminded her of Aidan, who had a blade very like it: straight, slender, with a silver hilt. There was a ruby in Aidan's pommel. Saladin's was plain, and lovely in its plainness.

She offered him such obeisance as her bulk and her rank would allow. He did not stare, she noticed, though the boy who sat at his right hand was all eyes and arrogance. That would be his son, no doubt. Al-Afdal, whose first battle had been Hattin.

Joanna had no time to spare for grief. She was too busy keeping the baby from coming in the middle of the hall, and keeping her audience from guessing it.

The sultan inclined his head to her. He was always a gentleman, even when he was murdering infidels. "My lady," he said.

The shadow of a man next to him began to speak in Frankish. Joanna overrode him in Arabic. "My lord sultan. I am grateful that you would receive us."

"It is my belief," said Saladin, "that the measure of a man is his conduct in victory."

"Not in defeat?"

Saladin's eyes glinted, direct on her for once, and more amused than annoyed. "In that, too, my lady. You have an admirable command of our language."

"No more admirable than yours, my lord. I am kin to the House of Ibrahim in Aleppo."

"Are you indeed?" Saladin asked. "I had been given to understand that you were a baroness of Jerusalem."

"That, too," she said. "Your lady, Ismat al-Din Khatun: she is well, I hope?"

"Well," said Saladin, "and prospering." He paused, eyes opening wide in sudden surmise. "Ah. Would you be the Lady Jahana?"

"So I am known in the House of Islam."

He smiled. His face was stern in repose, and rather grim; his smile transformed it, made it seem as lively as a boy's. "My lady, my lady! Well met indeed. Come, sit, you should not be standing, where is my courtesy?"

She sat because she did not know if she could go on standing, but she kept her head up. Akiva stood beside her like a young guardhound, all bones and fierceness. Ysabel insinuated herself under Joanna's arm and glared at Saladin.

Saladin smiled back. "This princess would be yours, I think, my lady? And the young warrior?"

"The son of a friend," she said. "As this is the near kin of one whom you call friend." She indicated Elen, who had refused to sit. "The Lady Elen of Caer Gwent in Rhiyana."

Saladin knew those names. He accorded their bearer deep respect. "I see your kinsmen in you," he said. "They are well, and would send you greetings, I am certain, had they known that I would find you here."

Elen started forward, caught herself. Joanna asked the question she would not, or dared not, ask. "They are well? And where would they be?"

"By now," Saladin answered, "in Damascus, recovering from the ravages of their battle."

"And awaiting ransom?"

"That has been seen to."

Joanna forbore to press. She had other concerns, for the moment. "My lord sultan, I hardly came here for the pleasure of your company, great though that has proven to be. I know that the city has surrendered according to its own chosen terms. I know also that those terms require Frankish citizens to take themselves elsewhere. So shall I do, but not, I fear, for some days yet. Will you grant us leave to remain until my child is born?"

"Allah forbid that I should refuse you," the sultan said. He sounded honestly shocked that she should hint at such a thing.

She inclined her head. "Will my lord also allow me the presence of my household and my kin, undiminished, and our departure unmolested when I and my child are able to travel?"

He raised a hand. "You have my word on it."

Again she bowed her head. "The world knows that Salah al-Din Yusuf is a man of his word. Now it may know that he is also generous and compassionate, as a lord of Islam should be."

She was not flattering him emptily, and he seemed to know it. He offered her food and drink. She did not want them, but she understood what they signified. She choked down a bit of bread sprinkled with salt, and a sip of something sweet and redolent of oranges. She made the others share both. None of them argued, for a miracle.

Saladin watched them in silence. The rest of the hall had gone back to its own concerns, whether brooding on defeat or celebrating victory. She wondered if any of them had laid wagers on her dropping the baby where she sat.

The sultan was not watching her, after all, or even the beautiful Elen. His eyes kept seeking the children, now narrowing and growing keen, now dragging themselves away, now flicking back as if they could not help themselves.

Ysabel spoke before Joanna could stop her, clearly enough for him to hear, but too soft to be understood at any distance. "Yes, we are. How is it that you can see?"

Saladin sat very still. He did not look frightened. Fascinated, more like, and even a little elated. "Would there happen to be more of you?"

"Three in Damascus," she answered boldly, "and the two of us. Aren't we enough?"

"Quite ample for the purpose," he said. Yes, he was pleased. He reckoned Aidan a friend, as much as any

Frank could be; that had not changed, as Joanna had been able to tell when he spoke of the two in Damascus. He regarded Ysabel in honest delight, and said, "Your princely kinsman tells me that I have a keener eye than most."

"He told me. I remember now." Ysabel was clearly as fascinated by him as he was by her, if somewhat more defiant than delighted. "He likes you. He's sorry you couldn't have been on his side of the war."

"As am I," said Saladin. "But God wills as He wills, and He has been kind to your kinsmen. When they have had time to rest and restore themselves, I shall send them back to you."

"Why not now?"

"It was a hard battle," he said, "and they fought more bravely than any. They took no more than a scratch or two, but they are very tired."

"You killed my father," she said. "I saw him die."

Her voice was rising. Joanna raised her hand to clamp it over the young imp's mouth, but paused. Saladin was speaking. He was calm, but there was steel in it. "Your father, madam?"

Joanna went cold.

"My mother's husband," said Ysabel. "His name was Ranulf de Mortmain."

Saladin frowned. It was not a comforting thing to see, though Joanna could detect no anger in him. "I did not kill him, my lady. He died of his wounds before we could save him."

"Your battle killed him. Your people cut him down."

"That is the way of wars and warriors, my lady."

Joanna could not move, let alone speak. Saladin addressed Ysabel no longer as a child; he gave her the respect, and the honesty, due a grown woman.

She gave him implacable will. "You owe us reparation."

Saladin's brows went up. "Yes, my lady? On what do you base that contention?"

"He died by your fault. You kept him waiting too long when he should have had water and tending. He might still be alive to be ransomed, if you hadn't left him dying in the sun. You owe us his blood-price."

"You know that for a certainty?"

"I saw it," she said.

He knew how she saw. He sat back, running his finger along his jaw, tracing an old scar that ran into his beard. Joanna did not think that he would drive them out and refuse them what he had promised them: he was much too honorable for that. But Ysabel had gone far beyond what was allowable for a child who owed her life to his clemency. When Joanna got her wits back, she would tan the imp's hide.

Saladin lowered the lids over his fine dark eyes. Ysabel stood with her chin up, glaring as formidably as ever. He looked her up and down calmly. "You are a very forward child," he said.

"I loved my father."

She did not put any charm into it, and she certainly did not choke with maidenly tears.

He nodded. "That is evident. Suppose that I were willing to pay your price. Have you considered that everyone who lost a kinsman in the battle might ask the same of me? How then would I pay my army?"

"No one else is forward enough," she said. "No one else saw her father die."

"Still," he said. "Is it fair?"

"War isn't fair."

Saladin stared at her. Suddenly he began to laugh. He was not laughing at her, not exactly. "My lady, you should be a *qadi!* You argue as irresistibly as one, and rather more cogently." He sobered; he leaned forward. "So then, you have your blood-price. But let it be understood that that removes all obligations between us, except insofar as they touch on my compact with your mother."

"I don't ask any more," she said.

"You might ask your mother to spare you the rod," said Saladin. "Out of the generosity of my heart, and because I reckon you a worthy opponent, I add my plea to yours. For this time, at least," he added cannily. "Future transgressions, I cannot speak for."

Ysabel's face was stony, but Joanna could sense her admiration. It was not often that Ysabel met her match; and never, up to now, had that been a human man. She curtsied, going down rather deeper than anyone might have expected. Admiration indeed, and unwilling respect. "Thank you, my lord," she said.

27

Ysabel would have to be punished. But, like Augustine and sanctity, not yet. The baby, having obliged its mother by holding off until she was out of the sultan's presence, now wanted to come all at once. The pains were coming sharp and close even before the litter rocked and swayed its way under Joanna's own blessed roof. She walked away from it; she insisted on that.

Zoe was there, that small dark woman with her astonishing gift for healing. Her assistant was new, and young. "Demetrios went back to the City," she said, meaning by that what every Byzantine did, Constantinople on the Golden Horn. "It was well past time, I told him. As if he would ever listen. He insisted that I still had more to teach. Even when he left he dragged his feet, for fear he might have missed one last, tiny secret."

Joanna smiled, though a new pain turned it to a grimace. She was sorry not to see the young eunuch with his great dreaming eyes, but glad that he had spread his wings at last. The new apprentice looked a little scared. "Your first birth?" Joanna asked her.

The child shook her head, dumb with shyness.

"Her first noblewoman," Zoe said. She crooked a finger. The apprentice ducked her head and scampered, transparently glad to have a signal to answer and an errand to run off to.

The bedchamber was ready. Dura knew, as she always did; though mute, she could command the servants well when she chose. The birthing-stool stood in its accustomed place. There were heaps of clean cloths, fresh sheets on the bed and fresh sheets waiting, swaddling for the baby and a cradle to lay it in, and water, and wine laced with poppy if Joanna should need it. She was not too proud to confess that she well might. William had come feet first, and nearly torn her in two.

This one was facing as it ought. She could feel it, and never mind who might call it nonsense. Zoe, searching, confirmed it with a smile. "All in good order," she said.

Much of birthing was waiting. The rest was sheer hard work, and pain, and pain ten times over. Joanna thought in the ever-shortening pauses of cattle, how easy by comparison it was to birth a calf. If man was wrought in God's image, then God was a preposterous, big-headed, totter-balanced, furless comedy of a creature.

She caught the blasphemy before it ran away. *Father,* she prayed, *forgive.*

There were eyes in the shadows beyond the bed. Joanna took them for a delusion born of pain, but they did not go away when she bade them. Eyes. Two pairs of them. One gleamed beast-green; the other, beast-red.

"Ysabel," said Joanna, low in her throat. "Come out of there."

They both came, humble enough to look at, but there was no contrition in them. Joanna must have been a sight to remember. Her hair straggled out of its braid; her shift was sodden with sweat; her belly was vast beneath it, rippling with the birth-spasms. A woman need never have shame of this that she was born for, but it was not an easy thing for a child to understand.

"We aren't children." It was Akiva who said it in his sweet, unbroken voice. He reached out half boldly, half shyly, and laid his hand on the summit of her belly. His touch was warm and cool at once. It made her think, somehow, of the way sunlight felt on her face, when it was still winter but spring was almost come.

She heard Zoe's brief, well-chosen words. "Children or no, you have no place here. Go."

Neither child deigned to hear her. Ysabel took her mother's hand and held it. Akiva seemed rapt in his own hand where it lay on Joanna's middle. "I can see it," he said. "How it all goes together. Why it does what it does. Why it has to hurt."

"If you can tell me that," Joanna gritted, "then you're even more than I took you for."

"It's to make you push hard enough. Pushing helps it; and when you push, the baby comes." He paused. Wonder dawned in his face. "I can make the hurt stop."

He could; he did. She breathed a great sigh; then she knotted with fear. "But if I have to hurt— Bring it back! For the baby's sake, bring it back."

"It's not the hurt that's necessary," Akiva said. His voice was dry, dispassionate, scholarly. "If your body does what is required of it, whether it hurts or not is unimportant. Therefore, why hurt?"

She could feel the muscles clench, but that clenching was without pain. It frightened her. "It has to hurt. God made it so."

"God made fever, too. Does that mean you have to die of it?"

Damn the boy. She wanted him out. She wanted him there, with his hand on her, taking away the pain. What would it do to her baby to be brought into the world without anguish, without taking its mother down to the borderlands of death? It was against Scripture. It was blessedly, blissfully easy.

It was still work. She had to push. There was no taking that away from her.

Akiva stayed, and Ysabel, for once subdued and silent. Ysabel did not look frightened, even at the blood. Someday it would be she who labored to bear a child, just as her mother did now.

It was not so ill to have her there. Zoe was not pleased, but Zoe, like Saladin, had a clearer eye than most. And she knew whose child Ysabel was. She had been there the night Joanna almost died, long ago in Aleppo, when Aidan—and, more deadly by far, Morgiana—learned that he had begotten a child. Joanna was alive because Aidan, who had no power to heal, still had known what human healers knew of how to remove a dagger from a woman's heart, and how not to kill her while he did it; but when that was done, it was for Zoe to see that she did not die of shock or wound-fever, or lose her baby.

When Ysabel was born, Aidan was there. Zoe had not liked that, either; it went sorely against her grain to share a birthing with a man. But Aidan was not to be quarreled with. "Our children are different," he had said to Joanna, somewhat before she came to childbed. "For your safety as much as for her own, I must be with her when she is born."

That had been a long birth. Longer by far than this one. Ysabel had fought it, her father said. Witch-children did. They had will for that, and consciousness. He had been talking to her as his kind did, in thoughts without words, since she began to move in the womb; he told Joanna that, well after Ysabel was born, when she could not recoil or grow afraid. But she had suspected something like it. She had been more aware of Ysabel within her than of Aimery before her, or than she would be of any of her children after. She was not shocked when the small, yelling, furious body was laid on her belly, and its howling stopped, and it opened eyes that, though stunned by the light, saw her with perfect and wondering clarity. Joanna saw that those eyes were not human. They accepted this world and her mother as Joanna accepted her daughter, warily but with growing gladness.

Ysabel-then and Ysabel-now blurred and came together. "Akiva has the gift," Ysabel said, envious. "The way the king does. I wish I wasn't so young. I wish I had my gifts."

"But," said Joanna, gasping it between contractions, "you have. As your f—your uncle has. He told me so."

Ysabel did not leap on the slip. Joanna prayed that she had not noticed it at all; had taken it for a breath drawn awry. Now was no time to tell her daughter that she had been lied to all her life.

Joanna focused herself narrowly on getting Ranulf's last child born alive. Akiva was tiring, or his power was not strong enough yet to take away the great pains that heralded birth. Each in succession made itself more strongly felt, though never as strong as if there had been no witch-child standing by her with sweat running down his face, every atom of his being fixed on making this birth go as it should. She could not persuade him to give over. After a while she stopped trying.

"Now," one of them said. "Once more. Once—*Now!*"

Silence. A prick of fear. Then, blessedly loud, the baby's cry.

Zoe lifted it. Her. Clotted with birth-blood, purpled-red, flailing, howling like a banshee: beautiful. Five fingers on each hand, five toes on each foot, arms and legs as they ought to be, down of damp dark hair, eyes and nose and mouth, small big-bellied body with the discreet fold of its sex. She stopped crying soon enough and settled into this new art of breathing.

Joanna let herself sink into the bed and opened her arms. Zoe laid the child in them, all wet as she was, still bound to her mother by the cord. "Salima," Joanna said. The name came out of its own accord; it was not the one she had chosen some while since. A Muslim name for a child born under the Muslim sultan. It was a kind of defiance. It meant, not *defeat,* but *peace.* And in peace, hope.

Part Five

TYRE

August 1187

28

Damascus was ancient and beautiful, a green city in the endless dun expanse of the desert, a vision of paradise: towers and minarets above the green of fields and orchards, watered by the myriad streams of Barada. There was no city older, and few more fair to see.

It was a prison.

Aidan was not, they all kept telling him, a prisoner. He was ransomed, he was an honored guest, when it was safe he would be permitted to depart.

"Safe," he said, spitting it. "For whom? I gave my word. Has Saladin forgotten all that I am?"

"He remembers," Morgiana said.

It was not her house in which the brothers and their companions were kept. This belonged to an emir who rode now with Saladin. His wives kept apart in the harem, but his servants were assiduous in seeing to the guests' comfort. They all knew Morgiana: the emir, whose name was Ishak ibn Farouk, had inherited her by way of his father, whom she reckoned the best sword-smith in Syria and perhaps in the world. Farouk, and his father and grandfather before him, had always forged her blades. Ishak had none of their gift; he was born not to forge blades but to wield them. His sister's husband pursued the family's calling, and his sister's sons showed signs of taking after their father. The succession, as Ishak liked to say, was secure. He could settle with a clear conscience to the life of a knight of Islam.

Ishak was with Saladin. He had been at the capture of Acre. He was part of the vast locust-swarm that swept over Outremer, devouring all before it.

Aidan prowled the tiled halls and the fountained courtyards as if they had been a cage. Each castle that fell, each city that surrendered, stabbed his heart to fresh pain. And he could do nothing. His word was given. He could not escape, he could not arm himself, he could not fight.

Morgiana gave him no comfort. He could not help but know what it meant that she was here and not with her sultan. She too had made choices.

But she kept him here. She tried to distract him. She walked or rode with him through the city; she took him hunting among the orchards; she took him with honest joy to her bed.

He cherished every moment of her presence, but it was driving him mad. Even Aimery was a better prisoner than Aidan. And why not? Aimery was biding his time. When he was freed, he would go back to war against the infidel.

Gwydion sank into deepening quiet. He too waited, not to be freed to fight, but to return to his own kingdom. Aidan's prowling and snarling barely ruffled his calm.

His calm ruffled Aidan more than enough. "O serenity! Who would guess that you turn madman in a battle?"

"I do not," said Gwydion. "I lose my temper. No more than that."

"So does the sea lose its temper when it swallows the fleet. Why do you bottle yourself up now? Why aren't you acting like a reasonable being, instead of making sure it will all come out again when you least want it to? When there's a sword in your hand and an enemy in front of you, and you go blood-mad."

"I," said Gwydion with the barest hint of tightness, "am a reasonable being."

"Now you are." Aidan turned away in disgust. Gwydion would never give him a decent fight. This was the best one he could ever get out of him: a suggestion of displeasure, a hint of ripple in his calm.

Morgiana would not fight, either. "Last time was enough," she said.

"Then let me out," he said. "Let me out of this trap."

She would not. No more than she would fight.

There were other knightly prisoners in Damascus, and some had been there unransomed far longer than Aidan. The king and the Grand Master of the Templars, once they had recovered fully from the ravages of the battle, were taken out of the city and compelled to ride with Saladin, living trophies of his victory. Humphrey of Toron rode with them to serve as their interpreter.

The king's brother remained under guard in the citadel. Aidan was permitted to call on him, and did, for charity; but Aidan had never been overfond of Messire Amalric de Lusignan. As a fellow in suffering, he left somewhat to be desired.

Most bitter of all was what had become of the lesser folk of the army. Twenty-five thousand lived and were taken prisoner. Those who did not die of wounds or ill-treatment were sold in the slave market of Damascus.

Aidan could not buy them all. Morgiana would not let him buy even one. "No," she said in front of one of many blocks with Franks chained to it, sullen or snarling or numb with shock. "What Allah has written, Allah has written. You have your mamluks who are left. Be content with them."

He would have bid for some of them in spite of her, but she had the purse and would not give it up. Her eyes, level on him, commanded him to see sense. If he beggared himself, well and good. But what of his mamluks here, his people in Millefleurs, his kin who had need of his wealth and his strength? What would become of them?

A prince, even a prince who was a witch, could not cure all the ills of the world. So should he have learned long ago.

"But some of them," he said with sudden passion, "some of them I can mend. However poorly. For however little a while."

Morgiana narrowed her eyes. After a moment she handed him the purse.

He bought as many of the captives as he could, and set them free; and they were properly grateful, most of them, if they still had wits left for it. But there were always more. There would never be an end to them.

"That man," Morgiana said, "is the worst captive I have ever seen or heard of."

"Then let him go," said Gwydion.

She glared at him. He had barely interrupted his reading to speak to her. He was reading holy Koran. To understand it, he said, inasmuch as he could with his imperfect Arabic.

"How can I let him go?" she demanded. "He'll only ride hell-for-leather for the war, and tear himself apart wanting to fight in it."

"Not if you go with him."

Her lip curled. "Yes. Then he'll simply tear me apart. I can't trust him, brother my lord."

"And why can't you trust him?" He did not wait for her to answer. "Because, sister my lady. He knows how little trust you place in his given word."

"I trust his word!"

"Then let him go."

She stood in thrumming silence. Gwydion went back to his reading. His lips moved slowly, puzzling out the intricacies of the Prophet's Arabic. He stopped, frowning faintly.

" 'Folly,' " she said harshly. " 'Folly' is the word you want."

He bowed his thanks. She left him to it.

Her friend the swordsmith's daughter had no time for her: one of the children was ailing, and it was not anything Morgiana could heal, nor anything deadly enough to shock the household by dragging Gwydion into it. She passed from place to place as her power moved her. None of them lightened her mood. Her cavern in Persia made it worse by far. There were too many memories in it. The swordsmith's daughter, Ishak's sister, estranged from her husband and given sanctuary there with her eldest son, who was now a well-grown lad apprenticed to his father; and Aidan, held captive then as now, and considerably less well disposed toward his captor. He had wanted her blood then. And so he had had it, if never in the way he had expected: not heart's blood but maiden blood. He had been startled to find her truly virgin. Startled and, somewhat to his credit, abashed. It was not in Aidan to be a ravisher of maidens.

Then, he had hated her, but he had endured his captivity because he thought that it accomplished something: it kept her from endangering his kin. Now he had no such comfort. He knew that Joanna and her children had been in Acre when it fell. He knew of her newborn daughter and of her departure, the moment she was allowed out of her bed, for Tyre.

Morgiana spun like a devil-wind, loathing that great, fecund cow of a Frank. But thinking clearly for all of that, and seeing by degrees what had been eluding her.

Tyre was safe. It was no more or less impregnable than Acre, but it was full of men who knew how to fight. They had all gone there, fleeing the sultan, Raymond of Tripoli first, but he left too soon and sought his own city. He thought Tripoli more easily defended than Tyre, less likely to tempt the sultan to attack it. So it was. But he reckoned without the one who came to Tyre after him.

Conrad of Montferrat, son of the marquis who had been taken at Hattin, kinsman to the kings of Jerusalem, was young but he was wily, and he had studied in the best school of intrigue in the world: at the court of the emperor in Constantinople. He had, unfortunately, outsmarted himself; someone died who had influence in high places, and Conrad's hand was evident in it. He left the City in haste, sailing well ahead of the news of Hattin. He brought his ship to harbor in Acre just after Saladin left it, but it was clear who held the city. If Saladin's son had been only a little wiser in the ways of war, Conrad would have been taken prisoner. But al-Afdal moved too slowly. Conrad escaped and sailed headlong for Tyre.

He found it on the brink of surrender. He was whitely furious to see the kingdom fallen so far; he disposed of Reynaud of Sidon, who had been in command of the city and who was about to hand it over uncontested to the enemy. He took command himself, drove the garrison to the ramparts, and made it clear that Tyre would not surrender without a fight.

Saladin was not minded to give it one. He had the rest of Outremer to occupy him. If all the rats chose to gather in that single bolthole, then so much the better; he could trap them at his leisure.

"Not when they have the sea at their backs and ships to sail on it," Morgiana said. The echoes of her voice rang faintly to the roof of the cavern. She could, if she willed it, step from this hidden place in Persia to the heart of the sultan's camp, and warn him that even rats were deadly under a strong king. Conrad wanted to be that. Morgiana could read him with ease, simply from what was said of him.

She did not move. She had left the sultan's service after Hattin. "You need me no longer," she had said. "Those against whom I defended you are in your power. Hereafter you need no more aid than mortal men can give."

Saladin had been less than pleased to let her go, but he had bowed to the inevitable. She was not his slave or his kinswoman, to be bound to him until one of them died. She had served him of her own free will, and been honest with him as to why she did it. Because it was holy war, yes. And because the Franks had a pair of white enchanters, and she did not intend them to gain the victory thereby. Mortal men had begun this war. Mortal men would settle it.

Even she could hardly have reckoned on the enormity of the Franks' folly.

She traversed the threefold cavern, circling round to the narrow gullet that was its gate and coming out under the sky. It was empty even of a cloud. "Allah," she said as she used to do when she was the Slave of Alamut, alone and solitary, with no one in the world to call friend. "Allah, what would You do? I don't want him to be tempted. No more do I want him to fret himself into a fever. He won't let me take him direct to Rhiyana. He says he can't abandon this country so absolutely. How can he make himself abandon its war?"

He could, because he had given his word. Was it more cruel to loose him into a war he could not fight, or to hold him prisoner against his will?

"Allah," she said. "Allah, I don't know. I thought I was being wise. He's learning to forgive me; he loves me in spite of himself."

But he wanted to be free to choose where he would go.

"He has to go to Rhiyana. He won't until he makes the Patriarch say the marriage-words over us."

Should he not then be freed to hunt down the pope's letter and its forger?

She paused. A slow smile bloomed. She dropped down on her knees and bowed three times toward Mecca, and leaped up, and danced for sheer exuberance. "Yes! Yes, that is it! Allah, *Allahu akbar!* Who but You could have conceived it? I'll free him to hunt. I'll hunt with him. We'll both be so intent on our tracking that it won't matter that he can't do any fighting. And when we've found what was lost . . ." She swept out her dagger and stabbed the air just where a man's heart would be, pounding in terror of the lady of the Assassins. *"So!* And the Patriarch says the words, and we have our night's lawfully wedded bliss, and we sail for Rhiyana, and so we live in peace forever after.

"Or as much peace as either of us can stand." She laughed and spun and flipped her dagger into its sheath. "O Allah, what a hunt it will be!"

Little as Aidan liked Messire Amalric, he went to the sultan's palace often enough to satisfy a saint, and for much the same reason. It was his way of mortifying his flesh.

The erstwhile Constable of the Kingdom of Jerusalem kept up his spirits remarkably well. He did not see fit
to study Arabic, even if he had had any talent for lan-
guages, but he managed to make himself understood. He
was allowed some freedom: to speak with his fellow captives and to walk under guard in one of the gardens.

Aidan found him engaged in both, and with no lesser
a personage than Humphrey of Toron. The young
scholar-lord looked all a Saracen from his bronzed, un-
shaven face to his slippered feet. Amalric, by contrast,
stubbornly refused to stoop to robe and trousers, but
kept to cotte and hose, and shaved his beard every week.

Humphrey turned to Aidan with a wide white smile.
"My lord prince! You look well."

"Well," said Amalric, "indeed. A perfect prince of
Saracens."

Humphrey laughed. "When in Rome—or in Damascus. Admit it, Amalric. You're melting away under all
that wool."

"At least I look like what I am," Amalric said.

Aidan fell in beside them. His head had begun to
ache, as it often did of late. Another price of his captivity. He firmed the walls about his mind and contented
himself with perceiving the world as humans did, with
eyes and ears and nose. The last wrinkled slightly. He
did not know which was worse, Amalric's unabashedly
human reek or the musk in which Humphrey seemed to
have bathed.

Humphrey flung a glad arm about his shoulders.
Aidan smiled in spite of himself, and forbore to edge
away. "I thought you were with the king," he said.

"I was," said Humphrey. "I came back with a message. The ransom is set. The sultan wants Messire
Amalric's word that, if he goes as envoy to collect it,
he'll come back to the sultan after."

"I'll give him my word," Amalric said.

"Ah, but will you keep it?" Aidan met their stares,
Humphrey's rather more indignant than Amalric's. "I
would, if I were you; and honor has nothing to do with
it. You know what Saladin does to men who break their
oaths."

"He holds my brother hostage," Amalric said. "That might keep me honest."

Aidan considered that. "It might. I'll wager that's what Saladin is trusting in."

"We all know," said Amalric, "that an oath sworn to an infidel is no oath. But an oath with one's brother as surety—that's binding."

"That's what your brother told the sultan," Humphrey said. "I won't say there's liking between them, they're too different for that, but they see the virtue in being honest with one another."

"So," Aidan said. "They're letting you go."

Amalric did not even pretend to be abashed. "I'm on a longer leash, that's all. I'll be yanked back soon enough. Do you have any messages for me to carry?"

"Thank you," Aidan said, "but no."

"Ah," said Amalric. "I forgot. Your lady—is she still running errands for the sultan?"

Amalric knew that she was not. Aidan showed his teeth in what might be taken for a smile. "No; now she runs them for me. She was in Nablus yesterday. The queen is well, she says, though she feels the absence of her husband. It's a pretty sight, a queen who adores her consort so unashamedly."

"Should she be ashamed?" Amalric inquired.

"That is hardly for me to say," Aidan said.

Amalric tired of the sport soon after, or perhaps of sweltering in wool and linen, and excused himself. Humphrey did not immediately follow him. Aidan did not intend to.

"It's like a tournament," Humphrey said, "watching you two talk. You'd almost think you hated one another."

"We do," said Aidan. "Cordially."

Humphrey eyed him sidelong. "I'm afraid I believe you." He shook his head. "I know how little good it ever does to say it, but have you considered how dangerous this game is? Amalric is a good deal more clever than he looks, and considerably less amiable. He's a bad enemy."

"So am I," Aidan said.

"My lord," said Humphrey. "If I presume, forgive me. But you may be more vulnerable than you know. There's always talk, I know, and now it waxes hysterical, but hysteria can be deadly. Some in what's left of the kingdom might find it useful to have a scapegoat. Not a king's folly or a sultan's superiority in numbers and in generalship, or even the ill luck that plagued the king beyond his own incapacities, but the sorcerers who rode with the army and refused to win the victory for it."

"We couldn't," Aidan said. "We weren't wanted when we could have done something; when we were wanted, it was too late."

"You could have shown the king where he was in error."

"No," said Aidan. "We have our laws. We don't compel. And compulsion it would have had to be, as set on his course as Guy was."

"What do you call what Ridefort did at Cresson?"

"Gerard de Ridefort convinced the king to do what he, himself, wanted most to do. It wasn't only the king, remember. Most of those he trusted thought it better to move then than to wait and sacrifice Tiberias. What Raymond did in convincing him to wait was as much as any man could do. Or any enchanter."

"People won't accept that. You could have changed Guy's mind. You wouldn't. You and your brother both—you kept to the letter of your word, and the battle was lost."

"It wouldn't matter if we had compelled him. There would be other, like circumstances; and others still. Eventually he was bound to fall."

"He might not have taken the kingdom with him." Humphrey paused to calm himself. "There, I'm forgetting how to be reasonable. You see how easy it is. People aren't logical, and they're even less so when their world is falling out from under them. They're looking for something to blame it on. They'll burn you if they can."

"Amalric, too?"

"Amalric more than any. And you encourage him."

"Are you telling me that I should lie to him?"

"I'd prefer to call it circumspection."

Aidan shook his head. "He's no danger to me. He still thinks he may have hope of escape—from here if he can persuade me to wield my alleged powers, and from Outremer if he can persuade my brother to give him the Lady Elen."

"It's not an ill match," Humphrey said reflectively, "while there's still a kingdom for him to be Constable of."

Aidan laughed without mirth. "I knew that would distract you. You never could resist a good intrigue."

"Well," said Humphrey. "Can you get him free of this captivity?"

"No." Aidan would have left it at that, but something in Humphrey's expression made him add, "Morgiana stops me. She's stronger than I."

Humphrey admired him for admitting it. Foolish, Aidan thought. There was nothing admirable in knowing one's own limits: narrow as those were when one stopped to consider them. The least of the angels had more power in the world than Aidan did. The masters of the black arts claimed more; and maybe they had it.

"What I can do," Aidan said, "is seldom what I should, and not often what is wise. I could have taken Hattin out of human hands and made it a battle of sorceries. Maybe, between us, my brother and I would have won. What then? Would people be any less eager to see us burn?"

"Victory at any cost," said Humphrey, "is hard to resist, when one has seen the horror of defeat."

"And we are very convenient targets." Aidan stopped under a rose arbor and plucked a blossom. Its thorns stung him fiercely. The pain was almost welcome. The scent was worth the price, and the beauty of the petals, each the color of heart's blood, but in the flower's heart a glimmer of gold. "You know what will happen to us in the end. We'll be hounded out of human lands; we'll be branded with anathema. It's the human way. Don't they do it to the old gods wherever they go, and to the beasts who hunt the forests, and to the land itself in compelling it to serve them? They make it in their image. What cannot or will not be so altered, they destroy."

Humphrey did not speak. He tried to understand, that was evident, but he was human and young, and no little afraid. Even he, who honestly liked Aidan, did not like to be reminded that Aidan was something other than a human man.

In Rhiyana people knew and accepted. They had the blood, if not the magic.

Aidan's fingers tightened on the rose-stem. Carefully, in a cascade of stinging pains, he worked them free. Not in years had he known so fierce a longing for his own country. The wind and the cold; the rain that blew off the sea with an edge of sleet; the green places and the grey stones and the mist on the headlands.

He could feel it, cool on his face; taste the salt in it; scent the sea. It was strange to look through it and see the garden of the Saracen sultan, and Humphrey standing in it, looking a Saracen himself, slender and dark and clad in silk.

"We could not have done other than we did," Aidan said. "If that condemns us, then so be it. We can do what we may to protect the humans who have dared to call us friends. Our leaving will help. If," he said, "we are ever permitted to depart from this city."

"You'll go," Humphrey said, understanding that much at least. "You'll go back to Rhiyana."

Aidan nodded.

"Good," said Humphrey. "For myself, I'll be sorry not to see you again. But it would be best for you to escape while you can."

"And for the kingdom, to escape the temptation that is our power. To use it. Or to destroy it."

"Both," Humphrey said. He took the rose from Aidan's fingers with a graceful gesture and bowed over it. "I'd best go. Messire Amalric is waiting, and so, at somewhat greater remove, is my lord sultan. God grant we meet again."

He said the last in Arabic. It was a farewell, as graceful as the gesture with which he had appropriated the rose. He did not linger for Aidan's response, or want to hear it.

Aidan gave him the gift of silence. He had been, after all, a friend. The last Aidan saw of him, the rose was tucked in his turban and he was rehearsing what more he must say to Amalric. A friend, was Humphrey of Toron, and a loyal ally, and a shameless sentimentalist; but with all of that, a sensible man. He would not weep for what he could not change.

An art which Aidan would do well to learn. He paused, weighing pain and purpose and considering what would be sacrilege for a blade of Farouk's forging. Quickly then, with his silver-hafted dagger, he cut a rose the color of wine.

Morgiana accepted the gift as she always did: with no attempt at artifice. She frowned at it as he set it in her hand, and then at him as he bowed extravagantly. "What is this for?"

"For you," he said. "Because you madden me, and yet I love you. Don't you like it? It's the exact shade of your hair."

Her frown deepened to a scowl. "My hair is preposterous."

"It's beautiful." He kissed it where it parted smoothly to ripple down shoulders and back and haunches. "You are the most beautiful woman in the world."

"Is all this in aid of something?" she asked. "Are you trying to bribe me, by any chance?"

He refused to lose his temper. "For once," he said, "no. I've made some choices. When you see fit to let me go, I shall go, and not stop until I come to Rhiyana."

"What, not at all?"

"Not for anything."

"Not for war? Not," she said, "for me?"

"For war," he said, "no. For you . . ." He looked down at her. She seemed like a child, looking up, with her great eyes and her pointed chin. "For you, I'll stop in

Rome, and browbeat the lord pope himself into making us honest sinners."

"You don't need to do that," she said.

He stilled. "So. You'll stay in Islam. Will you miss me a little when I'm gone?"

She struck him, not hard, but hard enough to sting. "Were you born a fool, or was it the humans who made you one? What makes you think I'd leave you again?"

"But—" he said.

"I left you once," she said, "because I let my temper get the better of me, and because you so obviously needed the lesson. Now that you've learned as much from it as you ever can—"

"If I'm so contemptible," he said bitterly, "why do you waste yourself on me?"

"You are not—"

"Listen to yourself. Child, you think me. Fool. Vaunting boy. Always in some degree of disgrace. Never capable of more than the most rudimentary good sense."

"Aren't you all of that? Aren't I?" She raised her hand, the one that did not hold the rose, and stroked his cheek. He stiffened against her. "My dear love, I never know how to talk to you. I say too much or I say too little, and what I say is never what I meant to say. How it is that you can love me in spite of it—surely Allah has a hand in it."

"God," he said.

"Allah." She frowned, but she wiped the frown away. "My lord, you are all that I am, and much that I could wish to be."

"Male?"

"Allah, no." She tugged lightly at his beard. "Can you imagine what I would look like?"

"Like Bahram the eunuch who serves Saladin."

"Served," she said. "I am my own woman again."

"And not mine?"

"Can't I be both?"

His head tossed. It had stopped aching shortly after Amalric left the sultan's garden; there was no pain in it now, but he was dizzy enough that it hardly mattered. She did that to him. Dangled him, spun him, befuddled him. He never knew what she would say or do. "A woman is not," he said, "her own possession. She has to belong to a man."

"Why?"

"Who will look after her? Who will protect her? Who will defend her honor?"

"I like to imagine," she said, "that I have some small facility in those arts."

He shut his mouth.

"You can look after me," she said, "and I can look after you. That's what being wedded is. Isn't it?"

"Then you won't be your own woman any longer. You'll be mine."

"And you will belong to me. And we will both remain ourselves. I won't be your shadow, any more than I'll ask you to be mine."

That was well, he thought, as anger gave way to wry amusement. He had never been able to teach her a woman's proper place. Even when she professed to have learned, she only played at it. In a day or a month she wearied of it, and became herself again.

And why should he bemoan his failure, when the whole doctrine of Islam could not compel her?

"You don't need to stop in Rome," she said with her infallible memory for the meat of any discussion. "We can find the pope's letter here, and the one who forged it, and the ones who abetted him. Then we'll have revenge as well as one another."

"Revenge isn't Christian."

"No more am I." She curved her arm about his neck. "I'm going to trust you. I'm going to let you go."

At first he barely understood her. Go? Trust? "What in God's name—"

"You're free. You can go. If you will promise to hunt with me, and not with the armies of Outremer."

"I can't hunt with what pitiful little is left of the army. I'm sworn."

"So. You're free to hunt with me."

He stood still with her arm about his neck and her hand cradling the rose between them, and her self all open to him. It was not given as his due. It was given because she chose; because she loved him.

Strange, that air of equality. Heady. More than a little alarming. It was heretical on both sides of this war.

"You're mad, I think," he said. She regarded him unblinking. "Yes," he said. "Yes, I'll hunt with you."

29

It was strange, Elen thought. The Kingdom of Jerusalem was overrun; the Saracens harried it in every hill and valley, every fold and inlet in the coast; the flower of its chivalry was dead or taken and its king was held in captivity. Yet Tyre kept its pride. Here the knights and barons came who had not fallen or been taken at Hattin; here the merchants of Acre gathered, cheek by jowl with the traders of Tyre; here was strength of purpose, embodied in the one who had taken over the city's defenses and held them against Saladin. Marquis Conrad would not allow the word *defeat* to be spoken in his presence. "We have suffered a reversal," he said where any could hear. "And not a slight one, either. But we can regain what we have lost. All Europe will rise and come to our aid. Only wait, and hold, and see."

The city waited, and held, and saw: that Saladin was not inclined to besiege it once he saw how strongly it was held. He departed in search of softer prey; the city held a festival. At the height of it they made a mummery, a mockery of the infidel who saw bright steel and strong walls, and fled with his tail between his legs.

Elen had expected at best to endure this last desperate refuge before she fled westward. She was startled to fall in love with the city. As old as Nineveh, they said, as old as Tyre. It was in Scripture; it was in the books which she had read, her Latin and her bit of Greek, and even the old, sweet, lying Latin story of Apollonius prince of Tyre. Its reality was this rock upon the sea, with its walls rising sheer out of the water and its great twin-towered harbor warded by a chain and its single gate upon the land. That was Alexander's genius and his madness, that causeway built by men's hands and mortared with their blood, to make an isthmus of the island because it would not yield to his kingship. The Roman road stretched die-straight down it, from the frown of wall and gate to the sun-scorched green of the fields and villages, and along it ran the lofty arches of the Romans' aqueduct, carrying water from the springs that never failed.

It was beautiful, was Tyre. It was full of fountains. There were memories of Rome in its houses, a fluted column or a jeweled pavement; more than a memory of Byzantium in the street of the glassmakers, under the crumbling portico with its sea-veined marble, as they plied their delicate trade. And in the sea, if the wind was calm and one's eyes were keen, one could see the sunken city, the Tyre that was as old as Nineveh: castles and markets, streets and palaces, drowned like Ys or Lyonesse, but older far, and beautiful, with its citizenry of fishes.

Tyre was as old as time, but there was no weariness in it. Its every house and hovel was full to bursting. Its churches rang with the voices of the faithful. Its markets thrummed with commerce; its harbor sheltered a fleet which would, its lord hoped, secure the sea for the Franks.

When the Mortmains and their guests entered the city, Elen at first feared that there would be no place for them; or that, at best, they would be sundered, quartered among strangers. But she had reckoned without Joanna. The House of Ibrahim was a kingdom of trade. Elen had been told as much without ceasing, but she had never quite understood it. Now she began to see. For a daughter of that great merchant House, there was indeed lodging to be had: a veritable palace, a caravanserai of a full five stories overlooking the harbor, with gardens and fountains and its own gate on the quay. It was not theirs alone, it could not be, but they had the better part of a wing to themselves, and the merchants who shared it were profoundly respectful of the lady and her following.

"It would be so wherever I went," Joanna said. "Wherever traders are, our House is known. We have a house in Rhiyana, surely you know it."

Elen did, vaguely.

Joanna laughed at her. "My lord prince is just like you. He admits, after long persuasion, that without us the world would be a far poorer place—and he a far, far poorer man. But still, to associate himself with trade . . . it goes against everything he was bred for."

"He is a prince," said Elen, "after all."

"That's what his mamluks say. Do you know how they kept the regent of Aleppo from executing him as a spy, when he was there as my guardsman? They reminded the regent that my lord Aidan is a Frank and a prince; could he possibly be so sensible as to take anyone's pay, let alone for spying on his enemies?"

"They played him for a fool?" Elen was indignant.

"They saved his life," Joanna said. "And it was true enough. Can you imagine him doing anything because he was paid to?"

"No," said Elen, after a pause. "But still, to mock him for being honorable—"

"He mocks them for being a race of merchants. Fair is fair."

Elen decided not to be angry. Her uncle hardly needed her to defend him; he was quite enough in himself. She turned her bit of handwork in her fingers. No pretty trifles, here; all the women had ample to do keeping the tribe of children in clothes. She was piecing together a chemise for one of the girls, out of an outworn one of Joanna's.

Joanna nursed the youngest of her daughters with every appearance of content. She was almost a stranger without the weight of pregnancy to bear her down: a big woman, yes, broad-hipped and deep-breasted, but light on her feet, and rather more handsome than she gave herself credit for. Black became her vilely, and she would not wear it until she must, when she had proof that her husband was dead; the deep blue of her gown was somber enough, and it looked well on her.

The third of their company sat in peaceful silence,

stitching a cotte for William. Lady Margaret had ridden into Tyre a handful of days ago with an escort well worthy of her: not simply her maid and a handful of grizzled men-at-arms but the pope's legate himself with all his entourage. In the face of her daughter's blank amazement she had said, "Father abbot's servants wish him to be where the strongest defenses are. I wish to see my grandchild."

"But," Joanna said. "All that way. With armies between. And you hate to ride."

"For my kin I can endure a hardship or two," said Margaret. "The armies were no danger. A wing of the sultan's cavalry kept us company from Nablus to Toron; they were most respectful. One of them was a cousin to our cousin Rashida, who married a man in Baalbek."

Joanna accepted that with fair equanimity, once she was past the shock of having her mother there. Elen, after months in Outremer, even after Raihan, still could not comprehend how a woman could live so easily on both sides of the wall. It was only Margaret, she was certain. The other little dark women she had seen were *pullani,* mocked and despised, their children scorned as mongrels. And those were not even Muslims; they were Armenians or Greeks, or Syrian Christians. Margaret's mother had been a true infidel, a Muslim from Aleppo, wedded to a Frank for the profit of the House. The Frank had been an oddity himself, a cloistered monk turned Crusading knight; what he did to earn a daughter of the House of Ibrahim, Elen had never quite understood.

The silence tempted her. She yielded; she asked.

"He was noble born, my father," Margaret answered her, "but there were sea reivers in his blood, and trader-pirates out of the Northland, and maybe a drop or two of blood from further back, all the way to Tyre itself. He was given to the cloister as a child, to pray for his father's soul, and for a long while it seemed that he was content. But his blood was strong, and in the end it ruled him. His abbot brought him to Rome for an audience with the lord pope; when the abbot left, my father stayed, and put off his habit, and took the cross. He came to Outremer with little but the clothes on his back, but soon his greatest gift revealed itself. He could fight well enough though he came to it so late, and he earned himself a knighthood by it, but more wonderful was what he did with the first booty he took in a battle. He sold it piece by piece; with what he earned thereby, he bought a share in a caravan which another knight had come by in a wager. The caravan was one of the House of Ibrahim. It came in soon after the battle, and he found himself a wealthy man. His gift being what it was, he did not rest content with that, or even with the castle which he won in another of the wars. He became an honored client of the House. He was a guest there more than once; he spoke with the then-mistress, and like took well to like.

"One of the daughters of the House was an adventurous soul, firm in her faith but not implacable in it. She had been married, but her husband died in a storm in the desert; the lone son of the union was old enough to depart from among the women. She had been offered another husband, and given to choose from among a number of men, but none came close to taking her fancy. The Frank, however, intrigued her. She bethought herself that the House might profit well from a kin-bond to the High Court of Jerusalem. The old coast roads, which the Franks closed at whim to the caravans of Islam or held open at the cost of ruinous tolls, were open without hindrance to the caravans of Christendom. If the House of Ibrahim shared kin with the house of a Frank, would it not be the stronger thereby?

"It was a firm choice, once she had made it, but it was never easy for her. She accepted her husband's faith, inasmuch as she could. Her kin were and are good Muslims, but they were merchants first. They understood how she could do as she did, and why. They would not, for that, accept her again into her family's house, although her husband was as welcome as before, and I who was born and christened a Frank had much of my fostering in Aleppo."

"She gave up her family to make it stronger," Elen said. "How brave she must have been!"

"She was brave," said Margaret, "and canny, and

only occasionally bitter. I will not say that she loved her husband, but they esteemed one another highly. They died within a year of one another, he of a wound gone bad, she, I think, of seeing no further use in living. I was grown and married, with a daughter and a newborn son; my husband was dead in the same battle which felled my father, and he had heirs by another, older union, leaving my son free to inherit my father's lands. She judged me fit to take her place in the demesne and in the House."

"Did she die a Christian?" Elen asked. "Or did she return to her old faith?"

Margaret smiled very faintly. "No one knows but God and she. She was shriven, rightly enough, and prepared for the dark road in proper Christian wise, but who is to say that, at the utmost, she did not say the words of the Prophet's faith?"

"I wish I could have known her," Elen said.

"She was a terrible old woman," said Joanna. "No one ever mocked her for what she was, to her face or otherwise. When she went to court, even the king gave her respect. 'Start at the top,' she used to say, 'and all the rest will follow.'"

"And so it does," said Margaret peaceably, biting off a thread. "Joanna, have you any more of this green?"

Joanna's hands were full of her baby, but Elen found what Margaret was looking for. The talk thereafter circled lazily round women's things, small and quiet and comfortably dull.

Ysabel liked Tyre even better than Elen did. It was heaven for children, if they could slip away from overburdened Nurse, or if Mother was too caught up in the new baby to notice that some of her brood were missing. The house alone was good for hours of exploring. They were forbidden the parts where people lived, unless they were invited. But there was much more to the caravanserai than warrens of rooms full of merchants and knights and knights' women and children. Its lower level was a vast cavern full of treasure, and under that were catacombs that went deeper even than the master of the house might know of, down into an older earth. There were pillars there, holding up the vaults of the roof, and floors that seemed made of jewels, and passages that ran away into the dark.

William and the girlchildren were cowards. They did not want to go down into the damp and the dimness, even with a lamp appropriated from the caverns above. Ysabel tried to be charitable. They were human, after all. They were blind outside of bright daylight.

But Akiva did not want to do it, either. He had been very ill after Salima was born, from stretching his power too far, too soon, with no one older or stronger to tell him when to stop. He was better now, but he was still weak; he spent most of his days reading, or simply sitting in the garden with the sun on his hollowed face. Ysabel knew—*knew*—that there were things one could do to help him. She could almost put her hands on some of them. But she was too young. Her gifts were only seeds, or straggly saplings with green fruit on them.

People worried, and his father most of all. But they could not understand. Simeon was afraid that he might die, because he looked so sick and so pale. It was not Akiva's body that Ysabel feared for. That would go on unless someone tried very hard to kill it. His mind and his power—those were what frightened her. He still kept trying to slide away, to go to sleep and not wake up. She had had her tanning at last, but not for being bold in front of the Saracen sultan; for refusing to let Akiva sleep when everyone was sure he should. For keeping his self from slipping into the deep places and never coming out.

Now they were sorry. Akiva had told them when he woke up more properly, what she had done and why. They believed him when they would not even listen to her. They still tried to make her leave him alone, but they did not whip her for disobeying.

He looked almost healthy today, sitting on his favorite bench under the lilac hedge. "I think I want to go for a walk," he said, startling her speechless. "Not underground. It's too dark. Too much—like—"

"I know," she said quickly, so that he would not have to go on.

"I want to be out in the light," he said. "Have you been up on the walls yet?"

"You can't climb up there. You're too sick."

A frown from him was so rare that when he did it he looked like a stranger. "Who says I'm too sick?"

She looked at him. He looked mostly like himself. Thinner, but he was growing so fast she could almost see it; he was all long and no wide. "You can lean on me," she said. "And we'll go slowly."

He did not like that, but he shut his mouth on it.

She was growing, too, if not as fast. Her shoulder was at a comfortable height for him to lean on, when he decided to stop being insulted and start being sensible.

They made a clean and quiet escape, with no one even stopping to ask them what they were up to. Usually Ysabel said a prayer to thank whichever saint was looking after her, but today she forgot. By the time she remembered, they were most of the way to the wall, and it was too late.

A little after that, she was sorry. Someone called her name behind her. Like an idiot she stopped to see who it was. There were people between; she was too small to see over them. But Akiva, taller, and trying to not to seem glad of the rest, said, "It's Lady Elen."

It was. She always looked cool and elegant and beautiful, even picking her way through refuse on the street. People stared as she went by. She never noticed them.

She did notice Ysabel. And Akiva. There was a faint line of frown between her brows. "Does your father know that you are out?" she asked him.

"Does he need to?" Ysabel broke in before Akiva could say anything. "We're going up on the wall. Are you?"

It was a desperate gamble. Lady Elen was grownfolk, and human, but she had a bit of wildness left in her. She frowned at Akiva, but he had his strength back now; he stood by himself and hooked his fingers through his belt. "I am so tired," he said, "of being an invalid. If I prom-

ise to rest when I get up there, and go right back when
I've rested, will you come up with us?"

Lady Elen's frown was almost a scowl, but all at once
it smoothed away. Ysabel would have liked to be able to
do that. "Obviously, if I refuse, you'll go up anyway, and
then who will look after you?" Elen shook her head.
"Akiva, you are a shameless conniver."

He grinned at her, his first grin since Salima was
born.

She grinned back and gathered her skirts.

They went up the stair one by one, with Akiva in the
middle and Ysabel going last. The guards on the wall
were watchful, but with no enemy in sight, they did not
mind if a woman and a pair of children wanted to see
what was outside of Tyre. Akiva was not up to walking
far, though Ysabel would have liked to see the drowned
city. They went a little way round instead, toward the
causeway. People were coming and going. Saladin had
burned a field or two, but there was still a great deal of
green, with the dun and purple of desert and mountain
beyond it, and in front of it the white sand and the blue
water and the great sweeping curve of the coast.

Akiva sat on a crenel of the battlement and tried not
to show how badly he needed to rest. Ysabel was not
deceived. Nor was Elen. Elen, who was tall, could lean
on the crenel just beyond him and let the wind blow in
her face. Ysabel could feel her wanting to strip off her
veil and fillet and let her hair fly free.

She would not, of course. It was indecent, and it was
appallingly public. She had to settle for the wind and the
sun, and conspicuously not caring if she burned her face
brown.

It was peaceful up here. Akiva was almost asleep.
Now and then a guard went by. It was always a different
one. They were taking turns admiring the lady, who did
not even know that they noticed her. Her mind was full
of someone else altogether.

Ysabel wandered a bit, came back, fit herself into the
crenel next to Akiva's. She would have dangled her legs
over, if Elen had not been there. If there had been no
humans there at all, she would have done much more

than that. Flown like a gull, now high up against the sun,
now skimming the water.

There were three gates in the wall, two smaller ones
flanking the great double one with its arches and its gate-
house. Only the middle gate was open. They were almost
beside the northmost one; they could see how people
went in and out, some mounted, most afoot, and how the
guards looked hard at every one. Ysabel could have told
them that a spy would be an idiot to look like one. Not
that there was any, that she could see. Saladin was not
interested in Tyre.

The first she saw of the company of riders, she
thought they were knights coming back from hunting.
There were about a score of them. But hunters would not
bring so many horses: a whole herd without riders, running in a tight knot in the middle. There were mules, too.
With packs. And, through the dust they raised, a line of
haughty camels.

More Christians escaped from the war.

Did Christians wear turbans? Some of the riders did.
But some did not, and those were clearly Franks: they
were wearing armor and surcoats.

Ysabel was standing on the crenel, barely holding on
to it, craning to see more. She knew—she knew—

It was agony to wait. Akiva was asleep. Elen was
oblivious. She must have seen the riders, but she would
be thinking as Ysabel had at first: more swords for the
defense of Tyre. There were more men than women, and
all the men were armed. Fighting men.

A handful of knights and squires. A tiny company of
men-at-arms. Five mamluks who had belonged, once, to
the Syrian sultan.

Only five?

Three white enchanters, a prince and a king and a
figure that was neither, but had been the most feared of
the Assassins. Ysabel's breath ran out of her in a soft
cry. It was. It *was*.

They crawled closer. They could not go faster. The
camels did not like it, and some of the mares had foals at
heel. Ysabel knew those horses. They were Aidan's best-
loved beauties from Millefleurs, and Raihan's precious

few. Maleka had a filly, bay with a white star. Raihan would be like to burst with pride.

But only five mamluks. Seven gone. She had felt them die. It had not meant anything real, until she saw how empty the ranks were without them.

The wind, the high fierce wind of Tyre, stung the tears on her cheeks. She dashed them away. Ranulf was not there, either. Would never be there again.

They checked for a moment, all of them, where the causeway joined the land. The guards on the wall were suspicious, seeing the turbans and the Saracen coats, even in the middle of all the Franks. Conrad had his wives with him, all three in veils.

But suspicion was not what the riders saw. They saw Tyre: the loom of the wall, the three gates, the city impregnable on its all-but-island. Some of them wept, because it was Christian, and safe, and beautiful.

Aidan on his grey gelding, in the coat of honor that Saladin had given him before Ysabel was born, rode ahead of the others onto the causeway. It was not far to the gate, but it could be a lonely ride, with the walls frowning down and the land falling away on either side to the sea. After a little the others followed him.

Ysabel reached out to him with her mind. He was closed against her. He could not even see her: his eyes were on the great gate, and not looking for a lone small figure in a crenel.

It hurt, that he could not know her. She ran along the wall, darting round guards and gawkers. She heard Elen's cry behind her. She did not stop for it.

The gatehouse stopped her. Aidan was almost under it. She scrambled out onto the edge of the wall.

He paused. To wait for the others, it was plain; but he was just below her. She called out to him. He started and turned his face up to her. She saw it in a blur, white inside of black. *Father!* she cried in her mind. *Father, Father, Father!* And leaped from the battlements, falling dizzily, swooping through the blue air.

30

Elen, dreaming in the sun, thought at first that her dream had taken substance. She saw them come riding in their company, Prince Aidan well ahead as he always was, Gwydion more quiet behind, and one in a turban whose face was a woman's, and a strong lad who but a season ago had been a child, Joanna's eldest son; and a few, a pitiful few, of those who had gone to the war with them. Of thirty Rhiyanan knights, she counted six, and Urien the king's squire. Of a dozen Syrian mamluks, she saw five. Five only in their scarlet coats, with heads high and haughty under the turban-wrapped helmets. A pair of slant-eyed imps who at this distance seemed to have no more beard than boys, and a golden lion of a man who, for once, was not singing, and a thickset Turk.

And somewhat behind, riding among the herd of horses, a tall wide-shouldered man with a handsome black beard and a face burned well-nigh black in the sun, and eyes shadowed under the turban. But they would be blue. Sea blue, sky blue, flaxflower blue.

The breath left her in a long sigh. He was alive. He rode lightly, no stiffness in him, no mark of wound or hardship. He was whole. He had come back.

She saw Ysabel dart toward the gatehouse. The child's face, flashing past her, was white and set, a little mad. Elen sprang in pursuit, calling. She doubted that Ysabel even heard her.

Elen stretched her stride. The child was as quick as a cat, and rather less inclined to serve any will but her own. Elen prayed devoutly that she would stop before she caught the guards' attention.

Someone else ran past her. Akiva. He had been asleep. How had he roused so soon? How could he move so fast?

Even he was not quick enough to catch Ysabel. Elen

saw her climb out onto a crenel, not even troubling to hold on. And saw her leap.

How Elen came down from the wall to the gate, she never remembered. One moment she was by the gate-house, watching a child fall to her certain death. The next, she was past the great echoing arch on the white sand of the road, and Akiva was beside her, and the riders were milling to a halt before her.

Ysabel was not dead and broken at her uncle's feet. She was in his arms, where she had flown—flown! Her arms were locked about his neck; he held her with his horse patiently still beneath them both, and rocked her and murmured words which Elen had no ears to hear.

Guards and hangers-on had run even as Elen had. They halted as she had, staring, and some crossed them-selves. A miracle, they said. That the rider should be there, precisely where the child fell; that he had caught her. No one said what most must have seen too clearly: that she should have come down a good horselength from where she clung and trembled and wept. And that she had come down as lightly as a bird landing, not even rocking the prince in his saddle. She wept because he had come back, and he was whole, and she was, when she drew up straight on the saddlebow, furious. "Don't you ever," she said clearly. "Don't you ever go away and leave me again."

Elen, caught between shock and dawning anger, saw more keenly than she had ever known she could. Aidan's face as he looked down at Joanna's eldest daughter. Ysabel as she clung there, hands fisted in his coat, glar-ing through tears. Ysabel was her mother's daughter, in-disputably.

She was also her father's.

It did not, on reflection, come as a surprise. Once one knew, one could see; and not only that the child was witchborn. She would grow to his length and lightness, and she would have his profile, though fined and soft-ened by her sex.

She knew whose child she was. Elen remembered

how Saladin had looked at her, and how she had spoken
to him. Yes, the sultan had seen it with his clear eye for
witchfolk. God's grace that no one else ever had.

Elen glanced at Morgiana, who had halted beside
Gwydion. Her face was unreadable. Not angry, it
seemed, and not visibly jealous. That she was fond of the
child, Elen knew. Fond enough to forgive her for being
Aidan's daughter?

The tableau shifted. One of the mares squealed; a
camel grunted; the world began to move again. In a
flurry of greetings and gladness, with the guards bidding
them *Move on, move on,* Elen took Gwydion's hand and
swung lightly up to ride pillion behind him. Akiva was
with Morgiana on her devil of a stallion, wide-eyed and
white-cheeked but loving it, laughing at something she
said.

Elen folded her arms about Gwydion's narrow waist
and hugged tightly. She could feel his pleasure and his
welcome, even without the hand he laid on hers. "Thank
God and all the saints," she said, "that you've come back
to us."

In all the confusion of riding to the caravanserai,
fetching Joanna and the rest of the family, meeting and
greeting and settling the beasts and the baggage, Elen did
not speak to Raihan, or even look at him except for
stolen glances. They had ridden back from Damascus by
the long way through Aidan's castle of Millefleurs; besides the horses, they had stores of food and wine, and
camel-loads of belongings, and coin and gems enough to
pay their share many times over. It all took an eternity
to settle; and then there had to be a feast, and more
uproar.

The joy of the riders' coming was muted by the news
they brought, that at last must be accepted: the lord of
Mortmain was dead. The lord of Mortmain, now, was
the boy who greeted his mother with such dignity, whom
war had honed and tempered into the strong beginning
of a man. Neither son nor mother wept. They sat side by
side at the table under the canopy of Mortmain crimson,

and showed their people how it must be. Grief, yes, but there was a war to fight; later would be time enough to indulge in wailing and gnashing of teeth.

"We buried him on the field of Hattin," Gwydion said. "He can be brought back if you will it, and set among his own people."

Joanna shook her head. "His own people are in Normandy. His lands are overrun. Let him lie where he fell. There's honor in that, and glory enough."

"He hated fuss," said Ysabel. Her voice was suspiciously husky. She would not leave Aidan's side for anything; it had taken main force to pry her loose so that he could bathe and rest. He laid his arm about her now, and murmured in her ear. Whatever he said, it seemed to comfort her. She stopped picking at her dinner, even ate a little.

It was Salima who put an end to the ordeal. Joanna had a wetnurse for her, like any sensible lady, but preferred to nurse the child herself. That she chose to do so now, was patently an escape, and for Elen at least, a reprieve. Most of the newcomers went to rest from their traveling; the household scattered to their tasks, the children to the ministrations of their nurse.

The house that had been so large for the number of them was hard put now to hold them all. Elen surrendered her solitude willingly enough, to share a chamber with Lady Margaret and their maids and, on her own recognizance, Ysabel. "My uncle thinks I ought to be your maid," the child said. "I know you have Gwenneth, but doesn't she get tired sometimes?"

"Your uncle," said Elen, very careful indeed not to set any burden of irony in the title, "is very kind. What does your mother say?"

Ysabel shrugged. "She'll be happy. She thinks I need reining in."

Elen remembered a leap from the wall of Tyre, and stifled an urge to laugh. "I think you need jesses and a hood. And a creance, for when you decide to fly."

"I forgot," Ysabel said with gratifying contrition. "I saw him, and all I wanted was to be with him."

"You should remember," Elen said severely. "Yes,

you may stay with me, but you must promise to do as I tell you, and you must do your utmost to remember what humans can and cannot do."

"I promise," said Ysabel, barely pausing to consider.

Elen nodded, unsmiling. "You may begin by helping me with my dress."

The others were asleep: Lady Margaret in the bed with Elen, and Ysabel; the maids on pallets on the floor. The air in the room, even with the shutters wide, was hot and close. Flies buzzed beyond the bed-curtains.

Elen lay stiff and still. Her mind would not stop circling. One word only; that was all. *Alive, alive, alive.*

He had never glanced at her. Not once. He kept to his own kind, more apart than ever: the alien, the enemy, the Saracen. In the hall they had sat alone, the five of them, and eaten only what their own servant brought them. They were not shut out, not precisely, but they were not wholly welcome, either; the less so now, since the debacle of Hattin.

She told herself that his indifference was prudence purely. Her uncles were wise, and she loved them, but they would not look kindly on a commoner who dared aspire to her favor. If they knew that there had been more than aspiration, they would be outraged.

So she told herself. It did not keep her from lying awake, hating herself for cowardice. She should have gone to him at the gate and embraced him as she had longed to do, and told the truth without subterfuge. She could protect him from harm. If Aidan sent him away, that would be grief, but it would bring him joy. He could go back to his own people, reclaim the honor he had lost, win wives and wealth, sire sons as a soldier of Allah should.

She rose quietly, found her chemise, put it on. Light though it was, little more than gauze, it weighed on her. But she could hardly walk naked through the house. Barefoot and bareheaded was scandalous enough.

There was a nightingale in the garden: pure gift of

God, and perhaps an omen. Its song made her eyes sting, so sweet as it was, and so sad.

She wandered aimlessly. The nightingale fell silent. The wind was blowing enough to keep the flies at bay; she could hear the hiss of waves on the shore, the creak and wash of ships riding at anchor beyond the wall. Tomorrow one would go out to Cyprus to summon Gwydion's fleet. He meant to offer passage to as many as his ships could hold: pilgrims put to flight by the Saracens' war, wives and children of knights slain at Hattin, and more than they, messengers to the courts of the west.

He had paid a price for his freedom, he and his brother. Elen wondered that Aidan had not come to hate his lady of the Assassins for buying him with such an oath as she had made him take. Never again to bear arms against Saladin: that was a bitter bargain. It robbed him of revenge; it made him seem a coward. It left him with no honor, and no recourse but to flee.

"It's not as bitter as that," he said out of the darkness.

She saw him then, a shadow within a shadow, a gleam of eyes. A white blur was his hand, offered to lift her up to the pavilion in which he sat.

The pavilion was small, an airy folly on a pedestal, with slender columns holding up the roof, and a ledge running round the rail at sitting-height. Elen perched beside Aidan, straining to see him in the thin moonlight.

"I'm not bitter," he said. "Unhappy, yes; I'd give much to deal Saladin such a defeat as he dealt us. But the price was fair."

"Do you ever regret it?" she asked him. "Loving Morgiana. Being loved by her."

"Neither of us had much choice in the matter," he said.

She looked at him, knowing that he could see her clearly.

"No," he said under her blind, bland stare. "No, I never regret Morgiana. Quarrel with her, yes; long to throttle her, all too often. But regret, no."

"Even with all she's cost you in honor and reputation and in battle with the Church?"

"Even with that."

She thought about it, unhastily, sheltered in his silence. After a little she reached out and took his hand. It was warm, warmer than a man's, and strong. She wanted suddenly to tell him her secret. He of all people—he would understand.

But she did not. It was Raihan's secret, too, and she did not have his leave. Bad enough that Aidan could know it if he chose, simply by walking in her mind.

She leaned toward him and kissed his cheek. "Thank you," she said.

He did not ask her what for. She was glad of that. If he had asked, she would have had to answer, and that answer might have had to be a lie.

It was easier to corner Raihan than she had expected. She waited a day or two, until the house had fallen into its new rhythm. She saw how its patterns flowed and where everyone was likely to be, and where one might go to find solitude. Raihan spent most of his time in the stable with his horses; she suspected that he slept there rather than in the warren of the house.

She found him there, and alone, at an hour when everyone was either sleeping through the heat of midday or doing something quiet that could be done in the shade. Raihan was with one of his mares, who was in foal and approaching her time.

He glanced at Elen as she approached, but kept most of his attention on the mare. "I knew I should have left her at Millefleurs," he said as easily as if they had never been apart. "The journey troubled her little enough, but now she'll foal on shipboard, and that's no way for a horse to come into the world."

"She's one of your best," Elen said. "How could you leave her behind?"

"That's what I tell myself. And the lord king, he knows how to heal beasts as well as men. But I'm human. I fret."

She came to stand beside him. All the mares were in this one stable, with its broad passage and its louvered roof and its stalls divided by thin walls, and each with a round window at horsehead-height to look out of. There were no doors on the stalls; one could, and Raihan did, leave the horses loose to wander as they would, although he tethered them at night and when he fed them. Or when, as now, he wished to examine one.

The mare was mettlesome and given to fretting, but under his hand she was calm. He smoothed her long mane. She lipped his shirt; he smiled and gave her the bit of apple she was asking for.

"You are going, then," she said. "With your prince. To Rhiyana."

He nodded. He looked neither happy nor sad.

"Why? How can you leave your own country?"

"My country is where my lord is." He ran his hand along the mare's back and round her barrel, probing for the shape of the foal.

"If you had a choice," she asked, "would you stay?"

His hand paused. He did not look up. "I don't have one."

"What if you did?"

He straightened. The mare flattened her ears. He caught her halter and held it, stroking her out of her temper. "Are you offering me one?"

"Yes," she said. "Yes, I am."

His face was unreadable under the beard, with his eyes in shadow. "Do you have that right, my lady?"

"I love you."

The words fell in silence. His voice came soft and slow, but there was iron in it. "Has it occurred to my lady that if I remain here, we will never meet again?"

"Yes," she said. "But you would be free. You would have your own people. You would not be a foreigner in a land of infidels. I see how they treat you here, where your people are known and familiar, and a few even understand your faith. What will it be like in the west, where there are no Muslims?"

"How would you go about setting me free?"

Her heart thudded. He was listening. He had not cut her off. He wanted this, then. He wanted to be free.

Free of her.

She crushed that thought before it could sink claws in her. "All you need," she said, "is to be caught with me. I promise you, you won't be hurt. My uncles will not be pleased, but they'll listen to me. They'll leave you alive and unmaimed. They'll send you away, and you'll be free."

He stared at her. "You would dishonor yourself for that?"

"They'll hush it up, of course," she said. "They're not likely to whip me or starve me, or do anything but sunder me from you."

"Is that love, then, my lady? Or disposal of an embarrassment?"

The heat rushed to her face. "I love you, damn you! I want you to be happy."

"An odd way you have of showing it," he said dryly, "my lady. Proposing that I smirch your reputation, shame your kinsmen, and abandon you to whatever fate they may propose for you."

"I know what my fate is. It is to marry a man of their choosing, to bear heirs to their house." Her hands were fists; they ached. She could not will them to unclench. "I don't want you to have to see it. Or suffer it. Or be torn out of your own place, thrust into one in which you are always, and only, a foreigner."

"As to that, my lady, I've never had a place that was mine. Except this one." He gestured toward his scarlet coat where it hung by the stall. "Seven of us died for my lord. Allah chose not to take me. I accept what Allah wills; that is what it is to be a Muslim. Would you have me refuse Him?"

"Surely your Allah would want you to worship him in his own country, among your own kind."

"If that were so," he said, "then He would never have given me to my lord."

Elen had begun to tremble. "What if I can't bear it? What if I tell you that, if you come, I will never be able to accept any other man? What then, messire?"

Now she could read his face. It was set hard, with his eyes glittering in it, the color of ice under a winter sun. "If you tell me that, my lady, I will tell you that you are not so poor a creature as that. You are a lady and a princess. You will do what is best for your house."

"No," she said. "No, Raihan. I am not that noble. I am not that strong."

He was. She could see it in him. He would give her up because he must; because his lord required it.

She raised her fists. She set them with trembling care on his breast. She wound her fingers in his shirt, and wrenched it down.

The soft cotton tore. He did not move. She stripped him of the tatters. Her mind was quite clear. White fury, that was the name of it. "I can't give you up," she said. "I can't."

"Therefore you would force your kin to do it for you?"

She combed her fingers through the hair of his chest. He shivered almost imperceptibly. He was not as calm as he seemed, or as cold.

"Every night I prayed for you," she said. "Every morning I dreaded that, that day, I would learn that you were dead. Every hour I thought of you." She tried to laugh. It was an ugly sound, dry and strangled. "I've gone mad, I think. And I can't even want to be sane. It must be in the blood. Prince Aidan is just like me. Just—like—"

The tears startled her. She was not a woman for weeping. But he could have died, and he had not, and she had to give him up for both their honor's sake.

He opened his arms and gathered her in. He smelled of horses and mansweat and musk.

He had a bed there, indeed: a heap of sweet straw in a far stall, with his box of belongings beside it, and his weapons hung up carefully, and a pot for his needs, for he was fastidious. He blushed a little. "This is no bower for a princess," he said.

There was too much that she could have said. She kissed him instead, long and deep, and pulled him down into the straw.

31

Akiva lay utterly still on his pallet. He was so white and
thin and elongated that he looked as if he had died.
Then, as Gwydion bent over him, he drew a breath. The
king laid a hand on his brow, his own face going still,
until it seemed hardly more alive than Akiva's. They
looked like kin, then, with their arched noses and their
black-black hair and their narrow bloodless faces.

Ysabel, mute, huddled in her father's lap on the high
bed that was Gwydion's, watched and tried not to fidget.
Morgiana was there, too, frowning over the king and the
boy, but she touched neither, simply stood guard. They
had had to send Simeon out. He was afraid, and Akiva
could not help but know it, and it slowed the healing.

For that was what it was. It did not look like much.
But to power's eyes it was a great flaming torrent, reined
and bridled to Gwydion's will. In the light of it they all
could see the places that had burned from being used too
soon, and the places that were raw and bleeding, and the
threads that ran, frayed and raveled, between body and
power. It was much worse than Ysabel had thought.
They had not even known, when he did it. Even when he
fainted. Power could do that, if one used too much of it.

*Now you know why I'm always after you to rein your-
self in,* Aidan said in her mind.

She hated it when he preached at her. But because
she was afraid for Akiva, and because she did know, she
only scowled; she did not say anything.

He smiled and tugged at one of her curls. *You're
growing up, catling.*

Not fast enough for me. She glowered at Akiva. *He's
starting to look like you.*

What, less homely?

Less human.

Aidan nodded slowly. *It happens,* he said. His mind-
voice was soft. *It will happen to you.*

She shivered. *I'm not human. Am I? In spite of Mother.*

You are what you are. He kissed the top of her head.

People call us witches. They want to burn us. They hate us. But why? We're not bad people.

We have things that they can't have, and wish they did. We don't get sick. We don't grow old. We have power.

She shook her head sharply. *I'd hate to give up power. But they can go to heaven.*

Not all of them. And the ones who hate us most are often the ones with the least chance of heaven. Aidan hugged her to him, tender but fierce. *None of them will ever lay a finger on you. I won't let them.*

One could believe him when he shaped the words so, each one distinct, ringing with truth. She looked at him while he watched his brother. He had no glamour on him now. He was tall and strong and splendid, as a prince ought to be. He did not look human at all. His face was too odd, his eyes too big, his skin too white. Human skin was different. Coarser and softer and darker, and it grew odd bits of colorless hair, even where it seemed bare.

People are afraid of us, she said, but deep within herself, where only she could hear.

She did not like it, that she was frightening. She ran her tongue over her teeth. Cat-teeth, to go with her cat-eyes.

She was only Ysabel. She never wanted to hurt anyone, except when she was angry, and even then she knew better. She tried to be good. It was not her blood's fault that she was a hellion.

The healing lasted a very long while. Humans were quicker, Aidan told Ysabel, and easier. They had no power to fight back. Power was like an animal in a trap. It fought to protect itself even from what would heal it; from anything at all that was outside of it.

But Gwydion was stronger. It was a fierce battle, but he won it.

When Akiva slept, and Gwydion stood up and staggered and needed Morgiana to keep him from falling, Aidan set Ysabel on her feet and went to help his brother. Gwydion needed sleep at least as much as Akiva did, but he insisted on telling Simeon that his son would be well. That was what a king was. He always put his people before his own comfort.

Ysabel hovered for a bit, but no one needed her. She was too young, again. Without her friend and with her father all caught up in looking after his brother, she felt horribly alone.

Everyone else was sleeping through the midday heat. She was not sleepy at all; she had seen enough sleep in the healing to last her for a while. She looked for Lady Elen, but did not find her in her room, or in the women's solar, or in the garden. The last place Ysabel looked, the stable, held the lady, but she was not alone. Not in the least.

Ysabel backed off before either of them could see her. She knew what they were doing. When animals did it, it was breeding. When people did it, it was loving. They looked hot and rather desperate, but to mind-eyes they were beautiful: a great, blooming flame, with two colors in it, shifting and blurring and mingling.

She was sorry to leave them, but they would be deathly embarrassed if they knew that she was there. Humans could only see the ugly, sweaty, heaving part, and they were odd about that even when the lovers were married. Some of Elen's worry spilled over, and it was full of defiance. Let her uncles find her; let them despise her; let them call her a whore. She loved this man. No one could make her recant it.

Raihan thought much the same, but he went all dark and blood-tinged, willing violence on anyone who spoke ill of his princess. He meant to find a way, somehow, to protect her honor and have her, too.

Ysabel wished them good fortune. Loving was nothing that she could understand, or wanted to, yet, but she liked the two of them; she would not want them to be unhappy. It had been bad enough when Raihan was gone to the war and Elen feared that he was dead. Ysabel had

never been able to tell her that he lived. She had been too
fierce about keeping him a secret.

Now Ysabel was all alone. Mother was napping with
Salima at the breast. The children never understood
Ysabel, even when she tried her hardest to be like them.
She wandered at loose ends, out into the garden, back
into the house, up all the way to the roof. There was not
much of a garden up there, but there was a lemon tree in
a basin, and a cote full of pigeons. Sometimes the keeper
let Ysabel hold one of the birds, and told her stories
about their noble ancestors. Some of them were descended from the very bird that flew the first message of
the Crusaders' coming into Outremer.

The keeper was gone now about some business of his
own. Ysabel talked to the pigeons for a while, but pigeons were not excessively good company. She perched
on the basin under the lemon tree and amused herself
idly, plaiting bits of light and shade, trying to see how
big a tapestry she could make before it escaped her fingers and melted into the air.

Aimery was in a mildly foul mood. He had come to
Tyre because Prince Aidan persuaded him, and because
he did not want to go to Count Raymond in Tripoli.
"Visit your mother," Aidan had said. "Tell her what you
have to tell. Then let her choose whether to keep you or
send you away. She is your lady mother, after all, and
should stand regent for you, now that you are lord of
Mortmain."

"Lord of Mortmain," he said aloud, with a curl of his
lip. Oh, he was that, no doubt about it. All the servants
called him *monseigneur* now, instead of simply *messire*.
But Joanna was still their lady, and she was the one they
listened to; she was the one they obeyed.

He did not mind that. He was young and his training
was only half done; and she was a very great lady. He
was proud of her.

But there was no substance in his title. The Saracens
had his demesne; Mortmain had an emir in its high seat
and soldiers of Allah in its guardroom. He would win it

back, he had sworn it, but the winning seemed farther away now than it had when he left Damascus. All they did here was sit and wait. Marquis Conrad had a war in train, but he had not answered the message Gwydion sent, that the King of Rhiyana was in the city. Gwydion would not call on him until the message was answered. A king did not play suppliant before a marquis; the message alone went well beyond what was necessary. Conrad had to know that: he was trained in Byzantium. That meant that he was silent because he chose to be.

Gwydion refused to speculate on why he did it. Aidan only said, "An asp bit Conrad in his cradle. He's been a venomous little snake ever since." Which gave Aimery a suspicion as to why Conrad insulted a king by ignoring him. The king's brother had never been noted for his tact.

Aimery smiled in spite of himself. Prince Aidan had a definite, if perilous, gift. People loved him immoderately or hated him passionately. Never anything between. But only raw newcomers failed to respect him. He showed the world what a prince should be.

He had made the weeks after Hattin endurable, because he was what he was. For the first time since Aimery was a baby, he had had Aidan to himself, and it was bliss. He did not speak of Ranulf unless Aimery began it, but when Aimery needed him he was there. He took Aimery riding and hunting; he taught him weaponry; he played chess and backgammon, and taught him strategy. They were uncle and nephew, kinsman and kinsman, knight and squire.

Now that was ended. Aimery could reckon the very moment. When Aidan sat his horse under the gate of Tyre, and Ysabel dropped out of the sky into his arms. Aidan had barely said a word to Aimery since. It was always Ysabel, Ysabel, Ysabel.

No one had even thrashed her for almost getting herself killed. Jumping off the wall, for God's sweet mercy. What if Aidan had not looked up when he did? What if she had misjudged her leap? She would have died.

Aimery did not want that. He detested her cordially, he hated her domination of their uncle, but she was his

sister. He simply wished that she could be his sister
somewhere else.

All his thinking had carried him through the Mortmains' part of the caravanserai from bottom to top. He
found himself at the foot of a stair which led to the roof.
He climbed it.

And stopped in the bright air, and almost groaned
aloud. Ysabel was there. Of course. She could not even
keep herself out of his solitary rambling.

He started to turn back, but stopped. She had not
seen him yet. She was doing something indecipherable. It
looked like weaving, the way the weavers did it in the
bazaar. But she had no loom. And no thread. Only dark
and light.

He watched her shape a shaft of sunlight that came
through the leaves of the lemon tree, rolling and spinning
it between her palms until it was a shimmering, burning
thread, and working it into her weft of air. She did it
perfectly calmly, with a line of concentration between
her brows, and the tip of her tongue caught between her
teeth.

Aimery stood very, very still. He did not want to
believe what he was seeing. But he had grown up with
Aidan and his Assassin. He knew what magic was.

It all began to make excellent sense. Why Aidan fa-
vored her so strongly. How she could be such a terror.
She would not have died when she jumped off the wall.
She could fly. Probably Aidan had taught her.

She looked up. The light was strong and strange in
her face. Her eyes were stranger still. Witch-eyes. "Hello,
Aimery," she said with perfect calm.

He refused to turn and bolt. "You," he said. "You're
one of them."

She nodded. "I'm surprised you never guessed."

"Why? You've always thought me stupid."

"I don't." That was more like Ysabel: sharp and indignant. "You're a boy, that's all. Boys are silly."

"Girls are worse." Aimery advanced on her. She
made no move to protect her weaving. His finger reached
of its own accord.

Solid. Like shadow, like sunlight. Cool, hot. Soft.

Carefully he reclaimed his finger. It did not shake. He was proud of that. "You're a witch," he said. "Like Morgiana. If the Church finds out, it will burn you."

"It's never burned the others."

"They never tried hard enough."

She showed him her teeth. Sharp cat-teeth, like Aidan's.

He hated her suddenly. Hated her so much that he said what the devil bade him say. "You're his, aren't you? You're his bastard."

If he could have eaten the words, he would have. He did not want her to be that. He could not bear it if it was true.

"It is," she said. Answering what he said in his mind. The way Aidan did. "He is my father."

Aimery leaped on her. She fell back against the tree-bole. She did nothing to stop him, except fend his hands from her throat. He seized her shoulders instead and shook her till her head rocked on her neck. "It's not true! *It's not true!*"

"Then why did you say it?"

His head tossed. "You made me. You drove me wild." He dragged her roughly to her feet. Her witch-weaving was all gone, torn and scattered into nothing. "Of course he isn't your father. You just said it to make me mad."

"No," she said. "I am his bastard. Why else do you think he'd spend so much time with me? He's trying to teach me how to be what he is."

"You *aren't*," said Aimery. He was almost crying. "You can't. How could he—how could Mother—"

"They loved one another," said the little witch, calmly and horribly certain. "They still do."

"No! She loves Father."

"She does. But she loves my father, too."

"No," said Aimery. "No." He could see them. His mother all naked and wanton, and the prince stooping over her. Ravishing her. Filling her with—

His cheek stung. Ysabel drew back her hand from the slap. Her eyes were fierce. "You are disgusting! It was only for a season, and it was only me. Do you think

Morgiana would have let it last any longer? That's why
she tried to kill Mother. Because Mother was pregnant
with me, and Morgiana was in love with my father and
wanted him for herself. Morgiana took my father away
to her cave in Persia, the way she's always told it, and
Mother went home to Father. Your father. Whom she
left because of you. Because she wanted you with all her
heart and soul, and he took you away, and she hated him
for it. My father was one of the people who helped her
understand why Father did what he did. She went back
to him, and she was faithful to him. She learned to love
him. She was never what you are thinking."

Whore, Aimery was thinking. Slut. Wanton and
wicked. Adulteress.

Ysabel hit him again. He tried to hit her back, but
she was too quick. Witch-quick.

He was crying. Dribbling and sniffling like a baby,
and there was nothing he could do to stop it. Father was
dead and Mother was a whore and his sister was a bastard, and his lord, his prince, his beloved kinsman, was a
—a—

"Don't think it," Ysabel said softly. "Don't you even
think it."

He swung wildly, knowing that he would not touch
her, but wanting her out, off, away. She retreated out of
reach. "I hate you!" he screamed at her. *"I hate you!"*

Aimery ran as far as he could run. Which was not,
after all, very far. He wanted to burst in on his mother,
fling it all in her face, hear her call him a liar. She would
beat sense back into his head. She would tell him to stop
his fretting; Ysabel was baiting him again, driving him
wild, because Ysabel was a hellion, and hellions could
not help what they did.

But he did not approach Joanna. He knew what she
would say. She would tell him that it was true. She had
put horns on her husband; she had played the harlot
with a jinni prince. A demon lover. Had they been surprised when he got her with child? Had they had the
decency to be appalled?

He could not face Aidan, either. It was not hate, what moved in him. It was grief.

He carried it to the one place he could think of. Aimery had been unhappy at first to be put in the nursery, made to share a room and a bed with William and the baby, who was no longer the youngest now that Salima was born. But it was not crowded as rooms went in this house, and now it was empty. He flung himself on the bed and cried, and when he tired of crying, he began to throw things.

Cushions and bolsters were hardly satisfactory: they struck the wall with a muted thump and dropped bonelessly down. Clothes flew at peculiar angles, even when one wadded them up. He was not ready for knives yet.

Morgiana caught the lamp just before it shattered against the wall. She hardly even spilled the oil in it.

She walked away from the wall and set the lamp delicately on its table. She had not come through the door, which was on the other side of the room. Aimery crouched, breathing hard, glaring at her.

She tucked up her feet eastern-fashion and sat. "So," she said. "The little witch told you."

Aimery stopped goggling at the spectacle of the ifritah sitting with nothing between herself and the floor but a yard's worth of air, and dropped back flat on the denuded bed. He dug his hands into his eyes before they could run over again. "Why did she have to tell me? Why couldn't she have lied to me?"

"Would you have wanted her to?"

"Yes!"

She was silent.

He let his hands fall. He turned his head. She was watching him, wearing no expression that he could decipher. Except that there was no contempt in it. He looked for that.

"No," he said roughly. "No, I wouldn't have wanted her to lie. I don't want the truth to be true."

"One doesn't, when the truth is as bitter as this."

"It is true, isn't it?"

"It is true." She laced her fingers in her lap, studying them as if they formed a pattern that she could read. "It is also true that he has not touched her, or gone to her, since the night I thrust my dagger in her heart. We quarreled over that, did you know? That was why I left him in Jerusalem. He taxed me with—" She shook her head slightly. "It doesn't matter. I taxed him with his old sin. We fought, and I sundered myself from him. We were both fools."

"You should never have come back to him."

"I should never have left him." She met his eyes. Hers were as clear and hard as emeralds. "I have no love to spare for your mother. But I can, if I wish, see why he loves her. She is bright and strong and fearless. She has become a great lady. She gave him the child I cannot give him. If ever a mortal woman was a match for him, that one is."

It was too much for Aimery. There were too many sides to it. That Morgiana could praise his mother for giving the prince a bastard. That she could understand it.

"And what about my father?" Aimery cried. "What voice did he ever have in any of this?"

"He never knew." Morgiana met his incredulity with a cool stare. "Your mother saw no purpose in giving him pain. He thought the child his; he cherished her. She loved him as much as any daughter should love her father. It speaks well for your sister, messire, that she has love enough to spare for two fathers, nor ever stinted either of them."

Aimery did not want to hear praise of his sister. "You all *lied* to him."

"None of us told him aught that was not truth. We let him think as he pleased, and did nothing to disillusion him. There were indeed nine months between his reunion with your mother and the birth of your sister. She had indeed been apart from my prince for a month and more before she came to your father. There was never need to explain that witch-children dwell longer in the womb."

Aimery was dizzy and sick. "Lies. Liars."

"No," Morgiana said.

The sickness rose to engulf him.

She held him all through it, and conjured a basin for it, and conjured it away when there was nothing left to

empty himself of, except grief and rage and bitter disappointment. Her touch did not revolt him. He was a little
surprised at that. She was not human enough to be repelled by. She was a pure thing, like fire, or like a spirit
of the air.

"Which after all is what I am." She smoothed his
sweat-sodden hair with disconcerting gentleness. "I'm
hardly a pure spirit, Aimery. What your prince is, what
your sister will be, I am. We make mistakes like human
folk. Worse than they, sometimes, because of what we
are. One of them was that I tried to kill your mother,
because I was jealous of her."

"You should have," he said bitterly. "Then none of
this would have happened."

"You know you don't want that," she said.

She was sitting on the bed now, still with her feet
tucked up, looking hardly older than Aimery. He
thought of all that he had said to her, and flushed hot
with shame.

"Don't," she said. She reached out her hand. It was
cool on his cheek.

He snatched it. It did not try to escape him. He
looked her up and down, hard, the way he had seen men
do in the army. "Maybe I should carry on the family
tradition."

She did not laugh at him. He was grateful for that.
Nor did she ask if he was capable. Though of course she
would know. Better maybe than he did.

"Not yet," she said, so softly that at first he did not
think he had heard it. "But soon."

His flush mounted all the way to his hair and went
down all the way to his belly. What was below his belly
was soft and slack and helpless, and doing its best to
crawl back into his body. He was not a man yet. He did
not want to be one. He wanted it to be yesterday, and all
this bitter truth untold, and his heart burdened with no
more than his grief for his father and his hatred of the
Saracen and his petty rivalry with his sister.

"I'll never be able to look at her again," he said. "Or
my mother. Or—her—father." He choked, getting it out.

"You will," said Morgiana. "You are stronger than

you know." She flowed to her feet, drawing him with her. He staggered; she held him until he steadied, then set her hands on his shoulders. "Aimery de Mortmain, listen to me. This is no easy thing to learn and no easy time to learn it. And you are going to have to do something harder yet."

"What?"

"Accept it."

He shook his head so hard that he almost fell. But she held him; her fingers were inhumanly strong. They hurt. He welcomed the pain. It kept him from running screaming into the dark. "I can't," he said. "I can't accept it."

"You will."

"No."

"Yes." She shook him lightly, but hard enough to focus all of him on her. "Not at first. Not all at once. You will begin by keeping silence. You will treat your mother no differently than before; you will continue as you have been with your prince."

"And my sister? My sister, too?"

"Even your sister."

He laughed, rough and short. "Is there anything else you'll ask of me? Maybe I should go to the Saracen sultan and kiss his foot? Maybe I should bow down to the caliph in Baghdad?"

"Don't be ridiculous," said Morgiana. "You can study to keep your tongue between your teeth. It will serve you well when you come into your inheritance. And surely you can be courteous to your kin."

"What will you do if I can't?"

"I, nothing. You will do it all yourself."

Maybe she made him see. Maybe she did not need to. The truth cried aloud in front of everyone. His mother repudiated, his kinsman rejected, his sister branded bastard. Even if he kept it among the four of them, it would poison all that they did and said to one another.

He was only twelve years old. People forgot it: he was so big, and his voice had always been husky, and maybe he knew how to act older than he was. Lords' heirs learned that, being what they were.

But he was being asked to be even more than he seemed. To be not only a man but a saint.

"I can't do it," he said.

He heard the whine in it. So did Morgiana. She raised a brow. She was a cold, hard, cruel witch, and he did not care if she knew it.

She laughed.

"All right," he said angrily. "All *right*, then. I'll try."

"You'll do it," she said.

She held out her hand. He stared at it. It stayed where it was. Demanding. Expecting him to seal it, so, like a wager.

Well, then. Let it be a wager. The family's peace was stake enough against his own heart's comfort.

He gripped her hand. He did not try to soften it. But she was stronger than he. Her smile was brilliant and wicked and a little—maybe more than a little—proud of him.

"And well you ought to be," he growled at her.

She grinned and pulled him out of the room.

"Now?" he cried. "I have to begin it *now*?"

"When better?"

He had a mouthful of answers for that, but she gave him time to utter none of them. He did get out a curse. "Witch!"

She only laughed.

32

Ysabel peered warily round the door. Gwydion was gone, which meant that his servant and his squire were gone as well, and Simeon with them, though he would not have gone easily. There was only Akiva, curled in a knot on his mat, a bundle of blanket with his curly head at the top of it.

It was quite an ordinary sleep by now, or Gwydion would never have left him to it. She set down what had given her an excuse to come here, the bowl of bread and

cheese covered with a cloth, and sat on her heels beside
it.

Akiva was changing so fast that she could almost see
it. Suddenly his nose almost fit his face, and his eyes were
not quite too big for it, and his chin made human chins
seem wide and clumsy. He was not getting pretty, she
decided. No more than Gwydion or Aidan were. He was
growing beautiful.

She would never let him know she thought it. He was
almost awake. His nose twitched, catching the scent of
cheese and new bread. She drew her brows together in
the beginning of a frown.

He opened his eyes. Sleep made them soft and
blurred, but his mind was clear enough. She watched
him focus all in an eyeblink, like a hawk. He saw her. He
reckoned where he was, and when he was, and what had
put him there. He sat up a little dizzily. His stomach
growled.

"The king was hungrier than you are," Ysabel said as
Akiva wolfed down his breakfast. "He ate so much that
he even made Mother happy. That's what power does, he
says. You should have eaten after you did your healing,
and then you should have slept. You'd not have been as
sick then."

"I didn't think I'd done that much," Akiva said between bites. He reached for the bottle she had brought. It
was almost all water, but there was a little wine, and an
herb or two that Gwydion had told Cook to put in it.
Akiva grimaced at the taste, but he drank it.

"It's odd," he said. "I didn't feel as if I was sleeping
at all. More that I was dreaming, the way trees do, and
growing, and mending where I needed to. I felt you
there. You kept me from fading, did you know that? You
gave me strength to feed on until the king came. It's a
gift, like healing, but different from it. Your father has it,
too. He's like fire. He warms more than himself."

"Sometimes he burns," Ysabel said. She filched a bit
of bread and nibbled on it, for something to do. "You
look all well. The king says you are. He says you'll want
to rest for a day or two until all your strength comes
back, but there's nothing wrong with you."

Akiva stretched. His bones cracked; he made a face. "Did I grow again while I was asleep?"

"A whole inch," said Ysabel.

He believed her, for a moment, until he saw the glint in her eye. He glared. "Just you wait till it happens to you."

"I wish it would. I'm tired of being a baby."

"Well," he said. "Girls grow faster than boys."

"I don't want to grow," she said, contrary. "I don't want to change. I wish I could be grown up without having to go through all the awkwards in between."

He looked at her. His eyes narrowed. "You could do that," he said. "You could make it happen."

She could. She saw it inside. One willed thus, and so. One made this change, and that.

She hugged herself, shivering. She could, but she did not want to. She thought that it might be a Sin. Children grew the way they did because God made them that way. If they grew themselves too fast, who knew what would happen?

Akiva was changing fast enough, and none of it was his doing. He was like a colt, all legs and awkwardness, but the grace was coming through. He walked to the bed and back, unsteady at first, then more sure of himself. He turned, feeling the way his body moved. A smile broke out on his face. "I feel so strong," he said.

"That's because you were so weak for so long." Ysabel offered him his coat. He put it on over his long linen shirt.

He needed to rest then. It surprised him; he was as angry as Akiva ever got. Ysabel bullied more breakfast into him, and more of Gwydion's potion. They helped more than a little, but he stayed where he was, sitting on his mat with his back against the wall.

After a while Ysabel said, "I did a little hunting while you were asleep."

He was not about to be distracted that easily, but he raised his brows. "Did you find anything?"

"I think they're here," she said. "All of them. And the pope's letter. The trader's son spends a lot of time trying not to think about it."

Akiva did not, as she had half expected, try to see what she spoke of. His mind was tender yet, and not inclined to stretch itself. "We ought to tell your father," he said.

"What makes you think I didn't?"

He looked at her.

Her cheeks went hot. "So. I didn't want to do it without you."

"You should have," he said.

"When? They were all too busy with you."

He had to admit the truth of that. "They'll know now. That all the grownfolk are here. Their walls will be higher than ever."

"But now we know where to look. I think we should go ourselves, and see what we can see."

"Without telling anyone?" Akiva frowned. "That's not wise. Remember what happened the last time we did it."

Ysabel did not want to, but it was hard to stop, with Akiva showing her wherever her power looked.

"I think," he said, "that we should go to your father now, and tell him. He doesn't know. My lord king didn't take it from my mind, or anything else but what he needed to heal me. He's scrupulous, is my lord."

"So is my father," Ysabel said. "He won't even read humans if he can help it. Morgiana says he's foolish. But she doesn't steal thoughts, either, except when she's being shouted at."

Akiva stood up again. "Maybe we should tell the king first. He's less likely than either of them to get angry and kill someone, and then be sorry after."

"No," said Ysabel. "It's my father's grief, and my father's right. He should know first. He's wiser than people give him credit for. He won't do anything hasty."

Akiva was not at all sure of that, but he granted that she was more likely to know what her father would do. He let her lead him to the fire of power that was Aidan.

*   *   *

Guillermo Seco was not by nature a nervous man. It was his boast and his pride that, whatever befell him, he greeted it with a calm face and a steady mind.

His son, unfortunately, took after his mother. A silly, flighty woman, much given to excesses of religion. Seco had taken her for her dowry, and for her family that was one of the greatest in Genoa; once she gave him an heir, he was more than pleased to leave her to her moaning and praying.

Marco had her looks at least: her fine fair skin and her big brown eyes. It was Seco's misfortune that the boy also had her propensity for foolishness. She would have seen him happily into an abbey in Genoa, and most of her dowry with him, had not Seco sailed headlong from Outremer to pluck both boy and dower free. Small thanks he had had for it, either. Marco sulked and pined and affected to loathe the slightest whisper of commerce. Seco had dared to cherish a hope or two in this conspiracy which they had entered, taking the boy with him against the others' wishes, but now it was evident that the attraction had been not hope of riches and revenge, but calf-eyed infatuation with the monk who had forged the pope's letter.

Now this Brother Thomas was in Tyre, attending the pope's legate, and there was no reasoning with Marco. "Why can't I see him?" the boy whined. "I don't have to stay long. I can just talk to him for a little. Shouldn't he know that the witch-king is here, and his brother and the Assassin, too?"

"I doubt very much," Seco said tightly, "that he can be ignorant of it."

"Then maybe he'll know what to do." Marco was shaking, God knew what for, whether eagerness or sulkiness or plain fear. "I tell you, Father, there are more witches here than we've been told of. That Jew's whelp in the caravan—"

Seco had heard all he ever wanted to hear of the Jew's whelp in the caravan. Incessantly. For months. Ever since the caravan left Jerusalem. He had long since given up trying to reason with Marco. He cuffed the boy to stop his babble, ignored the boy's black glare, and said, "What your monk will do, I hardly care. I care more that the witches have come, and they will be in no forgiving mood. If they discover what part we had in their discomfiture . . ."

"They know," said Marco. "The whelp knows. I tell you, Father. He *said* so. He haunts me. Night after night I dream of him. I pray, I hang myself with holy relics, and still he comes. Still he besets me. He *knows,* Father."

Seco considered another blow, but something in his son's face made him pause. "How can he know? Your monk said that we would be protected."

"Yes, but were we? The witches were gone to the war. Did you keep on defending yourself as you were instructed? I tried, but it was, is, so hard. It makes my head ache."

"Well, then," snapped Seco. "If he knows, why hasn't he done something about it?"

"Maybe he can't," Marco said. "He's a young one, after all. Maybe he needed to wait until the others came to help him." He fretted from one end to the other of the room, wringing his hands like a woman, plucking at his beardless chin. "They'll hunt us, I know it. They'll find us. They'll eat our souls."

Seco despised him. But months of his nonsense had not lessened it; and Seco himself was uneasy. Not because of Marco, he told himself. Marco was an idiot. Still, even an idiot need not be wholly blind. Seco had seen the witch-king and his brother in the city, and the Assassin riding beside them, fair and strange and terrible amid their human slaves. There was no mercy in those bloodless faces; no compassion in those eyes.

He was not unduly concerned for his soul. His skin, however, and his livelihood: those, he feared for.

Marco did not need to know that Seco had spoken with the monks, Thomas the sour-faced saint and portly Richard both. They had refused to tell him where the pope's letter was. No more had they consented to do as he proposed—he who was, after all, the fount of this conspiracy. *When the Constable comes,* they had said, *we will consider it.* As if there could be anything to consider beyond what Guillermo Seco intended: what they had all agreed to do, long ago in Acre, once the pope's letter was taken and forged and read. Messire Amalric was coming, they said, as perfectly immovable as ever Mother Church could be. He had set in train the gathering of the king's ransom; now he would come to Tyre, then and only then would they do aught but sit and wait.

Messire Amalric had come. Yesterday, in the morning. He had sent no word to Guillermo Seco; no reply to the message which Seco sent. Seco could argue that there had been no time. He knew that there had been no desire. He who had conceived this plot was closed off from it by those who had come after.

Marco dithered about the cell of a room that was all even a rich man could find in thronged and costly Tyre. Thomas had succeeded well with him: he was in abject terror of the witches and their spells. Now and again he crossed himself, muttering nonsense.

He stopped, quivering. "Father, let me go to Brother Thomas. Let me warn him at the very least. He's in terrible danger. If they find him—if they catch him—"

Seco would be delighted to feed him to them. Sneering, sanctimonious fool. What he wanted was no secret. He would thwart the witches for the pure joy of it. And if they found and seized him, he would play the holy martyr for all that he was worth.

What Seco wanted was simple. The others did not intend to let him take it.

He was not their menial. Let them thwart him as they would. He would do it in spite of them.

He rose, breathed deep. His heart was thudding under his breastbone. He was not a young man, nor a brave one. But for his skin's sake, and for his son, who though a fool and a witling was still his only heir, he could do what he must do.

33

Seco left his son at home, telling him that he had an errand, which was true enough. The boy, commanded to remain where he was, sulked but did not argue. It was not the first time Seco had left him so. He prayed, the servants said, and read from his book of saints, and played the perfect little priest.

Let him do it now to his heart's content. Seco intended to win him free from this war-mad country, and a fine weight of gold with him, to recover what they had lost in the debacle of Acre. Outside of Brother Thomas' power, away from the reeking holiness of Outremer, perhaps at last Marco would learn that he was never born to be a priest; he was a merchant's son of a long line of merchants, and his sons would be merchants after him.

Yes, Seco thought as he jostled through the streets. Sons for his son. They would go back to Genoa; they would survey the prospects; they would find Marco a wife. Someone pretty enough to fire his blood, practical enough to look after his house, and fecund enough to present him with a family. And rich. That, of course.

He shook his head at himself. Marco's mooncalf moods were infecting him; he was building castles before he had the land to set them on.

But this was what he had intended from the first. Or part of it. The others thwarted him; or dreamed that they did. Cowards, all of them. They would sit with folded hands and do nothing while all hope of profit passed them by.

He was made of sterner stuff. Not that he lacked for fear. Dear Mother Mary, not at all. His hands were damp with it; his heart lurched and stumbled. Now and again his feet dragged to a halt, his body begged to turn, his mind screamed at him to give it up. But he pressed on. For Marco, he was doing it. For silly, saintly, ingrate

Marco, he endangered his immortal soul and his precious skin.

The caravanserai loomed before him. Its doors multiplied to infinity.

He stopped. "Spells," he said. His voice was a rasp, but it cleared his head. The walls shrank to human dimensions. The doors dwindled to a mere half-dozen along the colonnade. He had ascertained long since which was the proper one. The farthest, heading toward the harbor, no different from any of the others, except that its porter was a turbaned Saracen.

The creature showed no sign of speaking Frankish, but he understood it well enough. Ugly little beast, with his yellow face and his narrow slanting eyes. "Tell Prince Aidan," Seco said, "that Guillermo Seco di Genoa begs the favor of an audience."

The infidel looked Seco up and down with purest insolence. He took his time about it. Seco endured it. He had met this beast before, or another like him.

At length the Saracen deigned to respond. He opened his mouth and bawled what surely was a name. In time another appeared, who might have been his fetch: ugly little yellow-faced devil, this one wearing a broad, gap-toothed grin. The porter gabbled at him in what was not Arabic. The newcomer gabbled back. Seco discerned his name amid the nonsense.

The second imp swallowed a last, guttural word and sauntered inward. The first faced Seco. "You wait," he said in dreadful *langue d'oeil.*

Seco waited. The porter leaned against the doorframe, arms folded across his chest. He did not invite the guest within, or even deign to notice him, now that duty was done.

Seco schooled himself to patience. It was cool in the shade of the colonnade, and he was out of the jostle of the street. He would have welcomed a cup of something cold, to soothe his thirst.

It was an hour, perhaps, before Seco was again acknowledged. People passed at intervals: another Saracen, this one with a Norman face, haughty as his own master; a pair of giggling women; a boy as tall as Seco, whom

Seco recognized as the heir to Mortmain. None of them spared Seco more than a glance.

It was almost exactly an hour, Seco reckoned. Just past the stroke of terce, with even the shade beginning to take on the sun's heat. The one who came was not the imp who had gone; it was a more proper servant, a Frank in a brown smock who said only, "His highness will see you now."

His highness waited in what, in a castle, would have been the solar: a room more large than small, with tall windows and a good carpet or two, and chairs, and a table. There was no light but what came through the windows; after the dimness of stairs and passages, enough. Seco saw the figure in the tall chair like a throne, settled at its ease, lazy as a great cat, and as subtly dangerous.

There was fear, great waves of it, but Seco rose above it. He bowed to the rank if not to the man, and straightened, searching the white hawk-face. "Prince Aidan," he said. It was not a question unless the prince chose to make it so.

He did not. He gestured slightly toward a chair. A servant offered wine.

Seco took both. If there was poison in the wine, then so be it. He doubted that there was. Prince Aidan was never one to poison a cup, when his tongue was enough.

It was excellent wine. He said so.

The prince smiled. It did not touch his eyes.

He was not going to make it easy. But then, he never did. Seco remembered. Memory roused hate, sudden and blinding. Seco quelled it with all the strength he had. This creature had made a mockery of him, and more than once. Now Seco had the means to master him.

The priest's nonsense babbled through Seco's mind. He hardly needed to think of it; it woke of itself and raised its wall. Foolish, perhaps, but perhaps not. This was not a man. He knew that, drinking wine from the fine silver cup, watching the prince out of the corner of his eye. Not a line on that face, not a thread of grey in that hair, and beauty to touch even a merchant's hardened heart. The long fair hands flexed on the arms of the chair, warning enough as he rose and began to prowl: proving beyond a doubt that he was Aidan and not the shadow-quiet king.

Seco willed himself to sit still, not to follow the prince with anxious eyes. Even when he passed behind, soundless on the carpeted floor, a bare breath of air and presence. He circled the room once, twice, thrice, sunwise.

A spell. Seco felt the panic rising. Soon, all too soon, he would have no power to quell it.

He spoke more quickly than he might have chosen, with none of the indirection which he had intended. "I have a bargain to offer you."

Seco's voice was steady, if harsh. It stilled the panther-strides; it brought the prince round to face him.

"A bargain," Seco repeated, "which may work to both our advantage."

Aidan stood still. His head was up, haughty, mettlesome as a stallion's. He looked as if he would have liked to sneer, but would not so condescend. "People are always offering me bargains," he said.

"Not such a bargain as this." Seco drank from the cup, struggling not to gulp it down. "I hear that your lady is with you here. That she ransomed you from the Saracen sultan; that you have sworn oaths which you might perhaps have preferred to forgo. Would you take her to wife still, if you could?"

"She is my wife in all but the name," Aidan said.

"The name," said Seco, "is all that you strove for. What price would you pay to gain it?"

The prince tensed subtly, like a panther braced to spring. Seco, weaponless, with only the monk's wall of nonsense to protect him, sat straight and firmed his wavering spirit.

"I never bargain with thieves," said Aidan.

Seco made himself smile. "Of course, your highness. But suppose that I offered you the wherewithal to gain what you seek. Would you refuse it for that you despise me?"

"What do you want?"

Seco sat back. He had him. Witch, prince, deadly beast this might be, but Seco had what the creature wanted; and now he knew it. "What do I want? Very little, your highness. Assurance of protection for myself and my son. Passage to the Italies, and the wherewithal to keep ourselves in comfort both on the voyage and thereafter. Your sworn word that we will be safe from reprisal, whether yours or any other's."

"And in return?"

"Knowledge that you need."

"The pope's letter?"

"The means to find it."

Aidan was absolutely still. That, in one so restless, was startling; disturbing. "Why should I pay your price? My brother sails within the fortnight. It is a matter of little moment to disembark in the Italies, journey to Rome, obtain a new dispensation."

"But, your highness, you swore to wed your lady in Outremer before the Patriarch of Jerusalem. Will you break that famous oath?"

"The Holy Father can dissolve it for me."

"Perhaps. Perhaps he may refuse. What then? Will you surrender this chance, which is certain, for one which may turn against you?"

The prince laughed, light and mocking. "What, you're no turncoat, either? Fool that I am, to think I knew one when I saw one." He drew closer, standing over Seco. His presence was almost more than Seco could bear: a heat like fire, a flare of white terror. "You never loved me, Messer Seco. I saw through you long ago; I ordered you out of my sight. You had gall to come back. I admire gall. I chose to receive you, to see what could have brought you here, knowing what I am and what I swore to do when next you inflicted yourself upon me. Are you truly so eager to be stripped and shorn and whipped out of my gates?"

"Are you so eager to be stripped of your lady and your wedding?"

Aidan drew back a very little. "Gall," he said as if to himself, "indeed." He smiled his sweet, terrible smile.

"Your price is low, Messer Seco. You'll pardon me if I mistrust it."

"I would hardly reckon your protection a small thing, my lord prince."

"That, it is not. But you know how greatly I desire what you offer. Why are you asking so little of what is mine?"

"I know how little it matters to you."

The truth, sometimes, could be a potent weapon. Prince Aidan saluted it. "My protection—that matters to you. I scent the fear on you. Of what, Messer Seco? Surely not of me?"

"You are what you are," Seco said.

"And my lady is my lady." Aidan paced to the far wall and returned, and stood where he had stood before, looking down at Seco. Seco, caught like the coney beneath the hawk, looked up.

"He's not afraid of you," said a child's voice, "or even, much, of Morgiana. He's more afraid of the people he's plotted with, once they find out he's played them false."

The Jew's whelp, indeed, and in the prince's presence Seco's eyes were sharper, or else the boy had changed, for there was no doubt at all that he was one of them. But it was not he who had spoken. The child who came forward was a Mortmain, and arrogant with it, setting herself beside the prince and eyeing Seco as if he were a coney indeed, gutted and roasted and laid on her trencher. "I can't get any sense out of him," she said. "Can you?"

The prince did not give her the back of his hand. He regarded her with the air of one besotted, although he had the sense to frown a very little and inquire, "Ysabel, is this polite?"

"He isn't," she said. "He's trying to sell you what belongs to you. You shouldn't let him. His son knows, too. Shall I tell Morgiana to go and get him?"

Seco's stomach was a cold knot. The prince was tall and strange and terrible. This human-seeming child, with her untidy brown braids and her wide blue eyes, was appalling.

The prince raised a brow at her. "What do you know of this?"

"We hunted," she said. "While you were in the war. We found a track; it's here in Tyre. We were coming to tell you." She fixed Seco with a glare. "We can tell you as much as he can, and not ask payment for it, either."

Prince Aidan laid a hand on her head, half to quell her, half to caress her. Seco shuddered. Even the serpent, no doubt, knew affection for its young. This new-hatched viper leaned against her kinsman, horribly like a human child, and nibbled on a braid-end. "Should I fetch Morgiana?"

"No," said the prince. "Not quite yet." He raised his eyes from her to Seco. "Well, sir. Are you prepared to tell us what you know?"

"If you already know it, your highness, then what is there to tell?"

"You have your life to buy," the young one said. "He's being very generous to let you, instead of just asking me. Are your friends as generous as he is?"

"My life?" Seco asked with the bravery of despair. "Is that all I gain?"

"Your son's, too," she said. "And maybe passage west, if the king has room for you. He's very charitable, is my lord Gwydion."

Seco grimaced. It should have been a smile. "Is it always so with you, your highness, that you suffer women and children to do your bargaining for you?"

"They're better at it than I am," Aidan said. His smile was wide and white and faintly feral. "There's your bargain, Messer Seco. Your life and your son's, and passage west if my brother consents; and in return, the names of your conspirators."

"We can always ask Marco," the little witch said. "He's terrified of us. He has nightmares about Akiva, can you believe it, uncle? He'd do better to have nightmares about me."

Seco had no doubt of it. He would not berate himself for a fool. That gained him nothing. He had gambled that the prince would be alone and therefore vulnerable, between his pride and his innocence in the ways of merchants. Seco had reckoned without this new nest of witches.

A merchant knew when to cut his losses. Seco spread his hands, accepting the bargain as the witch had proposed it. "For my life and my son's, and for passage west, and for such compensation as hereafter we shall settle—"

"Compensation?" Aidan asked, deceptively mild.

"Surely what I have to tell is worth a dinar or two."

"Or three, or a hundred. Or are you asking all that I have?"

"Not even the tithe of it, your highness," Seco said.

"The price of passage for two, and my protection," said Aidan, "should amply suffice. If I add to it a purse of gold bezants, will that content you?"

"That depends on the size of the purse."

The young ones were outraged. Their elder was amused: a white, cold amusement. "The price when last I looked," he said, "was thirty pieces of silver."

Seco sucked in his breath.

"I shall give you," the witch-prince said, "thirty bezants. And of my charity, one blood ruby set in silver. You won't mind, surely, the curse that lies on it. He who wears it on his finger is doomed forever after to tell the truth, and nothing but the truth."

That was, in more ways than one, a threat. Seco swallowed. His throat was dust dry. "We have a bargain," he said. He did not offer to seal it with a handclasp. He breathed deep, once, twice. "The man who forged your dispensation," he said, "and who hid the proper document, is known as Thomas. He has been a scribe in the papal chancery; he serves the pope's legate. The one who suborned him is another monk, Richard of Ascalon. Both are in Tyre in the legate's train."

"Yes," said the little witch, looking past Seco to the Jew's whelp. "Thomas and Richard, that is who they are. *We* want to know—"

"We want to know," said the Jew, "how they conceal their minds from us."

"To be safe," the little witch said. "You understand. If we know the weapon, we can make a shield for it."

"That was not in the bargain," Seco said.

The witch's eyes narrowed, but the prince restrained her, as Seco had gambled that he would. Knightly honor, even in a witch, could be useful. "It was not in the bargain," said the prince, dangerously soft, "and it doesn't matter. I know who they are now. I know where to find them."

"Now?" The little witch was dreadfully eager.

"Now," the prince said.

"Us, too," said the little witch. "You have to take us. We know what the truth feels like; we'll know it when we see it."

The prince's brow darkened. The Jew leaped into the breach. "My lord, you shouldn't go alone. It's too deadly. We know; we were almost trapped before, when we tracked them to their lair in Jerusalem. If you won't take us, then you should wait for your lady and your brother. Truly, my lord. We know what we're facing."

"Do you?" the prince asked. "And you want to come with me?"

"With you, we're strong enough. With your lady and your brother—"

"My lady," said the prince, "no. I'd prefer to finish this without bloodshed if I can."

"We can help you," the little witch said. "They'll underestimate you. Thinking you can bring children into such danger as that—you'll look contemptible."

"Such words, you have in you," said the prince, frowning, but wavering visibly.

She hastened to cast him down. "We won't say anything unless you ask us to. Haven't we proved that we can do it?" She ignored his lowered brows. "We won't say a word, I promise. We'll just watch and look harmless."

"One of us can stay outside," said the Jew. "And if there's trouble, go for your lady."

He nodded slowly. "That's not ill thought of," he said. "But I don't think—"

She widened her eyes and pleaded.

He fell before her. "But mind," he said. "No heroics. From either of you."

"Oh, no," said the little witch, brimming with sincerity.

He favored her with a long, level look. She did not flinch. He sighed, shrugged, allowed himself a rueful smile.

When he turned from her, it vanished. He fixed his gaze on Seco. Seco flinched from the fire of it. "You come with us."

"I did not bargain—" Seco began.

"You bargained for your life. How can I protect it unless you remain in my presence?"

Seco opened his mouth, closed it again. He had outsmarted himself. If he could only be protected within sight of the prince, then what was that protection worth?

The prince smiled almost lazily and stepped aside, freeing Seco from the captivity of his chair. "At your pleasure, Messer Seco."

34

Gwydion, with Urien the squire to keep him respectable, tasted for an hour's span the joy of playing truant. Though it was hardly dereliction of duty, as Urien pointed out, to dawdle along the quay, reckoning the count of ships and pausing now and then to speak with a captain or an officer of the port. He should know, after all, what anchorage there would be for his fleet when it came, and what tariff the city would place on the water and the stores which they would need.

But once he had ascertained that—and done his best not to choke on it; war brought out the worst in the sellers of necessities—he was free to go where he would. In his plain clothes, with only the squire to attend him, he seemed no more than any knight. It was pleasant not to be known for a king, or even for a prince. He lent a hand with a line, tasted good brown ale in a tavern near the docks, watched a fisherman bring in a boatload of

gleaming silver fish, and among them a store of spiny
shells.

"More precious than gold, these are," the man said,
setting one in Gwydion's hand. "They make the purple
that kings like to dress in."

The King of Rhiyana looked at the wet and glisten-
ing thing with its scent of fish and the sea. The fisherman
took his expression for incredulity: he took up another
shell, and a hammer from the clutter in his boat.
"Look," he said. He cracked the shell, baring the beast
within, soft and quivering, shaped like a slug. He stabbed
it. Ichor welled forth, cloudy, almost colorless. But as
the sun struck it, it turned as red as blood.

"Blood of the murex," the fisherman said. "Put
enough of it in the dyers' vat and dip your wool in it, and
it turns as red as this blood; then let the sun at it and it
deepens to royal purple. Use less of it and you get as
pretty a violet as you could ask for. Double-dye it and
you've got a robe for an emperor, pure deep crimson,
more costly than anything in the world."

"Why does it cost so dear?" Urien asked, intrigued.

The fisherman grinned at him. "Because, my fine
young lord, one of these beasties can just about dye the
tip of your finger. For a robe to wrap an emperor in, you
need a whole shipload of them, and hammers to crush
them, and vats to steep them in, and dyers to keep the
secret."

"Such as it is," said Gwydion, "if you're willing to
tell us who simply wandered by."

"Well," said the fisherman, "my father was a dyer,
and we had a falling-out, but not before I learned the
tricks of the trade. And you look like a lad who can keep
a secret."

Urien grinned. Gwydion quelled him with a look.
"I'm honored, sir," he said.

"Remember me in your prayers," said the fisherman,
"and if you ever put on the purple."

"You could charm a sermon out of a stone," said
Urien as they left the fisherman to his catch, both scaled

and shelled. He skipped round a knot of dogs snarling over a bit of offal, and nigh backed into a dray full of wine-casks.

Gwydion plucked him out of danger and kept him there with an arm about his shoulders. It was Urien's cherished secret that he was never the monument of dignity that everyone took him for, but a madcap boy. Like his king; and all too well he knew it.

Gwydion pondered turning back. Regretfully; but a king, even a king outside of his own country, could not idle away a day with only his squire for company. He was almost to the end of the harbor, where the wall stretched out into the sea. One gate opened in it, an arch of mortared masonry between two lofty towers, and the great chain to bar it, which the sea-guard would lower when a ship sought to pass in or out.

"Imagine this in the harbor at Caer Gwent," said Urien. "We'd be impregnable."

"I am imagining it," Gwydion said. "It's not for us, I think. Tyre is an island city with a harbor in its heart. Caer Gwent, but for the headland that is the White Keep, is like a torque about a lady's neck."

"That lady being the sea." Urien sighed. "I was glad to get away from it; I thought myself trapped there. Now all I can think of is going back, and being home."

"I, too," said Gwydion softly. "Soon now. When the fleet comes; when we settle the matter of my brother's wedding."

"As to that, my lord," Urien said, "do you think—"

"My lord! My lord king!"

Urien stopped. Gwydion turned. He was not precisely displeased to be recognized so publicly, but he would have preferred greater discretion. Even here, where the quay was almost empty. The guards on the wall, and the odd idler, stopped to stare.

The man who came, came alone, without even a servant to bear him company. He greeted Gwydion more circumspectly, now that he was noticed; he did not offer an embrace, of which Gwydion was glad.

"Messire Amalric," Gwydion said. Courteously; no

more warmly than he must. "The pleasure is unexpected.
I had thought you in Jerusalem."

"So I was," said Amalric, offering a sketchy reverence. "But the strength of the kingdom is here; I had a
mind to look at it before I went back to captivity."

"Did you, sir?"

Amalric showed a flash of teeth. "You can call it
spying if you like. I'd rather call it pondering alterna-
tives. The sultan holds my brother hostage, well enough,
but I doubt he'll put a king to death for his brother's
failure to walk back into the cage. Not with the ransom
still to pay."

"Is it?"

"The queen will pay it," said Amalric. "That's settled, though she'll need time to gather it all together."

"Yours, too?"

"Mine, too," said Amalric. "I have that much
honor."

Gwydion sat on a coil of rope, suppressing a sigh and
an urge to bolt for cover. Amalric would hardly have
hailed him for idle pleasure. The man had the look and
the air of one who had hunted for some little time, and
hoped to catch his prey out of its wonted runs.

The Constable of the embattled kingdom did not presume to sit uninvited in a king's presence. He clasped his
hands behind his back and surveyed the long curve of the
harbor, at ease, but with a subtle tension beneath. "I'm
glad to see you made it so far and prospered so well. The
marquis caused you no trouble?"

"The marquis would hardly vex a sovereign king,"
Gwydion said.

"Rude little bastard, isn't he?"

"I have not," said Gwydion, "heard calumny of his
lady mother."

Amalric laughed. "That's true: he's his father's son
to the bone. He calls you arrogant, as if he had a right to
judge."

"The marquis may call me what he pleases."

"He does," said Amalric. "He says you summoned
him—lord of this city as he is, or so he says, and no
vassal of yours."

"I informed him that I was present, and gave him to know where I reside. He did not see fit to respond. That is his right as lord of this city and no vassal of mine."

"He doesn't know when he's outmatched," said Amalric.

"That is as may be," said Gwydion. "Will you, then, be entering his service?"

"He's asked," Amalric said. "I've been in no haste to answer. My brother still holds my oath, after all."

"So does the sultan."

"Another oath," said Amalric. "Another and briefer binding."

"Enough at least to keep the marquis at bay."

"There is that," Amalric said. "And you, sire? You'll be going home, now that you've sworn yourself out of the war?"

"Out of the war, perhaps, but not out of the Crusade. Europe will learn from me what has been done to our holy places."

Amalric considered that and whistled softly. "So that's why you took oath so easily. The sultan would have done better to keep you."

"Could he have held me?"

"Probably not." Amalric exchanged glances with a gull on a bollard. The gull mewed and took wing. "My lord, if I asked a favor of you, would you grant it?"

"Have you earned it?"

Amalric turned on his heel. For a moment Gwydion saw him unmasked. Anger, yes, that was to be expected. And fear: for Gwydion was what he was. And, always, calculation. Plain, rough, unpolished Amalric was heart-kin to Conrad of Montferrat. Snakes of a scale, Aidan would say.

Amalric's eyes hooded. He smiled as if at a jest. "A king should be wary, yes, your majesty. It's not so great a favor. Only passage on one of your ships, for which I can pay."

"And?"

Amalric's smile slipped; then widened. "I forget, sire, what arts are yours. Yes, there is somewhat more. I asked you once, if you recall, for leave to pay court to your kinswoman. My condition has altered somewhat since, but my rank remains, and my kingdom, though diminished, has still its king and the core of its strength. In Europe we'll gather armies to win it back greater than before. With the Lady Elen at my side, I would find fire in myself to rouse such a Crusade as this world has never seen."

"And then? Would you ask the lady to ride into the jaws of war?"

"Hasn't she already done so?"

"So she has," said Gwydion mildly.

"May I address her, at least, sire?"

"Have you not already done so?"

Amalric failed to see the wit in that. "Your majesty was generous to allow me to speak to her on the road to Acre. But we never spoke of marriage. It wasn't time; and there was the war. Now, if we're to sail together—"

"That has not been settled," Gwydion said.

"If we should," said Amalric, "there will be time to talk of gentler things. If your majesty will grant his approval."

"The Lady Elen is a grown woman. She has been wed before; our custom in our country, from the old times, is to leave a widow free to choose whether she will wed again or remain faithful to her husband who is gone."

"Yet if she does choose to marry, surely her kinsmen have a say in it."

"The final word is hers," Gwydion said.

"Would she marry against your wishes?"

"That is for her to say," said Gwydion.

Amalric paused. Gwydion tasted his frustration: sour, with a tang of iron. It was not Christian and hardly kingly, but Gwydion knew a moment's pleasure.

"I may speak with her, then?" Amalric asked. He did not quite succeed in keeping the roughness from his voice.

Gwydion met the man's eyes. Amalric stiffened but held his ground. For that, Gwydion said, "I will speak with her. If she consents, then you may address her. If she refuses, you will abide by her wishes."

"I'll trust you to be persuasive, my lord," said Amalric.

"Indeed," said Gwydion. He rose. Amalric stepped back. Aidan, whom the monks had never managed to tame, would have smiled. Gwydion promised his God a penance. Later. When he was well away from this thorn in his side.

It was a king's privilege to dispense with greetings and farewells if it suited his pleasure. Gwydion did not often indulge it. He left Amalric standing there and turned his face toward the caravanserai.

Gwydion's mood had altered for the worse. He turned Urien loose; the boy, meeting his glance, swallowed argument and went. Alone but not content, Gwydion slowed little by little until he hardly moved at all.

It was neither kingly nor charitable, but he did not want Messire Amalric on any ship that was his. He knew nothing truly ill of the man; he had seen nothing to condemn, except an excess of ambition. But he could not like him.

Elen was safe enough from Amalric. Unless she judged, as dispassionately as royalty could, that what he offered would profit her family; and she could do that. Fourteen years old and betrothed to the man whom her father chose for her, thinking him old and less than pleasant to look at, she had gone to her wedding with her head high, like a warrior into battle. She had won what she fought for. It had never been a love match, but as marriages went it had been better than most. Riquier had cherished her even when she failed to give him the heir he longed for. She had grieved when he died.

This pilgrimage showed every sign of having healed her as Gwydion had hoped. When she returned to Rhiyana the suitors would gather; for she was the fairest prize in his kingdom. Yet to vex her now, when her joy was all so new . . .

"I should give her to Urien," he said aloud.

He had only meant to jest, however bitterly, but once he had said it he saw the logic in it. They liked one another. They were cousins, but what of that? Rome had dispensed before, and would again, for a king's asking. And it would rid them of Amalric.

Urien was younger than she, but that might be to the good. He was no monk nor virgin; he had a pair of sons by women whom he did not love, but who had had all honor from him, and ample provision for their children, and husbands who were kind to them. His family was well thought of, his wealth considerable, his prospects excellent. They would do well together, they two.

Gwydion allowed himself a smile as he threaded through the crowd. Elen would consider the match carefully if he proposed it, and very likely take it, wise child that she was. Yet it might be a greater pleasure and a sweeter victory to broach it subtly. To encourage them to come together; to set them in the way of one another; to let them think that they had chosen it for themselves.

Aidan would laugh at him. Aidan was certain that, left to himself, Gwydion would happily set himself up as a matchmaker, and make a new order of marriage. Love matches, such as he himself had made. Little as Aidan could afford to mock, who had chosen even more unsuitably than Gwydion himself.

Witchfolk were not as humans were. The Church did its best, but humans—human men, at least—were not made to mate for life. Witchfolk could do no other.

Gwydion reached down to the core of him where that other was, a cool soft presence, a hint of sweetness. She was in her garden with a wolf-cub in her lap. She smiled as she felt his awareness on her. *Beloved,* she said.

Soon, he said. *Soon I come back.*

She had never doubted it; nor ever could.

Tyre was harsh and strident after the green silences within, areek with human bodies, ababble with human voices. Gwydion passed by the public door of the caravanserai, the great gate that faced the harbor, and sought the postern, the small narrow door hidden in a fold of the wall, that opened on the garden. It was no such garden as his queen had made, being human and mortal and imbued with no more than earthly magic, but it was green, and it would be quiet. He needed both, for a little while. Then he would go. He would approach Elen and tell her that she had a suitor.

Green and quiet indeed, and the song of falling water, and a woman's laughter.

Gwydion, walking unwarily, lost in himself, paused in startlement. Deeper laughter echoed the woman's, and a murmur of words, endearments in a mingling of Arabic and *langue d'oeil.*

The garden's maze was deceptive: what seemed distant could be very near, and what seemed near could be impossible to reach. Even Gwydion's senses were of little use. He could only go on and hope that he did not stumble on the lovers. One of Aidan's Saracens, it had to be, with one of the flock of wives. Shy, veiled creatures, those, soft-voiced as doves where strangers could hear, but lively enough away from infidel eyes. They had all been given the choice to remain in Millefleurs and not be torn away from home and land and family. Not one had taken it. They had packed up their belongings and their children and ridden with their husbands, and refused to call it bravery. Bravery was for men, they said. Women did what they had to do.

The path bent round a hedge, opening on a bit of sun-seared grass and an arbor laden with roses, and a vision out of one of Morgiana's more interesting books: a cloak spread on the ground, greener than the grass it covered, and on it the two lovers. The Saracen with his turban laid carefully aside, his coat folded under it, but decorous enough else, though that was like to alter swiftly. His lady, even more modestly clad than he, with her veil over her hair and her gown demurely laced, teased his shirt out of his trousers, and laughed when he blushed. He swept in for a kiss. They tumbled together on their makeshift bed. Her fillet slipped from her brow; her veil fell, baring her head. Her hair was free. It cloaked them both, to his manifest delight.

Gwydion stood stock-still. He could not move to advance; he could not will himself to retreat.

The man was a Saracen surely, incontrovertibly. The woman, as surely, was not.

Gwydion was not angry. He was too old for that; too much a king. He would have preferred to have been less blind, or perhaps less trusting.

The man saw him first. Blue eyes; they were always startling in that face. They went utterly, perfectly still.

Elen, who had her back to him, perceived her lover's stillness. In human wise, and in the heat of her blood, she sought to stir him with kisses. He laid a finger on her lips, gently. She kissed it, but she stilled as he had. She turned to see what he saw.

It said somewhat for their perception, that neither took Gwydion for his brother. The blood drained from Elen's face.

They rose together, hand in hand. It was not meant to be defiance. They let go when they were up, but did not move apart. The mamluk was a handsome man. Gwydion could see that, dispassionately; as he had always seen the man's courage and his quality. A good man, a knight and a gentleman, a notable warrior, a trainer of horses.

None of it entitled him to a princess.

Elen raised her chin. She had never been more beautiful. Love did that, even to a woman whose beauty was not already worthy of a song. "My lord," she said, cool and proud.

The mamluk bowed as a Frank and not as a Saracen; as a knight to a king. He had grace, and pride enough.

"You could," said Gwydion, "have been more circumspect."

Raihan blushed like a boy. Elen's pallor never altered. "We ask your majesty's pardon," she said.

Gwydion drew a breath. "You may ask. You may not receive it."

"That is your majesty's right," said Gwenllian's daughter's daughter.

"Did you think," Gwydion said, "that I would accept an accomplished fact, when I would never otherwise consent?"

"I would not so insult your majesty's intelligence."

"And this?"

Her eyes were level, her voice unwavering. "This, I could not help. I love him, my lord. I know that I should not. I cannot bring myself to repent of it."

The mamluk said nothing. Wise, he was, for a mortal and a man. He loved her. It was written in his every line.

"Do you fancy yourself worthy of her?" Gwydion asked him.

"Insofar as any man may be, sire," said Raihan, "yes."

Gwydion closed his eyes. When he opened them, neither had moved.

A grown woman, Gwydion had said to the man who would have courted her for his own ambition. *Hers to speak; hers to choose.*

And while he said it, she had spoken; she had made her choice.

"I do not know," he said to her, "that I can forgive you."

She inclined her head. He was her king; she was his vassal.

He could command her. She would obey. It was bred in her.

It would not undo what she had done, nor alter what was unalterable. There would be no love match for her now, not with any Christian. Not, certainly, with Urien, whom she thought of as a brother· young and callow and very dear to her, but never as this other was. This freed slave, this infidel, this halfblood Syrian who could not even name his father.

"You are a breeder of horses," Gwydion said. "What would you do to a common drayhorse, a stallion of no lineage, who broke in upon the finest of your mares?"

Raihan's nostrils flared. He looked indeed like one of his own horses, and no common one, either. "I would wait, my lord, and judge the quality of the foal."

Gwydion stilled. But she was not with child. That grace at least God had granted them. "And if there was no foal?"

"Then I would remove him, and see that he did not approach her again."

"Yes," Gwydion said.

"And what of the mare?" Elen asked. "Has she no say in it?"

"Do you think that she should?"

Elen's lips tightened. Her hands were fists. She had begun to tremble. "May I have your majesty's leave to go?"

What Gwydion gave her, perhaps, was mercy. "Go," he said.

She went. The mamluk took the command to himself also, but waited until she was gone before departing in another direction altogether. Gwydion stood alone and still, like an image of a king.

35

Marco knew what his father thought of him. It was one of his less successful exercises in charity, to understand it. To Guillermo Seco, a man with a vocation was no man at all. Manhood was greed and venality and grubbing for gold.

When Marco thought of what his father wanted him to be, he had an irresistible urge to wipe his hands on his cotte. His too-clean, too-rich, too-elaborate cotte, which his father had chosen for him and bidden him wear. There was no hairshirt under it. His father had got wind of that and had it burned in front of him, with a lecture on conduct becoming a citizen of the commune of Genoa.

Honor thy father and thy mother, the Commandment said. But Scripture also said, *Render unto Caesar what is Caesar's, and unto God what is God's.*

Marco was God's. The call was clear in him. Every day it came clearer. The more his father strove to make him a proper son of Mammon, the more his soul strained toward the purity that was God.

Now he wrestled with an angel, or maybe it was a devil. His father had left him behind: a gift, it should

have been, and rare. But something in Seco's eyes made
Marco restless. He was commanded to stay. His heart
wanted to go. It had to do with Brother Thomas, this
errand of his father's. He knew it without knowing how
he knew.

Brother Thomas was more of God than Marco could
ever hope to be. He was a saint; a child of heaven. And
Seco loathed him.

If Seco went to him without Marco's knowledge,
what would they say to one another? What battle would
there be?

Marco did not flatter himself that he could do anything about it. Except witness it, and maybe prevent
something dreadful.

The angel tumbled down with Marco's foot on his
throat. Marco snatched his cap and pulled it on, and ran
after his father.

He was not much good at shadowing and lurking,
but Seco was not looking for pursuit. Marco kept his
head down and his cap over his eyes, and let the swirl of
Tyre's crowds obscure him. God was with him. No one
jostled him too badly; nothing held him back or got in
his way, or separated him from his quarry.

He began to wonder if after all his heart had played
him false. Seco did not turn toward the cathedral and the
archbishop's palace, where Marco knew Brother Thomas
to be, waiting humbly on the pope's legate. He turned, in
fact, in almost the opposite direction, toward the harbor.
He was only going to see to something worldly.

But Marco kept following him. Spineless his father
might think him, but he could be stubborn when he
needed to.

Seco did not go all the way to the harbor. He stopped
at a great tall building, one of the city's larger caravan-
serais. He spoke to a porter in a turban. Marco, shielded
behind a gaggle of pilgrims, heard the name he asked for.

It was not a shock. Marco was no more stupid than
he was spineless, and he knew his father rather better
than his father knew him. He remembered what Seco
had wanted to do, back at the beginning, before Brother
Richard came into it, and brought Brother Thomas, and

turned plain rancorous conniving into something much
higher and stronger. Seco wanted simply to discredit the
witch-prince and gain somewhat of the prince's wealth.
Brother Thomas wanted to cast the witches down and
condemn them with the power of holy Church.

Seco knew it, and despised it. He had been saying so
for days now. "What use is this? What have we accomplished but a few moments' discomfiture, and their
hounds on our trail?"

Not that he honestly believed in them. He laughed at
Marco when Marco told him that the Jew's whelp was
one of them. He thought that human guile was enough,
and human treachery.

Now he went to the prince. Just as Judas had gone to
the high priest, and for much the same reason. He
wanted more than he thought he was being given. He
reckoned to get it from his enemy, with no one else to
share it or to keep him from it.

Marco came within a breath's span of running to his
father and dragging him away. But Seco would never go.
He was as stubborn as Marco, and much more obvious
about it.

Marco dithered from foot to foot. He had to do
something. His father was about to go into the lion's
mouth. He would betray them all. And once the witches
knew what they had done, and who they were . . .

He was running before he had time to think, as hard
and as fast as he could, away from the caravanserai, into
the thick of the city. He did not even think of it as a
choice. He did what he had to do, that was all.

Brother Thomas was not difficult to get at. One only
needed determination, and a measure of gall. Marco's
cotte was good for something after all: it made the archbishop's guards salute him instead of stepping to bar his
way. The well-to-do were always coming and going
around the cathedral, especially now, with Tyre full of
nobles and their servants. One guard even told Marco
where to find the legate's secretary. "I saw him not an
hour past," the man said, as affable as if there had never

been a war outside the walls. "He and his friend, the monk from Ascalon, were talking about a bit of prayer, and then a turn around the cloister."

It was in the cloister that Marco found them, and a third with them, King Guy's brother as rough-hewn and opaque-eyed as ever, but looking remarkably pleased with himself. He did not seem to have suffered from his captivity among the Saracens. As Marco paused to take stock, Messire Amalric said, "I don't know that we need to do anything further. We did what we set out to do. The kingdom is safe from all of them. They'll be gone before the month is out, sailing back where they came from."

"Is that all you care for?" Brother Thomas demanded of him. "That they be cast out of your garden, even if it be into another's?"

Messire Amalric refused to be offended. "That's all I ever pretended to want. I saw this kingdom threatened by an unholy alliance. We broke it; it turned to our advantage and freed us from them all. Now let them mate if they will. They're no danger to Jerusalem."

"You would surrender the dispensation, then?" Brother Richard inquired. "Leave it under a stone, perhaps, and send a bird to guide them to it? Messer Seco may not like that. He had his heart set on a fat ransom."

What Messer Seco could do, in Amalric's opinion, was not for sanctified ears to hear. Brother Richard merely smiled. Brother Thomas suffered in silence.

"We might still reap a little advantage," Amalric said when the air had cleared again. "One of us can pretend to lead them to it, and accept what reward they may choose to offer. A princely one, I don't doubt. Whatever their faults, they've never failed of generosity."

"That one of us, of course, being you." Brother Richard was amused. He usually was. A good man, Brother Richard, but rather more a cynic than he ought to be. "Have you won the princess yet, my lord?"

Amalric rubbed his jaw. If Marco had not known better, he would have thought the man was embarrassed. "Not yet. But soon."

"Your courage amazes me," Brother Richard said. "I

could never play both sides as you so boldly do, still less contemplate allying myself with that family for the rest of my days. What if your guard slips?"

"It won't." Amalric was not even arrogant. He simply knew. "You should give me credit. I'll save the lady's soul and snatch her from the arms of iniquity. A good mortal marriage, a good Christian husband—that will rid her of the taint that's on her."

"And her dowry is improbably rich." Brother Richard shook his head. "Bold, my lord. I'll stop short of calling it foolhardy."

Marco listened, appalled. It had taken him a while to understand what they were saying. Messire Amalric was paying court to the Rhiyanan princess—Marco had seen it on the road to Acre, but he had not known enough to recognize it. How could he think to marry her, with such blood as she had? How could he imagine that her kin would let him do it?

Brother Richard saw Marco then, and told the others. Messire Amalric looked surprised. Brother Thomas did not.

"Your father has a message?" Messire Amalric asked. His voice was rough. He was never polite when he did not need to be.

Marco shook his head till his hair whipped in his eyes. They stung; he rubbed them furiously. He had been steady all this time, but now suddenly he began to shake. He knew he looked every bit the mooncalf his father—and surely Messire Amalric—thought him.

Brother Thomas was silent. Brother Richard was kind, if somewhat mocking. "No message? Did you come out of the goodness of your heart, then?"

Marco shook his head again, not as hard this time. If he spoke, he knew that he would stammer. But he could not help but speak. He fought the words through his stumbling tongue. "I—I—I come because I have to come." He flung himself down at Brother Thomas' feet and clung to the monk's coarse robe. "Brother, I'm sorry, I'm so sorry, I'd give anything not to have to tell you, but he's gone—he's gone—"

"Back to Genoa without us?"

Brother Thomas fixed his brother monk with a cold eye. "Levity is hardly called for here," he said. He turned that same eye, but the merest shade warmer, upon Marco. "What has he done? 'He' being, I presume, your father?"

"My father, yes," Marco said. He was calmer now, with the beginning out of the way, and Brother Thomas' habit in his hands. It was like an anchor. "He's gone to the prince. He wants to ransom the dispensation, I think."

"He doesn't know where it is," Amalric said so quickly that he could not have thought at all.

"He knows who has it," said Brother Richard. He looked as cool as ever. "We should have watched him more closely. He never lacked for intelligence, however low its order. He would know that he was being left out of our counsels."

"And whose idea was that?" demanded Amalric.

"Yours." Brother Richard rattled the beads that threaded his cincture, seeming to take an innocent pleasure in the sound. "So, then. The rat has gone to the cat. What do we do about it?"

"Pray," said Brother Thomas.

Amalric curled his lip. "That's easy for you to say. The king knew nothing of this when I saw him just this hour past. If we're lucky, he won't be home yet, and the Assassin will be hunting somewhere safely distant, and it will only be the prince."

"The most dangerous of them," said Brother Thomas, "and the one with least cause to love us for what we have done."

"You call him dangerous? More even than the Assassin?"

"The Assassin kills cleanly, with a dagger in the heart. The other is Christian and a Celt. He may favor teeth and claws."

"More likely he will challenge my lord Amalric to a passage in the lists." Brother Richard seemed to like the sound of that.

Amalric went faintly green. "I wasn't talking about mortal combat," he said.

"True," mused Brother Richard, "he is the least of them in name for witchery. I doubt that that makes him less than either of the others; simply more inclined toward battles of the body, and more adept in them. He, of them all, seems most fond of seeming to be human."

"He pretends badly," Brother Thomas said. "He is a warrior both of his hands and of the darker arts. The king would pause for conscience. The Assassin has none. He who falls between—him, truly, I fear."

"They'll hunt us wherever we go," Amalric said. "They'll find us wherever we hide, by our spoor among our kind."

"A hermitage in the desert might be good for all our souls," said Brother Richard.

"You may go," Brother Thomas said, "and hide if you can. You, my lord, have little to fear, I think; they lived and fought and suffered the grim defeat with you, and never marked you for their prey."

"And you?" said Amalric.

"I am the one they seek. I wrote the dispensation as it was read before them. When they have me, they will hunt no lesser quarry."

"A martyr," said Amalric, half in wonder, half in scorn. "A holy Christian martyr."

Brother Thomas took no notice of his mockery. "If you will go, you had best go now: I doubt that they will tarry, once they know where I am."

Messire Amalric barely hesitated. Nor did he thank the man who would suffer for his sake. He turned on his heel and left them, walking swiftly.

"A prudent man," Brother Richard observed, "and, thereby, a safe one." He shrugged, sighed. "I was never overfond of prudence."

"Nor I!" Marco cried. "I'll stay, Brother. I can't do much, I know that, I'm not good for much of anything, but maybe I can die for you."

Brother Thomas looked down at him in mild surprise. No contempt, Marco saw that. Wonder, a little, and a dawning of respect. "I am hardly worth dying for," Brother Thomas said.

"God is."

Brother Thomas nodded. The respect was clearer now, and the wonder. "I see that I have underrated you."

Marco shrugged, miserably embarrassed. "I'm nothing. Except maybe a shield for you."

Brother Thomas reached down and pulled him up, brushing him off with his own frail saintly hands and holding him by the shoulders and looking deep into his eyes. "Messer Marco, have you a vocation?"

"Yes." Marco's voice was hardly more than a squeak. "At least, I think so. All I ever wanted was to belong to God." *And you,* he added in his heart, but Brother Thomas did not want to hear that. "My father doesn't like it. He's a good man, Brother, you have to believe that. But he's of the world. He doesn't understand."

A great light kindled in Brother Thomas' eyes. It dazzled Marco; it made him blink and his heart swell. "We shall have to see," said Brother Thomas, "what can be done about that."

He let Marco go. Marco almost fell. "But now," Brother Thomas said, "we gird for battle. Shall we pray together, Brother, Messer Marco?"

36

As Aidan, with Ysabel and Akiva and a reluctant Seco in his wake, prepared to leave the caravanserai in pursuit of Brother Thomas, he met Gwydion coming in. Collided with him for a fact, as he strode blindly down the passage in a rare and inscrutable temper. Aidan would have wished to know what had caused it, but his own temper was rarer and more terrible. He caught his brother in a light strong grip and held him when he struggled, and shook him into something resembling consciousness.

Gwydion blinked at him, eyes pale and strange. Aidan gave it to him whole, as only witchfolk could.

He seized on it as Aidan had hoped, and came fully

into the world again. "Truly?" he whispered. "Truly, at last?"

"Truly and inarguably." Aidan grinned at him. "Will you hunt with us?"

His answer was to turn and stride before them.

The pope's legate greeted them with honest pleasure, unperturbed by the grimness of their faces or the white terror of Seco's. Aidan would not have brought Abbot Leo into it, but Gwydion was insistent. "For courtesy," he said. "And for a witness whom none will question."

It was Gwydion who told the tale as Aidan had given it to him: shock on shock for Seco, who was learning much too late what power could do. Abbot Leo listened in stainless quiet. At Brother Thomas' name, a shadow crossed his face. Pain, perhaps; sorrow. "He is the most promising of my servants," the abbot said when Gwydion was done. "Alas for his soul! What brought him so low?"

"Sanctity," Aidan replied. "Good men of God have forged lies before in holy Church's name. He thinks that he preserves it from the evil that we are, by committing a lesser sin."

"Hell has been bought for less," said Gwydion. He was all hunter now, and all implacable. Aidan eyed him narrowly and resolved to fathom his trouble. Soon.

Abbot Leo rose stiffly, refusing the proffered hands. He did not hate the brothers for being older than he yet knowing none of the frailty that beset him, but he had his pride. Aidan let him keep it. It was small price to pay for such a witness, and time was fleeting.

There was no joy like the joy of the chase, with the scent hot and rich in one's nose, and the quarry in sight, and the hunt closing in for the kill. Such a chase as this, across all of Outremer, through war and defeat, was sweeter yet, and its end more glorious when it came. Soon now he would taste blood. Soon he would hold the quarry between his claws, and sink his teeth in its throat.

Guillermo Seco, poor mortal craven, was paralytic with terror. The children half-carried him between them,

which only made his terror worse: grown witchfolk were
ill enough to bear, but their young were appalling. Aidan
showed him a smile much too full of teeth, and paused
on the threshold of the monks' chapel. The prey was
within. He had tracked it by its absence, through the
memories in men's minds: a servant who saw them pass,
a monk who left the chapel as they entered it, a sacristan
who saw them kneel within to pray.

The wall of nothingness which had so frightened the
children was stronger and stranger than ever. It beckoned. It seduced. It lured the power down into its light-
less dark. There was nothing of his own kind about it. It
was a human thing; a mortal horror. Not power, but its
utter, boundless absence.

Gwydion's presence surrounded him before he could
fray and scatter. The children wove themselves within it.
And all about it like a thread of silver and steel, the
purest of all presences, stronger than any and more
skilled, and furious that he had thought to leave her out
of it.

Protection! she spat at him where none but he could
hear. *Idiot! Brainless fool! Where would you be at all, if I
were not here to protect* you?

Actually, he said, *I was protecting our prey.* That
stopped her. He smiled as she shaped herself out of air,
and kissed her before she could toss him off.

All together they were a thing of light and splendor,
a weaving of magic more potent than any one of them
apart, or any five of them unwoven. What Gwydion had
seen on the Mount of Olives before his entry into Jerusalem, now shaped itself into solidity.

They braced themselves. Aidan drew his sword with
a soft hiss of steel. Morgiana's dagger was in her hand.
Gwydion and the children bore no weapon but their
power; but that would be enough.

"Now," said Aidan.

The wall of not-power swayed before the assault;
stiffened; held. Aidan smote it with all their conjoined
strength.

It shattered; and the door with it, in a rain of stinging
shards.

They sprang through the splintered door, Aidan in the van, Morgiana hard upon his heels. He was a tower of light, she a leaping flame.

They came like the wrath of God. No weapons met them; no last desperate stroke of not-power. Only silence and stillness and the scent of incense.

The monks' chapel was rather a part of the cloister than of the cathedral, small and almost bare, although its shape was beautiful: an aisle and a graceful curved bay with the altar set in it, and columns from old Rome holding up the roof, red stone polished bright beneath the flowering capitals, and a floor of colored marble. The hand of Islam had struck the faces from the mosaics above the altar, and the Frankish archbishops had done nothing to restore them. There was an odd power in the stiff elongated figures, faceless as they were, veiled as if in clouds of awe.

Those whom Aidan hunted knelt beneath the faceless Christ. Three together, each in his separate fashion: a thickset monk who seemed to lie at languid ease even on his knees, and a wizened monk as stiff as a carven saint, and a boy in a cotte rather richer than a commoner should venture, trying to be as stiff as the monk beside him, but trembling in spasms.

Guillermo Seco, whom Aidan had all but forgotten, lurched forward a step through the last of the magelight. He was oblivious to it. "Marco! What are you doing here?"

The boy lurched to his feet, tangling them as he turned. His face was white and defiant. "Father. What have you brought here?"

"Retribution." Aidan studied their faces. Such utterly human creatures, to have thwarted power for so long. The fat one was beneath contempt: a hanger-on, a seeker after entertainment, with no regard for the cost of it. The boy was merely young. The third—the third was the one he sought. He knew that, meeting those level dark eyes.

This one was dangerous. It was his not-power which warded them all, whispering its seduction even through Morgiana's potent guard; his will which held them. And his hand surely which had wielded the pen. He had written as if he were the lord pope, words which were his own deep conviction.

Aidan could find no hate in him, though better far for all of them if there had been. Hate was a simple thing. One found it, one measured it, one destroyed it.

This was worse. It was true faith, and pure conviction. Brother Thomas believed what he had written. He knew that Aidan and his kin were evil; that they should be named anathema.

Thomas stood firm under the weight of that stare. All of them had come after all, and the betrayer with them; and Abbot Leo, whom they had seduced long ago. It was better so, Thomas thought. Whether he lived or died, he would know, surely and incontrovertibly, that he had been tested to the fullest.

They were beautiful as the sons of God were, even cast down into perdition. A perilous beauty. God meant it, surely, as a warning; humans, flawed creatures that they were, might only see how it seduced. The eye strove to soften the edges of it, to blur its strangeness, to shape it to human measure.

Seen clear, it ceased even to be beauty. It was merely alien. The woman, the ifritah, most of all: humanity in her was patently a mask, and naught beneath but the beast, fanged and clawed and deadly.

Strange that she should have mated with the one who, of them all, came closest to a semblance of humanity. He spoke again in the silence. His voice was like a man's voice, indeed very like, yet it was not. It rang too clear, its music too flawless, no murmur in it of mortality. "Brother Thomas," he said. "You have something that is mine."

Such simplicity. Thomas smiled. "I do," he answered. He heard Marco's gasp of shock. Poor child. He understood so little, who sacrificed so much. Had he thought that Thomas would lie, or at least prevaricate?

The witch-prince himself seemed somewhat startled. "You admit it?"

"I can hardly lie to you," Thomas said.

"Tell me where it is."

Princely, that; imperious. Thomas answered it with perfect serenity. "No, lord prince. I will not. Not without a price."

Prince Aidan's lip curled. "So. Even you will bargain with the devil."

Thomas laughed. He had not felt so light of heart since he was a child. "Why not? Should my charity be perfect, and I imperfect man?"

The prince was barely amused. "Name your price."

"These," said Thomas, indicating the conspirators. "Set them free. Give me your faithful word that you will do no harm to any of them."

"And yourself?"

"I am nothing," said Thomas. "You may do with me as you will."

"A martyr," the prince said. Thomas could not be certain that it was scorn. Admiration, it was not. The grey cat-eyes flicked from Richard to Seco to Marco; held each, stripped his soul bare, cast him aside. There was no more compassion in it than in the death-play of a cat. "And do you trust me, once you are disposed of, to keep my word to these others?"

"Yes," said Thomas.

That raised the prince's brows. He spared no glance for those who had come with him, although the Assassin, at least, looked as if she would speak. "Very well," he said. "In return for your surrender and for the pope's dispensation, they may go."

"Unpunished," said Thomas with gentle precision. "Unmolested by you or yours, now or ever."

The prince barely hesitated. "They are free."

Thomas smiled. Richard seemed disinclined to linger. Seco wavered, his eyes not on Aidan but on his son. Marco was oblivious to him. Aidan patently was not. "If I were wise," the prince said very gently, "I would go."

The color drained from Seco's face. He shot a last, wild glance at Marco. Marco was aware of it: he stiffened, but he kept his eyes on Thomas.

Seco turned abruptly. Perhaps he strove for dignity. It mattered little. It was still, incontestably, flight.

Marco would not follow him. He clung to Thomas, white and shaking but immovable. "I want to die with you," he said. Through the chattering of his teeth, his voice was remarkably steady.

It was the Elvenking who spoke, soft and seeming diffident, but one could not help but listen. "Let him stay. He can hardly do more harm than has been done already."

The prince seemed inclined to disagree, but after a moment he acquiesced. Marco sank down at Thomas' feet, the look on his face compounded of terror and triumph.

He was safe enough, by the prince's own given word. Thomas believed that, if Marco did not: and all the braver of him to remain in the face of such fear. Thomas signed a blessing on his brow and stood straighter, meeting the prince's stare.

"Now," said Aidan. "Tell."

Thomas thought that he could sense the force of all their sorceries beating upon his inner defenses. His head ached dully, far back behind his eyes. He knew how he might lay himself open to them. So simple, it would be: to let down the walls, to relax the discipline which for so long had held his soul inviolate. But that courage was not in him.

The silence had begun to stretch. Aidan, ever restless, spoke to fill it. "Your game is up. You know that perfectly well. If you won't tell us what you've done with our dispensation, we'll find it. It will simply take a little longer."

Likewise, Thomas was certain, the death which they intended for him. The Assassin's hand was on the hilt of her dagger, her eyes hungry, needing but a word to spring upon him.

Her leman did not give it. He said, "Tell us."

Thomas sighed. The ache in his skull was rising to true pain. Five of them, all fixed upon him, all battering at his walls. How proud his teacher would have been. But pride was a sin, and Thomas was but mortal flesh.

He said, "It lies in the box of my belongings in the cell which I occupy here."

The ifritah was there, and then she was not: astonishing, even when expected. Kings would pay high for such a servant. So had the masters of the Assassins; and the Prince of Caer Gwent, who had fought so long a battle to win her the name of wife. Thomas considered pitying him. She was not, by all accounts, the mate of his choosing; that had all been her doing, and he had bowed to the inevitable.

God granted each man his just deserts; so too each man of the unhuman kind.

As she had vanished, so she appeared, with a parcel wrapped in silk. She held it out to her prince. His hands closed over hers.

Not all her choosing, then. If that kind could love, then he loved her with all the fire that was in him. Moving together, they folded back the silk. The vellum lay in their conjoined hands, heavy with its pendant seal, all as Thomas had left it. He had not even cut the thread that bound it. There had been no need.

"It is," the prince said as if to continue a colloquy long since begun. He offered it to his brother. "It is the dispensation which you won."

The king nodded. No doubt he could tell by his sorceries. "Will you read it now?"

The prince hesitated. The ifritah said, "Let the abbot do it. He has to bear witness, no?"

"Yes," said Abbot Leo. His hands were steady, taking the packet, cutting the bindings: even with the dagger which she gave him, Assassin's weapon, shimmering, sorcerous steel with a silver hilt. The vellum whispered as he unfolded it. His lips moved, reading what was written there. They watched the light grow bright in his face.

"It is," he said as the prince had said before him. "It is indeed."

"Keep it, Father," the prince said. "Guard it for us, if you will."

The pope's legate bowed to him. He inclined his head, a prince's courtesy, and turned again to Thomas.

"And you, Brother," he said. "Do you know of any reason in the world that I should suffer you to live?"

"Yes," Thomas answered. "I know one. Mercy."

"You know what I am, and yet you allow me that?"

"You were raised by Christian men," Thomas said. "What you may not know by nature, surely you have learned to know by art."

"And why should I be merciful? I have no soul," Prince Aidan said, "to endanger with my sins. Why should I not simply cut you down?"

"You may," said Thomas. "How can I prevent you?"

Aidan smiled. "You can't, can you?"

Thomas crossed himself. His palms were damp, betraying him; but the rest of him was strong. This was what he had dreamed of all his life. This was what he had prayed for. To die in the name of God. To take the crown of martyrdom.

The others had drawn back somewhat. Even the ifritah; even young Marco, though his body yearned toward Thomas. This battle was for the two of them.

Thomas considered his adversary carefully. Despite what he had said, he did not think that this was a cruel creature. Soulless, yes. Inhuman. Dangerous, as an animal is, by its nature.

"You will do what you will do," Thomas said. "What defenses I have are only that; I cannot fight against you. I knew that when first I took up my pen. I knew then what I did; I understood how, in the end, I must pay. I would do it again if I could."

"Why?"

It was an honest question. Thomas answered it honestly. "I envy you. I covet your youth, your beauty, and your magic. And I know that thereby I sin. You are temptation made flesh. How can I do aught but destroy you?"

"You might resist me. Other humans do."

"Do they?" Thomas regarded Abbot Leo; Marco, loyal in extremity; the children. One of whom was not human. One of whom . . .

Was not. In earliest youth they truly deceived. God's gift, or the devil's.

It did not alter what was true. "Humanity was not made to endure such trial as you are to it by your bare existence."

"Are you telling me that God has made a mistake?"

"God, never. The devil may claim infallibility, but he is the Lord of Lies."

"What are we, then? Satan's image as humans are God's?"

"It is known," said Thomas, "that the Adversary cannot create, only twist what God has made. You are humanity altered. All of it that is solely of earth, you are. All that is of heaven, you lack utterly."

The prince was not pleased to hear so stark a truth. His face tightened; his cat-eyes narrowed, glittering. "Someday," he said, "if God has any care for us, we will produce a theologian to match what you humans brag of. Then we shall see how the battle runs. I, alas, have no skill in the higher logic. I only know what is. I am no spawn of the Evil One. Nor is any of us. Far less than you who call yourselves children of God, can we abide the stench of the Pit."

Thomas shook his head in honest sadness. "Even your candor is a lie. The Adversary, it is said, truly believes himself wronged. Can you do any less?"

"Come now," said the ifritah, sharp and piercing-clear as a bell in the morning. "This is nonsense. Will you slit his throat, my lord, or must I?"

She had her dagger in her hand, ready to strike. Her temper was fierce. She was beautiful, like the lioness defending her lion.

Thomas was ready. Now at last it would come. Now, after so long, he would die.

The prince laid his hand on the ifritah's, restraining it. "No," he said. "You will not kill him. Nor shall I."

She was stiff with resistance; but no more so than Thomas. The prince saw it. His eyes glittered. "He wants it, do you see? A martyr would serve his cause. It would prove that we are what he says; it would fire his followers to greater passion against us. How better to take our revenge than to take no revenge at all?"

They stared at him, all of them, save only his brother. The Rhiyanan king smiled slowly, but said nothing.

Prince Aidan laughed a little wildly. "You didn't think I was capable of it, did you? Believe me, I'd happily tear out his throat, and never mind the nicety of a dagger. But that would be too gentle a punishment. Let him live and learn to see how all his truths are lies."

The ifritah regarded him as if he had gone mad. "You let him live? The others, yes, they count for nothing; let them go if you please. But this one, the king serpent—he has barely begun to distill his poison. Let him live, set him free, and we shall rue it down all the long years."

She spoke eminent sense. But her prince was in no mood to hear it. His face set, stubborn. "I said that I would not touch him, and I will not. Nor shall you. Any of you." His eye fixed on each, but longest and most particularly on the youngest. "We have what we came for. The reverend father may punish the sinner as he chooses. Our part is done, and well done."

"We did nothing!" snapped the ifritah.

"We have proved to human men that mercy is not purely a human province." He took her hand, clenched though it was, and raised it to his lips. "Is he or any of them worth your anger, my lady?"

She drew a sharp breath, perhaps to argue; but she let it go, hissing like a cat. "None of them is worth a hair of your head."

"Then why do we waste time that could be spent preparing for our wedding?"

Her scowl lightened as if of its own accord. She strove to sustain it; she said, "They will come back to haunt us."

"Let them." He was magnificent in his folly. He opened his arms wide, taking in all his following. "Come, my friends! Who'll sing at my lady's bridal?"

"Conrad," said the maidchild, facetious. Prince Aidan laughed and swept her up. With her still struggling and ordering him peremptorily to set her down, he bore her away.

It was grand insolence, well befitting a demon prince. In the moment before he was gone, his eyes met Thomas' once again. They laughed indeed, but that laughter was white and cold, demon-laughter, daring Thomas to do as his lady prophesied.

Thomas stood where they had left him. Marco, freed at last from the weight of their presence, tumbled in a faint.

Very slowly Thomas knelt beside him. He was deathly white, but his heart beat strongly enough. Terror only, and shock. Poor child, he had had more than his strength could bear.

He came round slowly. Thomas made no move to hasten it. He was numb, emptied. Mercy, had it been, that they let him live? The devil's mercy, and the devil's contcmpt. Thomas tried to exorcise it with a sign of the cross; with the words of piety. "I shall do as God wills," he said.

Marco stirred, murmuring. Thomas stroked his brow to quiet him. He started, thrashed. His eyes opened wide. White rimmed them. His mouth worked. "I can't—" he said. "I can't—I can't—"

"Hush," said Thomas. A little sharply, perhaps. Defeat was bitter; the scorn of his enemies more bitter still.

Marco's hands, groping, found Thomas' habit. They wound themselves in it. He pulled himself up. His eyes, still fixed in that wide, mad stare, rolled upward, over Thomas' head.

There was nothing to see. Only air.

"Light," said Marco. "All light. I can see— Brother, look! Do you hear it?"

Hysteria. Thomas raised his hand to slap the boy to his senses. But Marco had staggered to his feet. He swayed perilously, but he stood.

Now Thomas knew that stare. Blind.

"Blinded," said Marco, "by the light." He half-sang the words. "Don't you see, Brother? What they did? What they freed us for? Even the devil—even he must do the Lord's bidding."

Mad. When Thomas was himself again he would grieve. For a little while he had hoped that here was one who shared his true vocation. They had taken that from him as they had all else.

Marco turned, stumbling, and nigh went down. Thomas was there to catch him. He wound his fists again in Thomas' habit, like the child he was, and laughed. "Oh, Brother! Don't you know what they've done? They've shown us what to do. Like Saint Paul on the road to Damascus. They've made our faith all new."

It was an appalling prospect, as if these devils could stand in place of God Who had blinded Paul so that he might see the truth. But had not the Adversary himself been suffered to tempt Job?

Thomas was beginning, however dimly, to see. Pride and shame had robbed him of his wits. Now this child showed him the way.

Iblis' daughter had foretold it. Thomas said it in the words which God set on his tongue. "This is God's will," he said. "For this He set us here, and tried us so, and tempered us with defeat. For this and no other: to be the end of them." He paused. The light that dawned in him was nothing so feeble as to blind him. No; it made him see as he had never seen before, down to the very heart of things. "And not you and I alone," he said. "A whole army of us, an order sworn to the service of God, bound by our vows to destroy witchcraft and heresy wherever it may be."

"Yes," said Marco, rapt. "Yes."

Thomas seized the narrow shoulders; held them, shook them, clasped the boy to his breast. Tears ran unheeded down his cheeks. "I shall do as God wills," he said again: and now, truly, he meant every word of it.

37

Once Aidan was out of the chapel, he set Ysabel down, to her manifest relief. It had not come home to him yet, for all his show of exuberance. The hunt was ended. Abbot Leo had the dispensation, wrapped again in its bit of silk, laid carefully in the breast of his habit. The man who had forged it, the men who had abetted him, were gone and forgotten.

Yet Aidan could not summon the joy that had lain on him in Jerusalem. Its bright clarity was clouded, its purity stained by war and defeat and the long bitter hunt.

The hunters stood about him in the corridor. They had let him lead, even Morgiana, against Brother Thomas and his conspirators. It was his oath and his battle. Now they waited for him to say what they would do. Go back to the caravanserai, first, and bear the news to the rest; then consider how to go about wedding a Muslim woman to a Christian prince, with the Patriarch in Jerusalem and a war between.

He shook his head. "Why should we wait?" he said to them. "Why not do it as soon as may be? Not today, no, the poor cooks would never forgive us, but tomorrow —surely that's time enough."

"You did insist," Morgiana pointed out, "that the Patriarch say the words."

"So he shall, if you will fetch him for us. He can hardly refuse the pope's command."

"He might refuse to travel as I travel." But she was catching his mood. This was purely to her taste: sudden, headlong, and full of witchery.

They grinned at one another, he and she, well matched and knowing it. For a moment it was almost pain to know that they would be wedded at last. Now. Tomorrow.

Abbot Leo ventured to break in upon them. "I can understand your eagerness, my lord, my lady. But would it not be wiser to wait somewhat—two days, even? Three? Surely even you cannot effect a court wedding in an afternoon and a night."

"Would you care to wager on it?" Aidan asked.

The abbot looked so dismayed that Aidan laughed, laying an arm about his shoulders and embracing him, shaking him lightly. "Come, father abbot! Aren't you a man of God? Don't you believe in miracles?"

"Surely, my lord, but—"

Aidan overrode him, the gladness rising now, and the wildness, and the sheer, white exhilaration of knowing that he had power, and it was strong, and he was free to wield it. "My lady?"

She nodded, smiled, took the hand he held out to her.

"Brother," Aidan said, clear as on the battlefield. "If you will, go to our kin now, and tell them. Ysabel, Akiva, go with him; assure Lady Joanna that I haven't gone quite mad, and ask her if she'll tell the cooks."

Gwydion nodded. The children looked mildly rebellious, but he offered a hand to each and bent his glance upon them. They could hardly refuse a king. They went together, Ysabel with her chin on her shoulder, willing her father to change his mind.

Her father was hardly aware of her. "And I," he said before the abbot could say it for him, "shall have a moment's audience with my lord archbishop." He slanted a brow at Morgiana. "Will you come with me?"

She inclined her head. She was amused. She often was, when Aidan troubled to be decisive.

Precipitous.

Aidan refused to be discommoded, even by a whisper in his mind. He gathered the two of them, abbot and Assassin, and went to face the spiritual lord of Tyre.

The Archbishop of Tyre was no stranger to the lord of Millefleurs. Aidan had known him since he was Archdeacon William, chancellor of the kingdom and tutor to King Baldwin. It was William who first ascertained that the heir to the throne was a leper, and William who stood as friend and teacher to the young king, until Baldwin died and the throne fell, lurching and tottering, into Guy's hands.

William was still an elegant personage, although the years had thickened his middle. He received the prince and his lady at once, as much for policy as for friendship, and set aside the pens and parchment with which he had been working. "A history of our country," he said as he greeted his guests, "and a stone around my neck when I consider how much of it is still to tell. But I write a little every day, as God and my duties allow."

Aidan smiled. He would not at all have minded hearing William's new chapter; but time was pressing. "Your excellency, when you've a mind to read to us, we'll happily hear it, but now I have a favor to ask."

William was only slightly disappointed. If there was anything he preferred to the writing of history, it was the making of it. "Ask on, my lord," he said.

"Today," Aidan said, "we have won back what was taken from us in Jerusalem. My lord abbot has it now: the dispensation which was stolen, permitting my marriage to Lady Morgiana and obliging the Patriarch to officiate. We see no purpose in delaying past the morrow. My lady will go when it is time, to fetch the Patriarch."

"Wiser so," she said, "and more practicable. Even I would be hard put to bear all our friends and kin to Jerusalem, that they might see us wedded."

"Yes," William said. "That might be a strain even on your . . . capacities." He raised his brows. "*Fetch* the Patriarch? Here?"

"If you will consent," Aidan said.

"Heraclius is my metropolitan. Obedience binds me to him." William's tone was faintly sour. He was no admirer of his Patriarch.

"I'm not speaking of obedience," Aidan said.

William's face was perfectly still, but a spark had kindled in his eye. "You'll be wanting the cathedral, of course."

"By your leave."

"The canons will have to be consulted." He allowed himself a very small smile. "There are procedures, and precedents. We can hardly give you what we have always given the kings of Jerusalem, but what we can manage, you shall have."

Aidan was puzzled for a moment. "The kings . . . I had forgotten."

"Kings have often been wedded here," William said. "A prince will suit us very well."

He was enjoying himself, was William. Not Aidan alone would welcome the spectacle of Heraclius plucked from his comfort in Jerusalem, haled away to bless the union of a witch and an Assassin. That their haste was unseemly, not to mention ungodly, troubled him not at all. He went in his own person to speak to the canons of the cathedral, to bid them wreak a miracle.

Elen was happy—more than happy—to know that Aidan could have his lady at last and with the pope's blessing. She wished that she could have been as happy for herself.

Gwydion brought the news to them all. He did not speak directly to Elen. He had no glance to spare for her.

Certainly he had cause to be distracted. There was much to do, and precious little time to do it in. But Elen knew the many colors of his silences. This was indigo, with a flicker of scarlet: storm colors, thunder colors. His majesty of Rhiyana was not pleased with his kinswoman.

There was no comfort in Raihan. He was gone about his prince's business; he would hardly welcome her presence in his shadow, even if she could have followed him.

She told herself that it was best. She had had a little joy, more than either of them was entitled to. Now she must put it aside. Her body was her family's again, to bestow to its best advantage.

Her heart was her own, and it knew surely what it wanted. She was woman grown and no giddy girl; she could not fall out of love as easily as she had fallen into it. She did not think, in the quiet of herself, that she would ever fall out of it at all.

Sweet saints, she had a virtue. She had a constant heart. Alas for her good name, that it had fixed itself on so unsuitable an object.

"He is *not* unsuitable!"

There was no one to hear or to stare. She was in the garden cutting roses for the wedding. A thorn stabbed her finger, last and worst of many.

She straightened abruptly. "Enough of this," she said. Patience was not an art she knew much of; and she had never seen the good in suffering, still less in silence. Her secret was uncovered; her king was displeased. So then: let there be an end to it.

She was not entirely lost to good sense. She took the basket of roses to the kitchen, set them in the basin of

water which waited for them, paused to smooth her hair
and her gown. Someone called to her. She pretended not
to hear.

Calm, she could hardly call herself. But composed—
yes, she was that, as a princess should be. She went in
search of his majesty the king.

His majesty was in the room in which they enter-
tained guests, hidden away behind the hall. For a miracle, he was alone. He had been dispatching messages—a
pair of pages had shot past her as she approached the
solar, nearly oversetting her—but he seemed to have
paused, perhaps for a moment's quiet.

He would have it when she was done. She sank down
in a curtsy, as if this had been his hall and the plain hard
chair his throne. He regarded her steadily.

She stood erect. She had meant to lower her gaze like
a proper meek woman, but her eyes had a will of their
own. They met his boldly, and would not turn away.

Her tongue was as willful as her eyes. It would not
keep silence or wait humbly for him to speak. It said, "I
am sorry that I caused you hurt. I cannot repent of what
I did."

"So you informed me." His voice was quiet; calm.
Cold.

"I would," she said, "if I could. I will pay the penalty
as you decree."

"Will you, then? Will you take a husband if I command it?"

She faced him steadily. "I will do my duty to you and
to our family."

"Duty only? Nothing more?"

"Can there be more?"

For a moment she thought she saw his eyes flicker.
Then they were cold again, hard, grey as stones beside
the sea. "What if I bid you wed the Lord Amalric de
Lusignan?"

Her breath caught in her throat. She could not swallow. She choked out the words as she must, as her pride
demanded. "I will do as my king commands."

Gwydion rose, paced to the far wall, turned. So would his brother have done. It was altogether unlike Gwydion. "Will you? Will you do so much?"

"He is a suitable match," she said.

"He has asked for you."

"It is my king's right to bestow me as he wishes."

"You cannot abide him."

"Does it matter?"

She heard the hiss of his breath. She meant what she said. She would do as he bade, as she had been bred and raised to do.

"I failed of my duty," she said, "but that is done. You may be assured that I shall not transgress again."

Gwydion's eyes were wide and very pale, almost silver. "You would do it," he said. "You honestly would." He approached her slowly. When they were face to face, not quite close enough to touch, he halted. "What if I set you free to choose?"

"Why ask, when you will not?"

"What do you know of what I will or will not do?"

He spoke softly, but his words stung. Her own were all the more haughty for it. "You will do what your majesty must do."

"You have a brother," he said. "Your brother has sons."

At first she did not understand him. It was all her mind could do to sustain her shell of coldness, let alone to comprehend his subtlety. When she began to understand, she did not believe what she understood. Rhodri had a son, that was true. "What, is Luned pregnant again?"

"She was. They are two. Boys both, and as strong as anyone could wish for."

"Twins run in our blood," said Elen, hardly heeding her own words. Three sons. After Aidan, Rhodri was Gwydion's heir, unless Gwydion sired a son himself. Then Rhodri's sons. Then—

"I am still a valuable property," she said.

"You will always be that."

But not, any longer, quite so precious to the line. He was telling her that she was free. That she could choose.

"Then I choose Raihan," she said.

Gwydion's eyes were level on her. "Was there no man of your own faith to take, that you must have an infidel?"

"Did you think I had a choice?"

"You might," he said. "You well might."

"No," she said. "No more than you, or Aidan, or Morgiana. Humans can love, too, my lord. Sometimes even eternally."

There was no reading Gwydion, ever, unless he wished it. He was pure inhuman stillness. His eyes were grey as rain.

His silence, his mute intransigence, made her angry. And anger made her forget to be wise. "Apart from the cut of his privates and the count of his lineage, he is a thousandfold the man that your fine Lord Constable will ever be."

To her profound astonishment, the king laughed. "Truly, one bandit's son is very like another; even if one calls himself a lord." He stilled; he was unreadable again. "Do you expect that I will go to war in Rome for you, to win yet another dispensation?"

"No," she said.

"You know that without the Holy Father's decree, you cannot marry him."

"Then I will not marry him." She paused. "I will not marry anyone at all."

"Your children will be bastards."

"There is no bastardy in Islam."

"You would go so far?"

"I could," she said. Knowing it. Somewhat appalled herself, to see how shallow her piety ran.

"I have always done my duty," she said. "As child, as daughter, as wife. Even in my heart I have never asked aught but to be what a woman of my line should be. Now I know myself for a hypocrite. I was never sinless; I was merely untempted."

He did not deny it. He said, "I will not force you to wed against your will. Any man in Christendom whom you may wish to wed, you may have, whether he be king or carpenter, and I will bless you."

"But not Raihan."

He reached for her. She started. He laid his hand against her cheek. "Child," he said. "I never wanted you to be unhappy. When I saw how you were healed, here in Outremer, I was heart-glad."

"Until you saw the one who healed me."

He shook his head. The stillness had gone out of him; and with it a subtle, thrumming tension. "He was not," he said, "the one I would have chosen for you. But God is wiser than I."

Elen stared at him. "You're not angry. You're not angry at all." No: he was not. No more did he repent of his letting her suffer so painfully, and for naught.

For naught? His glance denied it. She glared. "You were testing me!"

"No," he said. "You tested yourself. I was never more than the mirror of your conscience."

True; but that was only half of it. "You are too wise a king," she said, "for the likes of me." She looked him full in the face. "Do we have your blessing?"

He barely hesitated. "You have it," he said. "You have always had it."

Her throat went tight. He opened his arms. She hung back, resisting. He did not move. She flung herself into his embrace.

There in the safety of his presence, with his blessing on her, all her temper shrank and faded. If he had tested her, then she had tried him sorely. He was man enough, and king enough, to forgive her. Could she do any less?

Such wisdom to come to, all late and unlooked for. It might almost have been witchery.

She stepped back, out of his arms. "May I go, my lord?"

"To your Saracen?"

His eyes glinted. She lowered her own. Her cheeks were warm. "Not if you forbid me."

"I set you free."

Like a hawk off the fist. She leaped; she soared; she flew.

*   *   *

"Well done," said the voice which Gwydion knew better than any in the world.

Gwydion turned, barely ruffled. Aidan grinned at him. Gwydion spared him the glimmer of a smile. "You'll bless our catling's sinning, then?" Gwydion asked him.

"How can I not?" Aidan said. "Raihan is almost good enough for her. He'll try to talk her out of this, you know."

"And fail."

"No man is proof against a determined woman." Aidan wandered to the winetable, found a bowl with pomegranates in it, took up a rose-red fruit and tossed it from hand to hand. "They'll probably call in a *qadi* and marry as Muslims do. Will you try to stop them?"

"Will you?"

"I am hardly in a position," said Aidan, "to preach against the marrying of infidels."

Gwydion plucked the pomegranate out of the air, cut it open with his dagger. They shared it between them, finding it ripe and honey-sweet.

"It could have been worse," Gwydion said. "She could have insisted on taking Messire Amalric."

"She could indeed," said Aidan. "And been wretched ever after."

"But properly, Christianly wedded."

"I don't feel very proper or Christian when I think of that man." Aidan licked his scarlet-stained fingers, frowning at the air. "He's in Tyre. Did you know that?"

"I know it," said Gwydion. "I saw him this morning."

"Did you?" said Aidan. He paused. "Do you know what his mind reminds me of?"

"Yes," Gwydion said. "A certain late conspiracy."

Aidan was not surprised that Gwydion had thought of it before him. Gwydion had always been the quicker to think, as Aidan was to act. "And yet," said Aidan, "none of them said a word about him. Not even Messer Seco."

"As if he had bought their silence," Gwydion said, "or been given it of their prudence. He is, after all, the only lord among them. That he would play so many sides in this game . . . that, I can easily believe. He asked for Elen this morning."

"Again?"

"Again. And for passage west, ostensibly to preach the Crusade."

"Bold," said Aidan, "if he had a hand in the forgery. And arrogant, to think that you would even consider him after what his brother did to this kingdom."

"Ambitious, and well convinced of his own worth." Gwydion met his brother's eyes. "Shall I summon him to hear the lady's answer for himself?"

Aidan smiled slowly. "You can do better. You can send me to fetch him. He'll fancy himself properly escorted."

"No," said Gwydion. "I think that I shall send Messire Raihan. If you will lend him to me."

"And tell him what, and why?"

"If you will."

Aidan's smile widened to a grin. "I do. Oh, I do indeed."

Amalric de Lusignan, though ambitious, was not a fool. He came warily, and he came in his own good time. The brothers were waiting for him, Aidan stretched out lazily at Gwydion's feet. Amalric raised his brows at the picture they made. "You should be woven in a tapestry," he said.

Aidan smiled with a white gleam of teeth. Gwydion wore no expression. He gestured; Amalric, after a moment's pause, sat where he was bidden. His smile was remarkably free of strain. "I've heard the news," he said. "I'm glad."

Aidan nodded, but did not speak. He did not trust himself to be wise.

Gwydion shifted slightly. Amalric's eyes flicked to him. Quietly he said, "I have considered what you asked of me. The lady has been spoken to. The choice, in the end, is hers. You may speak with her if you wish."

Amalric eased perceptibly. So, then: he had expected

other tidings. Of her refusal? Or perhaps of a certain conspiracy? "I'll speak with her, sire," he said.

Gwydion bent his glance on Raihan. The mamluk bowed low and departed.

They waited in silence. The brothers would not break it; Amalric, in courtesy, could not. He sat straight in the tall chair. Still though he was, he seemed subtly to fidget. His mind was a buzzing nothingness.

That, said Gwydion for Aidan to hear, *walled the king from me at Cresson.*

Aidan's response was wordless affirmation. It was indeed what he had sensed then and, like the fool he was, disregarded. It was like Brother Thomas' sleights of mind: not power, but not-power. But stronger. How much stronger, Aidan had only begun to see.

He laid his arm across his brother's knees, as much for reassurance as for his body's comfort. On the surface Amalric's mind seemed all harmless nothing-in-particular. Beneath, it was madness.

Gwydion was calmer, less openly revolted. *The man is eminently sane. The walls he raises are madness and confusion for any of our kind who may trespass.*

And he doesn't even know it. Aidan shivered in his skin.

I think he knows, Gwydion said. His mind-voice was deathly quiet. *Not what he is, but how; and why.*

Raihan returned, shadowing Elen. It seemed perfectly proper: the servant, deferential; the lady, regally gracious. When she made her reverence to her uncles, greeted the Constable, sat composedly under all their eyes, the mamluk took station behind her. A guardsman's place; or a watchful lover's.

Gwydion perceived it. A spark kindled in his eye, mate to that in Elen's. "My lady," he said. "Messire Amalric wishes to hear what you have chosen. Will you accept his suit? Make this, perhaps, an occasion for doubled rejoicing?"

She was not unduly disconcerted to have it direct, without the usual dance of preliminaries. She did not, Aidan noticed, glance at her lover. Raihan stood as a guard should stand, light and erect, at ease but alert; but his hand on his swordhilt was white about the knuckles.

Amalric was hardly more composed. His eyes flicked from face to face, avoiding the lady's. Until she spoke; then they fixed on her as if they had no power to move.

"I have considered," she said, "and pondered long. I am honored that so high a lord should seek my hand, and I once widowed already, and no proof that I can bear him healthy sons."

"As to that, my lady," said Amalric, "I'm sure I needn't be concerned."

She regarded him coolly, with no visible disfavor. "My lord is kind."

He rose and bowed with a passable flourish. "My lady is worthy of every kindness."

Elen inclined her head. "That is for my lord to judge."

"I hope I may do more than that," Amalric said.

Raihan quivered like an arrow in a target. Aidan wondered that Amalric could not see it and know it for what it was.

To Messire Amalric, no doubt, the mamluk was invisible: dark-faced, bearded, turbaned, Saracen.

Elen, well aware of all of them, glanced briefly at her younger uncle. He tried to warm her with a smile. She eased a very little and raised her chin a fraction higher. "My lord may hope," she said, "but alas, I fear I cannot be so gracious. My husband whom I loved is scarce a year in his tomb. To contemplate another in his place . . ." Her voice trembled. It was not all feigned. She was exerting all her will to keep her eyes down and not to feast them on the one who had taken her dear lord's place. "My lord, I pray your kind indulgence. You offer me honor and glory far above my poor deserts. How can I accept them? I would but bring a third into our marriage bed, a ghost who would lie ever between us."

A very solid ghost, Aidan thought, with eyes the color of sulfur burning.

Amalric mustered a clenched-teeth smile. "My lady

may find that there is no better exorcism for a lover's ghost than a new and living lover."

Elen's cheeks flushed faintly. "That may be so, my lord. But it is too soon. Please, my lord, if truly you have any regard for me. Someday, perhaps, when the pain is not so fresh . . . but now, my lord, now I cannot bear to think of it."

Gently, Aidan willed her. Not too broad a mime of grief, or milord would scent the mockery in it.

Milord, it seemed, was blind enough to take her at her word. She was distractingly lovely in her plain somber gown and her white wimple, with the slightest quivering in her chin, the slightest shimmer of dampness in her eye. She rose with pure unconscious grace and held out a slender hand. "My lord, I am most honored, you must remember that. I wish you well. I pray that you may find a lady who is worthy of you."

Her departure was graceful, queenly, and rather more precipitous than it looked. Aidan knew what she did once she was past the door: fell into Raihan's arms, choking with mingled laughter and tears.

Raihan would look after her. Aidan thought well of that pairing, now that he had seen them together. Christian marriage, no, they could not have that while Raihan held to his faith, but it would hardly stop them.

Elen, bless the child, had a wise head on her. If she was discreet and played her widowhood to its best advantage, she would serve the kindred nigh as well as if she had never taken a lover at all. She could play suitors like the lady in the story, who held off a pack of them for years, weaving on her loom all day and unraveling all night, and promising to choose a husband when the tapestry was done: thereby preserving alliances and appearances and some measure of peace.

Meanwhile there was Amalric, whom she had discarded rather more gently than Aidan would have been capable of. He stood where she had left him, mute and slightly stunned, and growing angry.

Aidan yawned, showing more teeth than humans liked to see. It drew Amalric's attention. Aidan held it with a sigh and a shake of his head. "My condolences,

messire. The lady was quite fond of her husband; she
took his death hard. You'll not fault her for it, I hope?"

"No." It was not quite a growl. "If I may have your
leave, sire, my lord? I've things to see to."

"In a moment," Aidan said. He rose, wandering as
he liked to do, but thinking of it more than he usually
did. It kept Amalric's eyes on him. The wall was higher
than ever about the man's mind.

Aidan paused. He drew his dagger, inspected his
nails, pared a rough edge. The blade shimmered. It was
damascene steel, Assassin steel, narrow and wicked and
deadly sharp, patterned like wind-ruffles on a calm sea.
Morgiana said that Aidan's eyes were the precise color of
that steel. No doubt they were now. Gwydion's were.

"You know how I've been gladdened, surely," Aidan
said, turning the dagger idly in his hands, playing a small
perilous game with it, tossing and spinning and catching,
tossing and spinning and catching. "My lady and I will
have our blessing at last, with the pope's decree to hal-
low it. As to where we found it . . . we would never
have guessed. It was a monk in the legate's own train
who did it, with a man or three of Outremer abetting
him. Can you credit such perfidy?"

"Shocking, my lord," said Amalric.

The buzzing of the wards mounted to pain. Aidan set
his teeth against it. "They had defenses against us, if you
can believe it. An eastern art, I understand; a discipline
for thwarting witches. It has a slight disadvantage. Once
known, it is as distinct as a beacon in the dark."

Amalric glanced swiftly, all but invisibly, toward the
door. Morgiana was in it in turban and trousers, smiling
very faintly.

"You wanted to sail west, my lord brother tells me,"
Aidan said, "thereby breaking your word to the sultan
and leaving your brother to his fate. Is that entirely wise,
messire?"

"My brother is safe enough," Amalric said. "My
lord."

"He would be safer, I think, if you returned to him
and waited for your ransom, and rejoined the war at his
side." Aidan smiled. "The Crusade has ample messen-

gers to preach it. I shall go, and my royal brother, and Archbishop William who will be sailing on our flagship, and the Holy Father's legate returning to his duties in Rome. The west will not fail you, messire. The Crusade will come to set your kingdom free."

Amalric had the look now of an animal in a trap. "The more messengers there are, the faster the news will travel."

"No doubt," Aidan said. "But you are needed here. What is the kingdom, after all, without its Constable?"

"The kingdom barely has a king." Amalric bit off the words.

"That is hardly any fault of mine," said Aidan gently. "Tell me, messire. What did you hope to gain from the disruption of my wedding?"

Amalric drew breath, perhaps to deny the charge. But he did not say it. He sat instead, stretched out his legs, folded his hands over his middle. "So. It's that obvious, is it?"

"I'm ashamed to tell you how long it took us to notice."

Amalric smiled thinly. His ease ran hardly deeper, but it was impressive to see. "All I wanted was to keep the kingdom safe. I wasn't at all sure it could be that, with infidels so close to all its counsels."

"Prudent," Aidan said. "Wise, after a fashion. Did you know that you were shielding the king, the morning before Hattin, when my brother would have talked him out of it?"

Amalric flushed, then paled. "I was guarding myself."

"Too well," said Aidan.

"God's bones," said Amalric. He straightened in his chair as if to shift his body with his mind, away from guilt and from the shame that rode with it. "You did nothing to the others—the ones who hatched the conspiracy. Why? Were you saving it for me?"

"No." Aidan caught his dagger by the hilt, slid it into its sheath. "I'm not going to do anything to you, either."

"Why?"

"I don't need to." Not precisely true, but true

enough. Aidan looked Amalric up and down. "You and your precious brother led this kingdom as badly as it could possibly have been led. The Crusade may win the kingdom back, but it will never be what it was before. Your fault, messire. Your brother can talk himself out of accepting the blame. You have no such fortune."

"Are you laying a curse on me?"

Amalric's voice was thick, torn between anger and fear. Aidan smiled. "You laid it on yourself in the king's tent at Cresson. What can I do to you that would be worse than that?"

"You share the blame, my lord. You were at Cresson. You fought at Hattin."

Aidan shook his head. "No, Amalric. My guilt is of another order altogether. I am removed from this war and this kingdom. You are bound to it. While it stands, you stand. When it falls, so shall you fall. There is no escape for you. The west will offer you no haven."

"A threat, my lord?"

"A promise."

Amalric stood. His mind was no more penetrable than it had ever been. His eyes were almost laughing. "My brother is right. You have no power to touch any of us. Mockery, illusion, sleight of hand—that's all you can offer."

"We never claimed to be gods." Aidan moved aside from the path to the door.

Amalric paused in taking it. "I'd hoped for more from you."

"What, hellfire and brimstone?"

"Something befitting your reputation."

Aidan laughed and called up the fire.

Amalric slitted his eyes against the pillar of flame that had swallowed Aidan's fleshly semblance. "Trickery," he said.

"If you wish," Aidan said. He quelled the fire; Amalric blinked, dazzled. "Or perhaps this body is the trickery. You saw me then as my own kind see me."

"What does seeing matter? I know what's real. You are nothing but the devil's lies."

"Not the devil," Gwydion said. He sounded ineffably weary. "Messire, I tire of you. Sister . . . ?"

"Brother," said Morgiana with profound pleasure.

Amalric had his marvel. He was there; and then he was not.

Aidan burst out laughing, though he knew that he should not. "Morgiana! Before the whole army of Islam? Naked? Backward on an ass?"

"It is," she admitted, "an insult to the ass."

"And I," said Gwydion, "am weary of kingly restraint." He rose and stretched and smiled at them both: as good as laughter in another man. "So then, my brother, my sister. Shall we see to the ordering of your wedding?"

38

Patriarch Heraclius was not at home to visitors. He was, in brief, indisposed. Very happily so, in the arms of his handsome mistress.

"Ah," said Morgiana, revealing herself in a lull. "Madame la Patriarchesse. I trust I find you in good health."

Madame la Patriarchesse, whose title was reserved strictly for tavern gossip, screeched and snatched at coverlets. His excellency the Patriarch, laid out like an effigy on a tomb but quite as bare as he was born, dived after his paramour.

He was rather a disappointment, after all the tales. But then, Morgiana reflected, size was not everything. Or beauty, either. She looked at him and remembered her hawk of the desert, and thought of clabbered milk.

He seemed determined to burrow through the featherbed and into the floor beneath. She plucked him out, blankets and all, and set him upright. Robbed of flight, he began to bluster. "Who are you? How dare you? What do you think—"

She shook her head at his obtuseness. Surely he of all

people should know what and who she was, from her mode of ingress if nothing else. She pulled off her turban and shook down her hair.

Its improbable color and her inarguable gender enlightened him remarkably. His bluster turned to fear; his crimson cheeks went white.

She smiled sweetly at him. "Good morning, lord Patriarch. And a fair morning it is. Would you not agree?"

Clearly he would not. She would have been pleased to change his mind for him, but her prince was waiting. "Come, sir," she said. "Would you be so good as to dress? We have need of you in Tyre."

"In—" He scrambled his blankets about him. He looked quite odd with his shaven crown and his straggling hair, his beard all fallen out of its curls. "The sultan has taken Tyre?"

"The sultan has nothing to do with it. We have our dispensation to marry; my lord has a mind to act on it. Will you dress yourself, or shall I do it for you?"

Heraclius dug in his heels. "The country is at war. I cannot leave Jerusalem."

"Or your paramour?" Morgiana glanced at the woman, who was a properly wedded wife, but not to the Patriarch. The woman regarded her with the calm of perfect horror. "We shall not keep you long. An hour only; surely you can spare us that."

"Nothing can take us there and back again so swiftly," said Heraclius.

"I can." Morgiana looked about. There was a chest at the bed's foot; it was, as she had hoped, full of clothing. Aidan would want him in vestments. There were none here. She cast her power like a net, closed it about a glimmer of gold, gathered it in. Heraclius jumped and gasped as it fell at his feet. Alb and chasuble, the latter of cloth of gold. Miter, crozier, odds and ends of silk and cord for which Morgiana had no name.

But Heraclius was no docile sheep. Even taken by surprise, he mustered a core of resistance. "I will submit to no witchcraft. No; not though you kill me for it."

"I have no intention of killing you," Morgiana said. "I will bring you to Tyre, where my lord is. You will say the words to marry us. Then I shall return you as I found you."

Heraclius' head sank between his shoulders. His jaw set, obstinate. "No."

"The pope commands you."

"Prove it."

"Come to Tyre and you will see."

"No," said Heraclius.

Morgiana drew a long slow breath. She did not want to abduct him. Aidan would not approve; and this day of all days, she wanted to please her prince.

Heraclius was not about to budge. Her clemency emboldened him; he stood straighter and glowered at her. She saw how he glanced at his mistress to see if she marked his courage.

Madame la Patriarchesse was oblivious. "For God's sake," she said. "Give her what she wants."

"She is a devil," said Heraclius. "She'll snatch me away to hell."

"Then go," said his ladylove. "It's only for an hour. Didn't you hear her?"

Heraclius gaped like a fish. Morgiana plucked the blankets from him and held up a garment at random. "Put it on," she said.

He put it on in its proper order, if slowly and with many pauses. Morgiana advanced toward him. He quickened then. He hated her. That was no novelty; if anything, it pleased her. She folded her arms and tapped her foot. His hands shook as he took up the miter and set it on his head.

He could have done with a comb, and a servant to curl his beard for him. But Morgiana was in no mood for trivialities. She thrust the crozier into his hand and swept him otherwhere.

Joanna was almost glad that it was over. The dispensation was found, the wedding begun. And so swiftly: so utterly like Aidan. Royalty was given to expecting the impossible of its servants, but Aidan knew what he him-

self could do. He never truly understood the limits of
human capacity.

She was up well into the night, and up again well
before dawn, mustering the family, rounding up the servants, setting the cooks to conjuring a feast out of air.
She gave Aidan his due: he was quite as preoccupied as
she, and she did not think that he slept. When she staggered half-blindly to bed, he was still awake; when she
staggered more than half blindly out of it, he was up,
lending a hand with the tables in the hall.

Now, for better or for worse, it was done. The children were clean, properly clad, and somewhat damp
about the edges. The household, all that could be spared,
made a suitably royal escort, even without the growing
crowd of onlookers. Rumor traveled fast in Tyre, and a
wedding was worth the running to, the more for that the
bridegroom was a prince and his bride an Assassin.

Tyre's cathedral raised its dome sturdily to the sky.
In the space before its door they gathered as they had in
front of Holy Sepulcher. There were fewer of them now
who were truly guests, but oglers enough. Some of them
even comprehended that the figure with the miter, re-
splendent in cloth of gold, was not Archbishop William.
One or two might have begun to suspect that it was
Heraclius of Jerusalem. A very stiff, thoroughly brow-
beaten, slightly wild-eyed Heraclius, who no doubt
would remember this as a particularly vivid nightmare.
It had not been kind of Aidan to send Morgiana after the
Patriarch, even if there was no one else who could have
done it.

Neither of them was in sight. Joanna saw Archbishop
William behind the Patriarch, coped and mitered himself, but properly subordinate. He seemed to be propping
the Patriarch up, or blocking his escape. The archbishop's expression was solemnly content.

Someone came quietly through the door behind
them. Heraclius started; William smiled. Joanna blinked
hard. Aidan had put on garb proper to a wedding, if he
was Aidan, and wedding his Assassin. His coat was that
which Saladin had given him in Damascus, the Saracen
robe of honor blazoned with the *tiraz*, the bands of scar-

let circling his arms, embroidered with his name and the name of the Syrian sultan. The cloth of the coat was silk, black subtly damascened with gold, and his belt was black inlaid with gold, and his sword hung from it, damascened scabbard, silver hilt with its great coal of a ruby. Most often he wore Frankish hose and shoes under the coat, but now he wore the trousers that were proper to it, and the soft boots with their upturned toes, and the inlaid spurs of the Saracen. He only lacked the turban to seem all infidel. His head was bare but for a coronet, the mark of his rank which he almost never wore. He passed Heraclius, bowing regally, and stood on the step, and waited.

The sun rose slowly to the hour of prime. None of them moved, not even the lookers-on. Either Morgiana would refuse it after all and flee away and never come again, or she would gratify them with a spectacle. They waited for it, either one.

They received neither, when it came. Simply a pair of nobles walking, her hand on his, through the cathedral close. Gwydion was in blue and silver, severely simple, with a hat on his head and no mark of his kingship. Morgiana was clad in green silk, seeming as much a Frank as Aidan seemed a Saracen. It was not the gown she had worn to that other, shattered wedding. This was simpler, such as a lady would wear in her own demesne, to please her lord and enchant her people. Her hair was free under the veil, confined only by a slender fillet, from which hung a single emerald to glow between her eyes. But they were brighter than any stone.

They did not seem to see anything in all that place but the one who waited for her. He was blind to aught that was not she.

Joanna's heart, which had broken long ago, throbbed dully as it rose into her throat. Now they came face to face. Now the pope's legate came forward, and in his hand a writ with a pendant seal. Now the monk who had read it on that other day, came to take it from him. The monk's hand shook a little, as if he too remembered, and dreaded what he might find.

The city itself seemed to stand silent, the wind to

still, the gulls to wheel mute in the vault of the sky. Joanna heard the whisper of vellum, the clack of the seal as it swung against its mooring, the clearing of the monk's throat. He began, somewhat unsteadily, to read.

"Urban, bishop, servant of the servants of God, to his dear son in Christ, Aidan, Prince of Caer Gwent in the kingdom of Rhiyana, Baron of the High Court of the Kingdom of Jerusalem, Defender of the Holy Sepulcher, and to the Lady Morgiana of the city of Persepolis, servant heretofore of the Masters of Alamut, greeting and apostolic benediction. In the matter of impediment, to wit, disparitas cultus, *disparity of faith, we dispense, we permit, we remove all obstacles to their joining in holy wedlock with the blessing of Mother Church and the countenance of the Holy See."*

None of them heard what more there was. Conditions, there were always conditions. Patriarch Heraclius or his chosen deputy must say the words; the children must be raised in the faith of holy Church; the prince would swear never to forsake that faith, on pain of anathema. None of it mattered. The pope had spoken. The dispensation was granted. Now at last Heraclius must begin the rite.

He did not wish to. That was evident. But still less did he wish to prolong the nightmare. He raised his hand on which flamed the ruby of his patriarchate, and beckoned. The king led the lady to her lord.

Their hands met, joined. Gwydion drew back forgotten. Heraclius, shuddering just perceptibly, laid his hand over theirs. In a voice which was, when it came to it, remarkably steady, he spoke the words for which they had waited so long.

Windy words, to matter so much. Aidan, handclasped with Morgiana, heard only that they were holy. Saw the ring brought out in Gwydion's hand, the circle of gold that Aidan had forged himself and set with an emerald. There was another beside it, gold and ruby, made for a larger hand.

He raised a brow. Morgiana would not look at him,

but her mind was on him. *Should the bridegroom be denied what is given the bride?*

He almost laughed. He should have expected it. She was Morgiana, after all.

Heraclius said the words twice, because they would give him no peace else. For her first, as was prescribed: setting the smaller ring on her thumb in the name of the Father, and on her first finger in the name of the Son, and on her longest finger in the name of the Holy Spirit, there to remain as Aidan set the bridal coins in her palm and said unprompted, " 'With this ring I thee wed, this gold and silver I grant thee, with my body I honor thee, with all my earthly goods I thee endow.' "

And for him it was the same, she saying the words gravely, to the shock of those who listened, he trying not to smile. She went down on her knees as the rite commanded, bowing low before him. And when she rose, he went down, sending a murmur up. He laughed for simple, wicked joy. Yes, this was how it should be, holy and splendid and, for all of that, somewhat of a scandal. So they were themselves, who raised eyebrows even in ancient harlot Rome.

Heraclius, for whom this was purest purgatory, spoke the blessing over them. " 'May the God of Abraham, and the God of Isaac, and the God of Jacob be with you, and may He join you together, and may He fulfill His blessing upon you. Take this thy kinswoman; henceforth thou art her love, and she thy beloved. She is thine this day and ever after. May the Lord of heaven prosper you both. May He grant you mercy and peace.' "

They bowed their heads to it, standing side by side, hand wound with hand. Aidan's mind was all perfectly Christian. Morgiana's, echoing beneath, spoke words of its own, words which were much the same, but to her infinitely more holy. *May the Lord of heaven prosper us both. May Allah grant us His blessing and peace.*

39

"You are grinning like an idiot," she said.

"So are you," he said.

They looked at one another. Vaults of stone arched over them. It was night in the desert of Persia, but the cavern was full of light. Hers, glass-green; his, fire out of embers. He remembered captivity, and walls of air. She remembered dancing for him just there, a long stride from where they lay, and learning the limits of her courage, and sealing a bargain with him.

"I never expected it to take us so far," he said.

"Nor I, to take us so long." She raised herself on her elbow, frowning down at him. "I feel no different."

"Should you?"

"There are words between us now. And the pope's will. Would he be angry if he knew how little he matters to me?"

"Probably."

She laid her hand flat on his breast, studying the shape of it, slender ivory fingers on his moon-white skin. His heart beat under her palm where a man's heart would not be: well she knew that, for when she drove the dagger home.

No longer. She was a princess now. When she killed, she would kill as royal folk did, in battle; not in secret, in the night.

He, woven in her mind, did not want her to know that he laughed, but she knew. "Princesses don't go to battle at all," he said.

"Queens do. When Eleanor was queen of Francia, she came Crusading with her king. She was a better general than he was."

"And he divorced her for it."

"Whereupon she found a fine young king and married him instead." Morgiana's hand moved slowly down, as if she had no part in it. "Was she the lady you made songs for, in Carcassonne?"

"One of them. Once." Thirty years agone. When he seemed no younger than he did now, and not a whit less wild. He lay all loose on the scarlet coverlets, stark black and stark white, but his eyes were the color of steel. He smiled at her. "I'm a married man now. No paramours for me."

"Not even your Frank?"

He shook his head, not trusting his voice.

Morgiana considered anger. They could quarrel. Again. They could accuse one another. They could ruin this night as they had ruined many another.

It would not change anything. What she was to him, she knew. Heart, soul, life. What that one was, was beyond any hope of altering. Beloved and lover; mother of his child. Child of fire though he was, he was a constant creature. He did not know how to fail of it.

She would not want him to. It hurt to know that she must share him; but that was part of why she loved him. There was enough of him for all of them.

Hers was a more niggardly spirit. There was only room in it for one great love; even that strained all its boundaries.

"Your heart is greater than you know," he said, so gentle that she almost wept.

She glared instead. "What, can you bear to share me with another?"

He blushed. He hated that he did it so easily; she thought it enchanting. "Won't you ever forgive me for that?"

"I thought I had." She bent down and kissed him where he was warmest, making him blush the more brilliantly: as above, so below.

He thought her blasphemous, or scandalous at least. Poor sometime Christian, he never knew what to make of her.

"I do know how to love you," he said.

"And you are beautiful." From her vantage, a most private and particular beauty. All hers now, by the pope's decree.

"That was not precisely what he was thinking of," he
said. His voice was dry, but there was a catch in it. A
little longer, and there would be no speech in him at all.

Their minds met, joined, wove and unwove, more
fully than their bodies ever could. This, the humans
could never know. For them it was only speech, and the
touch of flesh on flesh, and for a few brief moments,
body in body. She pitied them.

Forget them.

His voice, soft in her deep places. He could be wisest
when she least expected it. She let her gladness rise and
swell and bloom within her, and fill her full. There was
singing all about them, the old song, the wild song, the
sweetest song in any world. She made herself a part of it.

They had a night and a day and another night, and
full of joy they were, there where the world could not
come. But the world was waiting, and their kin within it,
in a rising tide of war.

Morgiana startled Aidan. She rose in the grey morning and said her prayer, and woke him with kisses. "It's
time we went back," she said.

He yawned, stretched, blinked the sleep out of his
eyes. "I was supposed to say that."

"Therefore I said it." She had bathed; she was
dressed in trousers and coat, her hair plaited and wound
about her head. As he watched, she began the winding of
her turban.

For an appalling moment he wondered if he had
dreamed it all; if she was still his captor and his vengeance still untaken, and the whole of it yet to endure.
Then she smiled. It was the same smile with which she
had heard the Patriarch's blessing: wide, white, and
wicked. He reached for her, turban, coat, and all, and
pulled her down.

It was, in the end, much closer to sunset than to
sunrise when they took the mage-road to Tyre.

*   *   *

They came back in the evening, the third after their wedding, when dinner was done and the family all together in the solar, drinking wine and talking. Ysabel saw them first. They looked splendid; triumphant.

She did not stop to shriek, or otherwise make a fool of herself. She flew into their arms, both of them, in a glorious, threefold tangle.

Gwydion came hard on her heels. Then the rest of them, laughing, babbling, even crying a little.

In a little while they settled, Ysabel in her father's lap, defending it against all comers. A servant, sent for, brought bread and meat, and sherbet for Morgiana. While they ate, Ysabel said, "We were talking about Messire Amalric. How he wanted a marvel, and how you gave him one."

Morgiana laughed. "We did indeed! He'll not forget it soon, I think."

"He played too many sides," said Ysabel, chewing the end of a braid as she thought about it. Her mother frowned at her; she lowered the braid-end and nibbled her knuckle instead. "He tried to make it so that he couldn't lose, no matter what he did. He'd have won, even, if we hadn't been so far outside his reckoning."

"He would never have won me," said Elen. Her voice was soft, but her will was unbending. Raihan was there, being her guardsman. They did not glance at one another, or touch, or make any move at all. They did not need to. Ysabel could not begin to tell which one of them was happier. Morgiana had given them a gift before she went away to be with Aidan: a long-bearded, deep-eyed, impeccably dignified *qadi* to make them man and wife as Muslims thought of it. The *qadi* seemed not to mind at all that he was there at the will of an ifritah, marrying a Christian prince's mamluk to a Christian princess. Odder things had happened where he came from, which was somewhere near Baghdad.

Gwydion was not precisely delighted to have a Muslim for a nephew-in-law; but he was glad to see Elen so happy. It seeped out of him like light out of a basket, casting odd bits of brilliance when one least expected it.

One dazzled Ysabel and almost made her miss what Aidan was saying.

Aimery had not spoken to her since he found her weaving sun and shadow on the roof, and he learned who her father was. He had not spoken to much of anyone else, either.

Now Aidan spoke to him, and he came out of his shadowed corner and edged into the light. "Aimery," Aidan said. "My lord of Mortmain. Hattin is over and done with and your ransom paid. What will you do now?"

Aimery stood in front of Aidan. His back was straight. He looked exactly like his father. "I'm going to fight," he said. "And win our lands back."

Aidan nodded gravely. He was seeing Aimery as grownfolk, as a man with lands and a lordship and the right to fight for them. "Have you decided whom you'll look to as your lord?"

Aimery's hands opened and closed, in and out of fists. "I promised Count Raymond that I'd go back to him—but—"

"But Count Raymond ran away."

Aimery swallowed. "You told me, my lord, why he did it. All about danger and prudence and someone needing to escape and muster what strength we had left. He'd only have died if he charged back through the sultan's lines. But, my lord, he ran."

"Sometimes a wise man has to run." Aidan said it gently. "It was bitter for him, too, Aimery. He had to see his city taken, his army shattered, his kingdom—the kingdom he should have been king of—thrown down for a fool's ill judgment."

Aimery shook his head, lips tight. "He ran, and he did nothing to stop what happened after. He is a very clever man, my lord, and a good ruler, and maybe he would make a good king. But how can I kneel in front of him and call him my liege lord, when I saw how his spirit broke and he ran away?"

"Then how much worse must I seem to you, who will run all the way to Rhiyana, and never raise my hand again against the Saracen."

"No, my lord!" Aimery was shaking, he was so vehement. "*No!* You aren't running. You are oathbound. You fought until you couldn't fight any more, and then and only then you surrendered. Your oath is your ransom. How could you have escaped it?"

"Raymond could no more have escaped what befell him, once he accepted the war as King Guy would wage it."

"I can't follow him," Aimery said, stubborn as he always was, even when it got him into trouble. "I've thought and I've thought, my lord, and I've tried as hard as I can, and I can't forgive him for what he did."

"Then you will swear your fealty to Guy?"

"No," said Aimery with a curl of his lip. "He would be a thousand times worse. I'm going to go to Marquis Conrad. People don't like him, I notice that, but they do what he tells them. I don't think he'll laugh at me. He knows how to use men, even men who aren't quite out of pinfeathers."

Aimery was hardly in them yet. Ysabel kept her mouth shut and watched her father's face. He approved of what Aimery was saying. "It's a baron's right, in default of a liege lord, to choose as he best may."

"I don't know about best," said Aimery. "I just don't want it to be worst."

"Conrad will do well enough," Aidan said. "If it were mine to choose, I would choose as you have."

The light in Aimery's face was as dazzling as it was brief.

"Of course," Aidan went on, "you've discussed this with your mother."

Aimery went all dark. He had not looked at his mother, nor had he spoken to her, either, except as he must, in days. Since he stopped speaking to Ysabel.

It was like a boy, Ysabel thought. Hate the woman, loathe the child, go on happily worshipping the man, and never mind that it took two to make a baby.

Joanna had been aware of Aimery's odd mood. She could hardly help it. But she had all the other children to think of, and the house to run, and a wedding on top of it. It was hard for her to keep track of every snit and crotchet. She looked at him with a small bit of worry, but not overmuch. "It's what I would have advised," she said, "if he had asked."

He had not, and he was not about to. He started to go back to his corner. His mother stopped him. "Is something wrong, Aimery?"

"No," said Aimery, mumbling it.

She did not believe him, but she let him go. Ysabel knew that look of hers. There was always a later, and Joanna always knew what to do with it.

"Tomorrow," Gwydion said, rather suddenly, "our fleet will come."

That stopped everyone. They all stared at him. The witchfolk knew. The humans had to have guessed.

"You'll leave, then," Joanna said much too calmly. "As soon as the ships are loaded and ready."

"Two days," said Gwydion, "or three. If the winds stay quiet and no storm comes."

None would, unless he wanted it. Messire Amalric was wrong to make light of the powers he had. He did not use them casually, that was all. And he believed that humans should look after themselves.

"You should come," Aidan said to Joanna. He looked a little wild, as if he had caught himself off guard. "What is there to keep you here? War and fear, and hunger if the enemy lays siege to the city, and worse than that if the siege drags on. It's no life for a mother with children."

Joanna faced him. It was as if the rest of them had dropped away, and there were only the two of them. Ysabel had never seen so clear what was between them. "What life would I have in a foreign country, dependent on another's charity?"

"My country would never be foreign to you."

"Would it not?" Her eyes flicked to Morgiana, who sat motionless, saying nothing, doing nothing, thinking nothing that went past her mind's walls.

Aidan could not help glancing at his hand, which had wound itself in Morgiana's some time since and was disinclined to draw away. But then he looked back at Joanna, and they were alone again in a world they had made for one another before Ysabel was born. "What of Ysabel?"

Joanna went pale. She had always looked younger than she was, a strong-faced, clear-eyed, handsome woman who bent her will to no one. Now, all at once, she looked old.

"You are her mother," Aidan said. "It is your right to command her obedience. But if she is here and I in Rhiyana, what will become of her?"

Ysabel felt the fear grow in her mother's heart. This was what Joanna had always dreaded. What a mother dreaded, no matter what her child was. The moment when she had to decide. To keep it and maybe smother it, or to let it go. Aimery had been taken from her too soon, and that was still a raw wound. She had given him up later, to be sure, and done it as a proper baroness should. She was getting ready to do the same for William; she would do it for the others, one by one. But all of them would go to fostering in Outremer. None of them would go across the sea.

And Ysabel was Ysabel. Joanna had never told her who she really was. Someday, she was thinking, she would have to. Someday she would have to surrender Ysabel to her father. She was of his kind and not of Joanna's. Joanna could not keep her.

Ysabel tried to make it hurt less. "Mother, don't hate yourself. I know. I've always known."

Joanna rounded on her. The pain was worse. It tasted like rage.

"I know who my father is," said Ysabel. "I couldn't not. It's written in my blood."

For a moment Ysabel knew that Joanna would hit her. But Joanna did not. She turned on Aidan instead. "You *knew*!"

He had to stand. This was nothing he could take sitting at his lady's feet, hand in hand with her. He stood in front of Joanna, who stood to face him. She was almost as tall as he was. "You lied to me," she said. "Both of you. You let me gnaw my soul with guilt. And fear—because someday I would have to tell her, and she would hate me, because I lied."

"I don't hate you," said Ysabel.

She might have been a mouse in the wall, for all the notice Joanna took of her. "Why?" Joanna demanded of Aidan.

"At first," he said, "because I didn't know she knew. Then because it never seemed to be time; and we were never where we could say it and not be heard. You avoided me," he said, "most strenuously, and most successfully, for ten long years."

She shook her head. It was not an answer to anything he had said. Not exactly. "You should have told me."

"I should."

She hated it when a person would not quarrel. Maybe that was why she loved Aidan: most of the time he would give her the fight she wanted. Now he refused.

She looked about half blindly. Her eyes found Aimery's face. What little color was left in her own, drained away.

"He knows," said Ysabel. "He found out."

She rocked back. She had not even seen her mother's hand until it hit her. She barely saw it drop to Joanna's side again. Joanna raised it, shaking, to her mouth. She looked as if she was about to faint.

Aidan seemed to think so. He reached for her. She beat his hands away wildly, in something that was almost terror. "Don't touch me. Don't *touch* me!"

He let his hands fall. His face was stark.

She scrambled herself together, alone, in the middle of them all. She looked from face to face. She did not flinch from any, even from Morgiana's. Even from Aimery's. "So that is what it is," she said. Her voice was rough but calm.

Aimery was as much a roil as she was. Hating her, loving her, adoring her, despising her. "How?" he asked her. "How could you do it?"

"I was young," she said, "and I hurt, and everything that I was and felt and did seemed too ugly to bear. And in the midst of it I found something beautiful."

He could not understand. He was too young, and he was a boy. "You were weak."

"I was weak," she said. "People are. Why else is there rape after battles?"

Aimery went bright scarlet. "That's different. Men are different."

"Yes," Aidan said. "Men aren't taught to rein themselves in." He met Aimery's furious stare with one almost as fierce, if nowhere near as angry. "Don't judge what you have no right to judge."

"I have every right!" Aimery cried. "She is my mother!"

"She sinned against your father once. Your father sinned against her a dozen times a year."

It was not Aimery who flew in his face, who struck him with such force that he swayed. He stared at Joanna, too shocked to be angry. "You will not," Joanna said, shaping every word with trembling care, "speak so of my husband. What he did was never more than the body's need. What I did was mortal sin. I betrayed my vows to him, in spirit as in flesh. And I never repented it."

"Not even now?"

"Now," she said, "I want you to understand. You have vows of your own. I will not give up my land and my country and my life because you want to keep me near you, though you can never let yourself touch me. That wanting is pure selfishness. It wrongs you, it wrongs me, it wrongs your lady. And it wrongs the child you begot."

The worst of it, the very worst, was that she was loving him through all of this. Wanting him so badly that it was an ache in Ysabel's own body, and resisting him so fiercely that it shook her within and without.

"You may take her," Joanna said. "She is yours. I cannot raise her as she should be raised; I cannot rule her as she should, and must, be ruled. But I will not go with you. This is my country. My children were born to it. I will die in it."

He shook, standing there, in the face of her mortality. Humans died. Love could not hold them; grief could not save them.

Her face softened as she looked at him. "My lord, we knew that it could never be more than a few moments'

pleasure, even when we did it. What came of it . . .
that, too, was only mine for a while."

"I am not a thing," Ysabel said angrily. "You can't
throw me back and forth like a clipped penny."

They both turned to her. Their eyes were frightening.
She tried to meet them steadily. "I may be an accident,
but I'm still me. I won't be given away."

"What will you do?" her mother asked. "I have to
stay here. He has to go away. One of us has to look after
you."

I can look after myself, Ysabel started to say, but she
stopped. It was not quite true. She was too young yet.
She needed training and teaching.

She could not get it as her brothers and sisters did,
from lords and ladies who owed her mother favors, or
who wanted an alliance with her father. She was not like
the rest of them. Humans could not understand her, or
even stand her, often.

It was not a choice that she stood in front of. Of
course her father would take her. He was the only one
who could. It was what would happen once he took her.
"I'll never see you again," she said to her mother. Not
whining too badly. She was proud of that.

Joanna tried to be light, to make her feel better. "The
world is not as wide as that. And children grow. You
might be like Morgiana. Then I'll see more of you than I
ever want to see."

Ysabel shook her head till her braids whipped her
face, making the tears spring. "I'll grow and I'll learn
and I'll forget how long time is, and when I come back it
will be too late, and you'll be gone."

"Your father won't let that happen," Joanna said.
She never cried when other people would lie down and
howl. She went quieter instead, and stronger. "I'm sending you the way I sent Aimery to Count Raymond, to be
Prince Aidan's fosterling and Lady Elen's maid, and
maybe when you're older you will be a maid-in-waiting
to the queen. Someday you'll come back to Outremer
and we'll see one another again, as gentlefolk do."

Oh, she was strong, to talk like that, who had always
hated passionately to let anyone touch a child of hers,

even a nurse or a servant. Ysabel would never have that kind of strength, rock-solid and rock-hard and more than a little merciless. It looked at Ysabel and saw what was best for her, and decided without wavering. It looked at Aimery and braced itself for a long hard war.

Men were not reasonable about women's sins. It was even worse when the sinner was a man's mother, whom he loved quite beyond measure and understood not at all. Aimery did not even hear what Ysabel said, no more than she heard it herself. Something about having to do as she was told, and coming back the moment she was able. She meant it, but half her mind had turned to her brother, seeing danger there and not knowing what to do about it.

He did not say much. Only, "That's brave of you, Mother. To hand her over to the one who sired her, and forget that she was ever born."

There was a sneer on his face. He wanted to strike and hurt, the way Joanna had hurt him.

"I will never forget," said Joanna, who was stronger than he was, though he lacked the wits to see it. "Nor will I beg anyone's pardon, short of God Himself."

"Not even the man you cuckolded?"

"That's an ill word for your father," she said.

"You gave it to him."

"He never knew it, nor did any other man. Will you be the one to do it, Aimery? Will you brand your father a cuckold and your mother a whore? Will that make you feel one whit better than you feel now?"

Aimery's eyes were the exact color of hers; the exact, thunderous blue, now almost black with pain. "I hate you," he said.

"Of course you do," she said. "Sometimes I hate myself. I can do two things about it. I can let it eat me alive, or I can go on past it."

He stared at her. His mouth worked. He started to say something, let it die unsaid.

"I am not asking for your forgiveness," she said. "All I ask is that you think, and that you try to understand. This war is going to need us both. If we cannot be friends, at least we should be allies."

"You could go," he said. "Turn infidel. Live in the House of Ibrahim and be safe from all the fighting."

"I thought of it," she said, "long and hard. I may still send the younger girls to Aleppo, where they will be safe and well looked after, and taught all that they need to know. But you and I, Aimery, we belong to the Kingdom of Jerusalem. We stand or fall with it. We can turn our private quarrel to a feud that divides half the kingdom. Or we can master it and swear a truce, and fight our war together."

He stood stiff. He was not ready to be that sensible. He wanted to scream at her and call her ugly names, and hear her scream back, and make her cry. He wanted to throw all his anger on her, and all his grief and loss and plain dull disappointment. His mother was human and mortal, and could make mistakes, and some of them were monstrous. She was not the shining saint that he had thought her.

Aidan spoke behind them. "Before you make your choice, Aimery, consider what you have to choose. The lands that you hold by right are lost until you can win them back, although you hardly lack for means, with your share in the House of Ibrahim. I had in mind to offer you more. I had my fief of Millefleurs from King Baldwin. I never submitted to King Guy, nor called him my liege lord; my fief is still my own though I abandon it for my own country. Will you hold it for me?"

"Is that a bribe to keep me quiet?"

Aidan did not lose his temper, though Ysabel would hardly have blamed him if he had. "You wrong us both in that, messire. That I would buy silence; that you could be bought. I have lands and a castle which have become very dear to me; my oath and my honor compel me to forsake them. Should I be faulted for finding them a master who can look after them and cherish them and hold them as they should be held?"

Aimery could not speak. It was too much for him all at once: all that they were asking him to understand.

"If you do accept the charge," Aidan said, "you can't do it alone. You'll need your mother. To be lady and chatelaine until you have a wife to do it for you; to be regent until you grow into a man. And she needs you, messire. You are her firstborn, the one she fought the hardest for. She loves you."

"Yes," said Aimery bitterly. "She loves me so much that she threw me away and got herself Ysabel to take my place."

"I see that you are her son," Aidan said, cool, almost cold. "She never forgot a slight in her life, either. Or forgave it. If you cannot practice Christian charity, will you consider Christian politics? You need her, messire. You need what she knows of trade and of the House of Ibrahim; of court and kingdom and the games of kings. You need a teacher. You will never have one better than she."

"You," said Aimery. "*You* say that. You are the one who seduced her!"

There, thought Ysabel. He had got to that. Blaming the one he had, for hero-worship, been refusing to blame. It had taken him long enough.

It was his mother who said, "He seduced me. I seduced him. What has that to do with whether you and I can hold Millefleurs?"

"Everything!" Aimery cried.

"Only if you let it," she said.

"Go," Aidan said, so gently that they all stared. "Think on it. Before I go, tell me what you choose."

"What will you do if I say no?"

Aidan raised a brow. "Will that be any affair of yours?"

"But," said Aimery. "If I don't take Millefleurs, or Mother doesn't, the enemy will get it. Or someone else, maybe worse. What if they don't know about the way the spring goes dry in August, but there's another and smaller one in the hill, that carries the castle through till the rains come? What if they knock holes in the door with the flowers carved on it, or tear up the mosaics in the chapel? What if they don't know how to be good to the people in the village?"

"Do you care?"

"Yes, I care!" Aimery stopped, breathing hard. "You're working on me. The way you do in councils."

"I'm telling you the truth."

"Yes," said Aimery angrily. "Yes, I'll take what you offer. I'm honored. I'm grateful."

"You'll swear a truce with your mother?"

That stopped him. He shot a glance at his mother. She stood still. She would not help him, one way or the other. She looked the way she always looked. He tried to see her as a whore the way he had seen them in the cities or hanging about the army: raddled, painted, with her hair done up in elaborate curls. He shied from seeing her in a dress so tight it strained at the seams, with her breasts bursting out of it and her ankles showing, and no modesty in her at all.

He could not do it. He could not forgive her, either. That would take more time by far than anyone was giving him.

"I'll swear a truce," he said. "I won't promise any more than that."

"It is enough," said Aidan. "For a beginning."

40

Beginnings.

That was what Joanna thought of, perversely, standing on the quay, watching the five blue-sailed ships as they took on their passengers and cargo. She did not want to think of endings. Of what was going away; of who would never come back.

Never, while she was alive to see him. She did not pretend to prescience. She simply knew.

It was all very orderly, as such things went. Inevitably the desperate or the frightened pressed forward now that it was too late, and tried to beg or borrow or steal a place on one of the ships. There would have been a fight, or more than one, but for the brothers, king and prince. It was unmistakable which was which, the one in royal blue, the other in Saracen black, but when they were so minded they had exactly the same voice. Soft, clear, and very firm. The contentious were encouraged to take their leave. The fearful were reminded, with apologies, that a ship could only hold so many.

Those who had won passage were remarkably quiet. The pilgrims huddled together and prayed. Some of the women wept. The children stared big-eyed from behind skirts or from enveloping arms.

The pope's legate came without fanfare and boarded under cover of Archbishop William's arrival. His entourage was somewhat less than it had been when he came. One had remained behind to do penance for a certain great sin. That one had a new novice to attend him, Joanna had heard: the merchant's son from Genoa. The merchant himself sailed on the smallest of the ships, as far from the king and his brother as the fleet would allow. Guillermo Seco was somewhat of a broken man since he gambled on Aidan's enmity and lost his son.

Abbot Leo looked as if he could not decide whether to be happy or sad: happy to be sailing home; sad to leave the Holy Land in such straits. The archbishop knew much less ambivalence. He was going to preach the Crusade. He spoke a few fiery words from the rail, promises of a return with the whole of Christendom at his back. A cheer went up even from those who had failed to win passage.

"That one will do well," Aidan said.

He was standing beside her. She could have sworn that he was over by the last of the ships, seeing to the loading of the horses. No one near her seemed to see him, except Dura, who lowered her eyes and backed away. Dura had great respect for the afarit, but she did not traffic with them unless she must.

Joanna could not breathe very well. They had all said their farewells in the caravanserai before they came out into the public eye. Aidan had offered her nothing but what he offered the others. Less in truth than he gave Aimery, or Lady Margaret. Joanna had been reckoning him wise, and trying not to hate him for it. Best to part so, watching him embrace each and every one of the others, engrossing herself in struggling not to cry and spoil her daughter's new cotte. People would not have thought it odd that he offered her no more than a formal word, with Ysabel clinging to her and the baby crying and, suddenly, too many goodbyes to say, too little time to say them.

He stood beside her now, not looking at her. The last of the horses, Raihan's best-beloved mare, was giving trouble. A slight figure slipped out of the press and caught her bridle. She calmed with uncanny swiftness. Joanna caught herself smiling. "Rather an unlikely horsetamer, that one," she said.

Aidan answered smile with smile. "It does go oddly with his Torah and his Talmud." A finger of wind waxed playful, tangling in his hair. Joanna's fists ached with clenching. He tossed his hair out of his face and slanted a glance at her. "When Ysabel is grown, she will come back. I promise you that. I won't let her forget you."

"Maybe you should."

"When did I ever succumb to plain good sense?"

"I won't be faithful to your memory," she said. "I'll do what I must for Aimery and the rest of my children. If I have to marry again, then I shall do so. If I am minded to take a lover, than I shall do that. You are not the beginning and the ending of my delight in this world."

"I never wished to be," he said.

He did not say what he could have said. That it was not his memory to which she should be faithful. Ranulf was another part of her, another wound that would, God willing, teach itself to heal.

"I have remarkably little guilt," she said, "when it comes down to it. Will I burn in hell, do you think?"

"I'm hardly an authority," he said. Light, almost. Accepting it.

She turned and looked at him. Looked, only, for a long while. Committing every line of him to memory. His eyes, unveiled, were hard to meet. She met them at last, to remember. Grey steel, grey stone. Grief, yes, and the bitterness of parting, but beneath them, deep and singing gladness. This had never been his country, well though he prospered in it. No more had he been her possession. "What we had," she said. "What, for a little

while, we shared . . . I'll remember. Be good to our
daughter, my lord."

"Yes," he said, answering both parts of it. For an
instant she thought that he would touch her. Perhaps he
meant to. But he did not. He bowed low and low, as to a
queen. "Prosper you well, my lady. May God keep you."

He was gone. A shadow and a light; then, all at once,
solidity, running lightly up the gangway. Morgiana was
waiting for him. Ysabel was close by her, silent for once
and subdued, attending Lady Elen. As Joanna watched,
Aidan came up beside his daughter. Her hand slid into
his; she leaned against him, seeking comfort. Morgiana
set her hand on the child's shoulder. They looked well,
standing so. They belonged together.

Joanna held her head high and thought of beginnings. There went the first cry of the Crusade, on the
flagship with the seabird on its sail. Here remained the
war, and a new demesne for herself and her eldest son,
and perhaps, with time, more than an armed truce between them.

Someone touched her. She started slightly. Where
Aidan had been stood her mother, offering a rare gift: an
arm about her waist, a warm human presence. Margaret
said nothing, did nothing but teach Joanna how to be
strong. Joanna let her own arm come to rest about the
plump shoulders, and stood with her, watching the fleet.

The gate of the horses' hold boomed shut. Gangways
slid rattling over rails. Sails ran up. Captains bellowed
orders in Rhiyanan, odd mingling of harshness and music, like the sea on their own cold stones. The ships slid
one by one out into the harbor, coming about in a stately
dance, making for the needle's eye that was the sea-gate
of Tyre.

Joanna's sight blurred. The ships, the men on them,
dimmed to shadows. But on the flagship as it pulled
ahead of the others, a great light went up. The sun on
Gwydion's crown, she told herself, though it blazed five-
fold. Blue fire and green, and two that were smaller, silver and ruddy gold; and a splendid, leaping flame, the
color of a ruby's heart. There was a vision in it. Lions on

a field of lilies, and an eagle soaring over them, and in the sky above them a blood-red cross.

Anglia, Francia, the Emperor of the Romans. Christendom would come and take vengeance for Hattin. Whether that vengeance would be complete . . .

"That will be as God wills," she said.

She closed her eyes, opened them on plain earth and simple sunlight. The world went on, unheeding of one lone woman, and the lover she had never truly had, and the child they had shared for a little while.

There were six who were all her own, waiting for her, and the baby would be hungry. She straightened her back and set her chin. The Crusade would come when it came. It would find her ready for it.

They linked arms, she and her mother. Their eyes met briefly. Understanding; agreeing. Arm in arm, proper in their dignity, they walked up from the quay.

Author's Note

THE HORNS OF HATTIN

The battle of the Horns of Hattin and the fall of the Kingdom of Jerusalem seem made to order for the novelist. King Guy of Jerusalem was much as I have shown him: a handsome man, a passable knight, and an inept ruler. He seems to have been constitutionally incapable of making a decision, unless it was the wrong one. He was badly overmatched by his adversary, the sultan of Egypt and Syria, Salah al-Din Yusuf ibn Ayyub or, as the Franks called him, Saladin.

For the events surrounding the battle, as well as for the battle itself, I am indebted as always to M. C. Lyons and D. E. P. Jackson's *Saladin: The Politics of the Holy War* (Cambridge, 1982). I have taken certain details of the battle, including the standard of Taqi al-Din, from Ian Heath, *Armies and Enemies of the Crusades 1096–1291* (Worthing, UK, 1978). This book, along with relevant volumes in the Osprey Men-at-Arms Series (particularly #75, *Armies of the Crusades,* and #171, *Saladin and the Saracens),* is invaluable for the novelist as well as the wargamer.

The battle of Hattin broke the back of the Crusader Kingdom of Jerusalem. Jerusalem itself fell at the end of September, 1187; on 2 October the surrender was concluded. By that time envoys had been sent to the West to preach the new Crusade, led by, among others, Archbishop William of Tyre. They were answered by Henry

II of England and then, after his death, by his son and
successor, Richard I, as well as Philip of France and
Frederick Barbarossa of Germany. This, the Third Crusade, plagued by internal dissension, problems of trans-
port and supply, and such distractions and disasters as
Richard's conquest of Cyprus and Barbarossa's death on
the march, failed of its end. Richard, deserted by his
allies, won back Acre but not Jerusalem. The city remained in Muslim hands for almost eight centuries, until
it was taken by British troops in World War I.

The Crusader kingdom limped along for another century, until its last outpost, the city of Acre, fell in 1291 to
the armies of Islam. Guy de Lusignan continued to call
himself King of Jerusalem, to which, in 1192 and until
his death in 1194, he added the kingship of Cyprus. Conrad of Montferrat, who managed to hold Tyre against
Saladin, laid claim briefly to Guy's crown; he was mur-
dered by Assassins in 1192, allegedly with the collusion
of Richard of England.

I have taken some liberties with the personality and
history of Guy's elder brother, Amalric (Ayméric). He
was in fact Constable of the kingdom, named to that
position by the leper-King Baldwin IV; it was he who
arranged the wedding of his brother to the Princess
Sybilla. He himself had married a great lady of the kingdom, Eschiva d'Ibelin; much later, in 1197, he would
take a second wife, Isabel de Courtenay, whose kinswoman, Agnes, was the mother of Baldwin IV. In the
end he fulfilled his royal ambition, inheriting from his
brother the title of King of Cyprus and, in 1197, that of
King of Jerusalem. From his capital of Acre he under-
took by various stratagems to incite a fourth Crusade.
The Fourth Crusade itself, by a concatenation of circumstances to which only history can be subject—in fiction
they would seem preposterous—ended in the conquest
not of Jerusalem but of Constantinople. Amalric, who
took no part in the actual, abortive Crusade, died in
1205. The line of Lusignan continued to claim the kingship of Jerusalem until the final fall of Acre.

MEDIEVAL MARRIAGE LAW AND
DISPARITAS CULTUS

The law of the Church in the twelfth century expressly and repeatedly forbade the marriage of a Christian and an infidel. For a concise historical and canonical summary, see Francis J. Schenk, *The Matrimonial Impediments of Mixed Religion and Disparity of Cult* (Washington, DC, 1924). The condemnation and threat of excommunication which Prince Aidan and his lady receive in Chapter 8 is, if anything, mild in its phrasing. That such a marriage was not regarded as completely unthinkable, however, is reflected in the proposal of Richard of England that his sister Joanna be married to Saladin's brother. If the proposal had gone so far as to be acted upon, it would certainly have required a dispensation from the pope. Equally certainly, only a king, and a strong and determined one at that, could have hoped to gain so extreme a concession.

The phenomenon of a forged dispensation is considerably less unlikely. Forgery in fact was a high medieval art, often for exalted ends—a notable example is that of the so-called "Donation of Constantine," which served as support for numerous abrogations of temporal power by the papacy.

I am indebted to Sandra Miesel for an introduction to the intricacies of medieval marriage law, as well as for the detail which signals the forgery, namely, the suspension of the papal seal or *bulla* (hence the later application of the term "bull" to all such papal documents) by a cord of either silk or hemp, depending on the import of the document. See under "Bulls" in the *Catholic Encyclopedia;* see also "Bulla" in the *New Catholic Encyclopedia.* Both are invaluable sources for details ecclesiastical and, often, historical.

A final note for the meticulous: Pope Urban III (who died in October 1187) was not in fact in Rome when my fictional king would have been suing for the dispensation. He spent his papacy in Verona, judging the political climate in Rome too hostile for safety. The five popes to whom the petition was presented would be Popes Alexander III (1159–81), Lucius III (1181–85), and Urban III, and Barbarossa's antipopes Callistus (III) and Innocent (III). Aidan, as a thoroughly medieval prince, would of course have undertaken to cover all eventualities—and all possible claimants to the papacy.